Embers
of War

RJJ Hall

Matador
9 Priory Business Park,
Wistow Road, Kibworth Beauchamp,
Leicestershire. LE8 0RX
Tel: 0116 279 2299
Email: books@troubador.co.uk
Web: www.troubador.co.uk/matador
Twitter: @matadorbooks

ISBN 978 1838594 664

British Library Cataloguing in Publication Data.
A catalogue record for this book is available from the British Library.

Printed and bound in the UK by TJ International, Padstow, Cornwall
Typeset in 10pt Palatino by Troubador Publishing Ltd, Leicester, UK

Matador is an imprint of Troubador Publishing Ltd

To the men and women who served in the
liberation of Italy – 1943 to 1945

And to my mother – Patricia Hall (1915-2015)

Outline Map of Italy 1943–1945

This map does not show the location of the following fictional places:
Castelnuovo, Sassovivo, Soglio and *Monte Tranquillo.*

PART I

– Late May 1944 –

CHAPTER 1

Captain Frank Hill wakes abruptly.

Last night, as he fell asleep, he had prayed that his luck would hold. But could it last till the end of the war?

A siren wails. He hears the bass growl of bombers overhead. Is that his answer?

Frank raises his head from the pillow and listens to the familiar din, but tonight something is missing. He sits up, stretching for his torch as his mind starts to clear. Where is the shudder of high explosives?

Damn them! The buggers must be dropping firebombs.

His watch shows 0235. He clambers out of bed and begins to throw on his uniform. The curfew applies to everyone, including officers, but that won't stop him. If he wavers, the theatre – *his theatre,* where for seven months he has entertained Allied troops – could burn down.

The theatre is close to Frank's heart. It has been his passion since October '43, when he reached Naples. Finding the abandoned building and getting the Colonel's permission to reopen it, had saved his sanity after the Battalion's drubbing on the beaches at Salerno.

Out in the street he flicks on his torch until he hears another wing of enemy planes. Anti-aircraft guns boom out a distant response. Searchlights sweep the sky, illuminating the planes and a thousand incendiaries. Frank raises his fists, aware that each stick of magnesium carries a detonator to ignite it on impact.

The bombers are heading for the docks where their targets will be the Allied supply ships and the warehouses near the quays. For the Fascists, Naples had been the port of empire; but now it's the main port of entry for the men and supplies the Allies need on the road to Rome.

Naples has seen many raids: the Allies bombed the port when the Germans were supplying Rommel in North Africa; before the Germans abandoned the city, they sabotaged the sewers and utilities; and since Naples was liberated, it has been a frequent target for German bombers. Mercifully, as the front has inched northwards, there have been fewer raids. Until now.

Frank keeps in the shadows as a fire appliance clangs by, its crew unconcerned about his theatre. *They* don't lie awake at night, worrying about its vulnerability so close to the docks.

Before landing in Italy, Frank had fought in North Africa where he often organised entertainments for the Battalion, but nothing on the scale of this theatre. Yet, as he recovered from Salerno, something drove him to stage a revue. It proved so successful that he was ordered to stay in Naples to provide daily entertainment for the troops passing through the city on their way to the front. And by keeping Frank away from the fighting, it had probably saved his life.

He hurries on. There's a blackout of course, intended to reduce the danger from air raids, but in Naples poverty ensures greater control: few inhabitants can afford electricity.

In the darkness Frank's boot strikes something solid. He tenses as a bottle shatters. That's the sound of his father all those years ago, stumbling over the empties – milk bottles on the front step awaiting collection.

He freezes as glass scrunches beneath his boots. He must avoid both the Military Police and the looters who come out after every raid. Briefly he flicks on his torch; the red unblinking eyes of two rats stare back.

He sets off again, walking as fast as he dares. He would like to run but can't afford to fall. Another fire appliance speeds past. He covers his ears as its bell resounds in the narrow street.

Frank was slow to join up when the war began. It had been different in '37 when he volunteered for Spain, but he had soon grown disillusioned with the horrors and treachery of that war. It was only when his wife, Maggie, was killed in the London blitz that he felt compelled to enlist again.

Somehow he had survived the brutal fighting in North Africa where he was part of the Eighth Army's retreats from Benghazi and Gazala before Monty got a grip in the summer of '42. But the landing at Salerno – south of Naples – was different. Days and nights of unending bombardment on the beachhead had killed a third of his Platoon, and by the time the Germans withdrew Frank feared he was becoming unhinged.

Reopening the theatre had changed his life; even after months at the helm he finds it hard to believe. He never dreamt that one day he would run one of Italy's great opera houses, the Real Teatro di San Carlo. In the midst of this interminable war, it feels like a miracle.

Frank knows, however, that his run at the theatre could end suddenly, if just one incendiary were left ablaze on the roof. Of course, opera houses often burn down – the San Carlo theatre itself was destroyed by fire in 1816 – but he couldn't bear that to happen again, especially not on his watch.

Frank had fallen on his feet when he was ordered to run the theatre. He had been fortunate to miss so much of the fighting, but he doubts this good fortune can last. Tonight he senses that the war has tracked him down. Is the moment finally coming when the army will change its mind and pack him off to the front?

From the next corner, he looks down towards the docks. A blazing building stands out against the moonless sky and the pitch-black sea. Its windows glow with an inner light, like a crowded church at Christmas. Then a windowpane explodes and tongues of fire start licking at the lintels, preparing to devour the roof.

Frank watches, mesmerised, as he had watched from Ealing while the heart of London blazed. The hot air is heavy with the reek of burning and the sight of buildings transmuted into pyres raises hairs on the back of his neck. He coughs as he presses on. With the road now illuminated by the conflagration he lengthens his stride. Through the smoke rolling up from the port he finally glimpses the theatre; and with a hundred yards to go he starts to run.

He hammers on the stage door. 'COME ON, GIOVANNI!' he shouts in Italian. 'HURRY UP!'

Silence. He considers drawing his pistol. When he first entered the derelict theatre, Giovanni, the night watchman, was waiting in the shadows with his rifle and forced Frank to raise his hands. Luckily, he relented when Frank offered him sufficient cigarettes.

Frank kicks at the solid wooden door. 'GIOVANNI! PLEASE! THIS IS URGENT!'

At last he hears slow footsteps.

'VENGO! PORCA MISERIA! VENGO!'

A bleary-eyed face appears. 'Ah, Franco!'

Giovanni sways as his words stumble out. 'You must be my guest. Have some wine.'

Frank glares at Giovanni, struggling to follow his Neapolitan dialect, which is hard enough when Giovanni is sober.

'NO, GIOVANNI! THE THEATRE COULD BE ON FIRE! I MUST CHECK THE ROOF!'

Frank brushes past and hastens towards the stone staircase.

'There's no need to hurry, Capitano!' Giovanni chortles as he lurches after Frank. 'The Lieutenant is up there already! She thinks there are bombs on the roof!'

'Good Lord! I hope she's all right!'

Frank accelerates. He had come to protect the theatre never thinking Vermillion would come too. He clenches his fists and presses on.

4

Vermillion Henthorpe, a Lieutenant in the ATS, has been at the theatre from the start, selling thousands of tickets each week to the troops. Without her, the theatre would never have flourished. She is clever, amusing, hard-working and charming. In short, Frank has been lucky to work with her.

He has also grown fond of Vermillion and has struggled to stop himself from falling for her, knowing she would never fall for him. She comes from a different social world: so perhaps it was fortunate that before she reached Naples she was already practically engaged – to Edmund Manley, a Major in Frank's old unit.

But while Frank was ordered to stay in Naples to run the theatre, Edmund led 3rd Battalion's C Company as the Allies pushed north into the mountains in late '43. The fighting, especially around Monte Cassino, was intense with the Germans desperately defending well-prepared positions.

In March Edmund was badly wounded, losing both legs. He almost died but has since made a good recovery and will soon go home. Initially he asked Vermillion to go too and she agreed. Frank likes to think she did this reluctantly, but when they said goodbye two days ago he was sure he had lost her. Then yesterday evening – just a few hours ago – the Brigadier had told him that Vermillion intends to stay.

Giovanni clicks a series of switches; but on the first landing Frank is greeted by a single bare bulb.

'Thank you, Giovanni,' he calls back, his voice echoing off the stone walls.

The steps are steep, and Frank isn't used to such exertion. At least here the air is clear, without the burning stench that fills the streets. But that doesn't matter: it's the prospect of seeing Vermillion that threatens to overwhelm him.

On the next landing he stops to catch his breath. His heart is pounding. He pictures her lovely face as he had held it between his hands when they last parted. He'd felt drained by the fear that he might not see her again. He longed to kiss her, but only brushed his lips against her cheek. Even that was too much: she spun round and fled up the steps to her flat.

5

Arriving at the top landing, Frank again encounters the stink of burning. He tries to hold his breath as he hurries towards the wooden stairs that lead straight to the roof. He looks up. The door at the top is open: Vermillion must be up there already.

The wail of the all-clear sounds from outside. Frank inhales the scorched air, and coughs. His mind is churning. He takes another breath and puts his foot on the first stair, which creaks in warning. He climbs slowly, stopping as he reaches the top. He wants to call Vermillion's name but holds back, afraid he might alarm her. He looks out across the city, lit by a thousand fires. Oily clouds stream heavenwards, pushing the barrage balloons aside.

Seeing no sign of Vermillion, Frank steps onto the roof. Something solid sweeps past his face and thuds against his shoulder. Pain shoots down his arm.

'BUGGER! What was that?'

A dark shape moves in the shadows. 'Vermillion, is that you?'

'Frank!' She drops the metal bucket and grasps his arm. 'Are you all right, Frank? I'm so sorry. I thought you were Giovanni. How's your poor head?'

Clumsily he feels for her hands. 'Don't worry, Vermillion. It was only my shoulder.'

'Thank God it's you, Frank. I was so afraid when Giovanni grabbed at me and gave chase. But I had to come to the theatre; I feared it might burn down. I've already put out one fire.'

'You're wonderful, Milione!'

'Frank, I can't tell you how glad I am to see you!'

'It was a funny way to show you were pleased! In fact, when you swung that bucket, I had a feeling you might be cross.'

'Why should I be cross with *you*?'

'I wasn't sure.' He pulls her gently towards him. 'Perhaps because I'd told the Brigadier I would go to Rome.'

'I'm sad you're going to Rome, not cross.' She holds him tightly. 'I thought you'd lost interest in the theatre.'

'I've changed my mind, Milione, but I haven't had a chance to tell you. The Brigadier says I'm staying here.' Frank points behind her. 'There's another incendiary!'

'There's no water up here! But there's plenty of sand.'

Frank grabs two sandbags and struggles through the smoke towards the blaze, which leaps up in greeting.

'Damn the bloody Germans!' He empties the load onto the flames, which vanish with a splutter. 'We mustn't let them destroy our theatre. Not after all we've done.'

Frank turns towards Vermillion. Dirt is streaked across her face and her hair is lank, but her eyes are shining. He hasn't seen her look more appealing.

'How wonderful Frank that you're staying in Naples,' she beams, 'I'm staying here too. Edmund's going home without me.'

Frank puts his arms around her. 'I know.'

'Frank!' She leans back and frowns. 'How could you possibly know?'

'The Brigadier came to see me at the flat. He wants me to stay at the theatre. He thought I wouldn't mind, as Edmund had said you intended to stay.'

'Edmund is incorrigible!' Vermillion glances at the Castel dell'Ovo, its walls glowing in the light of many fires. 'Even now it's over, he still wants to run my life.'

'Perhaps we should be grateful, Milione. It was knowing you planned to stay that made me check the theatre.'

'Frank, I've missed you so much in the last few months.' She looks up; the light from the burning buildings flickers across her face. 'Please don't go away. Tell the Brigadier you'll stay here till the war ends.'

Frank can't speak. He knows that any day he may be moved to Rome or returned to the front; but he can't think about that now. He clears his throat. The thick air makes it hard to breathe but he has to sing.

"Quanto è bella, quanto è cara!
Più la vedo, e più mi piace ..."

How beautiful she is, and how precious.
The more I see her the more she attracts me ...

7

He watches Vermillion who seems stirred by the song until she slides her hand behind his head and draws him down towards her. He has wanted to kiss her so often and has fought to hold himself back. Now he feels engulfed by the softness of her lips.

He holds her tightly, closing his eyes. Although he had longed to kiss her, he had never thought of anything more. Now he feels a strong desire to sleep with her; he wishes she would come to his flat.

Looking down at Vermillion's lovely face framed by her chestnut hair, he sees tears well in her eyes.

'You said you were pleased to see me,' he whispers.

'I am pleased, Frank ... and I'm very happy,' she forces out the words. 'And I'm so glad ... you're staying in Naples ... I thought I was going to lose you ... that would have been too much.'

She kisses him again. 'Thank you for making this time in Naples the happiest of my life. You've been very good to me.'

He pulls her gently towards him. 'You'll make me cry too, even though I'm very happy.'

'Frank ... I'm crying for Edmund although I don't love him anymore. And because of all the suffering in this dreadful war. And because I still hope we can make the world a better place.'

Frank looks out across the familiar bay, lit by pyres all around the harbour. In the east, the paler sky heralds the dawn and he can see the grey finger of the Sorrento peninsula. He lifts her onto the balustrade, gently wipes away her tears and kisses her again.

'Milione ...' he whispers. 'We will make the world better, but we've done what we can for tonight. Now we need some rest. We've still got a theatre to run.'

'You're right, Frank. We don't have to hurry. At last we have plenty of time.'

CHAPTER 2

Thick smoke belches from the smouldering buildings as they scurry through the foggy streets. But Vermillion is mainly aware of the grip of Frank's hand as he leads her through the shadows. She almost has to run to keep up with his long stride, but she doesn't care. "Quanto è bella …" still echoes in her head.

Frank pulls her into an archway as an army truck rattles by.

'I love you, Vermillion …' he kisses her gently '… and I always shall.'

She wants him to kiss her again and to talk about what has happened but the streets are dangerous during the curfew and Frank pulls her on.

Above them the brooding buildings are outlined in the twilight. It must be almost 0400. As they cross a small piazza, she glimpses the navy hue of the bay, where the silhouette of Vesuvius looks serene. She squeezes Frank's hand; she hasn't forgotten her feelings of dread when the volcano erupted in March.

'Frank, I love you too,' she whispers as they approach her flat. 'I think you're remarkable.'

Her feelings for Frank have grown silently. But she never dreamt he could love *her*: she doesn't feel clever enough. She has always admired him and what he has achieved. He knows so much about so many things; he isn't like the other officers who are mainly interested in the military, and in sport.

As the light increases, colour begins to return. Vermillion can now make out the khaki of Frank's jacket and the grey of his grimy face. Hers must be grubby too. And her fingernails are rough and broken from digging up sand to smother the first incendiary. It doesn't matter of course: no one will see her when she slips back into her flat without waking the other two ATS girls.

Frank slows as they approach the corner of her road. He peers round cautiously.

'Good Lord!' he grips her hand.

The street ahead is filled with a clamour of people milling about in their nightclothes. Someone shouts above a chorus of lamenting. Behind them smoke rises from the roof of a substantial building, the palazzo where Vermillion's flat is.

'Where the hell have you been, Vermillion?' Jackie rushes towards them, her service dress unbuttoned over her nightdress and her fair hair wilder than usual.

'We thought you were still inside, Vermillion. Barbara has gone back to find you. She could burn to death!'

'Oh, heavens! I just went to the theatre, Jackie ... in case it was hit.'

'In the middle of the night?' Jackie glances up at Frank. 'You could have told us, Vermillion.'

'I didn't want to wake you.'

'We must look for Barbara,' Frank says. 'How long has she been gone?'

'At least ten minutes.'

'You stay here while I find her.' Frank marches through the palazzo gates and up to the main door. Vermillion follows. He turns and quickly kisses her.

'No, Frank. You mustn't go ... alone.'

As he opens the door, smoke surges out. He pulls the door behind him but Vermillion slides through, coughing in the thick air.

'Keep down!' Frank kneels on the second stone step and sets off on his hands and knees. His khaki backside is the only thing she can see, until that too is absorbed in the murk. Vermillion follows, although the familiar staircase seems utterly changed.

The flat had originally been Edmund's. He had brought her here soon after she got to Naples. They had a delicious lunch at Settefrati, a black-market restaurant by the harbour, before Edmund brought her up to the flat. She remembers that he smacked her bottom as she walked in front of him and she scampered up four floors to get away.

But she can't run now: the lack of air makes it hard to breathe. Already Frank is well ahead; she can hear him half a floor away as he follows the staircase round.

High above a loud cracking records the progress of the fire which has enveloped part of the roof. A flaming joist tumbles through the central void, thumping against the banisters. She feels the draught as it hurtles past.

Reaching the second landing, she hears Frank on the floor above.

'Are you all right, Frank?'

Her voice doesn't carry in the fog and there's no response. She coughs again. Her throat feels raw and her eyes smart until her tears overflow. She pulls out a handkerchief and wipes her eyes. Then covering her nose and mouth, she presses on.

When asked what she's afraid of, she usually lists dentists and flying; in future she will add burning buildings.

'Dear God, please protect Frank,' she says several times. She cannot lose him now, not when she has admitted that she loves him. Being involved with the theatre and spending time with Frank has meant so much: he is the first man who has really trusted her.

'Vermillion!' she hears Frank's muffled call. 'I've found her. I'm coming down.'

A heavy footstep resounds above her head, and then another. She coughs but cannot clear her throat; she coughs again. She can hardly breathe. She squeezes her eyes shut and sinks down on the stone step.

She hears Frank's footfall above. The banister vibrates as he steadies himself. He is only half a floor away and she can hear his laboured breathing. Oh God, he is such a dear man. Another step. Then another. It must be hard for him, after losing his wife in the blitz. She wonders how he recovered.

A second joist plummets from the roof. It thuds against the wall, releasing a swarm of sparks. Vermillion jumps back.

'I'm here, Frank,' she calls hoarsely, afraid she may pass out. But Frank can't carry them both; she must get out herself.

She discards the handkerchief covering her nose, and hesitates; it will be harder going down. She wishes she were wearing something better than service dress: a pair of slacks would do.

Behind her, she senses Frank's looming shadow with Barbara slung across his shoulders.

'Milione ... you must ... go down.' His voice rattles. 'I'll come ... as fast ... as I can.'

She grasps the banister with both hands and bends almost double as she shuffles down step by step. She opens her mouth to suck oxygen from the soupy air. Another step. Another panting breath. Her head swims. Another step, another gasp. Her eyes are streaming. She can see no further than her hands. She has lost her bearings in the uniform greyness. Is she falling? She clings tightly to the handrail as the world starts to revolve. She closes her eyes but her head continues to spin.

Behind her, Frank follows. But his steps are slower now. Oh God, she mustn't faint. No matter that the staircase is whirling, she must keep going down. Another step. She must go faster than Frank. Another step. Frank's heavy tread echoes down the stairwell as he stumbles, but rights himself. She lurches on. One more step and she will start the final flight.

As she makes it to ground level something clatters down, shedding an intense white light. It must be the remains of the incendiary. She presses herself against the wall and gropes her way past the glowing timbers. She straightens up. There seems to be more air, and light is coming through the glazing above the door.

Should she wait for Frank?

She listens. She can only hear her own breathing. No sound of Frank. Oh God! Should she go back? She listens again. Still no noise from above. On the theatre roof she had panicked when she heard footsteps, fearing they were Giovanni's. Now she longs to hear footsteps again.

She tries to stay calm as she turns back. 'Frank!' Her voice is muffled. 'FRANK!'

Moving towards the stairs she hears a footstep above. Frank gasps for breath before taking another pace. Thank heavens! He's coming.

From outside she hears a clang of bells as a fire appliance arrives. She turns back towards the door. What will happen when she opens it? Should she wait for Frank? Or perhaps a draught through the door will help to clear the air. She turns the handle. The door flies open in her face, almost knocking her down. Cool air races past.

Thank God! But behind her the timbers burn with new vigour. Help! Frank will never get through. She throws her weight against door. The frame shakes as she slams it shut. Behind her the flames subside.

Across the hall, she discerns a shadow. It must be Frank and Barbara. She runs towards him, grabbing his free hand and together they grope their way to the door.

'She's still alive,' he breathes heavily. 'I felt a faint pulse.'

She watches as Frank lowers Barbara's ragdoll body to the ground. 'Thank God, Frank, you've come back.'

CHAPTER 3

Paolo Baldini sniffs the dawn air. Naples is a city of smells but even the worst of its drains seem muted since he was held in the rancid Poggio Reale gaol.

Growing up in these ancient streets Paolo learnt to use his nose to navigate the city where each alley has a distinctive scent: one has an aroma of roasted fake coffee, another stinks of cats' piss. But today, even in the cooler morning air, each odour is masked by the tang of burning following the raid.

Paolo, however, can breathe more freely, knowing the charges against him have been dropped. Of course, he should never have been arrested. He had only bought some lengths of copper telephone cable from the man who dug them up.

He extends his arms to touch both sides of the alleyway as he sidles along. He has lived in Naples since he was five and feels at home in the narrow confines of the old Greek heart of the city. His parents had moved here from Rome and he grew up thinking he was a Roman. But service in the

Italian army had shown him that he talked and thought like a Neapolitan.

Paolo is pleased with what he has achieved since the armistice in September '43 when he deserted from his barracks near Bologna in northern Italy and walked all the way to Naples. In a city where many are starving he has learnt to get by.

As usual he spent last night with Emma but he left her before dawn to visit his own flat. She lets him stay on condition that her children never see him. She has lost hope that their father will return from military service in North Africa, but she isn't ready for them to meet a *new father*. So each morning before dawn Paolo takes his leave and doesn't return until the children are asleep. Last night had been awkward because the raid had woken them and for more than an hour he had hidden in a wardrobe.

This morning he didn't want to get up, but Emma was adamant, and now, after changing his shirt, he feels ready to meet old friends to discuss opportunities for new business.

Despite feeling at home in the city, Paolo moves warily. With no sign of the bloody war ending, Naples – *his* city – is going to the dogs. Since the Allies arrived everyone must fight to survive. There's no work and no fucking money, and the food handouts are pathetic. The inhabitants have to take their chances, just as Paolo has taken his, by trading on the burgeoning black market. All right, it may mean bending the rules. But who cares? He smiles. Provided they avoid the Military Police, they can make a decent living. However, there are of course limits. He doesn't approve of how some of his compatriots behave: raiding isolated farms and selling the stolen produce not through the proper black market but through organised gangs.

He passes a group of half-dressed children squabbling in the gutter before an elderly couple totters by without looking up. All right, there's misery around. But there are opportunities too, for those with the balls to grasp them. How fortunate that Naples is full of witless young Allied soldiers, afraid of going to the front. They hang around in all parts of the city with too much money and too little to do. And the port is chock-a-block with their stuff. Despite the guards and barbed wire, the inhabitants – with a modicum of ingenuity – can divert a fair share of these supplies for themselves.

Still, Paolo wants the Allies to leave. The only thing to be said for their troops is they're not as bad as the blasted Germans, who occupied Italy after the armistice and now hold the north of the country in an iron grip. God, if he ever gets the chance, he'd love to kill some Germans.

Something which stands out about the Allied troops is that many of them come from British and French colonies in India and North Africa. Paolo has even seen soldiers with bushy beards wearing turbans. He laughed at first, but now he worries that just the thought of these troops will terrify the peasants in the countryside.

And why should foreigners run his country? Why can't Italians have the latest tanks and planes to defend themselves? Mussolini promised to make Italy modern and strong. But look at the result: the whole bloody place is on its knees. It wasn't this bad when the Visigoths sacked Rome!

At school Paolo had learnt about the benefits of Italian unification. Now the Risorgimento looks like a fucking big mistake: the country will soon break up again.

Paolo turns into another narrow alley, ignoring the stench of urine. Here it's dark and surprisingly cool. He looks up at the sunlight high above. The buildings lean over him. They stand so close together that only one double sheet can be hung between them and with a stretch the occupants can shake hands with their neighbours across the way.

He hears a noise like a boot slithering on broken glass. He spins round but there's no one there. He feels an emptiness in his stomach. Is he being followed? If only he hadn't quarrelled with Sandro.

Most of Paolo's family has left Naples. Only Chiara, his elder sister, remains. All winter she had lived with the giant English Capitano they call Franco or Generalissimo, but now the stupid girl has walked out on him. Bloody Chiara! And because Paolo was in prison, she moved into *his* flat with bloody Sandro, thinking he would never be released.

At first Paolo was appalled about Franco and Chiara. He even drunkenly attacked him with a knife – but it hadn't done much good because Franco had knocked him out cold. Over time, however, he had changed his mind and was grateful when Franco got him out of gaol. Now Paolo is livid that Chiara gave Franco up. *Porca miseria!*

Is it surprising he feels anxious? Chiara is only two years older, yet already she's going mad. Why else did she break off her engagement to Franco? And in favour of an army deserter? *Porca puttana!* Her madness brings shame on the family, although they no longer feel like a family since the fucking war split them up. *Porca Madonna!*

In '42, Paolo's father was sent to Germany – to work in an armaments factory – because he was too old to fight. But since Italy changed sides, he is effectively a prisoner. And after his father left Naples, his mother, who had never really settled in the city, returned to Rome with Francesca, Paolo's younger sister. Sadly his elder brother – poor Stefano – was killed on the island of Pantelleria during the dreadful Allied bombing.

Now only Paolo and Chiara are left in Naples. And Chiara is mad. Of course he hasn't forgotten that she was good to him when he struggled back to Naples in the autumn. And now she swears that once Rome is liberated she will go to live with Mamma. Paolo can't wait for her to leave so he won't have to feel ashamed. But thinking of Mamma pricks his conscience: he knows that soon he too must visit her.

Of course, there's nothing really wrong with Sandro. They had met as conscripts near Bologna where they did their military training. Several times they were moved in preparation for combat but – *grazie al cielo* – they never saw active service. And when the armistice was declared in September '43, they just walked out of their barracks while their comrades, who waited for the Germans to arrive, were disarmed and bundled off to labour camps.

From Bologna, Paolo and Sandro had walked right down the peninsula until they slipped between the opposing armies and crossed the front line. Then they split up. Paolo headed for

Naples to find Chiara while Sandro joined the Italian King's new army. But that didn't last long. Sandro soon acquired the distinction of deserting twice from different armies, although he still contends it was twice from the same army – before and after Italy changed sides.

Soon after his second desertion, Sandro turned up in Naples. Paolo was delighted to see him, until he realised that like a baby Sandro needed constant attention. Coming from Turin – where all his close family had been killed in the bombing – he was lost in Naples. He couldn't understand the Neapolitan dialect and the moment he opened his mouth everyone knew he was a foreigner.

For months Sandro has depended on Paolo to survive. And how does he repay him? By ensnaring the feather-brained Chiara. And when Paolo was released from prison – which Chiara should have predicted once Franco took up his case – they were suddenly three in one bedroom. *Santo cielo!* He can't wait for Chiara to go to Rome!

CHAPTER 4

Frank cries out as he wakes from a nightmare.

Clissold – Frank's Platoon Sergeant in 3rd Battalion, who had nursed him through at Salerno – had been ordered to lead his men into a burning building. Frank couldn't stop them. And when the building began to collapse, Clissold emerged engulfed in flames.

Frank sits up shivering despite the warm night. Clissold was shot during the attack on Monte Tranquillo, near Cassino. So why had Frank dreamt he was on fire?

Frank swings his legs out of the bed; slowly his brain follows. His heart thumps and his head aches. He rubs his hands across his sweaty face; his throat feels parched. He shakes his head and wrinkles his nose: something is burning.

Frank sniffs at his fingers and grimaces. Then he grabs his handkerchief and blows his nose, leaving two sooty rings. He tries to stand but his brain spins and he falls back onto the bed. He needs some water.

He rubs his face again and smiles. Vermillion is next door. He wonders whether she and Jackie are comfortable, sharing a bed. They had to sleep somewhere: they could hardly return to their flat.

Again Frank tries to stand. His head throbs as he grasps the back of a chair. Steadying himself, he steps towards the door but nearly falls before he grips the handle. He pulls on his dressing gown and rakes his fingers through his hair. With luck the girls are still sleeping.

He takes a deep breath and coughs, but then can't stop. His mouth is full of phlegm and his brain continues to whirl. He steadies himself again. He badly needs a drink. With heavy footsteps he makes it to the kitchen where he fills a glass of water. He takes a gulp and coughs again. He drinks more water and smiles: at least Vermillion knows that he loves her.

He remembers Clissold. Who ordered him into that building? It wasn't Frank but the dream has disturbed him.

He looks at his watch. 0840. It's only three hours since he got to bed but he must go to the theatre, now he's in charge again. But first he needs to wash. He thinks about lighting the wood-burning water heater but decides there isn't time. He will have to make do with cold water, even though he won't get properly clean. After a hasty wash and shave he gets dressed. Then, still moving from one piece of furniture to the next, he hunts for something to eat. He finds some stale bread and a piece of cheese but nearly chokes when he tries to swallow. He coughs violently. His throat feels scorched. Even water leaves it feeling sore.

It's almost 0920 when he's ready to leave. He wants to see Vermillion and check she's safe, but their bedroom door remains firmly shut so he leaves a note on the floor where she will see it.

* * *

'Good morning, Sir,' Corporal Huggins greets Frank at the stage door. 'Did you sleep through the raid, Sir?'

Huggins has been Frank's batman since they landed in Sicily in July '43. Having a personal servant meant little at the front but in Naples he has been invaluable. It was Huggins who had found the flat for Frank and he has proved adept at getting things done in the theatre, although Frank sometimes worries about his methods.

Frank tries to clear his throat. 'No, Huggins, I didn't sleep through the raid.'

He coughs. 'I spent half the night on the theatre roof, putting out incendiaries dropped by the bloody Boche.' He clears his throat again. 'You'd better take a look up there to assess the damage.'

'Crikey, Sir, you have been busy,' Huggins strokes his right hand which he holds close to his chest. 'I suppose you're back in charge, Sir, now the Doctor's in the clink. That's what I'm telling everybody.'

Dottor Malaspina had been the theatre administrator for many years and had stayed on when Frank took over. Frank found him hard to deal with and had recently discovered that Malaspina was hiding evidence about staff who were Fascist Party members. And when the Military Police came to arrest Malaspina, he drew a gun.

'Huggins, you really shouldn't guess. But this time you happen to be right. The Brigadier paid me a visit. He's pleased we put Malaspina away and for the moment I'm back in charge.'

'I haven't seen Miss Henthorpe this morning. I expect …'

'The Lieutenant had a late night too. I found her on the roof searching for incendiaries …'

'Blimey, Sir, it *was* crowded up there.'

'… and then there was a fire in the palazzo where she lives. She and Lieutenant Platt are at my flat getting their beauty sleep. However, Lieutenant Fortune was overcome by smoke and was taken to hospital.'

'You did have a night, Sir.' Huggins looks down at his

boots and then at Frank. 'Now you're back in charge, Sir, does that mean we'll be staying in Naples for a while?'

'It's hard to say, Huggins, now Malaspina has gone.'

'It sounds to me like quite a while,' Huggins glances at Frank. 'Don't get me wrong, Sir. I've had a marvellous time in Naples. But I'm ready to return to the front when the order comes.'

Huggins pulls out his cigarettes and strikes a match. 'Now Fifth Army has broken the Gustav Line, they're into the Liri Valley. In no time, they'll be in Rome. I just thought with the Germans on the run we might be needed at the front.'

Frank knows this breakthrough is important, but he can't forget that it has taken four months of bitter fighting at Cassino. For a moment he looks blankly at Huggins as it hits him that the officer in his dream who sent Clissold into that burning building was Roger Bewdley.

'I often think about the Battalion.' Frank says, wondering how Roger is faring at the line; he imagines he's all right, because Roger is adept at avoiding trouble.

'This morning,' Frank continues, 'I've been thinking about Clissold, who helped me though at Salerno. Perhaps I owe it to chaps like him to return to the line. But I have to confess I enjoy running the theatre.'

'What you've done, Sir, is bloody marvellous.' Huggins grins as he turns to Frank. 'You've made all the difference to thousands of lads who arrive in Naples with nothing to do. You've given them something real 'igh class to enjoy.'

'Have I told you why I joined up?' Frank asks.

'You said once you wanted to kill Nazis.'

'But did I tell you why?'

Huggins shakes his head. 'I joined up to save ammunition.'

'How come, Huggins?'

'My old man said he'd shoot me if I dodged conscription.'

Frank smiles. 'I joined up after my wife was killed. I couldn't do anything else. I kept remembering that moment of standing in front of our ruined home, staring at the holes where the windows had been. I was desperate to get into the building but an ARP warden held me back.'

Frank wonders why he is saying this to Huggins: usually he keeps such things to himself. He pulls out his handkerchief and blows his nose: the two sooty rings remind him of his flat's charred window frames.

Frank blinks. 'Sorry, Huggins. It still feels a bit raw, even after three years.'

'I don't know what I'd do if the bastards got my old lady. I think I'd go berserk.'

'I probably did go berserk. I can't remember much. I just knew I had to join up, to take revenge. Yet after a year of training and two months on the boat to Egypt I didn't have the same urge to fight. But the memories don't go away.'

* * *

Frank sets off to see what's happening around the theatre. He finds everyone hard at work and the arrangements for the afternoon performance of Un Ballo in Maschera are well in hand.

He is greeted warmly but discreetly. Everyone seems to know about Malaspina, but nobody mentions his name as though he no longer exists. Is this how they feel about the whole entanglement with Fascism, which held the country in thrall? Or do they fear that Malaspina may return? Frank doubts he will ever know the answers to these questions because no one will talk. After seven months in Naples he understands most of what he hears in Italian, but he knows he'll never understand the silences.

At the end of his tour, Frank slips into the auditorium and finds a seat. Even when it's empty, the place excites him. But as the quietness embraces him, he closes his eyes sensing the theatre's ghosts are at peace.

When he first entered the theatre it was dark except for pinpricks of light from the bullet holes in the ceiling where Allied planes had strafed a machine-gun post on the roof. Then Naples had no electricity; while the Allies repaired the power stations the first supply came from the generators of captured submarines tied up in the port.

The theatre had been abandoned but Frank was impressed by its faded grandeur and was determined to bring the place back to life. From the start, he revelled in its circus atmosphere as he mounted a string of revues. But what meant much more to him was staging a season of Italian operas for houses crammed with enthusiastic troops. Frank has loved opera for as long as he can remember but he doesn't know why: his parents had never even seen an opera house.

Frank had waited for several days before seeing the theatre with lights so it came as a revelation when he saw the illuminated auditorium with the great painting on the ceiling. He opens his eyes and looks up at Apollo. It seems right that the god of music and healing should preside over their shows.

The murmuring of voices and the shuffling of feet announce the orchestra's return to the pit. The maestro brings them to attention, and they start to play the frantic overture to Madame Butterfly, which will open soon. The rehearsal isn't fully staged but it doesn't need to be. The story is clear from the opening exchanges. Lieutenant Pinkerton knows his *marriage* to the fifteen-year-old Butterfly is temporary; but she believes she has found lasting love.

Frank feels transported by the richness of the sound. As he often tells Maestro Nanta, the orchestra and the chorus have improved immensely in the last seven months. And Frank feels confident that Butterfly's relevance to Naples will ensure its success with the troops.

Satisfied the rehearsal is going well, Frank has no pressing reason to stay but the music has caught him and he can't bring himself to leave. The tenor has a fine, light voice and catches Pinkerton's brash bravado as he sings:

"Dovunque al mondo
lo Yankee vagabondo
si gode e traffica
sprezzando i rischi.
Affonda l'àncora
alla ventura …"

Wherever in the world
a Yankee wanderer
enjoys himself and makes wagers
blind to risk.
He drops his anchor
and tries his luck …

Frank gulps. He bows his head, afraid someone may see the tears welling in his eyes. He turns away from the stage, pulls out his handkerchief and blows his nose before stealing back to his office. He closes the door firmly, shocked by this sudden surge of emotion. He sinks onto the solid wooden chair and leans on the desk with his face in his hands.

After several minutes he raises his head and surveys the bare room, furnished only with memories. Here he had battled for permission to stage a first opera when Brigadier Carburton demanded daily revues. Also here he had watched Vermillion with secret delight, long before he dared to hope she might reciprocate his feelings.

He wipes his eyes and stares at the blank expanse of the opposite wall where in the early days he often saw an image of Maggie, his wife, sitting at her piano. Sometimes she seemed to look up and nod approvingly. But over the months her image faded; instead he saw Vermillion's lovely face.

Looking at the wall now, he remembers the charred window frames of his flat. If only he had saved Maggie the way he rescued Barbara. He swallows, prompting another bout of coughing. It feels as though his lungs are still full of smoke. He pulls out a handkerchief, causing an envelope to drop onto the desk.

Frank picks up his father's letter, which had arrived a few days ago when Frank believed he had lost Vermillion. His father had urged him to fight for her although Frank had said little about her. Without even giving her name, he simply said he had met a girl he would like to settle down with. But he added that he knew she wasn't interested because she came from a different class and already had a boyfriend.

Frank's parents had divorced after his father returned from the trenches in a sorry state, made worse by alcohol. He has few memories of his father and what he does remember has been filtered through his mother's bitterness. It was only Frank's belief at Salerno that he might die and his sense that at last he understood what his father had been through, which led Frank to get in touch after more than twenty-five years.

But now he is established in Naples and has fallen for Vermillion, he isn't sure he wants to see his father again. He couldn't introduce him to Vermillion. And knowing his father has remarried, Frank faces the prospect that there might be half-brothers or half-sisters to come to terms with.

Frank sighs as he stuffs the letter away and makes a mental note to think about it another time. At the moment there are more pressing things. In particular, he's desperate for a drink. He looks at his watch. 1140. Ignoring the papers on his desk, he hurries down to the stage door.

'Come on, Huggins, let's find a bar. I'm parched. Last night has completely dried me out. And my head is full of fog.'

Huggins raises his eyebrows as he scans Frank's face.

'All right, Huggins, I know this is irregular, but spending half the night on the roof and rescuing Lieutenant Fortune was also pretty irregular.'

'Yes, Sir. Of course, Sir.'

'But there is one condition, Huggins.' Frank turns and grins. 'You must stop calling me "Sir" once we've left the theatre.'

CHAPTER 5

Vermillion opens her eyes and looks around. This isn't her usual bed. Where is she? Someone is breathing beside her. In the half-light she recognises Jackie's mane.

Frank's flat, of course. Last night's events come flooding back.

She checks her watch and slides quietly from under the bedclothes, keen not to wake her companion. She opens the bedroom door and is pleased to see Frank's note. She reads it as she drifts towards the bathroom. Longing to wash away the residue of last night's fumes, she turns on the hot tap, but the water runs cold. Frank hadn't lit the stove. Poor darling, he must have been exhausted!

She struggles to light the water heater but eventually the water is hot and she lowers herself through the steam. Her skin tingles. She finds a bar of army soap and washes vigorously. It's not just the smoke she needs to be rid of.

She cannot remember the details of her dream but Edmund had been there. She finds that odd, now their relationship is over. But he had been important to her. She had met him in Cairo where she served in Y Section, monitoring German communications. She was attracted from the first time she saw him, playing cricket at the Gezira Sporting Club. He was a natural sportsman who took soldiering in his stride, and had a way of never quite breaking the rules while bending them enough to do pretty much what he liked. Of course it helped that the Colonel was dazzled by his sporting prowess.

Vermillion was impressed too and also flattered when Edmund noticed her. He became a frequent visitor but as she refused to sleep with him, he continued consorting with other girls who were willing to share their beds. Nonetheless he took her out whenever he had leave from the desert. And over time she gathered that he saw her as an ideal wife and planned to marry her once the war was over.

After a year Vermillion relented and they began an affair, but when Edmund's Battalion landed in Italy Vermillion hated being left high and dry in Egypt. Eventually she was transferred to Naples where soon she started helping at the theatre. But when this work became full-time, Edmund did all he could to stop her. She was still in love with him, but increasingly she resented his efforts to run her life even when he was fighting at Cassino. In the end she concluded that their relationship couldn't continue and resolved to end their affair when next he came to Naples.

However, while she waited for Edmund to have some leave, she learnt that he had been wounded by a German mine, losing his legs. She was deeply shaken when she saw him in hospital and pictured him immobilised for the rest of his life. Visiting him every day, she sensed he was slipping away and in time she accepted it might be better if he died.

But with the help of penicillin which Vermillion obtained on the black market, Edmund slowly recovered. And soon he will go home to get his prosthetic legs.

She leans forward in the bath and scrubs herself energetically.

Edmund had asked her to accompany him. Feeling he needed her support, reluctantly she agreed. Then yesterday – yes, it was only yesterday – Edmund told her he was breaking it off and she should stay in Naples. He had learnt about her fling with a pilot in Egypt called Simon Lewis who had offered to fly her to Naples. Edmund knew it was a brief affair, but it was enough to make him change his mind.

Vermillion arches her back to wet her hair; it needs washing too, to remove the whiff of scorching. She closes her eyes and tilts back her head until her hair is under water.

Edmund's decision to leave Vermillion in Naples was what she had wanted, but it still came as a shock. And then on the theatre roof, Frank had told her he loved her. And she had said she loved him too. But can all this be true? She has known Frank for long enough – since October – but for most of that time it never entered her head they might fall in love.

She turns her mind to Barbara, wondering how she is. Thank goodness Frank had rescued her. She will visit the hospital later but first she needs to think about dear Frank.

She rinses her hair slowly, keeping her eyes firmly shut. Already she feels better as she sits up, wiping the water from her face.

She opens her eyes and gives a little start. 'Hello Jackie!'

'I asked a question, Vermillion.' Jackie stands over her. 'What on earth were you up to?'

'Sorry Jackie, I didn't hear.' Vermillion hunts for the soap, which has slipped into the water.

'What were you doing at the theatre?'

'I told you last night. I was woken by the noise of the raid. And when I saw they were dropping incendiaries I went check the place was all right.'

'Really? And you just happened to bump into Frank on the theatre roof in the middle of the night? Come on Vermillion, what the hell is going on?'

'It was lucky we were there. We put out two fires.' Vermillion stands up in the bath. 'Pass me the towel, Jackie.'

Jackie picks it up and extends her arm reluctantly, as though her decision to release it could depend on Vermillion's answers.

'Let me have it, Jackie! You can continue your interrogation when I'm dry.'

'There's no need to be crabby.' Jackie frowns. 'I just want to know what's going on.'

'Nothing's going on!'

Vermillion concentrates on getting dressed before speaking again. 'I wonder how Barbara's doing. Visiting starts at 1430.'

'You'll have to go alone. I can't take time off today. I'm on duty at 1200. And I must check what's left of our flat. Will Frank mind if I stay here tonight?'

'I do think you should see Barbara.'

'It's easy for you. Now you're having a fling with Frank.'

'He saved Barbara's life! He's hardly going to stop me visiting.'

'He's in love with you. I told you that months ago.' Jackie grins. 'And now you've fallen for him. It's all rather neat. And I suppose he's staying on in Naples.'

Vermillion hesitates. In a way Jackie is right. After seeing Frank and Vermillion together, Jackie had announced – in her usual forthright way – that Frank was in love with her. Vermillion hadn't believed her of course but she had started observing Frank differently and had briefly entertained the possibility that he might have feelings for her.

'I've no idea about Frank's plans, Jackie. For the moment he's back in charge of the theatre, but he'll probably be transferred before long. We'll have to wait and see.'

'Come on, Vermillion, admit it! You've landed on your feet. Edmund's off to England and your new man is staying here. They won't return Frank to the line.'

Vermillion's mouth tightens. She doesn't want to talk about Edmund. 'Frank was very brave rescuing Barbara. It was dreadful in there with all that smoke. I thought we'd never get out. And it must have been hard for Frank, after losing his wife.'

'I suppose so. But he could hardly have abandoned Barbara to be burnt to death, after she went back to rescue you.'

'Thank heavens it ended all right …'

'… assuming she recovers.' Jackie looks at her watch. 'I must run; I need to visit the flat.'

* * *

Vermillion aims to arrive at the hospital before the start of visiting time. But the streets are teeming with people, all jostling to keep in the shade. They seem oblivious to the effects of the raid, ignoring the debris, the usual stench of Naples' dilapidated sewers, the new smell of charring, and the air still thick with sooty smuts.

The signs of deprivation are obvious. At every turn, grubby children with matted hair and dressed in rags crowd around her with cries of "pane" and "biscotti". They scamper along shoeless in her wake.

The adults are better dressed, but their faces reveal their emaciation and exhaustion. Even with the Allies' food rations, most of them are close to starving. And the lack of sustenance for their families has led many women into prostitution. Vermillion wishes the Allies could help more but she knows the war is their first priority: everything else must wait.

Vermillion is used to being stared at in the street. Neapolitans are familiar with the sight of Allied troops from all round the world but women in service dress remain a rarity. Men watch her resentfully but then gesture or make eyes at her, hoping to provoke a response. But women, who with so many men away comprise most of the adult population, observe her with respect tinged with what she sees as envy at her independence.

As Vermillion is familiar with these streets and their inhabitants her thoughts soon return to Frank. Can it really be true he loves her? Everything has happened so fast. Yesterday morning she still expected to go to England with Edmund … and Barbara wasn't in hospital.

At the sight of the hospital gates, her chest tightens. Edmund was in a different hospital, but her feelings of apprehension are the same: a mixture of hope and fear. With Edmund there had been the desperate search for penicillin because the army's supplies had been stolen from the docks. In her despair she had turned to Huggins who led her to a young man called Paolo. He knew a chemist who miraculously procured the penicillin that Edmund needed. Only later did she discover that Frank knew Paolo already.

Vermillion still sometimes wonders how things would have been if Edmund had died. She wouldn't ever have thought about returning to England. But would she have fallen for Frank rather sooner? Or not at all? She can't be sure.

She stops at the gates and takes a deep breath. Then, clutching a bunch of flowers that are wilting in the heat, she marches into the lobby where starched nurses stride past followed by the hopeful eyes of waiting soldiers.

She has to ask several times as she tries to locate Barbara. Finally, approaching another long ward, a Sister stops her.

'May I help you?'

'I'm looking for Lieutenant Fortune. She was brought in during the night.'

'Ah yes. Smoke inhalation.'

'I'd like to see her.'

'I'm afraid she's sleeping and mustn't be disturbed. You could try again tomorrow; there should be more news by then.'

Vermillion opens her mouth to protest but the Sister catches her eye before she can speak. She knows there is nothing to be done after Sister has said no.

'Please tell her Lieutenant Henthorpe visited. And please give her these.'

The Sister looks at the flowers as though it were enough to care for dying patients.

'Of course, my dear,' she says without a smile.

* * *

Vermillion hurries up the steps to Frank's flat. She smiles as she takes out the key.

'Hello, Frank,' she says, not raising her voice.

No reply.

Is he asleep? She tiptoes to his bedroom, feeling a strong sense of his presence. The door is open.

'Hello Frank!'

Still no response. He must be at the theatre.

She looks around but it doesn't seem right to be here without him. She feels as though she has gatecrashed, although it isn't really Frank's flat: the Allies had requisitioned it after the owner died fighting in Sicily.

Vermillion sits down wearily and leans back, her head full of thoughts. Closing her eyes she sees Giovanni's face light up as he opened the stage door ... she remembers her fear that he would grab her ... and her headlong rush through the dark theatre to escape ... the climb up and up ... until she reaches the clouds where she looks down on Naples asleep ...

* * *

'Are you there, Vermillion?'

She awakes with a jolt.

'Frank, I'm in here. How was the theatre?'

He walks over and bends to kiss her. 'Would you like a drink, darling? The theatre was under control.'

Vermillion likes him calling her "darling"; it makes her feel secure.

'How are *you*, Frank ... darling? I'd love some wine.' She rubs her forehead as she stands up, wondering whether a drink will make it worse.

'I feel in a bit of a spin,' he hands her a glass. 'But my head is calming down and this will make it better. Where's Jackie?'

'Still on duty. I visited Barbara on my own.'

Frank studies her face and takes her hands; he looks pale. 'I meant what I said last night. I love you, Vermillion. And I always shall.'

'Thank you for everything, Frank. Especially for coming to the theatre last night and for saving poor Barbara.'

Frank moves her hands behind her back and squeezes her towards him. She lifts her face to be kissed, feeling very small beside him. He pulls her up till she's standing on tiptoe. Tears well in her eyes.

'Darling Frank,' she whispers between kisses. 'Thank you. I love you too.'

He lowers her slowly, until her feet are flat on the floor. She takes out her cigarettes and offers one to Frank. He doesn't usually smoke but perhaps tonight he'll make an exception. 'Was everyone all right at the theatre?'

'Things were much as usual.' Frank shakes his head and turns away as she lights a match. 'No one even mentioned Malaspina.'

He watches her as she slowly inhales.

'It's as though Malaspina had never been in charge. I wonder what they really think. They seem afraid to say.'

'They must worry that the Fascists will return.' Vermillion draws on the cigarette again and slowly exhales before continuing. 'They don't call themselves Fascists anymore but there are plenty of those people still around.'

'Huggins worries that I might leave Naples.' Frank waves his hand to clear the smoke and then rubs his forehead. 'I did my best to reassure him. He knows if it were up to me I'd stay here for ever. That might suit him too, now Paolo's out of gaol and there's a chance to do more business. I just hope Paolo has learnt his lesson and won't lead Huggins astray.'

Frank again waves his hand in front of his face.

'I'm sorry about the smoke,' Vermillion stubs out half the cigarette. 'You must have had enough last night.'

'You're right. The fumes had an odd effect.'

Vermillion sips the tepid wine. 'I visited Barbara in the hospital. But they said she was asleep and wouldn't let me see her.'

Frank looks intently at Vermillion. 'I was just thinking about your flat. It was lucky you all got out.'

Vermillion can see that the effort of rescuing Barbara has taken its toll on Frank. Has it reminded him of losing Maggie? Or is it the smoke in his lungs? Should *he* be in hospital too?

'Thank you for rescuing Barbara; you were very brave.'

'We had to rescue her. And thank you for coming too. Let me top you up.'

Vermillion pulls him towards her and kisses him. If only she could make things better. She wonders whether he wants to go to bed but she knows it would be too soon.

'Is Barbara all right?' Frank asks.

Before Vermillion can reply, the doorbell announces Jackie's return. Frank jumps away from Vermillion and goes to open the door.

'How are the lovebirds?' Jackie bursts in. 'Oh good, you've got some wine. I could do with a drink.'

'Sit yourself down, Jackie,' Frank says. 'You must be tired.'

Jackie looks at Frank. 'Is there something on the wireless? Let's have some music, and I don't mean opera.'

She takes a mouthful of wine. 'Did you see Barbara? Did she say when she's coming out? I hope it won't be too soon. It's already a squash in here.'

'I tried to visit her, Jackie. But they wouldn't let me see her. They said she was asleep. I'll go again tomorrow.'

Vermillion looks at Frank; she knows he would rather that Jackie weren't here.

'I visited our flat,' Jackie says. 'There's no damage inside, not even from the hoses. But there's a dreadful smell of smoke so I left the windows half open and I've brought some clothes we can wash. I'd like to move back this weekend.'

'You're welcome to stay here,' Frank says mechanically. 'But Jackie is right, it would be crowded with Barbara.'

'I was planning a day out on Saturday,' Jackie says. 'Mike promised to take me for a drive'.

'We'll have to move back on Sunday,' Vermillion says. 'Frank has the dress rehearsal for Butterfly, so we'll have to do it on our own. Staying here isn't fair on Frank.'

'Frank said it was okay,' Jackie empties her glass and stands up. 'All right, we can do it on Sunday. But I'm going out with Mike on Saturday, come what may.'

Vermillion glances at Frank; he looks completely done in.

CHAPTER 6

Flight Lieutenant Simon Lewis scrambles onto the wing of his Spitfire and steps into the cockpit. He stands on the seat before placing his feet on the rudder controls, as there's no solid floor. He twists round, easing himself down until he's sitting on his parachute. He raises the seat as far as it will go but he still can't see beyond the plane's nose, which rises in front of him.

He switches on his torch and signals to Mason, his fitter, who drops down from the wing. Simon has already inspected the outside of the plane, ensuring the flaps and rudder can move freely. Now he opens the left-hand breast pocket of his flying jacket and pulls out a dog-eared photograph of Vermillion, taken in '42 during the voyage to Egypt.

He presses the photograph to his lips before wedging it carefully amidst the switches. Only then is he ready to complete his final checks. Like most pilots he is superstitious: he knows it's only luck that has kept him flying when so many others have been lost.

He closes the canopy and confirms it's locked. Then he dons his helmet and connects it to the radio. He plugs in his heated flying suit and checks the oxygen supply to his mask. After adjusting the controls, he flicks on the ignition. The needles on the altimeter and the air speed gauge quiver before settling at zero.

Simon gestures to Mason to plug in the trolley accumulator that will start the engine. Then he flips off the covers from the starter and booster-coil buttons and primes the gas pump on his left. It takes six strokes before he feels increased resistance as the fuel gets to the priming nozzle. He places two fingers on the starter buttons and presses.

Suddenly the engine bursts into life before settling to a steady growl. Simon keeps an eye on the oil temperature while the engine warms. Then, satisfied the generator is charging the accumulator, he completes his routine by kissing the photograph again.

He is ready.

He signals to Mason to remove the chocks and prepares to taxi to the runway. He pulls the joystick fully back to keep the tail down and moves slowly forwards. He has done this countless times, yet he still feels apprehensive. He'll feel better once he's airborne.

At the end of the runway he pauses, awaiting instructions through his headphones. A measured voice from the control tower wishes him well as the runway lights are switched on. For a moment he hesitates, picturing Vermillion again. Then he accelerates across the rough airfield. The Merlin engine breathes heavily and in an instant he's off the ground and banking slowly towards the north.

Unlike a normal Spitfire with its machine guns and cannons, the PR.XI is built for long distance reconnaissance and is stripped of armour. Simon must rely on the plane's speed and altitude to avoid the enemy defences. He can outfly every enemy fighter except for the Messerschmitt 262 – the first German jet. But tonight's mission will take him to northern Italy and 262s are yet to venture south of the Alps.

In place of guns and bombs, the plane is armed with photographic equipment, including synchronised cameras designed to take pairs of photographs to be viewed in 3-D.

Simon's mission will take him to the Brenner Pass – the steep-sided valley, extending deep into the Alps, which provides the principal road and rail routes from Austria into Italy. There he'll record the damage caused by Allied bombing.

The plane climbs steadily. For two hours he'll fly nor-nor-west, arriving over the Brenner at sunrise. The weather forecast is good and already there's a first hint of light in the sky. The best photographs require strong light with shadows so every detail will be clear to the photographic interpreters at MAIU (West). But catching the light can be tricky in the mountains.

Allied aircrews have learnt to fear the Brenner because of the anti-aircraft defences that line the pass. They have suffered heavy losses in recent raids intended to stem the flow of enemy troops and supplies into Italy. Simon's pictures will help the Allies to target future raids.

But the Brenner is several hundred miles away. Here – south of Rome – he is over liberated Italy and should be safe, but soon he will enter enemy territory.

With no moon tonight, the sky is intensely dark. Simon will mostly rely on his instruments to maintain his course. But through the canopy he can see a myriad of stars against the wash of the Milky Way. He loves these moments alone in the heavens. It reminds him of Egypt and the wonders of the firmament seen through the pure desert air.

He was twenty-two when he arrived in Heliopolis as a newly trained pilot. With his interest in photography he was quickly assigned to aerial reconnaissance. It was unglamorous compared with flying a fighter. But in time he appreciated its advantages: not least that he's still alive.

He had noticed Vermillion at once on the troopship, but he didn't get a chance to speak to her until they reached Cape Town. He glances at the photograph. She was twenty-one but seemed younger. He thought she was beautiful and perfect and for the rest of the voyage to Egypt they enjoyed jolly times together, socialising and even dancing. He often tried to make her tipsy and sometimes succeeded, until she set a two-drink rule. But there were few opportunities for intimacy in the crowded confines of the ship; instead Simon dreamt of wooing her in Egypt. What a fool he had been to wait! No sooner had they made it to Cairo than she fell for Edmund; Simon has struggled to catch up ever since.

He starts to sing, blending the tune with the steady thrum of the engine.

"I've flown around the world in a plane..." He sings this line several times before continuing. And then at the end he keeps repeating the refrain: "... I can't get started with you."

After losing touch with Vermillion there were other girls of course, but none that mattered. It was only in the summer of '43, when Cairo was almost deserted, that he met her again. He was flying reconnaissance missions from the air base at Heliopolis and he regaled her with tales of his flights across southern Europe and the beautiful scenery and buildings he saw. She lapped it up, showing especial interest in Sicily because Edmund was there. So Simon embellished his descriptions of the beauty of the island: green after the winter rains, with golden beaches and snow high up on Mount Etna.

He felt again he had a chance – until he overplayed his hand. He is usually quite cool-headed, as pilots need to be. But in Vermillion's presence he struggles to think. He knows they should be together and he's sure she wants that too. He just needs to engineer the right occasion.

With the plane now over enemy territory, he pulls back the joystick and climbs again. Outside the temperature falls. Without his heated suit, he would soon freeze. He scans the sky all around, which he will now do continually. He lifts his left hand and rubs his neck below his helmet where his scarf chaffs from the constant movement. Then he pulls on the thick leather gauntlets over two pairs of silk gloves and starts a gentle zigzag to make certain there's nothing on his tail.

Tonight he's alone in the sky.

"I can't get started with you ..." he croons again.

With Edmund fighting in Sicily, Vermillion accepted Simon's invitation to go dancing at the country club. She danced well and with the baking summer evenings she would soon get quite flushed and would happily enjoy a few drinks. Then he would choose a moment to kiss her. She protested of course but sometimes she'd yield and kiss him properly. Yet despite his determined efforts things never progressed.

With the news of the landings at Salerno, Vermillion became desperate to get to Italy. She wanted to be nearer to Edmund and hated being left behind. With tears in her eyes she told Simon that her request for a transfer had been refused. By then he was flying there regularly and soon his squadron would be moving to Foggia. Feeling sorry for her and hoping to cheer her up, he offered to fly her to Italy.

It wasn't so unusual for pilots to take their girls on flights provided the sortie wasn't dangerous. Simon had felt sure he could get Vermillion to Italy. But that would have been the easy part: she could hardly have appeared in Naples without any papers. He assumed she knew this and was intrigued when she took his offer seriously. Suddenly she was flushed with excitement and gave him a resounding kiss.

Sensing she had lowered her guard, with a grin he added a stipulation: 'I'll take you to Italy, Vermillion … provided you sleep with me first.'

He knew she wouldn't agree of course, but he liked the way her cheeks flared as she hissed her response: 'Simon, you know I can't do that!'

He forgot all about the offer until a few days later when Vermillion telephoned the base and accepted his invitation. Simon could hardly believe his luck.

They agreed to meet at Shepheards Hotel where Simon planned they would dance and have dinner before going to bed. But Vermillion said she just wanted to get it done. Now he squirms to recall the dingy bedroom with the tawdry chandelier that quivered above the bed. Despite the bottle of champagne, it was a wretched place to make love.

At the time, however, Simon was delighted that Vermillion had agreed, even though she kept saying she was doing it for Edmund's sake. But a few days later Vermillion sent a message that her transfer had been agreed so he never did fly her to Italy.

It didn't take Simon long to discover he had made a huge mistake in overplaying his hand to get her into bed. Then it had been what he wanted more than anything. But ever since it has been a barrier between them.

Far below Simon sees the spectral reflection of a large lake, a key landmark on his journey. In the morning he will return this way to study a building he had noticed before and to take some photographs of his own.

The building, which appears on maps as the Castello di Montalera, looks like a fortified village with grey stone castellated towers. It's hard to gauge its age, but he guesses it's medieval. Italy is full of such buildings. But what makes this one special is its location at the top of a conical hill rising five hundred feet above the lake.

To Simon the place looks magical. He can picture Vermillion at the castle. Montalera: dedicated to Hera, the goddess of women and marriage. How perfect. When the war is over, he will buy the hill and the castle, and they will live there together.

"I can't get started with you ..." he sings again.

* * *

After crossing the Apennines at an altitude of 24,000 feet, Simon must now climb higher. Outside the temperature is minus thirty but when he reaches 35,000 feet it will be closer to minus seventy. As well as his heated flying suit, he will need pressurised oxygen to breath, with a steady counter-pressure from the bladder in his waistcoat to protect his lungs.

The light is stronger now and the jagged silhouette of the Dolomites is visible ahead. Snow has melted from the peaks but there are still white fingers on the north-facing slopes. From seven miles up Simon feels like a god as he watches the dawn unfurl.

He glances at the map strapped to his left knee. It shows the first target for his cameras near the head of the Brenner, close to Bressanone. Flying at 350mph he continues his slow zigzag, scanning the sky all around. Still no bandits.

He banks towards the east and begins a looping turn to bring him to the required course. He is approaching his northernmost 'target' just south of the town. He checks his course again and scours the ground for key landmarks. There's the church. And the bridge. He is set.

Along the length of the Brenner there are said to be a thousand German guns, many of them 88s with an altitude ceiling of 35,000 feet. But with some batteries located in the hills the Spitfire may come within range.

Simon leans forward to set the camera controller. He flicks the switch to on and watches as the counter spins. He scans the sky again before checking the counter, which has reached the required number. He flicks off the switch and pulls into a tight turn. A clean run. No ack-ack. With luck, they won't have spotted him and won't broadcast an alert.

He sets a new course south-west towards Bolzano. The town stands in the valley where it passes through a dogleg, swinging sharply east before curving slowly towards the north-east. He'll avoid the pass until the final moment, hoping to stay unobserved.

He has several targets in Bolzano. The mountains here rise above 5,000 feet, but because the valley turns north-east the town should be touched by the early morning sun.

Simon wills the Spit to climb further into the thin air. 36,000 … 36,500. The needle trembles. 37,000 … 37,500. He cranes his neck to search the horizon. He eases back slightly, levelling out at 38,000 feet. As he reaches his target altitude he zigzags again.

Below, the valley opens up until he can see the whole city. The railway line and the main road stand out and there's the camp he must photograph.

The plane judders. Telltale balls of black smoke burst all around. Shit! The gunners have seen him. A mighty bang and the oxygen pump misses a beat, but then restarts. Simon catches his breath and holds his course.

'Ten, nine, eight …' Another thud. 'Seven, six, five …' A louder bang. Shrapnel clomps against the fuselage. 'Four, three, two … one.'

He leans forward and switches on the cameras. The counter spins slowly until it reaches the required total. Thank God!

He swings the plane into a tight turn, levelling out as he flees across the mountains. It's time to leave the bloody Brenner and visit Vermillion's castle.

CHAPTER 7

Vermillion approaches the theatre cautiously, anxious about Giovanni, but she accelerates when she glimpses a familiar figure near the stage door.

'Welcome back, Miss,' Huggins greets her. 'The theatre hasn't been the same without you.'

She smiles as she looks around again. Still no sign of Giovanni.

'Have you heard the news, Miss?' Huggins pulls back his shoulders. 'VI Corps has broken through at Anzio and they've linked up with our lads from Cassino. In two shakes they'll be in Rome.'

'That's marvellous news, Huggins. Let's hope it means an end to the air raids. How are things at the theatre?'

'We've started repairing the roof! Those incendiaries didn't half cause some damage before you found them. If it hadn't been for you, Miss, we'd have lost the whole blooming place.'

'Captain Hill helped too.'

'Yes, Miss. That was quite queer. Both of you up on the roof with the Hun raining down firebombs.'

'We were both afraid, Huggins, that the theatre could burn down. By the way, there's a stirrup pump up there but no water. You'd better keep some buckets topped up.'

Huggins looks down at his scuffed boots. 'I hear there was a fire at your flat, Miss.'

'Lieutenant Fortune was taken to hospital, but she should be out soon. Luckily the flat wasn't damaged – just filled with smoke. Everything will need cleaning but we're moving back this weekend. Until then we're camping with Captain Hill. He tells me you found his flat. It's very nice but rather small for three.'

'Let me know if I can lend a hand.'

'Thank you, Huggins. That reminds, how is *your* hand? I heard you threw quite a punch.'

'A bit sore at first, Miss, but now it's right as rain.'

'I heard you laid out Malaspina with a single blow. You should try your talents in the ring at the Teatro delle Palme.'

'No thanks, Miss.' Huggins thrusts out his barrel chest. 'I'm the wrong shape for the fight game. I don't have Frank's reach.'

'It was still quite a punch by all accounts.'

'It was one of my better ones. But it's tough on the hands without no gloves.'

'Did you learn to box properly?'

'Yes, Miss. It was all Marquess of Queensberry with us. The old man has a gym in Poplar. He was a pro in his time and expected me to follow. I was still in my nappy when he first put me into the ring. But it didn't do no good. I can scrap with the best of them but I'm all the wrong shape. You see I'm an easy target for a bloke of five foot nine with a good straight left. I can't get to the b…'

'… but you can look after yourself.'

'Yes, of course, Miss. But I'm still a disappointment to my dad. That's why when the war started he made me join up, hoping the army would toughen me up – like the Great War had done for him.'

* * *

Vermillion settles down to go through the papers on her desk. The most urgent thing is a note from the box office saying ticket sales have dropped since the raid. She visits the box office manager to review the figures, which clearly show the decline started before.

With so many men required for the assault on the Gustav Line, Vermillion suspects there are simply fewer troops in Naples. She has seen these fluctuations before. What worries her more is what will happen as the line moves further north. Could there be a permanent drop in the numbers passing through Naples? That would be bound to affect the theatre. She needs to tell Frank, but not yet: the revival of Butterfly opens on Monday and in the winter it had sold well.

* * *

Vermillion is starting to feel drowsy in the afternoon heat when Huggins brings her a letter from her mother. Just the sight of her handwriting is enough to make Vermillion feel guilty: she has been a fitful correspondent, withholding important news since she reached Naples. Already, as she unfolds the sheet of thin paper, she begins to feel ill.

3rd May 1944

Darling Vermillion

I do hope you're safe and well. It has been a long time since we heard from you, but I expect there's a letter on its way. I suppose we shouldn't be surprised that some of them get delayed.

I try to imagine what you do in Italy but I expect it's very worthwhile. I hope your young man, Edmund, is keeping fit. Your father and I look forward to meeting him once the war is over. I hope that when he gets some leave you can enjoy your time together. Are there are any entertainments over there? Do you ever go to the pictures or see a show?

Penelope sends her love. I know she would be pleased to hear from you. Tucked away in the country with the babies she longs for any news. William is now in Burma, so she rarely hears from him, which is quite a trial. She lives for the day when he returns.

Your father sends best wishes. We look forward to your next letter.

Your loving mother

Vermillion buries her head in her hands. Then she gets up and edges across the room. She should have written of course: she knows her mother worries. She also feels sorry for Pen, her elder sister, who is stuck deep in the countryside with two small children, waiting for Bill's return.

Vermillion often thinks about writing, but things have grown so complicated. Her mother knows she met Edmund in Cairo and again in Italy but not that Vermillion had doubts about their relationship. And she still doesn't know that Edmund was wounded and had planned to take her back to England. Thank goodness she didn't tell her, or now she would have to explain she wasn't returning after all and that deep down she had always hoped to stay.

Oh dear! There's so much she hasn't said. She hasn't mentioned her work at the theatre, because her mother has a Victorian view that people who work in theatres are immoral. And she hasn't mentioned Frank. Sometimes she tries to imagine taking him to meet her parents. But in her mind's eye she never gets past the front door. They would be impressed by his charm and bearing but his lack of sporting interests and the fact that he went to university would arouse their suspicions. She does want them to like him of course; she will have to brief him carefully when the time comes.

Vermillion returns to her desk and sits down heavily. In Egypt she was a regular correspondent but life was simpler then. As she focuses on the urgent need to reply, she can see it was premature to think about Frank meeting her parents. Her letter must say enough without going into detail.

She addresses her reply to her parents and Pen together – avoiding the need to write twice. She begins with a fulsome apology for not writing before, which she combines with enquiries about everyone's health. Then she embarks on a long narrative about being posted to Italy and meeting up with Edmund in Naples where they had realised they weren't well suited and had decided to break it off. Then Edmund had been wounded and will soon return home. She makes clear her willingness to accompany him and his decision that she should stay here.

She has skated over painful details, but now comes the awkward part with her transfer from Y Section to the theatre. She tells them she is assisting a charming infantry Captain who reopened the royal theatre to entertain the troops. Referring to Frank as Captain Hill, she outlines the success of the revues and adds she is having a marvellous time seeing the great Italian operas. She is careful not to describe Frank in glowing terms.

Then she turns to the fire, outlining how she and Captain Hill had put out incendiaries on the theatre roof but she doesn't mention that this happened in the middle of the night. And when she describes how Frank had rescued Barbara she doesn't say that Barbara went back to find her. She praises Captain Hill's bravery but balances that by explaining how Barbara was overcome with smoke and is still in hospital.

She puts down her pen and closes her eyes. She had visited Barbara earlier and had seen her briefly, although she was still asleep. Barbara's hands had felt rather hot. Sister said she was running a temperature, which made Vermillion start to worry. She had heard that people sometimes die after inhaling too much smoke; their brains have been starved of oxygen and they never come round.

She opens her eyes and rereads the letter, which says what she needs to say. She signs off with love and sits back feeling tired but relieved that she hasn't given too many hostages to fortune. She makes a few corrections and seals the envelope.

'Thank goodness!' she says out loud.

CHAPTER 8

Major Roger Bewdley glances across at the wan face of Corporal Johns who had served with 3rd Battalion at Monte Tranquillo but missed the worst fighting at Cassino.

Roger grins causing his moustache to quiver. Johns will soon adapt to life at the front; they always do.

'God, that's awful … Sir.' Johns puts one hand over his nose. But soon he needs both hands to control the three-tonner. 'I thought the stink in Naples was bad, Sir. But this is worse.'

'It's the German soldiers, Corporal,' Roger clenches his pipe between his teeth, 'I always said they were rotters.'

The truck inches past the ruins of the town which once nestled below the towering Monastery Hill. In February '44 Allied bombers destroyed the abbey of Monte Cassino – founded by Saint Benedict in the Sixth Century – to prevent its use as an Observation Post directing German shelling onto Allied positions. And a month later the once thriving town of Cassino, here in the valley, had suffered the same fate.

Now hardly a wall remains. Rubble is heaped on rubble and only the road they are following has been bulldozed clear.

'I'd heard it was bad at Cassino.' Johns says. 'But I never pictured it like this.'

'I wish those desk-wallahs in Naples could see it,' Roger says, 'instead of sitting on their fat arses.'

They had set off this morning in darkness, following Route 6, the old Via Casilina. But now in the early dawn light they can see enough. Colour hasn't yet returned but that makes little difference: Cassino only exists in black and white.

The Battalion is returning to the line – wherever it will be when they get there. With the Germans retreating even Roger isn't sure. His orders are to muster C Company at the village of Le Querce where they'll spend the night, before entering the line at dawn. But at their present rate of progress – nose to tail at five miles an hour – Roger doubts they'll arrive on time.

UNEXPLODED MINES – BEWARE. They pass a large sign in English.

'I was thinking about Major Manley, Sir.' Johns still holds his nose intermittently and his voice sounds nasal above the rumble of the Bedford's engine. 'Do you know how he's doing?'

'Making good progress, Corporal. But after that blasted mine, he needs some new pins.'

Johns had once been Edmund's driver; Roger guesses he liked him, as many of the men did. But Roger was never a fan. He saw Edmund as typical of the sort who is born with a silver spoon, and sails through life without effort. All right he was a decent batsman but that was a talent he was born with. And yes, he could be brave, but he took unnecessary risks. No wonder he came a cropper.

For Roger, Edmund's one admirable quality was his way with the fillies. The Contessa was a stunner and then along came Vermillion. Everyone agreed she was a peach. Roger has pondered this a lot and has concluded it's just a matter of luck. But a chap needs to work on his luck and Roger can't wait to have another go: it should be one of the pickings of war.

'Is Major Manley returning to England to get his … his new pins?' Johns asks.

'I hope so, Corporal. Until then we can't pull his leg.'

Johns snorts at this remark and then grimaces as he breathes in more putrid air. Roger is surprised that Johns didn't laugh. Happily most of his men enjoy a joke. Perhaps Johns just lacks a sense of humour.

'It seems a miracle, Sir, that Major Manley survived, after the mauling he took.'

Roger doesn't reply. He has led C Company for more than two months. So why do people still talk about Edmund who was wounded in March in the third battle of Cassino? All right, it's a fact of army life that promotion comes from filling the shoes of the dead and wounded. Roger smirks at the notion that Edmund can't fill those shoes anymore.

The Company was one of many units broken at Cassino, where for four months the Allies had thrown young men in their thousands against the natural defences of Italy's mountains and rivers, made deadlier by German fortifications – minefields, barbed wire, gun emplacements and bunkers – and by the endless rain.

Cassino had formed a pivotal part of the Gustav Line, a defensive system that crossed the Italian peninsula from Minturno in the west to the Sangro River where it flows into the Adriatic. Only concerted Allied attacks two weeks ago – involving a colossal weight of guns and bombers as well as infantry – had finally broken this line. The Allied armies then surged past Cassino into the Liri valley. But a few miles further north they came to more German positions, the so-called Hitler Line.

After the losses in March there had been too few replacements to bring 3rd Battalion up to strength. Its remnants, including C Company, were therefore transferred to 4th Battalion, which was then held in reserve during the decisive fourth battle of Cassino.

Roger strokes his moustache as he stares through the windscreen at the queue of Allied vehicles stretching over the next hill, aware that even an infantry division needs thousands of vehicles to supply its men in the field. And the vehicles of several divisions are crammed onto this narrow and cratered road.

Above them a wing of medium bombers flies north to pound the retreating enemy. Roger wishes he were up there. In '38 he had wanted to join the RAF, but his mother begged him not to. He should have ignored her. Not that he wanted to fly bombers: fighter pilots are far more dashing.

Johns' attention stays fixed on the road as the traffic briefly accelerates outside Cassino but then stops completely. A truck has broken down and must be elbowed off the road. At least with soldiers everywhere there's no shortage of willing hands. But it all takes time and it's afternoon before they're under way again.

Past Cassino they start to see living trees. With their vibrant spring foliage they appear as signs of hope after lines of scorched and blackened skeletons. Yet in the next village they can't see a living thing and nothing remains standing. Aquino was a point of fierce resistance on the Hitler Line and had paid a heavy price. Although the corpses of soldiers have already been moved, they still pass the bloated carcasses of horses with eyes that gape in terror.

Roger's stomach nearly heaves at the sight of these innocent creatures. God, this war is cruel! He doesn't want to be seen to wipe his eyes, so he smooths his moustache again and opens the window further. 'Perhaps the Horsemen of the Apocalypse came this way.'

'I only remember Pestilence, Sir. What were the other three?'

'There's War … and there's Famine …'

Damn it! Roger says to himself. Why can't he remember the fourth? 'Pestilence, War, Famine and …'

'I suppose the last one must be Death … Sir.'

'That's it, Corporal. You got there in the end.'

Roger silently repeats the four names while he watches the road narrow. Here the wooded hillsides rise steeply and there's less sign of destruction. Where there has been shelling or bombing, the targets have been vehicles on the road. Wrecked trucks and occasional tanks salute grotesquely as the column passes by.

Ahead, several vehicles have stopped at the side of the road. A soldier waves Johns down.

'Keep back! There's a sniper in the trees!'

Several men are inching forward, their rifles raised. Roger follows their line of sight and glimpses a camouflaged figure moving along a branch. The figure drops his gun.

'I think he's coming down,' Roger says.

A shot rings out. And another. The figure cries out.

'He's certainly coming down now!'

The sound of a branch cracking merges into a stifled scream. The figure thuds onto the road.

'Couldn't you have taken him prisoner?' Roger addresses the Captain in charge of the men.

'Not bloody likely. Not without a mutiny. The men detest these snipers. We've lost three men already.'

Around the next bend, Roger glimpses Le Querce above on the hillside. The truck labours up through the woods until it emerges into afternoon sunshine. There's no sign of destruction here but now in the distance they can hear the rumble of heavy guns.

The road through the village is filled with waving Italians. Roger smiles; it's the first place to give them a welcome.

The men drum their fists on the side of the vehicles, shouting: 'BASTARDI! BASTARDI!'

'They don't seem very pleased to see us, Sir,' Johns says.

Roger removes his pistol from its holster. 'Drive on, Corporal. We'll stop at the end of the village.'

As the truck jolts to a halt, Roger leaps from the cab. 'Sergeant Major, line up the men over there. Then follow me. Be ready to give covering fire.'

Roger strides towards the centre of the village. From the houses lining the street he hears eerie howls. Then the crowd sees him and surges forward, shouting and shaking their fists. Some of the men carry scythes.

'VIA! VIA! VIA!' they yell.

Roger half raises his pistol. The crowd gasps.

'Does anyone here speak English, Inglese?' he shouts, 'Or French, Francese?'

An elderly man steps forward. The two men stand in the middle of the piazza in the sunshine with their respective retinues barely twenty yards apart. The crowd continues to barrack. The old man stares at Roger who returns his pistol to its holster.

'Major Bewdley of 4th Battalion.' Roger offers his hand, but the old man ignores it. 'What has happened? Tell your friends they shouldn't be afraid. We're here to liberate your country.'

'We've just come from the cemetery,' the man points up the hill, 'where I buried my daughter's husband.'

'I'm sorry …'

'He was killed …' The man's words contort into a cry of pain. He crumples, bending almost double before slowly pulling himself up. 'He tried to protect … my daughter … when they attacked.'

From behind him the crowd shouts: 'Bastardi! Bastardi!' Roger starts to feel impatient. The whole business is awful but there's nothing he can do. He feels for his pipe in his pocket.

'I'm sorry,' Roger says. 'You're right, they *are* bastards.'

Roger taps his pipe on his heel to empty it.

He listens as the man recounts the grim tale of multiple assaults. Roger finds the story hard to believe, but he can't quite ignore the conviction with which the old man tells it.

When the man finishes, Roger puts his arm on his shoulder, but he shakes it off. The crowd jeers.

'I can only say … I'm very sorry … I shall make a report.' Roger extends his hand but the old man has already turned away.

'All right, Sergeant Major!' Roger calls. 'I think we'll try the next village. We can't very well stay here.'

'Yes, Sir.' Singer turns towards the men. 'Attention! Shoulder arms! By the right, qui … ick march!'

* * *

Colonel Mortimer now commands 4th Battalion as part of II Corps.

'You'll be entering the line tomorrow morning,' he tells the assembled officers. 'I need to brief you now about the developing situation.'

He signals for a large chart to be hung over a tripod.

'With the success of Operation Diadem the two Allied armies have broken through the Gustav and Hitler Lines. II Corps has joined up with VI Corps from Anzio and now the reunited Fifth Army is heading north-west towards Rome. The other team are in full retreat, with VI Corps ready to cut them off.'

Roger's mind wanders back to Le Querce. There was no sign of any children. Of course, that was what was wrong apart from the obvious. Even in bloody Norfolk in '30 when people were miserable as sin there were always kids in the streets.

God, how he hates Norfolk! More then than now. But he still loathes what it meant for him: the humiliation of being removed from his public school and shoved off to the local grammar. Norwich wasn't such a bad place but coming from Surrey he stuck out from the other boys and they picked on him. It could all have been avoided if his mother had simply remarried after father died.

The Colonel catches Roger's eye. Roger flinches. Has he

missed something? But the Colonel continues talking and Roger soon picks up the thread.

'There's one more defensive line south of Rome – the Caesar Line – you can see it here.' He points to the map. 'VI Corps has made contact already and will soon break through. Our job is to drive the other team back until they're cut off. Tomorrow at 0500 the transport will take you to San Martino, a village in Allied hands. From there you'll climb these hills …' he points at the map '… to mop up enemy remnants.'

Colonel Mortimer beams; perhaps his enthusiasm is returning. Roger is still thinking about Le Querce. But when the Colonel asks for questions, he stays silent. He doesn't want Mortimer to think he's rocking the boat.

CHAPTER 9

After a string of meetings around the theatre Frank feels confident the new season's production of Butterfly will be a success. The cast and musicians are excited at the prospect and the stage crew is ready.

He feels great pride in what he and they have achieved but he still feels weary as he settles at his desk. He had slept badly again: after waking from a nightmare in the middle of the night he struggled to get back to sleep .

He remembers a fragment of a dream. Again Roger had ordered some men into a burning building but this time Frank was leading them. Oh God, how ghastly! Why on earth does he have these dreams?

Frank gets up and paces across the room. Why this image of soldiers entering a burning building? Is there a link with the fire at Vermillion's flat? But how can there be? Roger and Clissold weren't there and there were no other soldiers.

Even when Frank was with the Battalion – in North Africa, Sicily and Salerno – they never entered a burning building.

They had more sense. He wonders what Sigmund Freud would make of the dream. Would he say it had something to do with sex?

He strides along the corridor and into Vermillion's office. 'Have you had a good day?' He grins. 'Let's pop down to the Club. Jackie won't be back for a while: she's always late.'

Vermillion looks up. 'All right, but we must hurry. I promised Jackie we'd get back first.'

They walk through the theatre to the foyer, a grand room running along the side of the theatre with French windows overlooking the palace gardens. Frank had it restored as a canteen for the theatre staff after learning that many were undernourished. But when Brigadier Carburton, the officer in the Allied Military Government responsible for the theatre, discovered the splendid facility he requisitioned it for the Officers' Club.

Initially Frank was annoyed about this change, but he has come to see that the place is ideal for the Club and has brought more officers to see their shows. Tonight the place is busy, as so often after a performance. A small band is playing *The Very Thought of You* and several couples are dancing. But most of the men are crowded at the far end around the bar, where their banter drowns out the music.

Frank has been to the Club with Vermillion many times. But tonight is different. Before she was Edmund's girl having a drink with a colleague. He senses as she looks around that she feels nervous. He wonders whether the others can see their relationship has changed.

Vermillion clasps his hand. 'Let's dance. Just for a minute.'

'I'd rather get a drink first. Then we can dance.'

They stand at the back of the group jostling around the bar. The men are excited about the news from the front. Vermillion looks at her watch and then takes his hand again. Perhaps they should have gone straight to the flat and enjoyed a drink in peace.

A Major in front of Vermillion turns around with three glasses full of beer. He treads on her toes as he edges by. She winces.

'Frank, I'll wait over there.'

He watches her sit down at a quiet table. Soon her foot is tapping to the rhythm of the band. Then an Army Captain smiles and says something; he doesn't hide his disappointment as he moves away.

Frank wishes he could push the queue aside but finally he acquires two glasses of white wine.

'Sorry to have been so slow. There was quite a scrum. Your good health.'

She raises her glass and smiles before taking a sip.

Frank knocks the wine back. 'That's better. I really needed it. Perhaps it's the heat.'

'Well, it is almost June. And it's bound to get hotter. Edmund said that last year Sicily sizzled.'

Frank takes her hand. 'Darling Vermillion, it's marvellous to be with you here. We haven't had a moment to ourselves. It isn't anyone's fault, but I like seeing you on your own.'

The band plays: *You're Driving me Crazy*.

'Come on Frank. Let's dance for a minute and then we must get back for Jackie.'

He gets up at once – his face can't hide his disappointment, although he's glad to hold her. He pulls her closer and she slides her left hand behind his shoulder.

'I'm sorry we have to leave, Frank, but Jackie has an early shift tomorrow. Perhaps she'll go to bed early.'

She glances up at Frank who squeezes her hand.

* * *

They walk slowly back to the flat with their arms around each other.

'Frank, I know it's awkward with Jackie. She isn't easy at the best of times. But she can be fun and there's rarely a dull moment when she's around.'

'I know what you mean!' Frank pulls her closer. 'But just at the moment I'd like a few dull moments. Oh, I'm sorry! I didn't mean that being with you is dull! Of course not. I just mean I want to spend time with you alone.'

'We need Barbara to calm Jackie down,' Vermillion continues after a pause. 'I saw her today, but she was still asleep. I do worry about her.'

'She'll be all right, darling.' Frank tries not to show he's worried too. 'She's getting the best possible care.'

'I know the fire was hard for you too,' Vermillion says. 'Did it bring back memories of the blitz, and Maggie?'

Frank takes a deep breath.

'When we went into the palazzo … when we were going in … I thought of Maggie … I kept asking why I didn't save her.'

'But, you weren't there when she was killed.'

'No … but perhaps I should have been.'

'Darling, you can't be everywhere,' she catches his eye. 'You're not God.'

He turns to her again. 'When I opened the palazzo door I wanted to run away. Being trapped by fire is so horrific.'

'Thank goodness you brought Barbara out alive.'

'Yes …' he looks away.

'Frank, please tell me about Maggie. I know how important she is.'

'I really loved her. She wasn't beautiful like you, but she was loving and had a passion for music. She played the piano with a marvellous touch and had immense compassion for people and animals.'

Frank stops.

'But Maggie has gone.' He clears his throat. 'I grieved for her when I was in the desert. Perhaps that's why I can't remember much about those years. It was a grey time when even the desert looked grey. But that's in the past. Now I love you, and I always shall.'

She takes his hands again. He doesn't know what to say, so he envelops her in his arms and kisses her. With his heart ready to burst, he has to sing. What comes to him is Schubert's Erstarrung.

"Ich such' im Schnee vergebens.
Nach ihrer Tritte Spur,

Wo sie an meinem Arme
Durchstrich die grüne Flur.

Ich will den Boden küssen,
Durchdringen Eis und Schnee
Mit meinen heißen Tränen,
Bis ich die Erde seh'."

In vain I search for her footprints
Where on my arm she wandered through the fields.
Now the ground is covered in snow but my burning tears
Will melt it and restore the meadows to life.

Vermillion listens intently. She remains silent as the sound
fades away.

'Thank you, Frank,' she says at last as she blinks to clear
her eyes. 'Thank you for singing so beautifully.'

Frank takes her hand.

'When we were on the beach at Salerno things were pretty
grim. I was at the end of my tether with the German shells
raining down. I knew I had to sing to survive. I didn't choose
a German song but those were the sounds that formed inside
me. It's a song about a man who loses his love but keeps her
image frozen in his heart. And he knows if his heart ever
thaws then the image will melt. Maggie was my frozen image
and when I started to love you her image disappeared.'

* * *

All the way back to the flat Frank wants to sing. But he
contents himself with holding Vermillion's precious hand and
whispering every few yards that he loves her.

As soon as the flat door is shut, he wraps his arms around
her and kisses her. He hopes she will come to bed with him.
He takes her hand again to lead her to the bedroom.

'Not yet, darling. Jackie will be back in a minute.'

'Blow Jackie,' Frank grins, 'in that case we'd better have
a drink.'

'If we open a bottle we'll encourage Jackie to stay up.'

Frank struggles to contain himself. But when Jackie does appear, Frank and Vermillion are sitting well apart apparently reading.

'Where's the wine, Vermillion,' Jackie looks around. 'Don't say you've finished it.'

'Don't worry, Jackie, we've still got plenty,' Frank responds. 'I *could* open a bottle.'

'Don't open it just for me. I have to be up at 0500. I must go to bed. Vermillion, have you seen Barbara again?'

'I'll tell you about her tomorrow.'

'Good night, both of you. I feel done in and I don't intend to be a wallflower.'

Frank waits while Jackie traipses to the bathroom and then retreats to the other bedroom where the light finally goes out. He stands up and walks towards Vermillion intending to sit next to her on the sofa, but she gets up too and lets him kiss her.

'You'll have to be very quiet,' she raises a finger to her lips as he shuts the bedroom door.

'Yes, darling,' he whispers. 'I promise I won't make a sound. I won't even sing, although I shall want to.'

PART II

– *June 1944* –

CHAPTER 10

There they are again!

Paolo is sure he heard footsteps coming from behind, but the kaleidoscope of echoes makes it hard to tell. He freezes and listens.

Nothing.

High above the sky is brighter, but here in the alleyway the light has yet to penetrate. Has someone followed him? Emma's husband can't have returned: he was killed in Libya! Even if he had returned, he would have gone to her flat. He wouldn't be skulking around in these back streets.

Is he going crazy like Chiara?

Paolo accelerates. He must get out of the labyrinth. If he continues along here, he can escape into Via Roma.

Oh God! Those footsteps again!

He veers suddenly left and vanishes into the shadows. He stops, his back pressed against the wall. His heart is thumping. Someone *was* following him!

'You go that way!' An American voice calls. 'I'll check over here!'

A pair of boots advances along the side street. Paolo steels himself. He slips out his knife, gripping it behind his back. The footsteps slow as they approach. Paolo wants to run but his legs feel dead.

A head appears at the corner.

'Hi, pal,' the young man says conversationally. Then he yells: 'Carlo, the son of a bitch is over here!'

Paolo can't run now. He grips the knife.

'Paolo Baldini!' The man opens his pistol holster. 'Now buddy, why don't you drop what you're holding and raise your hands.' He speaks English with a sing-song American accent.

Paolo lets the knife clatter to the ground. He raises his trembling hands. 'What do you want?' he asks in Italian.

'Listen to me!' Carlo says, raising his pistol. 'We don't want you getting hurt.'

'I not understand,' Paolo pretends to struggle with English.

'Well, I'll speak a bit louder.' Carlo yells in Italian. 'Turn around! Face the wall! And keep your hands above your head!'

Paolo wheels round. One of the men kicks away his knife and checks his jacket and legs. Paolo starts to shake all over. He clenches his buttocks, terrified he might shit himself.

Damn these bloody Yanks, whose parents emigrated from Italy. How dare they return to lord it over their cousins! God, they're more arrogant than the British!

'Now buddy, listen carefully!' The first American grabs Paolo's thick black hair from behind. He pulls it back and then jerks his face against the stuccoed wall.

'Santa Maria!' The pain ricochets through Paolo's head. Something seeps across his eyebrow and into his right eye. A lump of stucco drops from the wall and bursts on the ground.

'Stay out of our business!' Carlo yells.

The first American tugs his head back again. 'No more dealing in copper wire! Do you understand? Or do I have to break your goddam brains?'

The message is clear, but Paolo can't think what to say. Then something heavy slams against his left foot. He cries out involuntarily, more from shock than pain.

'Legs apart!'

As Paolo slides his leg to the left, another kick on his right foot almost knocks him down. With his legs splayed apart, he trembles uncontrollably.

'Stay out of our business! NO MORE COPPER WIRE!'

'Yes,' Paolo whimpers.

'Louder!'

'YES!'

'And tell the Limey Corporal at the theatre the same goes for him. Any trouble from that lousy bastard and you'll both regret it. Is that clear?'

'YES!'

'Today is just a warning. Next time it will be for real.'

The first American releases Paolo's hair but slams a fist into his lower back. Paolo fights to stay on his feet. He feels a tug on his belt, which suddenly goes slack.

'I said legs apart, you bastard! Unless you want your pants falling down!'

'Farewell, pal,' Carlo says. 'Don't move a goddam inch until we've gone. And don't forget what we said.'

Paolo waits for several minutes. His feet don't move but the rest of his body convulses. The bastards! He'll kill them when he sees them again! Fucking foreigners! They claim to be liberating Italy when they're little better than gangsters. Oh God! What has Italy come to? He still wants to kill Germans but he wants to kill Americans too.

Paolo blinks, determined not to cry. He brushes his forehead to stop the blood seeping into his eye but looks around before lowering his hands to his trousers. He flings away the two halves of his leather belt, which he took from a corpse on the long slog south from Bologna. Then clutching his trousers, he hobbles towards the sea to bathe his face.

CHAPTER 11

Simon is struck by the calm inside the church, in contrast with the bustling streets. Without thinking he bows his head before looking up at the neo-gothic structure.

Christ Church, the Anglican Church in Naples, was built in 1863 on land gifted by Garibaldi in recognition of British help during the Risorgimento. To Simon it feels like a corner of Victorian England which has drifted into the Mediterranean.

With the pews already filling up, Simon advances up the central aisle, keen to sit near the front where he can see and be seen. He had met Barbara several times at the girls' flat in Heliopolis. She was always friendly, unlike Jackie, but she wasn't beautiful like Vermillion.

He settles down and looks around at the rows of khaki, mostly women in ATS uniform. He feels pleased to stand out in his RAF blue. From the corner of his eye he notices a nurse's white uniform.

'May I sit here, Simon?' Margery whispers.

'Of course, Marge. Isn't this sad?'

'Really awful.'

Simon had first met Margery in the winter when they gathered with friends after a show at San Carlo. They soon discovered they both knew Vermillion. Simon hadn't seen her since leaving Egypt in the autumn and Margery confirmed what Simon feared: that Vermillion was still with Edmund.

Learning that Vermillion worked at the theatre, he resolved to see her again. He chose to confront her at the Club when Frank was there. It was awful: another occasion when he tried too hard. It didn't help that he was pissed when he arrived. Then he insisted that Vermillion should dance with him. Not surprisingly Frank threw him out.

Soon after that encounter, Simon heard that Edmund had been wounded and might not make it. He was sorry for Edmund of course but also felt excited, hoping it might bring him closer to Vermillion.

Margery touches Simon's arm. Vermillion is walking slowly towards the front of the church. Although her head is bent forward she still looks marvellous. Jackie, next to Vermillion, turns and catches Simon's eye. Frank, walking behind the two girls, notices Jackie's gesture but ignores it. He looks grave.

Simon glances across at Margery. Does she know what Vermillion thinks of Frank? He is about to ask when the padre's raised voice from the back of the church interrupts.

"I am the resurrection and the life saith the Lord: he that believeth in me, though he were dead, yet shall he live ..."

Simon lets the words slide past. He has heard them too often ... memories of lost friends drift through his mind ... a wave of sadness washes over him.

"Man that is born of woman hath but a short time to live, and is full of misery. He cometh up, and is cut down, like a flower; he fleeth as it were a shadow, and never continueth in one stay."

Simon focuses on Vermillion. He can see the back of her neck until someone moves in the pew in front and blocks his view. He turns towards Margery. Her eyes are closed; she seems close to tears.

"In the midst of life we are in death: of whom may we seek for succour, but of thee, O Lord, who for our sins art justly displeased?"

As the congregation sits down, Simon watches Frank walk to the lectern and put on his reading glasses. He raises his head but looks disconsolate as he clears his throat.

'The reading is from the Gospel of John, chapter fifteen, starting at verse nine.'

Frank's large voice fills the church. Simon looks at Vermillion again: the slight shudder of her shoulders suggests she is crying. Simon wishes he could comfort her.

61

"As the Father hath loved me, so have I loved you: continue ye in my love. If ye keep my commandments, ye shall abide in my love; even as I have kept my Father's commandments, and abide in his love."

Again, Frank clears his throat.

"These things have I spoken unto you, that my joy might remain in you, and that your joy might be full."

Frank stops. That can't be the end. Simon looks up as Frank's voice wavers.

"This is my commandment … that ye love one another … as I have loved you. Greater love hath no man …"

There's another silence, fractured by a muted gasp. Frank pulls out a handkerchief and blows his nose.

"Greater love hath no man … than this … that a man lay down his life …"

Simon catches Margery's eye; she looks shocked. Simon has never seen anything like it. Poor old Frank. And how unfair on Vermillion.

The padre's flat voice fills the silence, as Frank blows his nose again and bows to the altar.

"We give thee hearty thanks, for that it hath pleased thee to deliver this our … sister … out of the miseries of this sinful world."

'Sister …' Simon repeats to himself. How strange to hear that word. Padres often speak of the death of 'brothers'. That's the thing about aircrew; few of them last very long. But 'sister'. He thinks of his own sister in Chester. God forbid she should be killed.

After what feels like an age, the padre announces the final hymn. The singing is stronger now as the congregation tries to expunge the awfulness of what has happened.

With the service over, Simon hopes to catch Vermillion. But Margery is still on her knees and he can't push past. He watches Vermillion slip away, with tears still in her eyes. Frank looks shaken, holding her arm.

Margery gets slowly to her feet and steps into the aisle. Simon pushes after her but now he can't see Vermillion or even Frank.

'Are you in a frightful hurry, Margery?' Simon smiles. 'I could do with a drink. I know a bar near here.'

* * *

'The service was awfully sad.' Margery sits down, resting her head in her hands. 'When I started to cry it was about Barbara, but then I kept thinking of Rob.'

Simon didn't know Rob. But he knew he was a friend of Edmund's – from the same Battalion – who was engaged to Margery.

'Marge, I'm terribly sorry about Rob. I should have guessed he'd be in your thoughts. It always happens with funerals. You think about someone else instead of the person who has died, unless you're very close, of course.'

Simon orders a Vermouth for Margery and some tonic water for himself.

'Simon, did you know that Rob proposed to me by letter from Cassino. I accepted of course and we planned to marry in that very church when he got some leave. Six weeks later he was killed.'

Simon remembers that after receiving the news Margery was beside herself for weeks.

'I was very close to Rob,' she says. 'And we still are close.'

'Of course, you are.' Simon raises his tonic water and almost downs the lot.

'But after he was taken away,' Margery turns to Simon, 'the only person I could talk to was Edmund, who was Rob's best friend. And when Edmund was recovering in hospital, he liked to talk about Rob. I visited him every day and learnt so much. He told me about Rob's family and what he was like as a boy. And then, as the pain of Rob's loss began to ease, I found I'd grown close to Edmund.'

Simon looks around the bar. He doesn't want to hear about Rob but the link with Edmund is interesting. He should have guessed: that was why Margery had urged Simon to visit Edmund in hospital.

'Is Edmund returning to England?' Simon asks absent-mindedly, wondering why he hadn't twigged what Margery was up to.

'He leaves next week!' Margery smiles, lighting up her whole face. 'He's very pleased. He can't wait to get his new legs.'

Simon studies Margery. With her large, dark eyes she looks wholesome but even with her face aglow, she's too gaunt to be attractive. After Rob died she became thin as a rake.

'Is Vermillion staying in Naples?'

'I believe so.'

Margery suddenly smiles. 'I haven't spoken to Vermillion since your chat with Edmund. Whatever you said, it had quite an effect.'

Simon smiles back. 'I just told him about Vermillion after he left her in Egypt. I thought he ought to know, instead of learning when it was already too late. I told him what happened when I …'

'Simon, I don't want to hear …' Margery looks away. 'Keep it to yourself. I'm not getting involved. Vermillion used to be a dear friend and I want her as a friend again, especially after that awful fire. I don't want her thinking I passed on messages from you.'

Simon can see that keeping close to Margery could be important. Since he talked to Edmund she's in his debt. Perhaps she will repay him by helping him get closer to Vermillion.

'I expect you'll miss Edmund.'

'Yes, he was so brave about losing his legs.' She looks up and beams. 'In fact, he wants *me* to go with him.'

Simon takes a deep breath. So that's why she looks pleased as Punch.

'Will you go?'

'I want to go of course, but the hospital said no. Since the fighting started again, there are too many wounded. I have to wait for another lull.'

Simon looks away. Despite the breakthrough at Cassino he doubts the war will end soon. Men and munitions are still pouring across the Brenner. The Germans show no sign of giving in.

'Marge, I'm sorry we didn't talk to Vermillion. Please give her my condolences. I hope to see her myself before too long.'

'Simon, you've been a good friend. We're both very grateful.'

CHAPTER 12

Vermillion scans the flimsy air letter. She has read it before but whilst her eyes move along the lines she doesn't take in the words. She just knows that Pen seems far away. They haven't been close for some time, probably not since Pen gave her the nickname *Vermin*, ten years ago. But today Vermillion misses her: she couldn't bear it if *she* should die.

She sits down, knowing she should try to reply but instead she peers at the blank face in the dressing table mirror.

After a while she returns to the letter.

"Bill sends his love. He has been away for almost three years and I can't wait for his return. Charlotte has never seen him, and Andrew is too young to remember him although he looks at his photos and talks about his soldier daddy all the time ..."

Vermillion closes her eyes as tears start to well. Oh God, this war is cruel. There's too much sadness in the world. Why does everyone have to die? And poor Pen, waiting at home! How can she bear it?

She thinks of the last time she saw her, in October '41. Bill had left for the Middle East but Pen was sure he hadn't gone for long. Vermillion would soon be sent abroad but she didn't know when or even where. It was a warm autumn day and Vermillion took Andrew for a walk because Pen was about to have Charlotte. He chatted cheerfully to Vermillion as they sauntered down the lane, stopping at every puddle. He seemed to know that in mummy's and daddy's absence it was his job to entertain his auntie.

Remembering that happy day reminds her why she had to get away, before her parents could marry her off as they had done with Pen. As it was they made her wait until her twenty-first birthday before she joined the Auxiliary Territorial Service.

Vermillion looks at the pile of Barbara's things she has gathered together. One day she will take them to Y Section where Captain Ashburn has offered to send them to Barbara's family. Vermillion's letter of condolence, written after that dreadful service, sits on top of the mound. She remembers what she had written word for word.

"… Barbara was a true friend. I never heard her say a bad word about anyone, which is a tribute to how you brought her up …"

Vermillion had agonised over writing the letter, not because she had nothing to say but because Barbara was such a kind and generous person and it's horrible she has gone.

'Dearest Barbara,' Vermillion says out loud. 'Thank you for going to rescue me. BUT I WISH YOU HADN'T!'

She squeezes her eyes shut as tears stream down her face. She pulls out a hankie to staunch the flow.

'Barbara, I'm so sorry! You shouldn't have died! It should have been me!'

She convulses into sobbing again, overwhelmed by the awfulness of what has happened. She never wanted to harm Barbara. And yet she knows … she killed her.

'BARBARA, BARBARA, FORGIVE ME!'

In time Vermillion's tears relent. She struggles to the bathroom where she washes and dries her face, carefully avoiding the image in the mirror. She doesn't want to see the face of Barbara's killer.

She hears a knock at the front door. 'Oh goodness! That must be Margery.'

She had forgotten that Margery promised to come. She isn't fit to be seen but she scrapes her fingers through her hair and drags herself to the door.

'Hello, Margery.' Vermillion fails in an attempted smile: the muscles in her face no longer work.

'I'm sorry, Vermillion,' Margery takes in Vermillion's face. 'This must be a bad time.'

Vermillion doesn't know how to respond. She doesn't want Margery to go but she doesn't want her to stay.

'I've been sorting out Barbara's things.'

'May I come in?' Margery steps forward, putting her hand on Vermillion's arm while she concentrates on closing the door. 'It's a real tragedy. Barbara was such a nice person. And how typical that she tried to rescue you.'

She expected Margery just to take the last of Edmund's clothes. But Vermillion's instinct to be hospitable hasn't gone and without thinking she points towards the kitchen.

'Would you like some tea?' she whispers.

Vermillion puts the tea things on a tray and leads the way unsteadily along the corridor. Aware that Margery is looking around, Vermillion recalls that the flat is impressive, despite the savour of burning. But she has started to hate the place: it's home to too many memories.

'Thank you for gathering Edmund's things.' Margery sits down in the armchair he preferred.

'Thank you for taking them. They have to go sometime.'

Vermillion carefully pours two cups of tea.

'How is Frank?' Margery asks. 'He did very well to rescue Barbara even though he arrived too late. But he was clearly shaken at the funeral.'

Vermillion doesn't want to talk about Frank; she fears it will make her cry. 'Frank was very brave but he's upset about the whole thing.'

'You're lucky he's staying in Naples.'

'He isn't quite himself at the moment. The fire brought back the loss of his wife, who died in the London blitz.'

'Sometimes men with shell shock find it hard not to cry.' Margery says gently. 'But it can't be that with Frank.'

What is she trying to imply? That Frank should be at the front? Margery knows perfectly well that the army ordered him to stay. Vermillion feels a rush of emotion.

'I saw Simon at the funeral,' Margery says after a while. 'He knows you've ended it with Edmund.'

'Simon didn't know Barbara.' Vermillion raises her head. 'He had no business coming to the funeral. And he had better watch out! Frank was livid in March when Simon came to the Club.'

'I don't think he knows about you and Frank.'

'What is there to know? Everything has happened so quickly.' Vermillion looks at the floor. 'Ten days ago I expected to go home with Edmund. I was fond of Frank of course, but I never thought he was interested in me.'

'It was a bit like that for me,' Margery smiles. 'I hardly knew Edmund before he was wounded.'

'You were a marvellous friend then,' Vermillion says. 'I would never have got through without you.'

'Then I got the news of Rob's death,' Margery says. 'Roger Bewdley wrote to me.'

'I didn't know who told you. It's hard when you're not the next of kin. Some women never hear.'

Vermillion drinks some tea and sighs, remembering Margery's frantic energy as she continued nursing despite her grief.

'When the news came about Rob,' Vermillion continues, 'I couldn't tell you my feelings for Edmund had changed. It seemed too ungrateful. But perhaps you thought I'd turned away.'

Margery finishes her tea. 'Thank you, Vermillion. I must go. But let's meet again when you have a moment. Let's see one of Frank's shows. Please remember me to him.'

Vermillion watches as Margery lifts the pile of Edmund's things. 'Can you carry all that? Let me help you down the steps.'

'Don't worry, Vermillion, I can manage.' Margery stretches forward and they half embrace.

'Goodbye,' Vermillion stands by the door as Margery sets off confidently. 'Wish Edmund "buon viaggio".'

She turns and walks slowly through the empty flat. Entering her bedroom she sees Pen's letter again. Oh dear! She really must reply.

CHAPTER 13

Frank spent the night after Barbara's funeral repeatedly going over what had happened. Even now he can't believe he had broken down in public. He feels mortified and has apologised a hundred times.

Vermillion has been remarkably understanding, considering how desolate she felt. Several times she has suggested that his distress was linked more to Maggie's death than to Barbara's. She also repeated that Barbara liked him a lot and would have understood his anguish.

This morning again he got up early with his head full of images of fire. At first light he set off, ready to throw himself into running the theatre, hoping to exorcise the memory of the funeral.

For several hours he drifted around the building, asking everyone how things were going but struggling to register their replies. When finally he settles at his desk, he is haunted by the image from last night's dream: the front of his Ealing flat after the bomb, with the windows blown out and the window frames scorched black.

Frank leans back on his chair trying to concentrate on the theatre but he keeps thinking about Maggie and why he hadn't saved her. He tries to drag his mind back to the schedule of forthcoming operas, reminding himself that he's in charge. But when he ran the theatre before, Malaspina was there. He was often obstructive but at least he knew the ropes and could explain how things were done before the war. Now Frank must manage without him.

Already he has met with Ingegnere Russo who is responsible for the stage crew and the technical aspects of the theatre. He had produced an endless list of problems, of which they only resolved the first few. And after lunch Maestro Nanta, who manages the orchestra, is coming to list his objections to the latest performance schedule.

Frank should start preparing to meet the maestro, but he feels too tired to move. He stares across the room but this time he doesn't see Maggie, nor even Vermillion. Instead he sees a white shape, rather like a head with two smaller dark circles which could be eyes. Frank rubs his hands across his face, afraid he's going mad but when he opens his eyes the image is still there.

He tries to focus on the papers on his desk and skims the first page without taking it in. Somehow he must survive his encounter with Nanta, before meeting Vermillion for supper. Should he tell her about the hallucination? No! She mustn't know he's going round the bend. He will just have to pray that the image won't reappear.

* * *

Frank gets to the restaurant early and downs a large whisky before Vermillion arrives. Then he orders a bottle of red wine and drinks half a glass to mask the whisky.

'How are you, darling?' he jumps to his feet. 'I've missed you at the theatre.'

'I'm all right, Frank. Margery came to see me, which was rather awkward, but I suppose it was nice of her to come. She may return to England with Edmund. Perhaps that's a good idea, but it came as a bit of a shock.'

'Have some wine. I'm afraid I've already started. Or can I get you something else?'

'No thank you. I haven't felt like drinking since the funeral. Just some bottled water, please.'

Frank is conscious that his response is quite different to hers. Since the funeral he has drunk much more in an effort to feel normal.

He takes her hands. 'Do you miss Edmund? He was a big part of your life.'

Vermillion smiles slightly.

'Yes, but I'm not sure why. We differed in so many ways. However, he *was* my first love. Of course, he was very demanding: everything had to be done as he saw fit. At his best, he made me feel special. It was a dream of course, but initially it was hard to resist.'

The waiter brings two plates of spaghetti. Frank starts eating immediately and empties another glass of wine. Vermillion says she no longer feels like eating. She takes out a cigarette.

'Do you have a light, Frank?'

Frank puts his hand over hers. 'NO! Please, Vermillion. I'm sorry but I can't bear it.'

She looks up. Her face is tense and drawn. 'What's the matter, darling?'

She puts the cigarette away.

'I'm sorry … it reminds me of the fire.'

'Of course.'

At last Frank looks up; his forehead is pocked with sweat.

'Dearest Vermillion, I'm such a lucky man, being here with you and loving you so much. And living in Naples and working at the theatre. Despite this terrible war, I have everything I could want.'

'Is something missing?'

He stares across the restaurant.

'What is it, Frank?'

He seems about to speak but no words emerge.

'How can I help you, darling, if you keep it all to yourself?'

'You can't help me, Vermillion. I don't think anyone can. I keep having awful nightmares. Usually I forget the details, but the images stay all day.'

She squeezes his hands anxiously. 'Let's walk back along the seafront.'

'Wait a moment, darling. I want to say again that I'm sorry about the funeral. I feel so ashamed for embarrassing you.'

'You don't need to apologise. I understand why you felt upset. People will forget the funeral.'

'I don't want anyone saying I should be at the front. I didn't choose to run the theatre. I'm lucky to be here and even luckier to be with you. One day they'll return me to the front and when that happens, I'll miss you terribly, but I'll have to go.'

CHAPTER 14

Vermillion again wakes early but today she feels stronger until a brief chat with Jackie saps her confidence. Alone after Jackie has left, she feels the empty flat close in, pressing its mournfulness into her.

Jackie had asked whether she still thinks about Edmund. Although the question came like an accusation, Vermillion answered truthfully that she thinks about him often, which she regards as only natural. Jackie's expression showed she disagreed.

Now Jackie has gone, Vermillion is alone with her thoughts again. She walks across to the window and looks down at the sunny street. She wants to go out but only if she has something to do. She no longer wants to think; she has thought enough.

She puts on her service dress, intending to go to the theatre. She isn't sure she can face it, but some instinct makes her try. It's mid-morning and the streets are crammed with people, all struggling to finish their daily tasks before the heat grows too intense. Being jostled repeatedly reminds her how fragile she feels.

Ahead a pregnant woman stops, propping herself against a shaded wall. She declines an offer of help. Vermillion wonders whether her baby is part of the unwanted army fathered by the war.

More than once she considers turning back, until the sight of Huggins outside the theatre strengthens her resolve. She finds it comforting that he watches her as she crosses the piazza keeping out the sun.

'It's a very good morning, Miss.'

Despite Huggins' broad smile, Vermillion doesn't really want to talk. 'Yes, Huggins, it's lovely but jolly hot.'

'It's not just the weather that's lovely, Miss. Did you hear yesterday's news?'

She studies him more carefully; he looks strained. 'No, Huggins, I haven't heard a thing.'

'Rome has fallen, Miss! Of course, it isn't surprising it took so long – it is the eternal city!'

'That's marvellous news, Huggins.'

Vermillion pauses as Ingegnere Russo hurries past with a rapid "buon giorno". Her pleasure at the news about Rome is tempered by the thought that Frank may now be moved.

'Let's hope the war will soon be over, Huggins.'

'Yes, there's another thing, Miss. Major Bewdley is camping in Frank's office. I told him Captain Hill is out, but he insisted he would wait.'

'Thank you, Huggins. I'll find out what he wants.'

She hurries up the steps. In the background she hears snatches of the Gossip Chorus from L'Elisir D'Amore. At another time she might have stopped to listen, but her mind is on Roger Bewdley. She has never met him, not even in April when, with the theatre closed for opera, he and Frank took a week's leave and Huggins drove them around Calabria.

'Good morning, Major.' Vermillion studies the fellow leaning back on Frank's chair with his feet on the desk. 'May I help you? I'm Lieutenant Henthorpe.'

Stepping forward, she is hit by the sweet smell of tobacco, which brings back memories of her father.

'Good morning, my dear.' Roger puts down his pipe and stands up. 'Roger Bewdley.' He smooths the ends of his moustache and extends his hand. 'You must be Manley's girl. They were certainly right about you.'

Vermillion coughs as she shakes his calloused hand, ignoring the reference to being Edmund's girl. 'I hear you're looking for Captain Hill. He won't be back for a while.'

'Well … perhaps *you* can keep me company. Sit down, my dear.'

Vermillion tries not to look at him too closely. But she can't quite ignore his nose, which bends slightly to the right, presumably from an accident. She wonders whether the asymmetry is accentuated by his moustache.

Roger resumes his seat. He slips the pipe into his mouth and sucks with apparent displeasure. Then he gets out his matches and lights the pipe again. He draws hard releasing a billow of smoke.

'I was with 3rd Battalion, my dear. I expect Captain Hill mentioned me.'

'Yes, of course. And you wrote to my friend Margery to tell her about Rob's death.'

'That was when 3rd Battalion was disbanded …' Roger tries to catch Vermillion's eye. '… after the botched attack on the abbey at Monte Cassino when poor old Manley copped it. Now it's 4th Battalion but with all the same faces. We miss Manley of course.'

Roger grips the bit of the pipe between his teeth, then places a matchbox over the bowl and sucks noisily. Vermillion wonders what she's meant to do. Is she a necessary acolyte at this ceremony? Or is she expected to keep talking?

In an effort to distract him, she says the first thing that enters her head. 'Edmund is leaving Naples. He's going home to get his new legs.'

'I know, my dear. It's a horrid business and very hard on you.'

She smiles but quickly wishes she hadn't.

'I expect you all miss him.' Vermillion blurts out the words before remembering Roger has said this already.

He removes the pipe from his mouth and gestures expansively. 'Of course, *I* command C Company now.'

'Did you help to take Rome?' she asks without raising her eyes.

'Not as such. The American Fifth Army entered the city.'

Roger puts the pipe back in his mouth and speaks in a stilted manner. 'We were part of Eighth Army, my dear, but they loaned us to Fifth Army. Our role was to drive back the Teds – the Tedeschi – once we'd winkled them out of Cassino. We've seen plenty of action, my dear. That's why we've got some leave.'

'You all did jolly well.' Vermillion feels nonplussed by Roger. She wonders how much longer Frank will be.

'You and Manley were lucky to serve in the same theatre – excuse the pun!' Roger chortles. 'Some of us are less fortunate.'

'Do you have someone at home?'

'It's a sad story, my dear.' Roger smiles as he takes the pipe from his mouth. 'Are you sure you want to hear?'

Vermillion nods slightly.

'I met Joan in '40. I was just back from France and in the excitement after Dunkirk we began an affair. We rubbed along well enough, but it was mostly a physical thing, if you know what I mean. Then I got my call-up papers to go overseas and a few days later Joan told me she was expecting. I didn't love her and didn't want to marry her, but I felt I should do the decent thing. We married just before I sailed for Egypt.'

'I'm sorry to hear that, Major. Now I really should do some work.'

Roger holds the bowl of the pipe in his hand and points the stem at Vermillion. 'Let me finish the story, my dear. I'm coming to the important bit. When I made it to Cairo, there was a letter from Joan saying she'd lost the baby. And now she can't have any more. It's sad for her of course but now she won't give me a divorce. So I'm rather stuck, my dear.'

Roger puts the pipe back in his mouth and talks through his teeth. 'I said it was a sad story.'

'I'm very sorry, Major. That's awful for you both.'

Vermillion wonders why he has told her all this. Clearly Joan was lucky that Roger had married her when she got into trouble. She doubts whether Edmund would have done the same. But is she meant to feel sorry for Roger or is he looking for advice? She can't think what she should say.

'Don't worry, my dear,' Roger says. 'I know it's a wretched story, but I don't let it get me down.'

Roger pulls out a used match and scrapes the bowl of his pipe. Vermillion tries not to watch but she can't help glancing back as heaps of dark dottle tumble into the ashtray.

'Before you go, my dear, tell me about Hill.' Roger looks up from the entrails of his pipe. 'He seems to have a cosy billet, well away from the line.'

Vermillion turns to face him. She feels her cheeks flush.

'Captain Hill reopened this theatre six months ago and has entertained more than a hundred thousand troops. What he has done is a minor miracle. *And* he rescued someone from a burning building!'

Satisfied with his pipe, Roger pulls out his tobacco and kneads a few strands into the bowl. He looks up and surveys Vermillion's face. She knows she shouldn't have let him see that his comments had rankled. But how could she help it?

'Do you like working with Captain Hill?' Roger tamps down the tobacco and strikes a match. He holds it to the bowl as he inhales, pulling in the flame. He blows smoke in Vermillion's direction.

'He's very interesting to work for. And the job is extremely worthwhile. Now, Major, I really must go!'

'Please call me Roger, my dear.'

Vermillion wheels round. Stretching to grasp the door handle, she is almost knocked down as Frank marches in.

'Roger, welcome back to Naples. Clearly, you two have met. Thank you for holding the fort, Vermillion. You look well, Roger. I hear you've got some leave. You must come to one of our shows. We're doing the Elixir of Love.'

Frank turns. Compared with Roger, he looks pale. 'Vermillion, are you heading off? Why not join us for a bite of lunch? Roger would appreciate some female company after weeks in the field.'

'I'm sorry, Frank. I really must get on. Roger and I have had a long chat and I've learnt a lot. I expect you two will want to reminisce.'

'All right,' Frank looks disappointed. 'Come on, Roger; let's wander over to the Club. I expect you could handle a pint.'

Vermillion slips into her office. She leans against the wall behind the door and doesn't move until the men's voices have faded.

CHAPTER 15

Roger stuffs the pipe into his pocket and follows Frank. He glances back hoping for another glimpse of Vermillion. She certainly is a fine-looking filly. She didn't say a lot – always a virtue – although she did imply it was over with Manley, which is hardly surprising. But is something going on with Frank? She was pretty quick to defend him.

Near the theatre entrance, several odd types push past. God knows what they do in the theatre. Then the Corporal saunters up and addresses Frank without saluting.

'We've landed in France, Sir!' The Corporal beams. 'The news has just come through. Does that mean the war in Italy is over?'

'Corporal!' Roger interjects, causing Huggins to come to attention and salute him. 'The war won't be over in Italy until every German is driven out. You should join us, Corporal. We need experienced men.'

'Thank you for the news, Huggins,' Frank says. 'You know Major Bewdley. He commands C Company of 4th Battalion. That's excellent news about the landings; let's hope it will end the war.'

Frank leads Roger into the Club, acknowledging other officers they pass. He seems to know everyone: clearly he's in here a lot. Roger is reminded of his public school before he was shunted off to Norfolk. The chaps he knew then had the same easy confidence. No wonder Frank fits in.

Frank orders a couple of pints.

'This is very decent of you, Frank. Are you sure you can spare the time? The Lieutenant says you're terribly busy.'

'Not at all. It's good to see you, Roger. Let's sit over here, where it's quieter. Now tell me how things are going. How is the new Battalion and how is morale since the breakthrough?'

Roger studies Frank's face. He looks pallid for a soldier but otherwise indecently well. Unlike Roger, Frank has put on weight. Yet despite living the life of Riley, he seems oddly subdued. Perhaps he had a heavy night.

'It was a bit like after Alamein,' Roger says. 'You remember the shambles when we were all chasing Rommel and we tripped each other up. But north of Rome the terrain should be easier.'

'I hear you've taken over the Company and you've been promoted. It can't have been easy following in Edmund's foot … in Edmund's wake.'

'That crack fell a bit flat!' Roger grins, pleased Frank has noticed his new rank, although it irks him that it's only a temporary field promotion.

'We picked up the remnants of C Company,' Roger continues. 'But with high casualties and few replacements we're still well below strength. There are too many bloody desk-wallahs. If only the chaps behind desks in Naples would hear the call of duty, that would swell our numbers.'

'You won't find many recruits here, Roger! The staff jobs have moved to Caserta, the new Allied HQ.'

'Don't get me started on that racket! I've heard they live in a bloody palace!'

Roger looks around the vast room that houses the Club. Already it's filling up. Are these officers really all on leave? He's sure he can spot the ones who've returned from the front: they look fit and alert; the others seem flabby in comparison.

Roger turns back to Frank.

'We've been in the line for four of the last six months. The men feel it's bloody well time for some other buggers to take their turn.'

'I'm not surprised they feel browned off. We should all pull our weight. Perhaps I should return to the line, if someone else could run the theatre. But the chap AMG selected proved to be an ardent Fascist. Happily, we've locked him up.'

'I didn't mean you, old chap. You're doing an important job.'

Roger pauses.

'Frank, if you could see things at the front, I think you'd be shocked. The Teds – the Germans – remain as tenacious as ever. They know they've lost the war, but they won't bloody well surrender.'

'They've all been bamboozled about German superiority,' Frank says. 'They can't now admit they were wrong. They find it easier to keep on fighting than to change their minds.'

'They're a lot more brutal now. Is that desperation? We've seen some grisly things. In one village there wasn't a woman in sight but we could hear them wailing indoors; apparently they'd all been raped.'

Roger is pleased that Frank now looks shaken; he needs to remember what war is like. 'That was a pretty rum business …'

Roger pauses, wondering what they really meant by rape. He thinks of Joan before he set off for Egypt. She needed encouragement: in Roger's experience women often do. He remembers pressing his hand over her mouth, forcing her back. *Shh! Darling, you don't want to wake the boys!*

'… the men in the village said they weren't German soldiers who committed the rapes. They claimed they were Allied troops but I didn't believe them. And when I told Mortimer, he was clear it must have been the Germans. He told me to tell Division that the villagers were confused. He didn't want to cause a stink.'

'That's shocking, Roger. My goodness, war is brutal, whoever was responsible. Imagine what those women went through. How will the village recover?'

Roger downs some beer and grins. 'Changing the subject, Frank, that assistant of yours …'

'You mean Huggins?'

'No, the filly! She really is a peach. With Manley out of the running, someone else must have a chance. What do you reckon, Frank? You must know her quite well.'

'Don't get ideas about Vermillion, whatever you do!'

'F*** me! That was quick work! Manley hasn't even left Naples. Jesus, you're a lucky blighter!'

Roger knocks back some beer. 'And what about the Eyetie filly who lived in your flat? Have you kept her there? Or have you turfed her out?'

'Steady, Roger.'

Frank drains his glass and signals for another pint. 'If you're referring to Chiara, she decided to leave. She moved to her brother's flat while he was in prison. Mind you, now he's been released, the place must be pretty crowded.'

'*She* wasn't bad looking for an Eyetie.' Roger gets out his pipe and matches. 'Frank, I don't suppose you could spare a bed, now Chiara has left. I just need a corner for the next few nights.'

'Of course, Roger,' Frank looks away.

Roger refills the pipe from his pouch of Dunhill's Royal Yacht, a birthday present from his mother. He strikes a match and holds it against the tobacco while sucking vigorously. It takes some time to catch. When he looks up Frank is already on his feet although he hasn't finished his beer.

'I must be off, Roger,' Frank turns away. 'I've a lot to do.'

Even from a distance, Roger notices beads of sweat around Frank's temples. Clearly the life in Naples doesn't suit him. Roger wonders how he can help. He must do what he can to get Frank back to the Battalion.

CHAPTER 16

Frank feels obliged to be hospitable, letting Roger stay although it's the last thing he wants.

'A small nightcap, Roger?' Frank asks as he clears the remains of supper.

'Don't mind if I do. Frank, you've been very obliging.'

'Say when.'

Roger raises his hand and settles back to enjoy the whisky. 'Do you remember Sergeant Singer?'

'Did he come after Clissold?' Frank leaves the washing up.

'That's the chap. Singer was a first-rate Sergeant Major … until we lost him last week to a blasted sniper.'

'I'm sorry! If Singer was half as good as Clissold, he must have been top-notch.'

'Clissold was okay, but Singer was better.'

Frank takes a large gulp of whisky. 'Clissold was a godsend at Salerno: he saved my bacon.'

Roger puts down his glass and taps the pockets of his jacket, searching for his pipe.

'NO ROGER!' Frank feels his heart beat faster. 'I'm sorry, but you can't smoke that thing!'

'Steady on!'

Frank coughs. 'It's my voice, I'm afraid ... the smoke affects my singing.'

'All right, old man.' Roger slips the pipe away. 'I didn't know you were so bothered.'

Frank takes a deep breath. He wants to tell Roger about Barbara and the fire. But what about Maggie? No, he can't say anything. At the front worse things happen all the time.

Frank pours an inch of whisky into his own glass. 'Have another one, Roger, when you're ready.'

'Is everything all right, Frank? You seem rather jumpy. You don't mind me staying, do you? Am I keeping you from one of your girls?'

'I'm okay. And it's a pleasure to see you, Roger. But once I've drunk this, I'll turn in. I need to make an early start.'

Frank takes a mouthful of whisky and downs it without noticing the taste. He wishes Roger weren't here. He doesn't need to be reminded about the Battalion, which is probably where he should be.

He looks across the room and again sees the white shape with the two dark patches. God! He rubs his eyes. He really is going nuts. He was thinking about rejoining the Battalion when it reappeared. Should he tell Roger what's in his mind? No, not until he has told Vermillion.

As Frank takes a larger swig of whisky, a knock at the front door makes him start. He charges across the room ready to do battle with the intruder. His last unexpected visitor, just before the raid, had been Brigadier Carburton. He hesitates. Could it be the Brigadier again? He half opens the door, bracing it against his boot.

'Chiara!' Frank opens the door wide. 'What has happened?' He says in Italian. 'Come in. This is Roger, a friend from the Battalion.'

'Franco, please! You must help!' Chiara grips his sleeve. 'I have to go to Rome, now the Germans have left. I have to see Mamma and Francesca to know they're all right.'

Chiara has always looked intense and in the early days

Frank was reminded of a young raptor waiting to be fed. But tonight she looks distressed.

'You must be pleased that Rome has been liberated,' Frank tries to sound calm. 'That's what you've always wanted? Why are you looking so sad?'

'Because Paolo has vanished!' Chiara brushes tears from her eyes. 'Sandro has searched everywhere, but no one knows where Paolo has gone. He promised to take me to Rome. But now he's missing. Franco, help me, please!'

Frank gestures to Chiara to sit down before turning to Roger to explain. He sees a look of disgust on Roger's face. Or is it envy?

'I understand Paolo is Chiara's brother,' Roger says. 'But who is Sandro? And why can't he take her to Rome?'

Frank asks Chiara and then translates. 'Sandro is Chiara's boyfriend. But he won't leave Naples until Paolo is found. He fears Paolo's in trouble.'

'You needn't translate, Frank.' Roger turns to Chiara. 'Capisco Italiano, ma parlo molto poco.'

Chiara looks at Roger and gives him a radiant smile such as Frank hasn't seen for months.

'Maggiore,' she addresses Roger in simple Italian, 'I'm so worried about Mamma and Francesca. I haven't seen them for more than a year. Paolo visited them in March and said they were well. But that was three months ago and there has been bombing and fighting and the Germans have done terrible things. I must go to see Mamma. Please help me, Maggiore.'

Roger leans forward, studying her appearance. But Chiara doesn't seem perturbed. She stares back with fierce determination.

Frank looks away. Chiara has always worried about her mother and was reassured in March when Paolo told her he had crossed the line and visited her. But recently Paolo admitted to Frank he never did go to Rome, but he insisted that Chiara shouldn't know. Has the time now come for Frank to tell her? But he can't see how it would help.

'*I* can take you to Rome, my dear,' Roger says with a grin. 'It will be a good way to spend my leave. I'm sure I can find a car.'

Chiara jumps up and tries to hug Roger although he's sitting down. He looks delighted. Frank is briefly concerned for Chiara but quickly concludes that Roger wouldn't do anything stupid. And if he goes to Rome, he'll vacate Frank's flat.

CHAPTER 17

Vermillion felt better being back at the theatre and had been looking forward to the new production of Rigoletto. But she hadn't allowed for its capacity to stir up the sadness of Barbara's death. As she emerges from the theatre she takes Frank's hand.

'I can't face the crowds at the Club,' she struggles to speak. 'Let's walk a bit and find a quiet bar. It's ages since I've seen you alone.'

Outside, the air feels like a warm oven.

'Thank goodness Roger has gone.' Vermillion blows her nose. 'I hope he stays in Rome and never returns.'

They find a suitable bar where Frank orders a bottle of wine. Vermillion is aware that he is studying her with concern; she fears that her eyes are red.

'Rigoletto is awfully sad,' she squeezes his hand.

'Rigoletto never fails to move me. Imagine killing your daughter by mistake. It's like a Greek tragedy.'

Vermillion turns the stem of her glass. 'I know. But I didn't cry for Gilda or Rigoletto. I was remembering Barbara.'

'I'm so sorry you've lost your dear friend. I know she was very important.'

'Shall we go, Frank. We can get some spaghetti at that place in the Galleria.'

'In a minute. There's still some wine left.'

Frank knocks back another glassful. 'Rigoletto reminded *me* of Roger. He looks old enough to be Chiara's father.'

'Will she be all right? Roger seemed rather keen to drive her to Rome, but he's hardly the paternal type.'

'He wants female company after so long.'

'He won't try anything?'

'I don't think so,' Frank laughs. 'Chiara can look after herself. She quickly got Roger's measure. You should have seen his face when she climbed into the back seat, leaving Roger looking like a chauffeur.'

'Do you miss her?'

'She was good company at first and the flat felt empty when she left. But she was often low, and I don't miss her dark moods.'

'I feel sorry for her. She has had such a tough life.'

'She's a fighter. When she turned up at the flat again, I remembered her first appearance last autumn. The army had requisitioned the flat and I moved in not knowing Chiara still lived there unofficially after her fiancé was killed in Sicily. That night she let herself into the flat, unaware I was there. When she saw me, she screamed blue murder and attacked me, knocking over the candles. In the dark, as I tried to restrain her, she sank her teeth into my hand. No, you don't have to worry, Chiara can look after herself.'

Before they leave the bar, Frank orders a refill. He seems sober enough, and she knows it's just the effect of the fire and the memories it has awakened. But she still wishes he would stop.

'What worries me,' Frank says, 'is what Chiara will find in Rome. She still believes that Paolo visited in March. I wouldn't want to be in his shoes when she learns the truth. She'll be fuming.'

While Frank empties his glass, Vermillion watches a girl in a nearby doorway as she bargains with an amorous GI, insisting there's a price for what he wants. In the end she settles for a day's pack of army rations.

'I think we should go, Frank.'

As they walk through the quiet backstreets, Frank wraps his arm around her waist. Although she feels close to him, she keeps thinking about that girl who had sold herself for so little. But would it have been better if the GI had paid 10,000 Lire? It would still be prostitution, but surely less bad than risking disease and pregnancy for just one day's rations.

They pass a group of soldiers who eye Vermillion. One mutters something about "an ATS tart".

Frank spins around.

'WHAT THE HELL DID YOU SAY, LANCE CORPORAL?'

The man attempts to salute. 'I shaid good ev'ning, Sir.'

'That's not what you said!'

Frank grabs the man's upper arms lifting him off the ground.

'WHAT DID YOU SAY?' he bellows into his face.

'Frank, it's all right! Let him go!'

Vermillion is shocked by the violence of Frank's reaction. She has never seen him so angry before. She fights back the urge to burst into tears.

Frank drops the man.

'NEVER SAY THAT AGAIN!' He glares at the group as they shrink away.

When the men are out of sight, Vermillion again takes Frank's hand, which is burning with fury.

'Damn the fellow's impertinence! I wanted to kill him.'

'I know you did, darling. And *he* thought you did too. You should have seen the fear in his eyes.'

'I can't bear rudeness to you.'

'I know, Frank. But he didn't deserve to die. There are worse things in this world.'

They walk on silently. Vermillion is deep in thought. She feels increasingly worried about Frank but she can't think what she should do.

At last they reach the Galleria, the nineteenth century arcade which had been full of smart restaurants and shops until Allied bombing destroyed the glazed roof. Recently it has reopened without the roof and is now a favourite haunt for servicemen who come to drown their sorrows or pick up the girls who hang around the bars.

They sit down at a small table and order some food. While they wait, Vermillion tries to concentrate on Frank but she finds it hard to ignore several solitary soldiers whose vacant expressions suggest they have much to forget. They don't even respond when a scruffy young boy tries to sell them phallic charms.

'Did I tell you about my Ealing flat?' Frank says suddenly.

Vermillion tries to smile as she looks up. Frank looks strained.

'The bomb that blew out the windows left black scorch marks on the frames.'

'Is that what you see in your nightmares?'

Frank doesn't reply.

'Is that what you see, you poor old thing?'

'Yes.' Frank looks down. 'That's often what I see.'

'I know you loved Maggie very much.' Vermillion squeezes his hands. 'You must miss her dreadfully.'

Frank looks up. 'I did love her, of course. And eight months ago when I came to Naples, I still felt her presence. I often used to see her, usually sitting at the piano she loved to play. I found it reassuring. But over the months the image faded until I didn't see her anymore. And I don't miss her now.'

Frank strokes her hand. 'Then in the last two months … after I realised I loved you … I started seeing your lovely face, instead.'

Vermillion smiles, but she wants to cry.

CHAPTER 18

Paolo stalks through the old city's narrow streets, stopping every few strides to check over his shoulder. Now and then he doubles back, making certain no one is following. He had been too cocky before but he can't go on like this, unable to do any business and with his money running out.

What can he do with those Yankee thugs waiting to pounce? God, what a wretched world! At least with his black eye fading he no longer looks like a fugitive from a drunken brawl.

As midsummer approaches, Paolo must rise increasingly early in order to leave Emma before dawn. But since his encounter with the Yanks, he daren't return to his flat. In the time since Chiara moved in, he has only stayed there once. *Porca miseria!*

Paolo's first problem was where to spend his days. But it wasn't long – *grazie al cielo* – before he found an ideal place and established a new routine, spending his days amidst the splendour of Naples' main cemetery. During daylight the place is quiet, with plenty of shade, and after a busy night Paolo is happy to sleep through the heat of the day. He feels safe, able to observe the entrance from a point where he can't be seen.

In the evening, after Paolo leaves, the cemetery changes. Neapolitan lovers, at least those not blessed with a bed they can enjoy together, often visit to seek their ancestors' blessings on their efforts to procreate or avoid procreation. Then they settle onto one of the many horizontal surfaces, where on warm nights the cold marble against the skin brings added pleasure. But by then Paolo has slipped away.

This morning, as always, he is vigilant approaching the cemetery. The sun is rising and for several minutes he watches and listens from a corner across the street. Satisfied the way is clear, he trots across the road and slips through the imposing gates.

Inside the cemetery he moves in a crabwise fashion, never heading straight to his destination. He pauses. The lovers have left and the mourners are yet to arrive; everything is quiet except for the hum of foraging insects.

Paolo reaches his vantage point and lies back, intending to sleep for a while. But today sleep doesn't come: he is preoccupied. Even with Chiara gone, he will soon run out of money. And what options will he have then?

All right! The Italians were bloody stupid to ally themselves with the Germans! But now they've done the right thing by changing sides, it seems they're still bloody well fucked!

It sickens Paolo that Naples used to have a flourishing black market where hard-working fellows like him could make an honest living. Now the bloody Yanks have ended all that, what the hell is he meant to do?

DAMN THE BLOODY GERMANS! DAMN THE BLOODY AMERICANS TOO!

* * *

It's almost noon when Paolo stirs and consciousness returns. The place is silent, except for insects buzzing on their roisterous rounds.

Paolo slips out from his refuge and stretches. He strolls towards the entrance but suddenly wheels to the right and disappears into a shaded corner. He listens again before sauntering on. Then he slides into a bay beside a family vault that's hidden from the path. He leans against the stonework and waits. In the heat, he feels drowsy again.

A noise from behind startles him.

'Ciao, Paolo. How are you?'

Paolo glares at Sandro's cheerful face.

'Ciao, Sandro. Everything is marvellous. I've been beaten up, I can't visit my flat, and I've no fucking money. Yes, everything is marvellous, except that you're bloody late.'

'I couldn't find the right vault. They all look the same. I had to ask.'

'For Christ's sake, Sandro! Only the Caporale should know we're meeting. I told him to give you a map.'

'The map was useless.'

'Santa Madonna!'

'I thought you'd be pleased to see me, Paolo. I stayed in Naples to find you when I could have gone with Chiara.'

'Of course, I'm pleased to see you. But you must be careful. I don't want you beaten up as well.'

'Why are you here? Do you come to spy on the lovers?'

'Don't be stupid, Sandro! I'm not here at night. I've better things to do.'

Paolo looks away. He likes Sandro and is glad to see he's looking well. The trouble is he's far too nice, despite two stints in the army.

'The Caporale said you'd like some food. I've brought you these.'

Paolo examines the contents of a sagging brown paper bag. 'What the hell *are* they?'

'Ravioli, of course.'

'Cold?'

'They're cold now but they were hot when I cooked them.'

Paolo puckers his face as he slides his hand into the bag. He raises a couple of ravioli to his mouth and nibbles at a corner.

'That's not bad.' He stuffs in the rest and grabs another. 'What the hell are we going to do, Sandro?'

Sandro watches as Paolo guzzles. 'We need to find more business. I'm almost out of money.'

'But what the fuck can we do without getting beaten up?'

Sandro grins. 'We could join the CIL.'

'Are you cut out for the Italian liberation army?' Paolo looks Sandro up and down, surprised that he should suggest it. It might suit Paolo, but he doubts Sandro could cope.

'At least they'd feed us.'

'With pigswill.'

'Otherwise, Paolo, we'll have to fight against the damn Americans.'

'Those boys have powerful families in Naples. If we cross them again, they'll eat us alive. A bit of looting from the Allies was different, more like war reparations.'

'What can we do?'

Paolo tries to picture himself back in the army. 'I've no bloody idea.'

He takes some ravioli and then some more, under Sandro's watchful eye. 'Do you want one, Sandro?'

'The Caporale sent you a message.' Sandro pushes his hand into the bag. 'He said the Maggiore is back.'

'That was bloody quick. Did Chiara stay in Rome?'

Sandro nods.

'That's one less worry!'

'The Maggiore says Chiara's all right. But he needs to see you.'

'Whatever for?'

'I don't know. He says it's urgent.'

'I can't see him; it isn't safe.'

'I've thought of that, Paolo,' Sandro grins. 'He's coming here.'

'He'll never find me.'

'The Caporale is bringing him.'

'Jesus! You must stop him! It could be a fucking disaster! Imagine it! Two British soldiers shambling around the bloody cemetery. Everyone in Naples will know they're here. Sandro, you must fucking well tell them not to come.'

'I can't.' Sandro looks away. 'They'll be here in a minute.'

'Merda! What the hell does the Maggiore want?'

'I don't know.' Sandro eyes the paper bag. 'Do you want the last one?'

'No, I bloody well don't.'

Sandro takes it in his fingers, stuffs it into his mouth and squashes the greasy bag. 'Paolo, is it because you lied about going to Rome? Perhaps Chiara is angry.'

'Don't be crazy! She'd hardly send the Maggiore to tell me she was cross. I had to say I'd been to Rome, in case Malaspina found out. If he'd learnt that I'd misled him, he'd have strung me up. And probably you as well!'

Paolo still regrets the deal with Malaspina, but at least the Dottore is locked away. 'When did they say they'd be here?'

'One o'clock.'

'Then you'd better go and find them, before they get lost and ask everyone for directions.'

Paolo squeezes further into the nook where he can't be seen. He waits, his arms hugging his stomach. He runs his fingers across the furrows of his ribs. God, this is impossible! What the hell does the Maggiore want?

'Paolo, are you there?' Sandro whispers.

Peering around the angle of the vault, Paolo sees the Caporale next to a tall, dark-haired Maggiore with a pipe resting in his mouth. He looks him up and down, deciding he wouldn't fancy his chances if it came to a fight. Why are British officers all so tall?

'Buon giorno,' Huggins says. 'This is Major Bewdley; he drove Chiara to Rome.'

'Good morning, Maggiore,' Paolo smiles. 'This is my friend Sandro; he doesn't speak English.'

Roger shakes Paolo's hand and then advances another half pace towards him. He inclines his head and speaks with the pipe still wedged in his mouth. 'Paolo, I've a message from your sister. She's all right but …'

Roger looks along the row of marble monuments as though reviewing a line of soldiers on parade. '… but your mother and younger sister … Chiara said they'd been molested.'

Paolo has heard rumours about Allied troops going on the rampage after Cassino, raping women and girls; but he had assumed it was German propaganda.

'What do you mean *molested*? Are you saying they were raped? Santa Maria, spare them!'

'I'm afraid so.'

'WHO DID IT?'

Paolo grabs Roger's arm.

'TELL ME, WHO DID IT?'

'Soldiers.'

'What's he saying?' Sandro asks in Italian, but Paolo turns away.

'WHICH FUCKING SOLDIERS?'

Paolo pulls at Roger's arm again. 'Tell me! Which soldiers?'

'I don't know.' Roger brushes his sleeve.

'Didn't Mamma tell you? Which units did they come from?'

'I didn't see her. Chiara said your mother was too distressed to let me into the flat. She made me sleep in the car, despite the curfew.'

'WHO WERE THESE FUCKING SOLDIERS? WERE THEY BLOODY GERMANS?'

'You're probably right,' Roger says. 'It probably was the bloody Germans.'

'NO!' Paolo's blood boils. 'How could it happen?'

Paolo starts to tug at his hair. 'PORCA MISERIA! I feel so ashamed!' He draws a long-bladed knife from his jacket and pokes it at his chest.

'What the hell are you doing?' Roger grips Paolo's arm. 'What bloody good will that do? Kill some Germans instead.'

Paolo peers at Roger. In his mind's eye he sees a German soldier on his knees. He jabs at him with his rifle butt, until he finally keels over.

'Find me some bloody Crucchi.' Paolo pulls Sandro towards him, 'I shall kill every bloody one.'

'What did the Maggiore say?' Sandro asks but Paolo ignores him again.

'What do you mean *Crucchi?*' Roger asks.

'Jerries!'

Roger relaxes his grip on Paolo's arm. 'I'll tell you what you should do. You should both damn well join up. Then you can kill Crucchi and liberate your country too. Now, put away that knife.'

Paolo fingers the knife before slipping it into his jacket.

'I'll do it,' he says in English. 'I'll do it now.'

He turns to Sandro and explains in Italian what he had said.

'I told you we should join up.' Sandro says.

'That was for different reasons!' Paolo glares at Sandro as he wipes his eyes.

'What about you, Corporal?' Roger turns to Huggins. 'Isn't it time that you returned to the front? We need experienced men.'

'Yes, Sir. I'll talk to Captain Hill.'

Paolo looks at Sandro. 'I don't suppose *you* can join up. You've already deserted from the CIL.'

'It should be all right,' Sandro grins. 'This time I'll use my real name.'

CHAPTER 19

Frank awakes from another nightmare. He can't remember the whole dream but there was something awful, involving fire. He lies in bed exhausted, wishing Vermillion were there. He needs to sleep but he can't face another bad dream.

Deliberately he turns his mind to things at the theatre that need doing. Convinced he won't get back to sleep, he clambers out of bed. The sun is only just rising as he sets off for the theatre, hoping to leave these images behind.

He hunches over his desk in the half-light, studying plans for coming productions. But he feels disconnected from his body and from the world outside. He is no longer sure who he is: it's not that he has forgotten but rather that the person he used to be no longer seems real; perhaps he doesn't exist.

... *Frank is inside the burning building* ...

His pulse races as he stares at his office, desperately seeking reassurance from the familiar surroundings. Ahead he sees that rounded white shape again. But this time he can make out the features of a skull, sun-bleached white except around the eye sockets which are scorched black. 'Damn and blast!' He buries his face in his hands. Is this an admonishment for forgetting why he came to Italy?

'All right,' he shouts at the skull, 'I came here to fight. I'll return to the Battalion. But I have to find a successor. And I must tell Vermillion. There, damn you, I've said it! Now for Christ's sake, leave me alone!'

After a while he opens his eyes and assesses the papers heaped on his desk. If only he could lose himself in work. He puts on his reading glasses and pulls out a schedule with the audience figures for every production since the theatre reopened. They had sold most seats for Traviata, followed by Butterfly and Bohème. Rigoletto and Tosca weren't far behind. He isn't surprised; the shows are roughly in the order he expected. Still it's good to see the numbers clearly.

Bang! Bang!

Frank leaps up, knocking over his chair. He thunders across the room ready to do battle. 'WHAT THE HELL WAS THAT?'

'Sorry, Sir,' Huggins says from behind the door. 'I didn't mean to disturb you. I thought I'd heard voices.'

Frank throws the door open, still braced to fight. He looks at Huggins and starts to drag himself back from the brink. He unclenches his fists and breathes deeply to absorb the pressure.

'What was all that racket, Huggins? It sounded like a bomb had gone off.'

'I just knocked on the door, Sir.'

Frank recognises the concern on Huggins' face.

'I'm sorry, Huggins.'

Frank's body starts to tremble. 'I'm sorry I was brusque … you startled me … I was trying to keep my head down with all this damn paperwork …'

'I'm sorry I disturbed you, Sir.'

Frank squeezes his eyes shut briefly, trying to clear his head. 'What was it you wanted, Huggins?'

'Nothing urgent, Sir. I'll come back when you're less busy.'

'Thank you, Huggins. We'll have a chat then.'

Frank picks up his chair and sits down at his desk. He is still breathing heavily. Had he really reacted like that to just a knock on the door? It had sounded like an explosion. The moment he heard it he was back at the line, ready to fight.

Frank pulls out his handkerchief and mops his forehead. Then he picks up the schedule again and tries to remember where he had got to before Huggins appeared. But his mind soon wanders again; he feels guilty for reacting so abruptly and for sending Huggins away. He wonders what he wanted.

He walks back and forth across the room. When at last he feels calmer he settles at his desk. He returns to the audience analysis and the forward schedule until he's engrossed again.

He is interrupted by a faint call from the corridor, followed by a gentle tap on his door. He reacts strongly again, jumping up and hurrying across the room. 'Who's that?'

'Excuse me, Sir!' Huggins says.

Frank takes a deep breath. 'I'm sorry, Huggins. I'm not ready yet.'

'It's not that, Sir. I just wanted to remind you about your meeting with the Brigadier.'

'Damn and blast!'

When Frank arrived in Egypt in '41, Colonel Carburton, as he was then, commanded 3rd Battalion. He had a reputation for pugnacity but it seemed to Frank this was based more on his service in the Great War than on anything he achieved in Egypt. And after the chaotic withdrawal from Gazala, the Colonel was moved to a desk job, which led to his current post with the Allied Military Government in Naples. Surprisingly this transfer hadn't stopped his promotion to Brigadier.

Frank's first direct encounter with Carburton came after Frank submitted a paper about the unnecessary losses of British tanks at Gazala. After a lengthy delay he was summoned to meet the Colonel, expecting to discuss the paper. Instead Carburton threatened to court-martial him and reduce him to the ranks.

It therefore came as a shock when Frank learnt the Brigadier had responsibility for the theatre. From the start he was distinctly peppery, demanding that Frank should present endless revues. Eventually Frank had to tell him there was only one way to provide daily entertainment: by using the theatre's own performers to stage operas. After fierce initial resistance, Carburton changed his tune when the operas proved popular with the troops. And since then he has basked in the theatre's success.

'Is it really time to meet the Brigadier?' Frank points to the papers strewn across his desk. 'When on earth can I finish all this?'

'Perhaps the Brigadier could help, Sir.'

'That would be something!' Frank laughs. 'Now tell me, Huggins, why on earth does the Brigadier want to see me at AMG's blasted HQ?'

'Would you mind very much,' Huggins raises his eyebrows, 'if I don't try to answer, Sir?'

* * *

Frank is led through the corridors of AMG's labyrinthine HQ, stopping at a tiny room, which looks more like a police cell. It's unfurnished save for a bare table and two rickety chairs. With no room to pace, Frank sits on the stronger-looking seat and leans on the table with his head in his hands.

The image of the skull reappears. But now the charred eye sockets slowly fuse with the window frames from his Ealing flat. He shivers, rubbing his face again. He doesn't need an apparition reminding him of Maggie.

'Damn you! That's enough!' he says out loud.

'Oh good, Captain,' a voice booms in Frank's ear, 'I see you *are* alone.'

Frank jumps to his feet and pulls himself up to his full six foot three, bracing for battle. In his time at the theatre he has learnt a lot about dealing with the Brigadier, but this sudden arrival causes Frank's hackles to rise.

'Good morning, Sir.'

Frank watches as Carburton squeezes into the cell and looks around in disbelief. He sits as far away from Frank as possible, but still their knees nearly touch. Frank pulls back his boots beneath his chair and holds his arms across his belly. He hates the Brigadier being so close.

'Now Captain, well done for saving the theatre. We'd have been in quite a pickle if those incendiaries had taken hold. And well done for standing-in since we locked up the doctor chappie. But that isn't why I'm here.'

'Is there any news about your boys?' Frank asks, hoping to slow down the Brigadier by asking about his two sons who were captured in February '42 when Singapore fell.

'All I know, Captain, is they're still prisoners of those blasted Japanese. But I'm not here to gossip.'

Carburton looks critically at Frank before continuing in a stage whisper. 'Please understand, this conversation is strictly hush-hush. Is that clear?'

'Yes, Sir.' Frank's mind starts to whirl with speculation.

The Brigadier looks round the cell again but finding nothing to focus on, he studies the table. 'AMG wants you to move to Rome.'

'Rome, Sir?' Frank tries to smile.

'Yes, Captain, that's what I said. Intelligence in Rome wants to meet you, to see if you're the right material. They insist your visit must be secret but don't ask me why.'

Thoughts race through Frank's mind as his head sinks. How will he tell Vermillion? Who will run the theatre?

'Cheer up Captain,' the Brigadier shows his teeth in a crocodile smile. 'If Intelligence needs you in Rome, we'll find some other bugger to run the theatre.'

Frank forces a grin. 'Do they want to see me in Rome, Sir?'

'They expect you the day after tomorrow. But before you go, you'll need a cover story. No one must know the reason for your visit. What excuse do you have for visiting Rome?'

Frank is more concerned about what to tell Vermillion, but an idea enters his head. 'I could visit Signor Gigli and invite him to Naples to sing.'

'Excellent idea, Captain! Here are your papers. My Adjutant will arrange a Jeep. Will you need a driver?'

Frank wonders whether it's sufficient to tell Vermillion that Gigli is the reason for his journey. 'No, Sir, Corporal Huggins will drive.'

'Enjoy Rome, Captain. And don't tell a soul why you're going. Don't forget: "walls have ears!"'

'Yes, Sir! Of course!' Frank looks around the cell. 'To fit in here, Sir, their ears must be pretty small.'

CHAPTER 20

Frank spends half the night awake. Then he oversleeps and has to scramble to be ready for Huggins but when he reaches the Jeep, Huggins sends him back for his helmet. It feels strange to wear it after all this time.

Since October '43, when the Battalion reached Naples, Frank has only left the city once. Then he travelled south where the fighting had been less intense, whereas to the north, after months of fierce fighting, the country has suffered immensely. Frank feels apprehensive but he wants to see things for himself.

He looks across at Huggins from time to time, grateful for his company and glad he's driving. Much of the road is like a riverbed and Huggins is absorbed in piloting the Jeep. Stones and assorted debris are strewn across the surface in the aftermath of military vehicles. Tanks of course are the worst: their tracks tear at the roadway as though in preparation for ploughing.

Once they leave Naples, the sea to the west shimmers in the morning sun. As the shadows shorten and the air loses its bite, Frank's mind begins to settle. Vermillion was right that he would find it helpful to escape from Naples. As he gazes out to sea, he starts to feel oddly calm as though Barbara and the fire are fading.

For much of the morning, progress is slow as they drive along narrow roads following military vehicles. Breakdowns or minor accidents frequently bring the traffic to a halt. And occasionally they encounter a roadblock where their papers are briefly examined.

'Frank, would you mind if we stop for a minute?' Huggins says after a couple of hours. 'I'm hearing nature's call.'

Frank sits on a low wall not far from the road. He shields his eyes from the glare and looks out to sea. Far to the south he can make out the island of Ischia; to the west is the headland at Gaeta with the Capo Circeo in the distance. Frank is struck by the contrast between the tranquil flow of Allied shipping across the flawless sea and the muddy devastation on land.

Huggins clambers onto the wall beside him and together they watch as another herd of trucks crawls by.

'Isn't this grand, Sir? You wouldn't think there's a war on. Apart from the transports!'

Frank smiles.

Huggins turns towards him. 'I wanted to have a word, Sir.'

'Oh yes, Huggins, what is it? And please don't call me Sir.'

Huggins peers out to sea before clearing his throat. 'I want to join up with 4th Battalion.'

'Bloody hell!' Frank half turns. 'Are you sure that's what you want? I thought you liked Naples. You've always seemed so much at home.'

Huggins looks down. 'I'm an experienced soldier, Frank. And now the lads are pushing forward, they need all the men they can get. And there's another thing. Naples isn't what it was. There are too many foreigners!'

Frank resists a smile. 'The Battalion will be glad to have you back, of course.' Frank's voice doesn't hide his astonishment. He had heard from Vermillion that Paolo had decided to join up, but he never thought Huggins would go too.

'Paolo has chucked in his business dealings.' Huggins resumes the study of his boots. 'That's another consideration, Frank. I've had a smashing time in Naples but one day it had to end. I hope you don't mind, Sir.'

'Of course, I bloody well mind.'

Frank studies an approaching tank carrier. 'If it's what you really want, Huggins, then of course you must go, but I shall miss you. And the theatre won't be the same. How will we manage without your frequent bulletins of news? I won't try to change your mind, but I would like to know why you want to go. Is it something Roger said?'

'Oh no, Sir.'

Huggins swings his legs back and forth; his boots thud rhythmically against the wall.

'Well not mostly, Sir. There's another thing that made me think. Naples is getting too hot. Tommies, on leave from the line, have started picking on soldiers who've avoided action. It's not hard to tell us apart because men who've been at the line look different. And then there are the Yanks who drove Paolo away; sometimes they hang around for me. I can look after myself in a way Paolo can't, but it's not a fair fight. If those Yanks come after us again, they won't play by the rules.'

'Huggins, we can't have you run out of town by some nickel-and-dime mobsters. Can't you gather your chums and sort the Yankees out.'

'The problem is my pals are in 4th Battalion. If they were in Naples, they'd soon deal with the Yanks. But it's more than that. I want to be with my mates again, which means going through things together. It's the only way to be part of the gang. And the war can't last much longer. If I wait, I may never get back in. I don't want it to end, feeling I was left behind. I'm sorry Frank, but I have to go.'

'Don't be sorry, Huggins. You're right. God willing, the war will be over soon. Then let's hope there'll be peace for a long time when we'll all have to live with ourselves and our friends in the knowledge of what we did … or didn't do … in the war.'

'I shall miss the theatre, Sir. And you've been good to me. I'll never forget your singing in the first revue. The Toreador's Song was a ruddy marvel. But I can't stay there for the rest of the war. What would I tell my old man? That I was working at a flipping Opera House? We'd never live it down. I've had a good run. And don't get me wrong, I'm very grateful. I've seen every bloody opera that's ever been and it's all been blooming marvellous.'

Frank stands up and brushes himself off. 'There's one other thing, Huggins. You said it was mostly not to do with Roger. Did he play some part?'

'That's simple, Frank. He said I could return to 4th Battalion and rejoin my pals; it wouldn't be the same joining up with a different crowd.'

They clamber into the Jeep. The air is hotter now. Frank jettisons his helmet, glad to feel the breeze around his head. Perhaps Huggins is doing the right thing. If Frank isn't moved to Rome, should he rejoin the Battalion too? Either way he'd have to leave Vermillion and the theatre.

* * *

They reach the outskirts of Minturno at the western end of the German's Gustav Line. Frank shudders at the utter devastation, which looks like something from the end of the world. Yet Allied soldiers had fought here a few weeks ago and the remains of some of them are entombed beneath the rubble.

Frank closes his eyes, trying to comprehend that this is the world to which Huggins will return. It's as though a giant wave has smashed its way across the peninsula. And without the theatre, Frank would have been part of that breaker.

He looks over at Huggins, who drives on unperturbed. How can he be so sanguine? Frank's eyes light upon a piece of wall, perhaps five feet high, one of the few sections still standing. For a moment he sees the skull. He is so shocked he almost addresses it out loud.

Frank swallows and starts to interrogate the skull in his head. *Must I join up? And if I do, will you leave me alone? Would a transfer to Rome be enough?*

Receiving no clear answers, Frank becomes angry. *Why are you haunting me? Why are you ruining my life?*

Huggins swerves suddenly to avoid a pothole. 'Sorry, Sir!'

The jolt brings Frank back. He looks at Huggins, relieved he couldn't hear his conversation with an imaginary skull. Had he heard it, he'd have known that Frank is going nuts.

'Dear God, please make me sane!' Frank repeats to himself. 'Dear God, please make me sane!'

* * *

From Minturno they follow the coast road to Terracina where the Ausonian Mountains meet the sea. Then they turn inland, skirting around the coastal plain where the Germans had flooded the Pontine Marshes to slow the Allied advance. Eventually they return to the Via Appia and head north towards the Alban Hills.

The sun is high overhead and they look for shade to park the Jeep. Huggins unwraps their sweating sandwiches while Frank opens a bottle of warm beer. Around them the world is silent apart from the thrum of insects, seemingly unaffected by the war.

Across the valley a group of sappers is rebuilding a railway bridge.

'Those chaps do an amazing job,' Huggins says between mouthfuls, 'throwing up ruddy bridges everywhere. And finishing them in no time.'

'At least here there's no enemy fire, not like at the Volturno.'

'I've heard the Naples to Rome railway will reopen in July.'

They are silent for a while. Frank downs a large draught of beer. 'Huggins, you know I plan to visit Signor Gigli.'

'Yes, Sir. How will you track him down?'

'I expect the opera house will help. But that's not the only reason for my visit.'

'But I heard you tell Miss Henthorpe that was the reason.'

'I know, Huggins,' Frank gulps some more beer, 'I haven't told her the other reason. And I'm relying on you to keep this cat securely inside the bag.'

'Yes, of course, Sir. You can rely on me.' Huggins looks up. 'Anyway … I'll be off to 4th Battalion when we return. Where else have you got to go?'

'The Brindisi Hotel. Near the centre, I believe.'

Huggins glances at Frank, hoping for more information. Frank takes another swig of beer.

'The thing is, Huggins, the Brigadier wants to move me to Intelligence in Rome. But I don't want to leave Naples and I don't want to worry Miss Henthorpe unnecessarily. That's why you must keep mum.'

'My trap will stay firmly shut, Sir. But why does the Brigadier want to send you to Rome?'

'He thinks I can help Intelligence, because I speak Italian.'

'That's a bleeding tragedy, Sir. You've done wonders at the theatre.'

'It's kind of you to say so. I don't want to go but it may be Hobson's choice. And by the way Huggins, there's a third visit we'll need to make. You remember Chiara. I want to see how she is.'

'Aren't you getting in at the deep end, Sir? But I won't say nothing about that neither.'

Frank smiles. 'There's nothing secret about visiting Chiara. After hearing the awful news about her mother and Francesca, Vermillion insisted I should go.'

'Right, Sir, so it's just the meeting with Intelligence that I'm keeping under my hat.'

'Yes, thank you Huggins. I need to tell Chiara about Paolo. Vermillion said you were there at the cemetery when Roger broke the news. How did Paolo take it?'

'He was suddenly shit or bust – ready to kill every German he could find. If a POW had marched by, he'd have torn him limb from limb. He was in a right old bate.'

'Poor man! It must be terrible to hear news like that about your loved ones, especially while you're away.'

'Paolo feels bad that he didn't go to Rome in March. And the Major laid it on thick about the dreadful things the Teds have done.'

'What did Paolo do?'

'You mean after he stopped jumping from leg to leg as though he'd caught St Vitus's dance. Well, he lapped up what the Major said and swore he'd join up at once.'

'Do you think he meant it? It might be better if he went to Rome.'

'He can't do that, Frank. Not before he takes revenge. No, he's bound to join up.'

* * *

When they set off again Frank dons his helmet to shield his head from the sun. But despite the shade afforded by its rim he still needs to raise a hand to reduce the glare.

Approaching the Alban Hills, they enter the outskirts of Velletri, part of the Caesar Line until the American advance destroyed it at the end of May. They drive past the ruins in silence. Frank wonders what Huggins is thinking. But when they stop again Huggins is in buoyant mood.

'Doesn't Velletri figure in one of your operas?' Huggins grins.

'Do you remember which one?'

'Wasn't it the Force of Destiny?'

'My word, Huggins, you're right. There's a scene at the Battle of Velletri in 1744.'

'That's funny … 1744 and 1944 … two hundred bloody years ago.'

'Then the Bourbons from Naples were fighting the Austrians.'

'Blimey! Some things never change. I hope the bloody Bourbons won.'

'Yes they did!'

'Well that's a bleeding relief, when the force of *my* bloody destiny is returning me to the line.'

* * *

Driving through the outskirts of Rome is different to anything they experienced on the journey, or in Naples. Rome hasn't been bombed and has largely avoided any fighting. Yet there aren't the crowds that throng Naples' teeming streets.

Frank knows the Romans greeted the Allies when they first arrived. He had seen photographs of the crowds garlanding Allied tanks with flowers. But today there's no sign of celebration. The streets are clean and orderly but apart from police and soldiers they're mostly empty.

Frank's meeting with Intelligence isn't until tomorrow morning and there are still two hours of daylight, so Frank decides to visit the opera house. But they find the place deserted. Outside the entrance there's an array of ageing posters. One announces a performance of Un Ballo in Maschera on the second of June, a couple of weeks ago. Gigli was here then.

Frank tries several doors and then resorts to hammering, but with no effect. It reminds him of his first visit to the San Carlo theatre. Then he found an open door but was confronted by Giovanni with his rifle.

Frank continues nosing around. German posters on the ground carry warnings about the mortal dangers of assisting partisans. They give Frank a disturbing feeling of the Germans' recent presence, as though they had fled part way through a meal.

Soon it starts to get dark but the street lamps don't come on. Frank is ready to abandon his search when a middle-aged man appears. Frank asks him where Gigli can be found. The man studies Frank with suspicion until he explains his business and produces a letter for Gigli written on San Carlo paper.

'Piacere, Capitano,' the man shakes Frank's hand. 'My name is Grisi, Angelo Grisi.'

'Piacere. I'd like to invite Signor Gigli to sing in Naples.'

'Ah yes, the San Carlo. The maestro loves that theatre. He was so happy to hear it had reopened.'

'How can I get in touch? I'd like to meet him.'

'I'll see what I can do. Things are difficult in Rome, but if you give me the name of your hotel, I'll send a message. For how long are you staying?'

'At least one more day.'

'Please await my message, Capitano. ArrivederLa.'

CHAPTER 21

With Frank away, Vermillion throws herself into organising her office, determined to catch up before he returns. At first she feels pleased having time to herself, but once her work is up to date she can't ignore the hole that Frank's absence has created.

She tries to imagine what it's like for Pen with Bill away for three years. She *must* write to her again. Margery is coming to see Butterfly in half an hour, which gives her just enough time to scribble a reply.

16th June 1944

Dearest Pen

Thank you for your letter with all your news.

Again, a thousand apologies for my slow reply, but I hope you saw my letter to parents which was addressed to you as well. That letter contained the bare bones of what has happened. Now I would like to tell you more but I must ask you not to pass this on to parents. I don't want them worrying unnecessarily.

This has been a difficult time. I told you about the fire in our block and how dear Barbara was overcome by the smoke. Sadly she died just after my letter, without ever coming round. We had shared a flat ever since we arrived in Cairo. She was a close and dear friend and I feel her loss deeply.

Dear Barbara went back into our building looking for me, not knowing I was already outside. I feel responsible although there was nothing I could have done.

Losing Barbara has reminded me how lucky I am to have you. But in the autumn it will be three years since we were last together. Then I was desperate to go abroad with the ATS, but now I miss the family. I've had a chance to spread my wings which are now quite stretched enough.

In the letter to parents, I mentioned working for an infantry Captain. Frank Hill is a marvellous man – tall and good looking – who has put the opera house back on its feet, despite the war. He reminds me of James.

James was Pen's first great love: their affair had to be kept from parents. Vermillion hopes that mentioning his name will encourage Pen's discretion.

>*The truth is I love Frank, although he's seven years older than me. And he says he loves me. I feel so lucky he's here in Naples when Bill is so far away. But Frank may soon be transferred, so I'm enjoying his company while I can, although today he's in Rome.*
>
>*Please send much love to Andrew, who must be five by now: what a big boy! Please also send my love to Bill; I hope he'll be home soon. I long to see you all and to meet Charlotte for the first time.*
>
>*With lots of love*
>*V*

* * *

Vermillion seals the envelope and sets off to find Margery. She decides to wait outside the theatre where it isn't so hot, but Margery is nowhere to be seen. Khaki uniforms hurry past, but there are fewer now.

Vermillion scans the road at the bottom of Via Roma: still no sign of Margery. She turns back towards the theatre, determined not to miss the show.

'I'm sorry I'm late, Vermillion,' Margery calls out.

'Come on, Margery, this way.' Vermillion leads the scramble. 'It's only two flights to our box. You'll find a synopsis in the programme.'

As they enter the box a sprinkle of applause greets the leader of the orchestra.

'Oh dear, the lights are going down. You'll have to catch up later.'

'Sorry to keep you waiting,' Margery whispers. 'It has been a frightful rush. I was caught in the operating theatre.'

Louder applause announces the maestro. The theatre quietens. Vermillion has seen the show several times, but she is still moved by Butterfly's devotion to Pinkerton and her unwavering belief he will return.

Margery is also captured by the story. Perhaps with Edmund heading for England, she sees herself in Butterfly's shoes. Vermillion feels Margery shudder when Pinkerton's wife appears. And by the end they are both close to tears.

'That poor child,' Margery says as they make their way slowly towards the Club, needing sustenance. 'I could hardly bear to look when Butterfly put the Stars and Stripes in his hand and blindfolded him.'

'How awful that Butterfly felt she must die.' Vermillion says as they find a table. 'She was little more than a child. How many girls in Naples are in the same position?'

Vermillion remembers that Margery wouldn't sleep with Rob for fear of becoming pregnant. She wonders whether she regrets that now.

'But women here can't hand over their babies.' Margery says.

Vermillion lifts her glass, giving silent thanks. She puts the glass to her lips and lifts her head but stops, aware that someone is approaching.

'Simon!' Margery says with a smile.

Vermillion almost chokes on her wine, but Margery doesn't look surprised. Is this something she planned?

'Hello, Margery, Vermillion,' Simon grins. 'May I join you?'

'Of course,' Margery smiles again. 'Did you see the opera? Wasn't it moving?'

'Very touching,' Simon looks at Vermillion as he stubs out his cigarette. 'Frank must feel jolly proud about the theatre. Is he around tonight?'

'Are you afraid he'll throw you out?'

'I'd be grateful if he didn't.'

'Don't worry, Simon,' Margery says. 'Frank's in Rome, scouting for opera stars.'

'I flew over Rome yesterday,' Simon offers his cigarettes and then takes one himself. 'The city looks magnificent from the air.'

'I'd love to fly,' Margery says.

'You should try it some time,' Simon smiles at her. 'I offered to take Vermillion up, when we were based at Heliopolis, but she pulled out.'

Vermillion's cheeks burn. Bloody Simon. How dare he mention that in front of Margery?

'Did you really turn Simon down?' Margery laughs. 'I'd do *anything* for a chance to fly.'

'Be careful what you say,' Vermillion says. 'Simon might hold you to it.'

'I'm sure he's a perfect gentleman.'

'Margery, you know very well he's not!'

'I don't want you two to quarrel,' Margery gets to her feet. 'But I must go. I'm on duty early tomorrow. Thank you, Vermillion for the lovely show.'

'Thank you for coming,' Vermillion prepares to leave too. 'I must be off …'

'Don't go, Vermillion!' Simon puts a hand on her forearm. 'Stay for a minute. I'm sorry, I shouldn't have said all that.'

'No, you shouldn't!'

'I was carried away by the excitement of seeing you. I still miss you, Vermillion …'

'Simon, stop! I'm leaving …'

'Vermillion, please listen!'

He draws on his cigarette again and then stubs it out. 'I'm so sorry about what happened in March. I should never have turned up drunk. I was drinking because I missed you. I was stupid and I got what I deserved. But now I'm sober as a judge and I'm telling you I still love you …'

'Simon, you mustn't say that. You know I'm with Frank.'

'Perhaps you are, when he's around. But don't worry, I can wait. When you're ready, I shall still be here.'

Vermillion stands up.

'May I have just one dance?' Simon asks.

Vermillion hesitates. Simon takes her hand.

'No, Simon. I'm not going to dance. I'm going home.' She moves towards the entrance but then turns back. 'Did Margery tell you we'd be here?'

Simon looks down.

'Ruddy Margery! Simon, please don't do this again!'

Outside the light is fading and Vermillion doesn't relish walking alone. If only Frank were here.

'I'll walk you back to the flat,' Simon says.

Vermillion glares at him.

'I won't try anything, I promise. I'll just see you safely home.'

CHAPTER 22

Huggins drops Frank outside the Brindisi Hotel. A gang of children gathers around the Jeep chanting the familiar 'Pane e Biscotti'.

Frank had slept well but this morning he feels confused. Although moving to Rome might be better than going to the front, it would still mean leaving Vermillion and the theatre.

Frank marches into the hotel where a trestle table in the lobby is manned by a Sergeant and a Private. Frank is told to wait, but a few moments later the Private calls his name. He leads Frank up the uncarpeted stairs and along a dark corridor. He taps on one of the doors.

'Enter!'

Frank strides into the crudely panelled bedroom. The Major – Frank assumes this must be Rummage – doesn't look up but gestures at a chair with tired-looking upholstery on the near side of the desk. Frank pulls the chair back and sits down, keeping his eyes on the Major who continues to write. From what Frank can see of his face he's about fifty, with a dome-shaped forehead, thinning short hair and a neat moustache.

It feels like several minutes before Rummage looks up and registers surprise at Frank's size. He addresses Frank in an upper-class accent.

'Bone, jaw, no. Comb a star.'

Frank can't think what he's saying. 'I'm sorry, Sir, no one gave me a password.'

Rummage repeats the words again. 'Bone, jaw, no.'

Was it "no" or "know" or even "nose"?

'Comb a star,' he continues.

Frank's skin pricks as he starts to sweat. He tries to follow the restricted movement of the Major's lips, repeating the strange sounds in his head in an effort to decipher them.

Suddenly the penny drops. Of course! "Buon giorno. Come sta?" Rummage had spoken with such taut vowels that the words had been unintelligible.

'Molto bene, grazie.' Frank exhales. 'Anche Lei?'

The Major writes something down before asking in ponderous Italian what Frank has done since he arrived in Italy.

'I landed with 3rd Battalion at Salerno on 9th September '43,' he replies in Italian. 'We were there for a week under the German bombardment. Then we headed north towards the Volturno …'

'All right, Captain!' Rummage interjects in English. 'That's enough. It's all very well speaking a bit of the lingo, but you were fearfully slow on the uptake when I was speaking. I'm afraid, Captain, you've put the cart before the horse. In Intelligence it's more important to listen and understand than it is to speak.'

Frank struggles to suppress the laughter rolling around his diaphragm. He swallows as he stares at the Major in disbelief.

'And why do you hope to transfer to Intelligence?'

'I might be able to help, Sir.'

'That's very good of you Captain,' Rummage sits back. 'And what have you done in Italy that makes you think you *might help*?'

Frank watches Rummage, intrigued that his moustache hardly moves when he speaks.

'I've had dealings with a lot of Italians, Sir, and have learnt to work with them quite well.'

'And where have you had these *dealings*?'

'In the San Carlo theatre, the opera house in …'

'So you think your meetings with Italians in an opera house can help British Army Intelligence.'

'Brigadier Carburton seems to think so, Sir.'

'The Brigadier isn't here, Captain. You'd better convince me yourself.'

'Well, I'm good at winning people's confidence, Sir. It encourages them to …'

'You've done nothing to win *my* confidence. I shall write to inform the Brigadier.'

'Major Rummage …' Frank is about to tell him what he thinks of his frightful Italian, but he catches himself in time. He doesn't want to burn his bridges. 'Thank you very much, Sir.'

* * *

Huggins is waiting as Frank emerges into the sunlight.

'That was bloody quick, Sir.' Huggins looks at Frank brightly, unable to hide his curiosity.

'Not quick enough,' Frank grins. 'The Major was an idiot, a typical Intelligence type.'

Huggins lets in the clutch and sets off into the maze of streets.

'Do you know where you're going, Huggins? I haven't worked out the geography yet.'

'Don't worry, Sir!' Huggins shouts above the noise of the Jeep. 'While you were having fun with the Major, I tracked down Chiara's flat. It isn't far! A whisker over a mile!'

* * *

Frank is grateful to Huggins for locating where Chiara lives, but he wishes he had taken a bit longer, giving him more time to think.

Frank's feelings for Chiara have never been simple. With no official record of her living in his requisitioned flat, Frank should have turned her away last autumn. But he felt responsible and found her intriguing. He couldn't throw her out.

Frank had therefore agreed to share the flat. He found Chiara attractive but knew it wouldn't be right to start an affair when he was expecting to return to the front. But when the success of the first revue led to Frank remaining in Naples, they did make love although he soon regretted it. He was fond of Chiara, but he didn't love her and he didn't want her to love him.

Over the months their relationship cooled further, as Frank was drawn increasingly to Vermillion. Finally, Chiara took up with Sandro and to Frank's great relief she moved out. Their affair seemed to have ended amicably, but for Frank it left a raw edge of guilt, which meant he preferred not to see her. If Vermillion hadn't insisted, he would have stayed away.

The Jeep stops outside a tenement block. Frank climbs down, carefully avoiding a dog asleep in the gutter. He keeps an eye on the mongrel until he sees a streak of blood and bile piped across its side, where the flesh had split.

'Wait here, Huggins. This shouldn't take long.'

The nails in Frank's boots ring out as he marches up to the entrance and enters the empty lobby. He starts to climb, stopping on each bare landing. As he makes it to the fourth floor, he remembers that Chiara hadn't let Roger in.

While he catches his breath, he studies the ill-fitting door. He knocks, and listens as light footsteps approach the door and the door slowly opens.

Frank glimpses half of a girl's head before she lets out a piercing scream. He claps his hands over his ears as she slams the door in his face. The whole wall shakes.

That must have been Francesca. Frank mutters, steadying himself against the side wall. Her screaming reminds him of Chiara's. He rubs his hand where Chiara bit him all that time ago. He wants to walk away but restrains himself: he doesn't want to frighten them any more.

'Chiara!' he calls. 'CHIARA! Sono Franco!'

His voice echoes in the stairwell until silence returns. Looking around, the dinginess of the building starts to get him down. He covers his nose; surely the mustiness is tinged with urine.

'Damn it!' Frank raises his fist. 'This is too much!'

He is about to hammer on the door when it opens, catching him in an apparent Fascist salute.

'Hello, Chiara,' he drops his arm.

'Franco!' She throws herself towards him. 'Thank goodness you've come. Everything here is terrible.'

'I'm so sorry, Chiara.' Frank tries to slip from her embrace. 'Are you all right?'

'What do you think, Franco?'

Frank feels an undertow of emotions: anxiety about seeing Chiara; pity for her and her family; and irritation that already he feels responsible for what has happened.

'May I come in, Chiara, so we can talk?'

'Don't be stupid, Franco!' Chiara's sunken eyes, circled with dark rings, flash a look of disgust. 'You saw what your arrival did to Francesca. We must go down to the street.'

Chiara turns back into the flat, closing the door behind her. Frank clenches his fists. He shouldn't have come. He tramps down the stairs. If Chiara wants to talk, she will have to come and find him.

'Was everything all right, Sir?' Huggins smiles. 'Shall we return to the hotel?'

'No, it damn well wasn't, Huggins. It makes me despair. Chiara is upset, but she won't let me into the flat even though we've come all this way.'

'It's lucky you had other reasons for coming to Rome.'

'But seeing Rummage was a waste of time and I haven't heard a word from Gigli. We'd better wait here for a bit, in case Chiara reappears. I still haven't told her about Paolo.'

Huggins climbs into the Jeep while Frank strolls along the pavement. He kicks at a stone which skitters ahead of him. A group of young boys watch him warily.

Further along, a large house is set back from the road. It seems solid enough, but the window frames are blackened by fire. He squeezes his eyes shut.

'Frank! Sir!' Huggins calls along the street. 'Chiara's here!'

'Damn!' Frank turns and watches Chiara shuffling towards him with her head down.

'Let's go this way,' Frank points away from the burnt house.

'Did you hear what happened, Franco?'

'Yes, Roger told us. Chiara, I'm so sorry. How are your mother and Francesca?'

'Terrified!' Chiara glares at Frank. 'How could those soldiers do it? How could you let them?'

'I'm terribly sorry, Chiara. There are so many dreadful things in this war but attacking women must be the worst.'

'Mamma has aged twenty years: she's already an old woman. Francesca was only a child. But now … I don't know what she is. She won't even talk: her life is ruined.'

Frank slumps his shoulders, wanting to be sick. This is too much to bear. 'Have you heard from Paolo?'

'No! I never want to hear from him again! He betrayed us! He lied about visiting Mamma. And he ignored my plea to come to Rome.'

'I haven't seen Paolo either,' Frank catches her eye. 'But I know he's distressed and angry and hell-bent on taking revenge. He has joined the CIL, determined to kill German soldiers.'

'What fucking use is that?' Chiara grabs Frank's arm. 'They weren't *German* soldiers!'

'That's what Paolo believes.'

'Then he's a fool as well as a liar. Who told him that?'

'I think …' Frank hesitates, '… I think he heard it from Major Bewdley.'

'Why would the bloody Major say that?' Chiara buries her head in her hands.

Frank puts his arm lightly on her shoulders.

'I never told the Major they were Germans.' Chiara looks up through her tears. 'Franco … it happened AFTER the Germans left, just days before I arrived. Santa Madonna, forgive me for coming too late.'

Chiara weeps for several minutes. Frank doesn't know what to do. He turns towards Huggins who stares at his boots.

'Chiara, I'm so sorry.' Frank says, above the sound of sobbing. 'I hope your mother and Francesca will be all right. Have you heard from Sandro?'

Chiara looks up. Her nose is running and her face is puffy around the eyes. Frank pulls out a handkerchief.

'Did Sandro give you a message?' she asks from the middle of the handkerchief. 'When is he coming to Rome? I miss him so much.'

'Sandro has gone with Paolo.'

'The stupid boy!' she looks up. 'Where the hell have they gone?'

'I don't know, but I'm sure he'll write soon.'

'How could Sandro be so daft? He hates the bloody army! He has deserted twice already!'

Chiara drums her fists on Frank's chest until he pulls her towards him and holds her.

'FRANCO! WHY DON'T THOSE BOYS UNDERSTAND! TELL THEM TO COME HOME NOW!'

For a moment Chiara is limp in Frank's arms.

'Why can't they understand?' She braces herself. 'As girls we were taught to depend on men, who then embarked on this dreadful war. Now they've left us to these foreign soldiers. How can we cope on our own with so little food, so little of everything?'

'I'm sorry, Chiara.'

Frank feels close to tears. Clearly Chiara wants someone to look after her, but he knows it can't be him. 'I'm sure Sandro will write soon. Then you can write back and tell him you need him here.'

Frank braces for another outburst, but Chiara just sobs into his handkerchief.

'I'm so sorry, Chiara. If I see Paolo or Sandro, I promise I'll give them your message. But now I must go.'

Briefly she clings to him. Then she stands silently on the pavement while Frank clambers up beside Huggins and they drive away.

* * *

'Come on Huggins, let's get a drink.'

Frank walks towards the entrance of their hotel. 'After seeing Chiara, I feel whacked.'

'Excuse me, Sir.' A voice comes from behind the desk.

Frank turns and takes an envelope from the outstretched hand. He pulls out a single sheet of paper.

'Bad luck, Huggins. There's a summons from Gigli.'

'Well, Sir, it is your lucky day!'

Frank takes a deep breath. 'First we have to get there.'

'Don't worry, Sir. You go and have a brush up, while I take a squint at the map.'

* * *

They drive past the Villa Borghese and its neglected park but the area is clearly prosperous with streets of detached houses. People are well-turned-out: even the girls wear stockings and silk dresses.

'This must be the one, Huggins!' Frank shouts above the noise of the Jeep. 'Can you stop here?'

'Blimey, Sir.' Huggins stamps on the brakes. 'It's a bleeding palace.'

'Yes, Huggins, Gigli *is* royalty.'

Frank drops down to the pavement. He never believed he would meet the maestro to face. He steadies himself before marching past a group of unkempt policemen and up to the front door.

'All right, Huggins,' he calls. 'I'll see you at the Jeep.'

Frank has hardly grasped the bell pull when a footman appears, bowing slightly. Frank gives his name and is ushered in. At least they're expecting him.

The footman leads him to an ornate side-room which feels cool after the heat outside. Left alone, he surveys the chequerboard of Gigli photographs that lines the walls. He tries to identify the costumes but keeps looking back at one of Gigli as Nemorino in L'Elisir d'Amore in which he looks like an oversized schoolboy.

The pictures are formal and there isn't one where Gigli smiles. Frank wonders why, but his thoughts are interrupted by the arrival of a middle-aged man.

'Good evening, Captain 'ill,' he says in English. 'I'm Signor Gigli's secretary. The maestro looks forward to meeting you.

But I should warn you, he feels rather anxious. This war has caused a lot of strain.'

'I understand; it has been dreadful for all of us.'

'Come this way, Captain.'

The Secretary leads Frank to a large reception room, where the windows are shaded by thick blinds. The room is dominated by a grand piano with the lid raised. Frank feels apprehensive as he looks around. Perhaps Gigli's anxiety is infectious.

From behind the piano a middle-aged man appears. Gigli looks shorter and rounder than Frank remembers from '39, but of course no one looks the same offstage.

'Ben venuto, Capitano.'

'Onorato,' Frank bows his head a little, feeling uncomfortably tall.

'I am told, Capitano, that you reopened the San Carlo theatre,' Gigli continues in Italian. 'I thank you on behalf of all Italians. The San Carlo is a wonderful theatre. Its acoustic is second only to the Teatro Bellini in Catania. I've sung in Naples with much pleasure and I look forward to singing there again.'

Frank responds to the warmth in Gigli's voice although his face shows no hint of a smile.

'We keenly anticipate your visit, Maestro. It will be a special pleasure for me. I heard you sing at Covent Garden and I long to hear you again.'

'Ah yes, Covent Garden! Did you see me as the fireman in Bohème?' Gigli catches Frank's eye.

Frank laughs. He had read a newspaper report about Gigli extinguishing an unplanned fire in the garret whilst continuing to sing. 'No, Maestro, I missed your Bohème, but I saw you in Aida.'

'With Maestro Beecham.' Gigli's eyes brighten. 'That production was magnificent, my finest Radames without doubt.'

Frank hesitates, still imagining that fire in Bohème. His palms start to sweat. 'We look forward to hearing it in Naples.'

'One day, but not yet.' Gigli lowers his head. 'Some people don't want me to sing. They say I'm a traitor. Last week a mob besieged my house. Now I have policemen outside, but I've sent my family to Recanati. All this because I sang for the Germans.'

Gigli lifts his arm towards the far wall but quickly turns away. Frank notices blank spaces where pictures once hung, presumably photographs of Mussolini and Hitler.

'Come over here, Capitano; make yourself comfortable.' Gigli gestures towards a sofa. Frank would rather stand but he forces himself to sit. Relief soon arrives in the form of a maid with a tray of drinks.

'What was I meant to do?' Gigli looks taller sitting down. 'Hitler and Goering loved my voice and asked me to sing. Was I meant to refuse? Has everyone forgotten that Germany was our ally? I'm a singer, not a politician. I only understand the politics of music, which says that people throughout the world want to hear my voice.'

Gigli gets up. He stands with his feet spread as though about to perform.

'Capitano,' he addresses Frank directly. 'I've sung for the Americans and the British. I sang for the Fascists too. And if they asked me, I'd sing for the Communists. Tell me, Capitano, does that make me a traitor?'

'I'm shocked, Maestro,' Frank says. 'I never thought the people of Rome would treat you like this. But I trust it's just a summer storm.'

'I'd like to think so. But I fear this squall will blow itself out only slowly. Until then the mob won't let me sing.'

'I understand, Maestro. But I want you to know our invitation stands. When you're ready to come to Naples we'll be waiting. Thank you for seeing me.'

'Farewell, Capitano.' Gigli steps forward and shakes Frank's hand warmly; but there's still no sign of a smile.

CHAPTER 23

Vermillion pours herself a cup of tea and walks slowly to the sitting room where she turns on the wireless. With Huggins away she hasn't heard the news. She waits for the valves to warm up before the reassuring chimes of Big Ben.

'How do you manage it, Vermillion?' Jackie puts her head round the door. 'Anyone would think you have all the time in the world.'

'Shh. I want to hear this.'

Jackie sits down and they listen in silence to the report of a flying bomb which hit the Guards' Chapel in Wellington Barracks. It's not the first V-1 over London but this one struck the heart of the capital. Other flying bombs were shot down, but Vermillion feels sick.

'That's awful,' Jackie says. 'It wasn't far from the Palace.'

The bulletin moves on to reports of Allied progress since the Normandy landings and it's not long before Jackie has heard enough.

'What's going on with Simon?' Jackie asks when Vermillion looks up.

Vermillion doesn't respond.

'Come on, Vermillion. I saw him leaving last night, when I was coming home.'

'How can you think about that when the news is so serious, Jackie? Anyway, it was perfectly innocent ...'

'I didn't say it wasn't. I just asked what was going on.'

Vermillion turns off the wireless and faces Jackie. 'I saw Butterfly with Margery – it was desperately sad – and then we went to the Club and Simon appeared.'

'What a coincidence!' Jackie sips her tea.

'It wasn't a coincidence at all. I'm sure Margery arranged it, knowing Frank was away.'

'That was nice of her,' Jackie laughs. 'There's more to Margery than meets the eye.'

'You know I'm not interested in Simon!'

'Is Frank really the one? Will you move into his flat?'

'I don't know, but I may stay there from time to time.'

'I don't like being left alone. Even with two of us, we rattle around. I've asked Margery to join us; I think she'll agree.'

'I don't mind Margery, provided she leaves me alone, but I sense that she doesn't like Frank.'

'That's jolly ungrateful. If it hadn't been for her, you'd still be hitched to Edmund.'

'*She* didn't tell Edmund. It was Simon. But I suspect she arranged that too, and not for my sake.'

'I still think you should be grateful. You always swore you wouldn't let yourself get penned in. And Margery freed you. Of course, you didn't take long to shackle yourself to Frank. How long was it between finishing with Edmund and starting up with Frank? How many hours?'

'Shut up, Jackie! You can't talk! How many boyfriends have you had in Naples? Do you even know? *I've* completely lost count.'

Vermillion hurries towards her room. She wants to slam the door. God, Jackie can be so annoying! She wishes Barbara were here. She still often talks to her, telling her how sorry she is. Poor Barbara; she was always the peacemaker. Vermillion is trying to come to terms with Barbara's death but this clash with Jackie brings back feelings of vulnerability.

'My goodness, Barbara, I miss you.'

* * *

In the morning Vermillion sets off for the theatre wondering how Frank is getting on in Rome. She doesn't relish the prospect of another day alone. although when he does return, she'll have to tell him that Simon walked her home. If only she hadn't agreed. And she still hasn't told Frank the whole story of what happened in Egypt. She fears that the moment may have passed.

'Huggins! Good heavens!' Vermillion smiles broadly, pleased to see him and excited that Frank is back. 'I didn't expect to see you today. When did you return?'

'At the crack of dawn this morning, Miss. It was bloody marvellous seeing Rome. And now I'm enjoying the last of the Naples' air.'

'When are you off?'

'I leave tomorrow, for a week of bloody training. Then I'll rejoin the Platoon. Major Bewdley arranged it before he left.'

'I didn't think you'd leave so soon, Huggins.' Vermillion swallows, wondering whether Frank will go too. 'We'll miss you, Huggins. You must promise that you'll visit us whenever you get some leave.'

'Did you know, Miss …' he looks up from his boots '… we've liberated Orvieto and Assisi, a hundred miles north of Rome? The front is moving blooming fast. At this rate, Miss, the Battalion will reach Berlin before my ruddy training ends.'

'That's excellent news. Thank you … Huggins … for all your help … and very good luck.'

Vermillion hesitates, wishing she could embrace him, but of course she can't. With nothing else to say, she takes a deep breath, lifts her head and tries to smile. Then she walks slowly up the steps.

Ruddy Roger! Why is he taking Huggins away? And why can't Frank see what he's up to?

She accelerates into Frank's room. He opens his arms and strides towards her, a large smile illuminating his face. She clings to him, excited and relieved that he's home. He kisses her, lifting her off the ground. She feels an ache inside: she wants to make love but knows she'll have to wait.

He lowers her to the ground, and she tidies herself a little. 'How was Rome, darling, and how was Chiara?'

'Are you sure you want to hear?' Frank sits down at his desk and she settles onto his knee.

'It was awful seeing Chiara. She has had a ghastly time. It's not just the assaults. Before the Allies arrived, her mother and sister were starving, like the rest of the city. Chiara is deeply distressed about her mother, of course. But she is even more worried about Francesca, who hasn't spoken since Chiara returned.'

Frank kisses Vermillion before continuing.

'Chiara's mother blames herself for what happened to Francesca. And Chiara feels guilty for arriving too late. And they both blame Paolo for not going there in March. If he had visited, mother would have had some money and they wouldn't have been desperate for food. The rape might never have happened.

'How was it caused by lack of food?'

'Chiara said her mother was driven to go with the soldiers to get something to eat.'

'That's terrible!' Vermillion briefly closes her eyes. 'Imagine choosing between starvation and rape. And Francesca's only twelve, for heaven's sake. It's too awful to contemplate.'

Frank wraps his arms around her. 'I just don't understand how these things can happen. War makes beasts of us all.'

'I saw Huggins downstairs. He told me he's off tomorrow. I hated saying goodbye. I wish ruddy Roger hadn't made him go.'

'Please don't blame Roger. He didn't make Huggins join up. He only pointed out that men with Huggins' experience are needed at the front. And Huggins is cock-a-hoop about rejoining the Platoon. Roger is probably right: we should all do a stint at the front.'

Vermillion glances at Frank and then looks away. Is Frank really thinking of returning? If Roger tries to persuade him, she couldn't forgive him.

'I don't understand, Frank. How you can be so calm about Huggins? I shall miss him awfully. He's been a great support in the theatre, and he's devoted to you.'

'Of course I shall miss him. I hate to see him go. I don't know what it's like to have a brother but if I had one, I hope he'd be like Huggins, someone I would trust with my life. But please don't blame Roger. Blame this blasted war.'

Vermillion is silent for a while. She is aware of the pressure on soldiers with desk jobs now troops on leave have started to pick on them. And she fears that people are talking about Frank behind his back. She wants them to see how brave Frank has been but he mustn't end up like Edmund or Rob.

'What if Huggins doesn't come back?' she asks at last.

'Darling! You mustn't worry about Huggins. There are men in every unit who have a way of dodging the bullets. Huggins is one of them. I'd stake my life on Huggins coming through.'

'Excuse me, Sir.' Huggins calls from the staircase. 'The Brigadier is here!'

'Damn and blast!'

Vermillion slips off Frank's knee and smooths down her uniform. She walks towards the door as two sets of footsteps echo along the corridor.

'Good morning, Lieutenant,' the Brigadier smiles warmly at Vermillion before turning to Frank. 'Good morning, Captain. How was Rome?'

Vermillion studies Frank as he greets Carburton and his Adjutant. Frank looks more solid than when he left; the journey must have done him good.

'Gigli wants to come to Naples soon, Sir,' Frank says firmly 'but he isn't ready yet.'

The Brigadier raises his eyebrows and grins at his Adjutant. 'All right, Captain, but what about your meeting with the Major.'

'Isn't that confidential, Sir?'

'I'm sure the Lieutenant won't spill the beans. Come on, Captain, spit it out! What happened when you saw Major ...?'

'Major Rummage ... Sir.'

Frank glances at Vermillion.

'The meeting went badly, I'm afraid, Sir. He wasn't impressed with my Italian.'

Vermillion stares at Frank. He hadn't mentioned Rummage before. He only talked about visiting Gigli and Chiara.

Frank's attention doesn't waver from the Brigadier.

'You've let me down, Captain.' Carburton raises his hands in an Italian gesture of incomprehension. 'I told Intelligence you were fluent in the language, but Rummage says you aren't. Mind you, I can't think how he would know; he hardly speaks a word himself. I suppose you bungled it on purpose to keep this cushy billet. But even if Rome won't have you, we've identified a chap who ran the theatre in the dim and distant. The Major will let you know when AMG tracks him down. You might care to meet him, Doctor Pitz …'

'Pizzetti, Sir,' the Adjutant interjects. 'Dottor Pizzetti.'

'Pizz … etti will replace that other doctor chappie. Mal … Mala …'

'Dottor Malaspina, Sir.'

Vermillion looks at Frank again. What has he been up to?

'Of course, I'd be pleased to meet him, Sir.' Frank bristles.

Vermillion can see Frank is shaken, but she doubts that Carburton cares. She watches in silence as he files out with his Adjutant.

Frank turns to Vermillion.

'Thank God they've gone! I'm so sorry, Vermillion. That was awful! Bloody Carborundum swore me to secrecy before we went. Even so, I'd decided to tell you today. But I never thought he would blurt it out. Come here, I want to hold you again.'

He folds his arms around her. 'I'm so sorry you learnt like this.' He tries to kiss her but she holds back.

'You didn't mention any meeting with Intelligence. You said you were going to see Gigli.'

'Gigli was my prime interest. But the Old Man insisted I saw Rummage. I didn't think it would come to anything and I didn't want you to worry. The interview was a disaster: Rummage talked Italian with such a ghastly accent that I thought he was speaking English. God knows why Carborundum still wants me to move.'

Vermillion hates secrets. She thinks of her father who suddenly retired from the army and went into a steep decline. But nothing was said till years later when she learnt that the army had pushed him out.

She leans away. 'Promise me, Frank, that you'll never hold anything back, even if you think I might worry. I won't be treated like a schoolgirl. I need to know what's on your mind; otherwise I'll just imagine. And if this wretched war is going to separate us, I need to trust you completely.'

'I'm so sorry. You're right, of course. I just didn't want you worrying needlessly. I never thought Carborundum would reveal his own secrets before I could tell you.'

Vermillion remembers about meeting Simon. She must tell Frank.

'I ...' They both speak at the same time.

'Frank, I'm sorry, I interrupted.'

He pulls her towards him and hugs her. 'Forgive me. I should have told you about Rummage.'

'I understand. But you must tell me in the future. There's another thing ...'

'Darling, can we talk about it later? Now I must run. I'm late for Ingegnere Russo. I'll see you at the Club.'

Vermillion catches Frank's arm, hoping he'll stay at least for a minute. But he smiles and sets off in search of Russo. She listens as his footsteps fade before drifting towards her office.

Why hadn't Frank told her about Rummage? And now AMG has found Pizzetti, does it mean that Frank may be moved at any time? Vermillion feels for her opal ring and twists it around her finger. To think that once she had said they had plenty of time. They've had so little time, especially since Barbara died.

Vermillion sits down to reread the programme for Carmen, which will open shortly. But she doesn't take it in. She crosses to the window and contemplates the neglected courtyard below, which had once been a garden.

Frank had let her down by not warning her about the meeting with Rummage. But supposing he *had* warned her, would it have made any difference? She would still be in the same position. He said he wanted to protect her. And given the way she's responding, perhaps he was right that she needs looking after.

She doesn't know what to do; but she seems to have little choice. Everything now depends on Frank. She had always sworn not to get stuck like Pen. But how can she avoid it?

* * *

Vermillion and Frank squeeze themselves onto the dance floor and battle their way through a Charleston. Then the tempo slows and they can hold each other again. Vermillion feels relieved. She hates arguing with Frank.

'Let's sit down,' he says after one more dance. 'I'll get you another drink.'

Frank returns with a bottle of wine. After filling their glasses, he downs most of his.

'Vermillion, I'm so sorry about Rummage. It was awful that you heard like that. Carborundum was adamant about the need for secrecy. But I was wrong. I should have ignored him.'

'Promise never to do that again, Frank. I want to trust you completely and I want you to trust me. Please don't leave me in the dark.'

He takes her hand and presses it to his lips. 'I'm so sorry, darling. I promise it won't happen again.'

'Thank you.' Vermillion takes a sip of wine. 'Why is the Brigadier so set on sending you to Rome?'

'I don't want to go to Rome and I've had enough of him interfering.'

She squeezes his hand. 'Would it really be so bad in Rome? Worse things could happen.'

'You're probably right,' Frank smiles. 'But I'd still rather stay here.'

'Are you cross about Pizzetti?'

'I'm sorry. I don't really know why I'm so annoyed. But when Carborundum announced that AMG had identified Pizzetti, I felt completely undermined. He said Pizzetti will replace Malaspina but he didn't say he wants us to stay. It felt as though everything we've done suddenly counts for nothing.'

Vermillion squeezes Frank's hand again before he continues.

'At least he acknowledged that we stopped the theatre burning down. But my goodness, he makes me angry! When he said they had found Pizzetti, I had the feeling he likes to taunt me.'

'And what do you suppose this imposter will want from us?'

Frank catches her eye and laughs.

'If the fellow ran the theatre years ago,' Vermillion adds, 'he must be getting on, in which case he'll need your help. Perhaps you'll like him. He might be a father figure.'

Frank looks away. Does he want a father figure when he hasn't resolved the issues with his own father?

'You're right, of course.' Frank takes a large swig of wine. 'But even if Pizzetti is a charmer, I hate Carborundum interfering.'

He picks up the bottle. 'Good Lord, we seem to have finished it. I'll get another one.' He gets to his feet.

'I think I've had enough, Frank.' Vermillion stands up as well. 'Let's go back to your flat. I've missed you while you were away.'

Frank gives her a huge hug, lifting her off her feet. 'Darling, it's marvellous to be back.'

CHAPTER 24

Frank squints at the weathered sign. Through the smoke he can make out the words: BEWARE OF MINES.

He looks around but there isn't the usual white tape to show where the minefield has been cleared.

He hears a cry.

'FRANK! HELP!'

Through the murk he sees Vermillion fifty yards away, waving her arms.

'STAY THERE, VERMILLION! I'M COMING!'

Frank rushes towards her but flames leap up between them, veiling her in smoke. He can't bear it; he wants to scream.

As the flames subside, he glimpses her again. She's wearing a simple cotton frock and her hair ripples in the hot wind. Frank presses forward again. More flames spurt up. The heat is intense. He raises his arms to shield his face and tries another route but the blaze drives him back again.

'FRANK! FRANK!'

Now he can see that Vermillion's head is surrounded by a halo. Dear God, her hair is on fire!

'NO! NO!'

Frank cries out as he throws back the sheet. He sits up and wipes his hands across his dripping face.

'Gently, Frank.' Vermillion turns over and is asleep again.

Frank shivers. He lowers his head to his raised knees and weeps. In the darkness he feels alone.

He rubs his eyes. He can hear Vermillion's gentle breathing. He longs to wake her, to be comforted. He can't cope with these horrors on his own. He feels for her arm and squeezes it lightly but she doesn't stir and he doesn't have the heart to press harder. Even if she were awake, she couldn't understand.

He wipes his face again and takes a deep breath before swinging his legs off the bed. He stands, swaying uncertainly in the darkness. He hitches up his pyjamas and reties the cord. His head throbs.

He waits until the world stops spinning, then he gropes his way to the corridor. He makes little effort to be quiet as he shuts the bedroom door and sets off for the bathroom. He turns on the light and glares at the face of the wretched stranger. He no longer feels real. Tears return before he stirs himself, splashing his face with cold water and mopping his body with a towel.

He glances again at the blank face in the mirror before traipsing into the sitting room and opening the shutters. But it's dark outside so he closes them again and turns on a lamp. The room looks unfamiliar and he feels he doesn't belong. Where is home? He stands in front of the sofa considering whether to sit down but he can't really see the point. The clock across the room shows 0220; it will be ages before the dawn.

Eventually he sinks onto the sofa and buries his head in his hands. Oh God! He can't cope with these nightmares. And tonight his precious Vermillion was involved, with her hair on fire! He can't bear it, especially after Maggie.

These images are ruining his life. Since Huggins left, they've been conspiring to make him join up with the promise that then they'll leave him alone. Frank feels stuck. If he stays in Naples with these nightmares he fears his madness will drive Vermillion away. But if he leaves her alone in Naples, he could lose her anyway.

In Naples he has everything he wants. He loves working at the theatre. But above all he loves Vermillion, who's lying in his bed a few yards away. He should be happy but he seems to have forgotten how. He knows in his head that he loves her, but he doesn't feel the old surge of delight whenever she's nearby. Of course it isn't just about her: even listening to great music has lost its thrill.

He stares emptily across the room, trying to face the fact that his soul has died. Is this what they mean by lack of moral fibre?

'Damn you!' he shouts as the skull reappears; tonight it seems larger than usual. Is it closer? 'Oh God! I'm going mad!'

He scrambles to his feet and sets off along the corridor. He must wake Vermillion. He can't manage alone. Even if she can't comfort him, at least she can share his torment. He has talked about his nightmares before. But how can he tell her about this one? He can't say her hair was on fire and he could do nothing about it. And she mustn't know about the blasted skull.

He stops outside the bedroom but decides he mustn't wake her when he doesn't have anything to say. He turns around and shuffles back to the sitting room before pacing down the corridor again. As long as he keeps moving, perhaps the rhythm of his footsteps will deaden the pain.

He marches back and forth across the flat. At first the skull goes with him but in time it tires and starts to fade. He chides it for its lack of stamina but keeps walking until he can move no more.

Finally, he sinks onto the sofa. It's 0335. He turns off the lamp and leans back. It's still dark outside. He doesn't want to sleep because he can't face another dream. But soon he closes his eyes and starts to doze.

* * *

He awakes with a start.

'What are you doing, Frank?' Vermillion touches his arm. 'Are you all right? Come back to bed.'

'I couldn't sleep,' he shivers in response to her warm hand. 'I had a bad dream.'

He's conscious of the contradiction in his words but he doesn't explain.

'Come on, Frank,' Vermillion pulls slightly on his arm. 'Come back to bed.'

He feels torn. He wants to follow her and embrace her. But part of him feels too sad and separate to let her help. He remembers as a boy pushing away his mother when the thing he really wanted was to be comforted.

'I'll come in a minute,' he says.

She looks concerned and tugs again on his arm. But he doesn't budge. She smiles. 'Darling, come to bed soon.'

He watches her slip away. Already he regrets not going when he had the chance. He wants to hold her in his arms. But something makes him wait before he gets up and follows her.

By the time he climbs into bed, she is asleep. For some time he lies in the darkness, listening for cues that she has woken. He wants to hold her. He curses his stupidity in not responding sooner. Perhaps she wouldn't mind if he wakes her now: he may not be in Naples for long. But he can't tell her that. And besides, if he wakes her, what does he have to offer? Could he be loving and attentive and concerned about her? He wants to be all these things but he doubts he still knows how.

Benighted in his bed Frank feels completely stuck. He wants to stay in Naples with Vermillion and the theatre, where he may soon be replaced. Yet he feels he should rejoin the Battalion to help end the war, which is what he came to Italy to do. But how would he tell Vermillion? And could he cope? Whichever way he turns something blocks his way. He has lost his grip: he no longer knows where his life is going.

Silently he starts to sing as he had before when he'd lost all hope.

"Ich such' im Schnee vergebens.
Nach ihrer Tritte Spur,
Wo sie an meinem Arme
Durchstrich die grüne Flur.
Ich will den Boden küssen,
Durchdringen Eis und Schnee
Mit meinen heißen Tränen,
Bis ich die Erde seh'."

In vain I search for her footprints
Where on my arm she wandered through the fields.
Now the ground is covered in snow but my burning tears
Will melt it and restore the meadows to life.

PART III

– August 1944 –

CHAPTER 25

'Hold tight, everyone!'

Paolo listens to the disembodied voice crackling over the intercom; it sounds calm in contrast to the racket at the rear of the Dakota.

The plane is stripped to its essentials to increase the payload and performance. Behind the cockpit, eight men wait to jump. A ton of supplies will drop with them.

An ack-ack shell explodes nearby. There's a burst of light and a thunderous crash. The flash freezes their faces which look blanched against the bare metal of the plane as it shudders and bucks.

It won't be long before Paolo is sick – the result of fear and the motion of the plane – but he's determined to jump and not to throw up until he's out.

He digs Sandro in the ribs and the next flash illuminates his grinning face. Why the fuck is he is so cheerful?

A cluster of explosions makes the fuselage rear up, as though a large predator has taken the plane by the throat intent on shaking it to death.

Behind Paolo someone crumples forward in the dark, emptying his stomach.

'We're approaching the DZ.'

Paolo has received intensive training in the two months since he re-enlisted. He had completed nine jumps, but only one at night, when their training was suddenly curtailed at the end of July. Everyone knew it had been too short, but the Allies were desperate to drop Italians into the north to bolster the partisans. Given the dangers, Paolo wasn't surprised there were few volunteers.

Paolo, however, had revelled in the training alongside fellow Italians who were dedicated to killing Germans. But even in this single-minded group, Paolo's determination to fight and kill had impressed his instructors, who quickly singled him out. Then they gave him the codename "Pigeon", just one of many indignities he suffered after joining up, but things improved a lot once he volunteered for parachute training. And now, finally, the moment is coming when he will take his revenge.

It had taken rather longer for Sandro, now known as "Swallow", to be selected too. But his knowledge of the Bologna area, from the year they were stationed there, had been decisive. His moment is coming too.

The Dakota took off from Foggia before sunset. Flying northwest along the Adriatic coast they had watched the day slip away in a rainbow of colours before fading into midnight black. In the three-hour flight northward, Paolo and Sandro are reversing their three-month slog from Bologna to Naples after the armistice whilst below the two armies continue to battle it out.

Paolo closes his eyes, trying to picture Mamma and Francesca. But all he can remember is the small blurred photograph he always carries. Chiara is clearer in his memory. Although their recent relationship has been stormy, he would give anything to see her now before he jumps. But he knows that he must wait until he has taken his revenge.

The plan is that once they're on the ground – assuming they hit the dropping zone – they will team up with a group of partisans from the hills south of Bologna, an area under

German control. Paolo had doubts about working with partisans again after their frustrating experience last year with one of the Garibaldi groups. But he hopes things have changed now that the Allies are arming these groups and have officers on the ground advising on targets and strategy. The Allies' desire to work with the partisans had been underlined by General Alexander – Commander-in-Chief of Allied Armies in Italy – in his June broadcast urging all Italians to rise against the Germans.

Light from the next explosion illuminates Sandro's face. Paolo wonders whether he will marry Chiara. As Sandro no longer has a home or a family, Paolo expects he will come to Rome after the war. But Paolo will only let him marry Chiara if he deserves her.

The crew opens the starboard door letting air blast in. Paolo gets to his feet. He pulls at his leg bag, stuffed with ammunition as well as explosives and incendiary charges. He glares at it, praying nothing will detonate as he lands.

The plane is dropping fast. Ahead Paolo glimpses the line of flares. They're approaching the DZ.

Falcon – that's not his real name of course – gets up. He's the English officer who will jump with them. He moves to the open door where his uniform gleams in the moonlight. He waits for the signal to send the others on their way. Once they're launched, he will jump himself.

He clasps the first man by the shoulder.

'Go!' The man vanishes into the night. The others shuffle forward. Paolo bristles. There's no bloody need for Falcon to push them out. They were trained to leap from the plane, not like the British who just step into the void.

Falcon shoves the next man out. Now it's Sandro's turn.

'Good luck, Sandro!' Paolo shouts but Sandro has already jumped. Paolo shuffles forward. Falcon grips his shoulder. 'Jump! Damn you!' Paolo wants to protest. A sharp pain in his shoulder propels him into space.

He spreads his limbs as he'd been taught but the air whips at his face. Shit! He's falling straight to earth.

The straps between Paolo's legs jerk tight, as his parachute billows out, slowing his descent. But the wind is blowing him sideways. He blinks until his vision clears.

Down to two hundred metres, he watches the flares recede. The others are some way away. The ground is approaching fast. He sees a steep slope with grass but trees to the right. He hears his equipment thump down. He bends his knees waiting for the ground to leap towards him.

No impact. He sways in the air.

'MADONNA!'

His damned parachute is caught in the trees and he dangles several metres off the ground. 'PORCA MISERIA!' He prays the Crucchi didn't see them coming down.

'Pigeon, are you going to roost up there?' Falcon calls. 'I suggest you cut those bloody straps and come down to join us. Unless you prefer it on your perch.'

Paolo feels for his knife, which is pinned behind the webbing. He works it free and hacks at the first strap, forcing the blade away from his body so as not to cut himself. But the webbing is bloody tough and he has no leverage.

'Are you all right, Paolo?' Sandro calls.

'Code names only, Swallow!' Falcon barks. 'You know the bloody rules.'

'I'm almost through, Sandro.' Paolo whispers.

The tree groans.

'Out of the way for Christ's sake!' Paolo shouts. 'I'm coming down!'

Paolo tries to grab the webbing to break his fall but only succeeds in dropping his knife. His feet thud against the sloping ground.

'Shit!' Pain stabs into Paolo's right ankle as it hits the incline badly.

'Get up, Pigeon!' Falcon extends a hand and pulls Paolo to his feet.

'Thanks.' He winces as he puts his weight on the foot.

'Quick, Pigeon! We've missed the DZ. Leave your parachute. The reception committee will collect it.'

Falcon grabs his own leg bag, throwing it over his shoulder, and sets off at a steady pace. Paolo lifts his bag and starts to follow. His ankle screams. God, it had better not be broken. He hobbles forward.

Sandro comes up beside him. 'I'll take your bag.'

'Can you manage two? They're fucking heavy.'

'Of course. It isn't far.'

Paolo limps on. Pain shoots up his leg but at least he can move.

After several hundred metres, they hear voices. Falcon calls out a password. The answering reply drifts across the hillside. They move forward again. Soon Paolo can make out a group of some thirty men; at least he assumes they're men although many partisan groups use girls to carry messages.

They exchange handshakes and words of welcome. Then Spartaco, the partisan leader, shouts his orders. Two of the men will retrieve Paolo's parachute from the tree while the rest collect the other supplies which came down with colour-coded parachutes.

Spartaco leads the new arrivals through scrubby woods until they reach a clearing where a hut affords some shelter.

'Are we staying here for the night?' Paolo slumps onto a tree stump.

'No. We must move on. This place is dangerous. The Brigate Nere have spies everywhere. But don't worry we've a truck to move the supplies. The rest of us will cross the hills and prepare for the attack. Are you ready?'

Paolo rolls up his right trouser-leg and folds down his sock. He can see little, even in the moonlight. His ankle feels swollen, but he can't be sure. He just knows it's bloody painful.

'Are you ready, Pigeon?' Falcon asks. 'Get what you need from your leg bag; they'll put the rest in the transport. But you'll need your Beretta, ammunition and grenades. We leave in five minutes.'

'I'm ready.' Paolo grimaces. 'Come on Swallow, bring my bag! I need some ammo.'

They set off shortly, moving first through woodland but then on an open hillside where they must be visible if anyone is watching. Paolo surveys the dark countryside. There isn't a light to be seen.

A dog barks in the distance. Has it heard them? Or is it registering a passing animal, perhaps an owl? When they started training, Paolo was surprised that dogs still existed in the countryside. None had survived in Naples where no one could afford to feed them and their flesh had provided vital nourishment. In the country, however, where food is less scarce, dogs still earn their keep by warding off marauders. But for soldiers they're a constant danger, always liable to disclose their presence. Paolo finds himself wishing that all dogs everywhere had been eaten.

Paolo's ankle starts to stiffen. The pain claws at his foot but he decides it can't be broken: it must be just a sprain. He limps on. After half an hour they come to another wood but here the trees are only six or seven metres tall. Their twisting roots make the way uneven and Paolo slows even more. Sandro hangs back to support him.

Soon Spartaco calls a halt. 'We're close to the rendezvous so I'll go forward with Falcon. You'll stay here to give us cover. I'll whistle when the way is clear! Then in the morning you'll see your target – the San Michele railway bridge.'

CHAPTER 26

Vermillion stretches her arm as far as it will go, but she can't grip the suitcase stuck beneath her bed. She lies back and stares at the high ceiling, feeling cross and sticky.

She had intended to leave the theatre early to collect more things from her flat. But another letter had arrived from Pen and stupidly she had stayed to scribble a reply.

When she finally made it to the flat, she raced around

gathering what she needs and now everything is laid out neatly on the bed. But she needs the suitcase.

She tries again but can't quite grasp the handle. Exhausted and frustrated she lies back, wiping her hands across her face. Briefly she closes her eyes. If only she could climb onto the bed and go to sleep.

It was a lovely letter from Pen, full of commiserations about Barbara and pleased to learn about Frank. But she is even more concerned about Bill. Letters from Burma are so much slower than from Naples and the advance seems to have stalled. Poor Pen: she aches to see Bill again. And now, sprawled on the floor, Vermillion feels closer to Pen than she can remember. She wishes she could see her again.

She resolves to make one last effort to reach the suitcase, until she hears a familiar voice.

'Is anyone at home?'

Vermillion starts at the sound of the door opening. She sits up and yawns.

'What on earth are you doing on the floor?' Jackie peers down at her. 'Are you all right?'

'I was trying to get my suitcase.' Vermillion shifts herself onto the bed.

'Are you going somewhere? You could have told me first.'

'I need more of my things at Frank's.'

'Why don't you tell him to come here.'

Vermillion hesitates.

'Frank prefers his own flat.' She doesn't like to say she prefers it there too, away from reminders of Barbara.

'And what Frank wants, he must get!'

'On this occasion.'

'So, you're deserting me for good. Thank God, Margery has agreed to take Barbara's room.'

Vermillion stands up, brushes down her service dress and walks to the door. 'I need to find the broom.'

'Is that for Frank too? Whatever for?'

'Of course it's not! I'm trying to retrieve my case.'

Vermillion goes into the corridor and remembers the long-handled mop, which lives in the bathroom. It should do just as well. She opens the bathroom door and sees several men's shirts hanging over the bath.

'Whose are these?'

Jackie doesn't respond.

'Whose bloody shirts are these?' She calls a bit louder as she emerges with the mop.

'Sorry, Vermillion. I'd forgotten they were there. I hope they weren't in your way.'

'They're not in the way. But whose are they? Who is staying here?'

'They're Mike's. He's here for a couple of nights. I didn't think you'd mind.'

'Jackie!' Vermillion laughs. 'You could have told me!'

'How could I? You weren't even here.'

Having retrieved the suitcase, Vermillion packs her things and sets off, much later than intended. She needs to hurry to make it to Frank's flat before the curfew. But the leather suitcase, one of her father's, weighs a ton even when empty. Every few yards she puts it down to swap arms.

The sun has set but the residual August heat of the buildings makes the streets feel baking. Indoors it's hotter still and families have brought out tables which they sit around in the street. Vermillion is forced to push past.

Groups of drunken Allied soldiers are everywhere. Rounding a corner, Vermillion sees the backs of three GIs as they urinate against a wall. From a window above a woman screams at them before launching the contents of a bucket in their direction. To judge by the swearing it wasn't water she was throwing. Vermillion presses on; such events are commonplace.

Despite the heat Vermillion pulls her cap well down and keeps her service dress buttoned up. She scans the route ahead. She doesn't look up when soldiers speak to her, not even when they offer to carry her case.

She stops to contemplate the steep steps up to Frank's flat and to catch her breath. She lowers the suitcase. She isn't sure about Margery moving in. How would she feel with Margery ensconced, if ever she has to move back? She hopes it won't be necessary.

In her reply to Pen, Vermillion didn't mention moving in with Frank. But she did say he had been married to Maggie who died in the blitz and that Frank is still troubled by nightmares about her death. She added that he's waiting for news about a possible transfer away from Naples.

Vermillion tidies her hair and starts to climb the steps.

'Frank,' she pushes at the door. 'Can you me help with this? It's fearfully heavy.'

Frank kisses her and wraps his arms around her. She notices his breath smells of toothpaste.

'My goodness … it's light as a feather.' Frank picks up the suitcase. 'I'll pop it into the bedroom. You'd better sit down while I get you a drink. How was Jackie?'

'Oh, that's better,' Vermillion flops onto the sofa. 'No, I won't have a whisky, but I'd love some wine.'

From the kitchen she hears the sound of a cork being pulled. Frank brings her a glass and sits down beside her. He raises his large whisky. 'Cheers!'

But before she takes a sip he leans over and kisses her again. 'Welcome home.'

'You'll be pleased to hear that Jackie was fine. She laid it on pretty thick about being left on her own until I found Mike's shirts in the bathroom. And Margery is going to share the flat, so Jackie can't really complain.'

Frank stares across the room.

Vermillion wonders what he's looking at. 'Are you feeling better, Frank?'

'I'm mostly all right, during the day. The problem is at night.'

Vermillion looks surprised.

'No, it's not that! It's wonderful you're here. It's just these confounded nightmares …' He raises his glass and drinks.

'Is it only at night?'

He takes another sip of whisky. 'It's mainly at night. The

images can haunt me at any time, but they have less power during the day.'

'Darling, I'm so sorry.' She almost adds something reassuring about his rescuing Barbara, but she doesn't want to mention her name.

'I hate the nightmares. But the worst thing is being half awake in the middle of the night, caught between waking and sleep. That's when I feel defenceless and most alone.'

'But I'm here,' she takes his hand.

'I know. And that's wonderful. But in the middle of the night you're asleep.'

'Then you must wake me.'

'I can't do that,' he leans across and kisses her. 'It wouldn't be fair.'

They sit in silence for a minute. Vermillion wonders what she's meant to do. She knows he wants her to comfort him, but she doesn't know how.

'I've heard from Carborundum again,' Frank says. 'I'm meeting Pizzetti tomorrow. I feel like I'm taking an exam.'

'You mustn't worry, Frank,' she squeezes his hands. 'You're bound to pass with flying colours.'

CHAPTER 27

'Quickly, Paolo, wake up!'

Paolo feels a hand on his shoulder as Sandro leans over him. He gives a little cry as he comes to.

'Shh!'

'What's the time?'

'0445. We move at 0500. How's your ankle?'

'Bloody sore!' Paolo grimaces, although it hadn't kept him awake.

'Here, let me pull you up.'

Paolo rises on his good leg. 'Thanks.'

He releases Sandro's hand and lowers his right foot to the ground. It feels stiff and heavy. He winces as he shifts his weight. He fears that his ankle has ballooned. Thank God he kept his boots on when he went to sleep.

'I think it will be all right, Sandro.'

'You always have trouble with your boots.'

'No, I don't.'

'When we walked from Bologna to Naples you were always complaining. Do you have odd feet?'

'Shut up, Sandro.'

'Come on you two.' Falcon calls out. 'Are you ready? We'll be walking for half an hour to reach the start line.'

* * *

'Come here. Where you see map.'

Sea Eagle, one of the partisans, spreads a hand-drawn map across the sloping rock. He had been captured by the Germans on the Eastern front and forced to join the German army, serving in Italy. But since he escaped he has acquired the weathered look of an Italian *contadino*.

He speaks limited Italian and with a heavy Russian accent but Paolo understands that the San Michele bridge lies between two hills in a curving valley.

'Monte Castello north,' Sea Eagle continues. 'We here – south side Monte Fiume. Between two hills is river. Railway line – here – run through mountain tunnel, except crosses river. Between is bridge: eighty-five metre long; fifteen metre height.'

Sea Eagle passes round a faded photograph of the bridge. He refers to the Allied strategy to cut off German supplies by destroying every railway bridge north of the front. The main bridges have already been bombed from the air, forcing the Germans to use this branch line. But the narrow valley and steep hills have thwarted Allied efforts to hit it from the air. So the job has passed to the partisans, who have the men and kit to blow it from the ground.

There is no road access to the bridge. When it was built, everything was brought through the tunnels. But the partisans can't use that approach because the outer ends of the tunnels are guarded. Sea Eagle points to the map where a minor road crosses the river upstream. The plan is to attack from this point. As the water level is low today they will follow the riverbed downstream until they find the target after two kilometres.

'When bridge blown, comrades withdraw up river. Is clear?'

'Who will place the charges?'

'Two teams. North side – Finch, Sparrow. South side – Pigeon, Swallow. Falcon lead group on top Monte Castello – give cover from above. I stay at road to cover rear. Questions?'

'Should we blow up a train as well as the bridge?'

'No. Please be clear. Blow bridge with Jerry not know we do it from ground.'

'How the hell do we do that?'

Sea Eagle explains that the air force has tried to bomb the bridge before and will appear to try again today. A bomber will make two runs over the bridge. The partisans will blow the bridge when the bomber is overhead so the Germans will think it was bombed. If they discover that partisans were involved they will take reprisals from local villages. The timing of the explosions is therefore crucial.

Paolo has heard about these *rastrellimento* operations where the Crucchi take multiple reprisals for every soldier killed. The bastards! How can they be so savage?

'What if the Germans attack?' Sandro asks.

'We fight. But withdraw soon possible. Good luck!'

* * *

The sky is light when they leave the road, but deep shadows still obscure the valley. Paolo and Sandro scramble down the bank through thick undergrowth. The riverbed is full of smooth rocks, some rising above their heads. It must be quite a torrent in the winter but today little water is flowing and it's easy to step from stone to stone. Paolo looks at the sky; there's little risk of a flash flood.

'Be careful here!' Sandro calls. 'The rocks are wet!'

But the warning comes too late for Paolo. His right boot slithers across a boulder and into a pool. The cold water feels soothing on his ankle.

'Do you think Chiara's all right?' Sandro says over his shoulder. 'I feel I should have gone to Rome.'

'Of course she's all right!' Paolo presses on, ignoring his wet boot. 'It was the others who were raped.'

'I *know* that. But I still worry. It must be hard for her, looking after the family on her own.'

'She can manage till we return.'

'Supposing we don't return?'

'She'll still manage. And she'll remember us as heroes – who died to liberate Italy. Isn't that better than hanging about in Rome, flogging trinkets to the troops? This way she can be proud.'

'Perhaps,' Sandro says, 'but I still worry.'

Paolo doesn't reply. He'd rather not think about his family. He wonders whether he'll see them again, although in his heart he's sure he will. He sees himself after the war being welcomed home, with Mamma filled with pride and delight at his return and Francesca looking prettier than ever as she smiles approvingly. That's how he'll return. Until then he must fight.

Paolo watches Sandro ahead of him. Usually Sandro follows, which is why he's here. He would never have rejoined the army if Paolo hadn't taken the lead. But it's right that he's here. He says he loves Chiara and now he can fight for her family's honour. When the war ends, Sandro can claim her as his bride. Yet in Paolo's dreams of his return, Sandro never appears.

'Look Paolo,' Sandro points ahead to where one end of the bridge is visible. As they clamber forward, the bridge rises quickly until it towers above their heads, black against the brilliance of the sky.

Paolo lays out their equipment: explosives, cable and detonators. But across the river Finch is already climbing.

'Come on Sandro. We've thirty-five minutes to fix the explosives. Falcon said we should place them in the Y-sections five metres below the track for maximum effect.'

Paolo starts to clamber up. His ankle feels numb; he suspects his wet leather boot has shrunk, restricting the flow of blood. While Paolo gets into position, Sandro has already fixed the charges on his side.

Across the river, Sparrow is rolling out the cable towards the detonator a hundred metres upstream.

'Paolo,' Sandro calls from below. 'I'll bring the cable up on your side and tape it to the bridge. You need to get down.'

Paolo begins his laborious descent, first lowering his sore right leg at each step. He gets to the riverbed just before Sandro. Together they roll out the cable, which they hide amongst the rocks, and connect the detonator. Then they squat down to review the scene. They still have twenty minutes before the bomber is due. Finch waves from across the river.

High above them, the bridge trembles.

'Quick, Paolo. Get under cover.'

Paolo hobbles forward and crouches behind a boulder. Above, the bridge shakes as though an earthquake has started. A train whistles as it rumbles out of the tunnel on the near bank. As it's heading north, it should be lightly loaded, probably with wounded soldiers or prisoners of war.

The valley echoes to the squeal of brakes. Steam is released with a loud hiss. There's shouting, followed by the drumming of boots high up on the bridge. Then comes a single shot.

Paolo looks up but his vision is partly obscured. Several seconds pass before something heavy falls from the bridge. He hears the thud as a spread-eagled body ricochets off the rocks and splashes into the water.

Silence.

Paolo grips the handle of the detonator, desperate to blow the train and its hellish cargo out of this world.

'PAOLO, DON'T!' Sandro grips his arm.

More shouting. A door slams and the train hisses back into life. It grinds its way slowly across the bridge until, with a final whistle, it disappears.

'Jesus! Poor man!' Sandro mutters, moving towards the body.

'Forget it, Sandro. He's dead. There's nothing we can do.'

'We should bury him. We can't leave him there.'

'We can't touch him, Sandro! Remember we shouldn't be here!'

They peer at the wretched bundle. Nothing suggests it was recently alive but the surrounding water is turning pink. Paolo walks forward. The body looks like a young woman. Why would the Crucchi have women prisoners? Damn them! He turns back to Sandro who is staring at the ground; he guesses he's thinking of Chiara.

Paolo has heard the stories of women from partisan groups being dragged from their homes and sent to Germany. What the hell do the Crucchi do with them? He wishes they had blown up the train together with the bridge, crashing the whole fucking thing into the river.

Paolo hears the rumble of a light bomber. He grabs the detonator handle and watches the plane appear over the hill as it starts its approach. When the plane is directly above the bridge, he plunges the handle down. Nothing happens. Then clouds sprout from the explosives. Finally, a loud report fills the valley. A second blast follows the first and then two more. The superstructure starts to bend, as though the steel struts have grown soft. Pieces clatter down until the bridge hangs in shreds.

'Come on, Sandro.' Paolo shivers. 'Let's get away.'

CHAPTER 28

Frank pushes his way through a crowd of well-dressed men who have come to the AMG HQ to prove they were never Fascists. Seeing Frank's uniform in their midst they start to importune him, as though he were there to judge their cases.

Inside, he is led to a room little larger than the one where he met the Brigadier. Frank blames the Brigadier's damned

Adjutant who makes these ridiculous arrangements. He wanted to meet Pizzetti at the theatre, but Carburton insisted they should meet on neutral territory. Frank suspects it's his way of showing he's still in charge.

Frank sits down and leans back. He tries to imagine Pizzetti. Will they like each other? If they don't, Frank may have to leave pretty soon. He clenches his fists at the prospect.

Suddenly the door opens and before Frank can get to his feet, Pizzetti walks in. He is tall for an Italian and his well-cut grey suit, cream shirt and claret silk tie make Frank's uniform seem shabby and tired.

'Captain, I'm sorry to keep you waiting.' Pizzetti says in fluent English with a slight American accent.

'You haven't kept me, Dottore, I was early.'

'I'm very pleased to meet you,' Pizzetti bows his head. 'I've been so impressed with what you have done at San Carlo. The place has never been busier – well, not since Rossini was in charge in 1815. What you've achieved is remarkable.'

Frank feels nonplussed. He was set for a difficult meeting like his other first encounters with Italians. Last autumn Chiara bit him, Giovanni threatened him with a gun, Paolo attacked him with a knife and Malaspina bellowed at him. In contrast Pizzetti seems friendly and appreciative. Frank feels that sudden surge of emotion which can be triggered by unexpected kindness.

'Thank you, Dottore.' Frank swallows, afraid his voice may crack. 'It has been a privilege working at the theatre. I feel proud it's back on its feet. But mine was a small part of course compared with the performers.'

He contemplates Pizzetti's face. It reminds him of someone. It's not so much his looks as his style.

They talk about the recent productions. Pizzetti has seen them all. Frank wonders why he hadn't noticed him before.

'The company doesn't have great singers, of course,' Pizzetti says. 'But even in my day we invited the big names for one opera at a time. And now Rome is liberated, we can do that again.'

'I should tell you, Dottore, I've already been to Rome to meet Maestro Gigli. I heard him sing Radames in London before the war; I hoped he would sing the role here.'

Pizzetti gives a thin smile while studying Frank from beneath his dark eyebrows.

'I can see you're intrepid, Captain; perhaps that is how you've achieved so much. But I'm a cautious Italian and I perceive certain difficulties.'

Frank frowns.

'Beniamino Gigli is a great singer,' Pizzetti continues. 'But people say he was close to the Fascists. Naturally he performed for them because that's what singers do, but it's rumoured he was a member of the party. There are even stories that the walls of his villa in Rome were hung with signed photographs of Mussolini, Hitler and Goebbels.'

'That was in the past.'

'Perhaps for some people. But the Communists are powerful, and they won't welcome him here. People have suffered greatly and I don't want to add to their pain. What did Gigli say?'

'He said he isn't ready to come. He was shocked by the protests.'

'He will come one day. But perhaps not to sing in Aida, which was a favourite of the Fascists. For now, Captain, there are other fine singers who don't carry this stigma.'

Pizzetti looks up but then continues. 'The Brigadier says you would be willing to remain at the theatre, liaising with the Allies. That seems a tenuous role, rather wishy-washy, if that's the right expression. I'd rather you became my deputy.'

'That's a generous offer.' Frank smiles. 'Perhaps my assistant, Lieutenant Henthorpe, could stay too.'

'The Lieutenant would be most welcome,' Pizzetti continues. 'Although I'd like the chance to meet him.'

Frank laughs. Pizzetti raises his eyebrows.

'I should have explained: Lieutenant Henthorpe is a woman. I'll introduce you. For myself, I appreciate your offer. What would you want your deputy to do?'

'We would need to decide that together,' Pizzetti says. 'But I know you've done the work of two. There will be plenty to occupy us both, with more singers and more productions to choose from. I hope you will consider my offer.'

'I'll consider it very carefully and discuss it with Lieutenant Henthorpe. Perhaps, Dottore, we could all meet at the theatre to talk about future plans.'

Frank stands up and shakes Pizzetti's hand. He wants to embrace him – he seems so different to Malaspina – but he holds himself back, determined to avoid disappointment.

* * *

Away from the AMG offices, Frank feels a weight has lifted. But the fact that he likes Pizzetti makes it more likely Pizzetti will be successful. Frank may soon have to move.

He hastens towards the theatre, ignoring the heat. At least moving quickly keeps away the flies. He arrives just in time for the first performance of Carmen. Maestro Nanta, the orchestra manager, and his assistant join Frank and Vermillion in their box and stay for a drink afterwards. Frank can only whisper to Vermillion that the meeting had gone well.

Frank is surprised to see Vermillion wearing a cotton dress and a little make-up. He keeps gazing at her; she looks wonderful. 'Come on, darling,' he says when the others have gone. 'Let's not go to the Club tonight. I've so much to tell you.'

He leads her out into the piazza and puts his arm around her waist, pulling her towards him as they stride along.

'Pizzetti was very positive about what we've done at the theatre. He even said he'd like us both to stay. But you should have seen his face when I explained that Lieutenant Henthorpe was a woman.'

'Frank, that's wonderful news!' She draws him towards her and kisses him.

'Of course, everything has to be agreed with AMG and I expect Pizzetti will drive a hard bargain. But there must be a chance he'll take charge.'

They cross the piazza towards the Galleria where they find a quiet bar and settle down for a drink.

'I want to hear all about Pizzetti.' Vermillion raises her glass. 'What was he like? What did you make of him?'

He smiles. 'Pissetti was all right.'

'Frank, you mustn't call him that. You might forget and say it to his face.'

'It was all rather extraordinary,' Frank raises his glass and downs a large swig. 'Pitz-etti was a complete surprise. He reminded me of my benefactor. They don't look alike but there was something about Pizzetti's manner.'

Vermillion declines Frank's offer of a refill. 'You haven't told me about your benefactor.'

Frank pours a small measure into his glass and catches her eye before filling it up. He raises the glass but doesn't drink. He hesitates, wondering what to tell her. He prefers not to talk about his upbringing, which he has tried to leave behind.

'To my darling Vermillion – mio tesoro!' Frank raises his glass again. He puts it to his lips but still doesn't drink. Instead he puts the glass down and kisses her from across the table.

He raises the glass once more. 'To my benefactor … who paid for my musical education and voice training.'

'Frank, I'd like to hear all about him.'

Frank drinks some wine and breathes in slowly.

'I was a choirboy at our local church from the age of seven. But after my voice broke, I dropped out of the choir. Then, to my surprise, I found I had a decent baritone voice. So, I rejoined the choir and sang every Sunday. I also sang in occasional revues.'

He drinks some more and refills his glass.

'It could have continued that way. But when I was eighteen my dear mother entered me for a local singing competition. No, I didn't mind, I was pleased she supported me. But I didn't take it seriously and I can't even remember what I sang. To my surprise I won first prize, which was nice but meant nothing. However, as I left the church hall, a man approached me. He seemed old but was probably only sixty. He was well spoken and smartly dressed. He complimented me on my singing and said he would like to help.'

'How marvellous and how lucky.'

'Yes, but also strange.' Frank sips more wine after every few sentences. 'I had just started at university and had little money. But he introduced me to a singing teacher and said he would pay the bills. And once I had made some progress, he invited me to a musical evening at his home. With half a dozen of his friends we sang madrigals and then he asked me to perform.'

Frank refills his glass.

'It wasn't just a single evening; these events occurred quite often. Sometimes I accompanied myself on the piano and sometimes he would play. After the first occasion, he sent me to his tailor to have a suit made in order to smarten me up. He was extremely generous and I'm very grateful. I can truthfully say he changed my life. And yet …'

Vermillion takes his hands. He wonders whether she's bored, but he feels he should press on.

'… and yet there was something odd. I felt he wanted something from me, but I never learnt what it was.'

'Was he a pansy?'

'Perhaps. There were never any women or girls at these gatherings. And only young men were invited to perform.'

'You weren't the only one?'

'No. There were usually two or three of us – all from modest backgrounds. He may have been queer, but he never made advances to me, nor to the others as far as I'm aware.'

Frank wipes his face with his handkerchief.

'I've every reason to be grateful, yet I still felt relieved when I got away.'

Frank signals for another bottle.

'Frank, haven't you had enough? Let's walk down to the sea where there may be some breeze.'

Frank wants to protest but he can't look Vermillion in the eye, so he jumps to his feet and slaps some coins on the bar. He turns and sees her waiting patiently.

'My God, I'm lucky!' he says under his breath. 'Frank, don't mess this up!'

They stroll towards the sea hand in hand. Frank stumbles slightly but rights himself. He thinks of his father coming home drunk. That was his response to the Great War. Did his drinking start like this?

'How did you part from your benefactor?' Vermillion asks.

'It was the war. No, not this war. It was in '36 with the start of the Spanish Civil War. I was appalled at what was happening and attended rallies in protest. I'd left university and was trying to find my way. It was easy to be a Communist then, before the Nazi-Soviet Pact in '39, because no one else was standing up to Hitler. Many of my friends were Communists, and, although I never joined the Party, I hated what the Nationalists were doing. So, when my friends went to Spain in '37, I volunteered too. I told my benefactor, who said I could resume my lessons when I returned. But when I got back, I learnt he had died.'

They cross the road into the public gardens that run along beside the sea. Other couples are out enjoying the fresh air. Groups of children dressed in little more than rags dart from couple to couple begging for coins and sweets.

'That must have been a blow, Frank.'

'I didn't really notice at the time. I was more concerned about my mother. I'd learnt in Spain that she was ill. I did everything I could to get back, but I arrived after the funeral.'

'I'm so sorry.'

'Thank you. Yes, that was an awful time – a real crossroads.'

'A bit like today, Frank,' she takes his hands.

'In what way?'

'That was a moment when things could have gone downhill. And you've had another difficult spell since the fire. But now you've heard you can stay in Naples.'

'You're right, Milione. Are you thinking we have plenty of time?'

'No, Frank, I'll never say that again. I've learnt not to waste precious time. Let's go back to your flat.'

'I think it's *our* flat now.'

CHAPTER 29

The Allied armies were held at Cassino from January '44 until May. But since breaking through the Gustav Line, they have driven the enemy back in a series of actions which have followed a predictable pattern.

The Germans would withdraw a few miles and then dig in to make a stand. The Allies would bombard the new positions before making a frontal assault, often at night. Once the objective was taken, the Germans would counter-attack before the Allies could dig in. Heavy fighting would continue until the enemy would withdraw again.

After a succession of these operations, 4th Battalion reached Florence – a hundred and seventy miles north of Rome. But this success came at a cost. Nine of Roger's men had been killed and more than twenty wounded in the past month alone, so C Company, normally a hundred and forty strong, can now muster fewer than a hundred. And Roger fears this need for replacements can only grow, given rumours that a major battle is coming and that seven Allied divisions are leaving Italy for new landings in southern France.

To Roger's relief, before the battle for Florence began in early August, the Battalion was taken out of the line and given a spell of leave. Today he feels full of hope, with thoughts of the war shoved to the back of his mind. Instead he is savouring an image which he has nourished through the icy winter and the long sweaty summer of fighting.

He had seen the Contessa only briefly and from a distance, when C Company reached Castelnuovo last September. But the image of her dismounting – slender, almost boyish, with her black hair pinned up on back of her head – has continued to dazzle him.

It was typical of Manley to choose the Contessa's house for his billet and then discover she was a widow. He was always bloody lucky with the fillies: the Contessa, Vermillion and those others in Cairo.

But now it's Roger's turn to enjoy good luck. He has planned his leave for weeks, even researching the Contessa's pedigree in the *Libro d'Oro*, a sort of Italian Debrett's. And now he's on his way. She doesn't know he's coming, of course, so his arrival will be a marvellous surprise.

The Battalion's journey south to Foggia, near the Adriatic coast, was slow and Roger spent the night in an overpriced brothel awash with overpaid Yanks. But this morning he had borrowed a Jeep and set off across country. Now, south of Benevento, he feels more certain with every mile that his journey will bring a fitting reward. The Contessa will be thrilled to see him, and they'll start a passionate affair.

Memories of the campaign still invade Roger's mind and for miles at a time he forgets where he is. But a broken signpost marked Castelnuovo brings him back. He remembers his image of the Contessa and smiles. This is his lucky day! He presses his foot to the floor and hums the tune of Lili Marlene. Getting into his stride he adds new words he had heard in Foggia.

We're the D-Day Dodgers out in Italy
Drinking all the vino, always on a spree
8th Army skivers out in their tanks
We go to war in ties like swanks
We are the D-Day Dodgers in Sunny Italy

We landed at Salerno, a holiday with pay
Jerry bought his bands down to cheer us on our way
Showed us the sights and gave us tea,
We sang all the songs and the beer was free
We are the D-Day Dodgers, the lads that D-Day dodged

Rounding the next bend, Roger jams on the brakes, bringing the song and the Jeep to a stuttering halt.

'Bloody hell!'

He scowls at the barrier blocking the road. Another blasted bridge is down. How can anyone get around when every bridge is closed? If it weren't for the bridges the sappers built, the whole blasted country would grind to a halt.

Stationary in the open Jeep, Roger's weathered skin burns in the sunshine. He moves the vehicle into the shade and pulls out an old handkerchief to wipe his face. Then he studies the map, already spattered with Xs where roads are closed. It should have been easy to find Castelnuovo but he has tried from most directions without success. He marks another X on the map and revs the engine again. The tyres screech as he swings the Jeep around. There's only one road left.

> *Palermo and Cassino were taken in our stride*
> *We didn't go to fight there, we just went for the ride*
> *Anzio and the Sangro are just names*
> *We only went there for the dames*
> *For we're the D-Day Dodgers out in Italy*

The road passes through a small town. In the central piazza Roger glares at the young men, hanging around like spivs.

'Why don't you join the bloody army and liberate Italy yourselves?' Roger yells in English. 'At least you could repair the bloody bridges! Or must we do everything for you?'

They watch him blankly.

'God, what a hopeless country!'

The road winds uphill through woodland. Roger feels he can breathe again. The image of the Contessa reappears. Now there's a worthwhile Italian! She had better be glad to see him. She owes it to a British officer who has risked life and limb for her country. Roger can't wait to see her face when he arrives.

Coming round the side of a hill he glimpses a village, half-hidden across the valley. He stops the Jeep and leaps out. Surely that's the place. He raises his field glasses. Yes, there are the medieval walls and the two towers just as he remembered them.

Roger grins as he vaults into the Jeep. He follows the winding road until he encounters another broken bridge. Damn and blast! But below the bridge the river is completely dry. How hard would it be to repair the whole bloody thing?

Roger knows there's no other road but he isn't giving up now. He abandons the Jeep and clambers on foot across the riverbed. Ahead an archway leads through the massive walls; it looks dark in contrast to the sunlight outside.

He marches on. As his eyes adjust to the gloom, he notices two youths propped against the left-hand wall. His right hand slides towards his pistol holster. Neither of the Eyeties moves. They both have one knee bent, with the foot placed flat against the wall behind them. They hold their cigarettes – stolen from the Allies of course – down by their sides.

Roger's blood boils. They look so fucking supercilious! He wants to grab each one by the scruff of the neck and march them to a recruiting Sergeant. They raise the cigarettes slowly to their lips, seemingly oblivious to his furious stare.

He enters a small piazza which he recognises immediately. But this isn't where *he* was billeted last year. Only Manley stayed here. And it wasn't until they got to Naples that he started crowing about the Contessa's special welcome.

Roger's understanding of what this meant was confirmed a few days later when Manley left the C Company garrison near Vesuvius and sneaked back to spend the night with the Contessa. Of course that was before Vermillion arrived.

Roger looks at his watch. 1735. He strides across the piazza towards a handsome stone house but stops a few yards from the door, hoping a servant will greet him. When no one appears he straightens his tie, smooths his moustache and marches up to the door.

He grabs the bell pull and waits, but still nobody comes. He is about to try the bell again when the heavy door starts to open. In the hallway an elderly manservant tenses at the sight of Roger's uniform.

'La Contessa?'

'La Contessa é fuori.'

'Quando sara qui?' Roger asks with the shadow of a smile.

'Fra poco.'

The servant tries to close the door but Roger jams it with his boot. Uncertain what to do next, Roger hears the distant sound of a horse's hooves. The door opens again. A change in the servant's expression confirms the Contessa is coming. Pleased with his timing, Roger graciously steps back with a broad smile.

His attention is on the rider as the horse enters the piazza. Although dressed as before in a fine cotton blouse with a neatly knotted tie, the Contessa isn't quite as he remembers. She seems older, and not as slender. But she's still a fine-looking girl, a cut above the tarts in Foggia.

He holds the horse's head and admires the Contessa's polished boots before studying the strain on her breeches as she dismounts.

'Buona sera,' she hands the reins to the servant before turning to Roger and studying his uniform. 'Can I help you?'

'Buona sera,' Roger smiles, relieved she speaks good English. 'I'm Major Bewdley from 4th Battalion, which was 3rd Battalion.'

'Do you know Major Edmund Manley?'

'Yes, of course!' Roger's smile widens into a grin. 'Major Manley's a good friend and I have some news about him.'

The Contessa scans the piazza. Roger watches her. She has certainly changed since last year. Her figure is no longer boyish and her bosom presses against her blouse. It seems a long time since he first planned his visit.

'You had better come in.'

She leads him into a drawing room, dominated by a piano, and gives instructions to another servant who quickly departs. Roger chews at his lower lip as he observes her, feeling embarrassed to take out his pipe.

'You have some news about Major Manley? How is he? Please don't say he has been killed.'

'Oh no, he's very much alive,' Roger grins again. 'Edmund – Major Manley – is back in England.'

The Contessa hesitates. 'When will he return to Italy?'

The servant reappears, bringing a silver tray and two small glasses of wine. Roger takes a glass and waits for the servant to leave.

'Major Manley won't return. He was wounded.'

The Contessa puts down her glass and glances at Roger as she raises both hands to her face.

He smiles, pleased to have her attention, but decides he should avoid any preamble.

'Major Manley trod on a mine. He lost both his legs.'

'Santa Madonna!' She screws up her eyes to hold back the tears. 'What will I do? I was sure he would return.'

Roger raises his glass and mutters a rapid thank you before downing a large draught. 'Don't worry, my dear. Edmund will be all right. He went home to get his new legs.'

'What will I do?'

Roger is about to say there are other officers in Italy, when the servant re-enters. He looks at Roger's empty glass and refills it less than halfway. Then as he opens the door to leave Roger hears an odd noise, which could have been a baby crying. But with his ears still muffled from the thunder of heavy guns, he isn't sure. He raises his eyebrows as he looks at the Contessa again. Could it be her child? She didn't react to the sound.

Roger smiles, remembering Manley said her husband was killed long before the Battalion arrived. Silently he counts the months since September. 'It must be possible,' he says to himself.'

'Will Major Manley return when he has his new legs?'

'No, my dear. I don't believe so. His soldiering days are over. He will probably settle down at home.'

'Poor Edmund,' she looks up through soft eyes. 'I don't suppose we shall meet again. Poor Eduardo.'

Roger empties his glass, conscious things aren't going to plan. 'Do you play the piano?' he asks, saying the first thing that enters his head.

'I used to play, once. I played for Edmund but now it just makes me sad.'

'I expect the war has been very hard.'

'Of course, but not just the war. We had twenty years of Mussolini first. The war just continued the destruction which Fascism began, destroying a generation. Nothing will ever be the same.'

Roger gets to his feet and ambles across to the Contessa's chair, where he stands looking down at her. Then gently he reaches out and strokes her arm.

'Do you have to leave so soon?' She grabs a small bell on the table and shakes it fiercely.

The door opens at once.

'Have some supper before you go, Major,' she says calmly. 'Meanwhile, I shall write to Edmund.'

She issues a string of instructions in Italian before turning to Roger again.

'If you follow Matteo,' she points the way, 'he will get you something to eat.'

Damn and blast! Roger is sure he could flatten Matteo with a single punch. And then he could deal with the Contessa in his own good time. God, he wants to sort her out. Yet something holds him back, perhaps the fear that other people are in the house. He grits his teeth and follows Matteo to a room off the large kitchen.

Roger subsides onto a chair, still thinking about the Contessa. He considers walking out, but before he can make up his mind the supper arrives: a platter covered with cold meats and several cheeses; and a basket of fresh bread. His nostrils fill with the smell of cooked ham and he starts to tuck in. After the first mouthful, he isn't going to stop.

He consumes more meat than he has seen for a month before turning his attention to the cheese. He cuts a thick slice and balances it on a chunk of bread. His mouth is still full when the Contessa reappears wearing a long skirt and a fuller blouse. Frankly she looks middle-aged.

'Do you have everything you want?' she asks.

Roger tries to swallow.

'I'm so sorry. You need a drink. MATTEO! It was kind of you to visit, Major. Here is the letter for Edmund. Please make sure he gets it.'

Roger finally manages to swallow. 'I promise to send it.'

He wipes his moustache and takes the crisp white envelope. He feels the wax seal at the back as he stuffs it into his breast pocket. He looks up at the Contessa, searching for a

161

sign she might soften. But her expression erases any lingering hope.

He gets to his feet and offers his hand just as Matteo brings a glass of red wine. The Contessa sidesteps, leaving Roger's outstretched hand ready to take the glass.

'Thank you again for visiting, Major,' she turns away. 'Have a safe journey.'

Roger raises the glass and takes a sip. He wishes Matteo would stop gawping. He sits down again, determined to enjoy the wine. He won't let some bolshie Eyetie put him off his stroke.

CHAPTER 30

'Does AMG really plan to move you to Rome?' Vermillion helps Frank clear away the supper.

Frank turns to her with a pained expression.

'If you do have to go,' she continues, 'You will be all right. And you mustn't worry about me.'

'I can't help worrying about you, but that's not what my nightmares are about.'

'What are they about?'

'They're horrible; I don't want to burden you.'

'But they affect me too, seeing you upset.'

Frank downs some whisky. 'I don't want to describe them. They're too horrible ...'

'I'm ready to share the horror ...'

Vermillion starts. 'That was a knock at the door.'

'Bloody hell!' Frank jumps up. 'Who is it? It can't be Chiara, it's well after curfew. Roger! What the hell brings you here? Are you on leave *again*?'

Vermillion puts her head in her hands. That ruddy man! What does he want this time?

'I'm fearfully sorry, old chap, but I'm in a bit of a hole.'

Roger strolls into the sitting room still looking at Frank. 'It's a bit of luck you're still up.'

He looks round and catches Vermillion's eye. 'I didn't mean to interrupt … or anything. I'll keep myself to myself.'

'I'm sorry, Roger. You can't turn up in the middle of the night and expect to find a bed.'

'Frank, let him stay tonight,' Vermillion says. 'He can't leave now with the curfew.'

'All right. But just for tonight.'

'Roger,' Vermillion smiles but without quite looking at him, 'put your things in the bedroom and come and have a drink. We'll be retiring soon. Tomorrow I'll talk to Jackie. I'm sure she won't mind if you stay in my old room there.'

'That's very civil, my dear. It's only for a few more nights. I won't be any trouble.'

'I expect you'll have a whisky, Roger,' Frank yawns.

'I don't mind if I do.' Roger takes the glass from Frank and drops down on the sofa beside Vermillion, where he sits stroking his moustache.

Just Roger's presence makes Vermillion feel exhausted.

'I saw the king!' Roger says suddenly. 'Yes George VI – a couple of weeks ago – at an investiture near Perugia. It's good to know Eighth Army isn't entirely forgotten.'

'How exciting, Roger,' Vermillion smiles. 'And how brave of the king to venture so close to the line.'

'Before he arrived, we were expecting a General Lyon, apparently that was his alias.'

Vermillion smiles again, uncertain how to respond.

'Frank, you'll never guess where I've been,' Roger says.

'Have you been back to Rome?' Frank asks. 'Did you see Chiara?'

'No, Frank,' Roger glances at Vermillion. 'Wrong direction.'

'I give up,' Vermillion says.

'Frank, you'll remember the Contessa. Manley was billeted in her house. Well, I decided to look her up!' Roger pauses. 'What do you think of that?'

'You went all the way to Castelnuovo?' Frank asks. 'That's quite a journey. Was the Contessa there?'

'She most certainly was.' Roger drinks some whisky and licks his lips. 'She gave me a very warm welcome.'

Vermillion catches Frank's eye. What does Roger mean? Well, if that's what he means, the Contessa must be a fool.

'And listen to this,' Roger looks up at Frank who is still standing. 'She's had a little one.'

'Goodness!' Frank lifts the whisky bottle and tops up his glass.

'And … you'll be interested in this, my dear … she thinks the baby is Manley's.'

'Gosh!' Vermillion says. 'Did she tell you all that?'

'No, but she gave me this: a letter for Manley.' Roger flourishes a sheet of thick writing paper, the sort people used before the war. Vermillion stares at the letter as he pushes it into her hand.

'Read it. Go on, it's interesting.'

'I can't read it, Roger. It's private.'

'It can't be private or she'd have put it into an envelope.'

Vermillion shakes her head: she wouldn't put it past Roger to have discarded the envelope.

'Well, have it your way, my dear. I've read it already. It says the Contessa has a nipper called Eduardo and she's sure it's Manley's. He was the only man she'd been with since her husband died.'

'Poor girl!' Vermillion is thinking of Margery. 'What an awful thing! Goodness what should we do?'

'You needn't do anything, my dear,' Roger empties his glass. 'I gave the Contessa my word that I'd forward the letter. And that's what I'll do. Then it's over to Manley.'

Vermillion doesn't know what to say. She looks away as Roger drains his glass.

'Roger, I think we should all turn in,' Frank says at last. 'You've given us plenty to think about. We'll see you in the morning.'

CHAPTER 31

Paolo was thrilled with the operation to blow up the bridge. But since then the partisans have lain low, awaiting another supply drop which hasn't come. Spartaco blames the British. He believes they've lost interest in Italy, preferring partisan groups in Yugoslavia and southern France.

Paolo had challenged Falcon about this, demanding to know why they were waiting around when they'd come north to kill Germans and end the war. At first Falcon was evasive but finally he acknowledged that Spartaco's politics might be the problem, because of British fears that after the war the Communists could use these weapons to seize power.

Paolo expressed his disgust that this British myopia would simply prolong the war; it wasn't as though *all* of Spartaco's men were Communists. Falcon promised to do what he could, but still no supplies arrived, forcing the partisans to take matters into their own hands.

* * *

Paolo waits on the wooded hillside, forcing himself to keep still. He must catch the first sound of a vehicle approaching. As he listens, he senses the stillness of the pine trees all around, with their thick resinous smell.

He glances at the other partisans, dressed mostly in old British Army garb, enhanced with items from many sources, even from the Carabinieri.

The partisans' politics are as motley as their dress. Sea Eagle, the Russian, believes in Uncle Joe, while Pheasant, an English Corporal who deserted at Cassino, lectures the others about class war. But they are the exceptions. Sparrow, an RAF officer who was a POW with the Italians, loves goading Pheasant, telling him the revolution will never happen. And Merlin, an anxious young Italian desperate to avoid conscription into Mussolini's new army, claims to be a Liberal, whatever that means now.

Generally, the partisans rub along well enough. But when the subject of Russia comes up, tempers tend to fray. The Communists still see Russia as a beacon of light and welcome all Russians as brothers. But most Italian soldiers hate the Russians for the way they slaughtered their comrades especially on the River Don, near Stalingrad.

Spartaco tries to keep a lid on these disagreements to stop them boiling over and endangering the group. This means keeping them busy, which makes today's operation – seizing ammunition and other supplies intended for German outposts and Fascist militias in the Apennines – so crucial.

What was that? Paolo strains to hear. Was it the rasp of an underpowered engine? The sound briefly echoes through the foothills before fading at the next bend. Silence returns.

Paolo glimpses the grey van. Usually it travels alone but this morning it has an escort, a black saloon which follows a few metres behind. It's a sign of growing German alarm.

'There are two vehicles, Spartaco!' Paolo yells.

'Stick to the plan, Pigeon!' Spartaco slaps the butt of his gun. 'You disarm the men in the bloody car! We'll unload the van! Make sure that no one gets killed!'

The labouring engine sounds louder.

'Get to your positions!'

Leaving Sandro with Spartaco, Paolo leads four partisans running down the hill to the place where they plan to cut off the vehicles' escape. He glances at his watch. Sunrise away from the hills was an hour ago, but the valley is still in twilight.

For a moment Paolo struggles to spot the vehicles through the trees. But he picks out the grey van as the driver slows for the next bend and crunches into first gear. The vehicles are now close enough for Paolo to feel vibrations through the road. He flexes his trigger finger and checks his grip. He flicks the safety catch to the firing position and crouches behind the boulders lining the road. The van grinds past, briefly imposing its grey presence. Paolo turns towards the saloon. Merda! There's a passenger in the front: a German officer, judging by his uniform. If only he could warn Spartaco.

As the convoy approaches the next bend, Paolo signals to the other partisans to roll the trunks of two small trees across the road. Without waiting for the men to finish, he sprints up the narrow track to meet the convoy at the top.

The van struggles on up the hill. Here with fewer trees, more light gets through. Paolo sees the passenger hand a beer bottle to the driver, who takes a swig before returning it. He just has time to wipe his hand across his mouth before changing down again.

Ahead the road is blocked by two large rocks, behind which the partisans' guns are visible. The van shudders to a halt. Spartaco gestures with his Tommy gun for the driver to get out.

Behind, the driver of the saloon bangs his hand on the horn until two partisans appear. The officer yells at the driver who rams the gear lever into reverse and swings the car across the road. The gearbox grates again as he searches for first. He wrenches the steering wheel round and the vehicle leaps forward.

Paolo fires a burst of bullets over the car which the driver ignores. He fires a second burst, shattering the windscreen. The car careers into the hillside and stops. The front passenger smashes the side window. He aims his pistol at Paolo who fires at the emerging hand. The man shrieks. The pistol clatters to the ground discharging a round which ricochets off the rocks. The left headlight goes dark as the glass splinters. Paolo thumps on the car roof. Then he gestures with his gun for the passengers to come out.

The officer slowly emerges from the front and raises his arms. A handkerchief is wrapped around his right hand. Blood seeps down his sleeve.

'Christ!' Paolo murmurs under his breath. 'He's a bloody Colonel! Porca puttana! There'll be hell to pay!'

Paolo moves towards the Colonel just as the rear doors open. From behind the driver a Corporal climbs out with his hands up; Merlin jumps forward to search him. On the far side a Lieutenant moves more slowly. Paolo watches until the car obscures the man's movements.

Paolo turns back to the Colonel as he thrusts his good hand into his jacket. Paolo steadies himself to fire if the Colonel produces a weapon. But a shot rings out from across the road and the Colonel sinks to the ground.

'Merda!' Paolo glares across at Sea Eagle who grins back. 'Bloody hothead!'

Other partisans grab the Lieutenant and the Corporal. Paolo approaches the car where the driver is slumped over the wheel. He jerks open the door and the driver topples onto the road.

'Santa Madonna! Two dead!'

Paolo hurries up the path towards the van, leaving the other two Germans tied together, guarded by Merlin.

At the rear of the van several men are extracting boxes of ammunition, which they heave onto the backs of the waiting mules.

Spartaco lowers the cigar from his mouth and grins, blowing smoke into the clean air. He half turns towards Paolo.

'Two Germans dead!' Paolo tries to sound calm. 'One's a Colonel.'

'Idiot! How the hell did that happen?'

'They drew their pistols.'

'But you've got a Tommy gun, damn you!'

'They tried to kill us.'

'Fuck!' Spartaco draws on his cigar. 'Put the bodies in the car and push it over the edge. We'll lock the others in the van and abandon it somewhere quiet. We can cross the mountain before they're found.'

Paolo looks down at the villages in the valley still sunk in twilight. He wants to be sick. The partisans should survive because they can slip away. But in the valley, the Germans will take reprisals. Ten or more innocents will die for each German killed, as General Kesselring has decreed.

CHAPTER 32

Frank sleeps for the first part of the night but as the effects of the whisky wear off he wakes up, sweltering in the sultry air. With Vermillion sleeping peacefully, he slips out of bed and wanders around the flat as usual until snoring from the other bedroom reminds him about Roger. Frank scrambles back to get his pyjamas.

In the morning, Roger is as bumptious as ever. He seems happy to move to Vermillion's flat but reacts when Frank declines to accompany him there.

'Come on, you lazy desk-wallah! It'll do you good to stretch your legs.'

A desk-wallah! So that's what Roger thinks of him! Frank has half a mind to retaliate but the urge to see Roger move out is stronger still, even if it means visiting Vermillion's flat. Watching Roger lead Vermillion into the street, Frank already feels green at the gills.

All the way to the flat Frank trails along behind and by the time he enters the building the others are halfway up the steps. He stops as sweat trickles down inside his shirt. At 0800 the air is already muggy but it isn't the weather that bothers him: this is his first visit to the flat since the fire.

He hears the others chatting away and is happy to leave them to it. But as he contemplates the first flight of the circular staircase he nearly buckles. Images of fire rage inside his head as he mounts the first step.

'There's no sign of the fire up here,' Roger says loudly, probably for Frank's benefit.

'It was enough to kill Barbara!' Vermillion says.

'Oh, I'm so sorry, my dear. I didn't mean any offence.'

Dear God! They must be rid of Roger!

Frank forces himself to follow by focusing on the fourth step ahead. But the skull is already there. Today the charring around its eye sockets seems more pronounced. How ghastly to feel one's eyes burn.

Frank makes it to the first landing. He feels exhausted, but he won't give up. He can hear Roger still babbling on, but happily the words are muffled. As Frank gains the second landing his hands are shaking, his legs feel drained and each step is an effort. He grips the banisters, pulling himself up, one step at a time.

Approaching the third landing, he hears Roger knock on the door. Why can't he wait for Vermillion to unlock it? Then he hears Margery's voice. Oh God! She mustn't close the door. He can't be left alone with Barbara's ghost. He runs up the last few steps, across the landing and into the flat.

'Of course, Roger can stay,' Margery says from the end of the corridor.

Thank goodness for that! Frank follows the voices into the sitting room.

Roger thanks Margery excessively but she responds with considerable charm and they chat for several minutes.

'I'll have to ask Jackie, of course.' Margery says. 'But I don't think she'll mind, will she Vermillion?'

'She'd better not. After all, I agree, so that makes two out of three.'

The conversation lapses into silence. Unable to bear it, Frank says the first thing that comes to mind. 'Margery, did Roger show you the Contessa's letter?'

Roger recounts his tale enthusiastically and Frank soon regrets raising the subject. But Margery listens intently, especially when Roger repeats his promise to forward the letter.

'May I see it, Roger?' Margery asks. 'As it isn't sealed.'

Roger looks at Frank before passing it over. Frank expects Margery to destroy it, but instead she folds it carefully and smiles at Roger. 'I'll send it to Edmund today.'

Roger seems poised to snatch it back but then changes his mind. He grins at Margery and they talk quietly together for a while.

Frank needs some air. He strides across the room and throws open a window. He wishes he were down in the street. He wipes his hands on his uniform, hoping no one will see.

'Thank you for arranging this, Frank,' Roger joins him at the window. 'It will make a splendid billet.'

'It's better than my pokey place.'

'Why didn't you move in here, Frank, when Edmund left?'

Frank turns away. Roger won't understand and Frank doesn't intend to explain.

'Your chap Huggins has settled down,' Roger says. 'He's fitter and happier. He was probably bored at the theatre. Back with his mates he looks like a proper soldier.'

Frank hates the way that Roger talks perfunctorily about Huggins; but it has the intended effect of making Frank feel guilty.

'We should liberate Florence soon.' Roger adds.

Frank takes a deep breath. 'I hear it's been quite a battle. I hope the old city isn't destroyed.'

'Once Florence is under our belts, we'll be ready for the Gothic Line.' Roger laughs. 'They say this line will be tougher than Monte Cassino. We'll need every man we can get.'

Is this another recruitment drive? Is Roger expecting Frank to volunteer?

'Roger, you must look after Huggins.'

'We look after every man; we can't afford to lose a single one.' Roger raises his eyebrows. 'Have you heard about your transfer to Rome?'

Is this the moment for Frank to say he's not inclined to go to Rome and if he must leave Naples he'd rather rejoin the Battalion? But he can't say anything until Vermillion knows.

Frank coughs. 'Nothing so far, Roger, and Pizzetti hasn't arrived. But I should hear soon. The Brigadier is sure to have something planned.'

Roger steps towards Frank and lowers his voice. 'You'd better take care, old chap, when you leave Naples. Keep a close eye on the Lieutenant. I hear she met that pilot chappie when you went to Rome.'

Frank stares at Roger's grinning face. He wants to hit him. 'Do you mean Simon?'

'That's the one.'

Frank looks across at Vermillion who's still talking to Margery. If she really did meet Simon, why the hell didn't she say?

'Is there anyone at home?' Jackie's voice echoes along the hall.

They all turn to watch as Jackie appears.

'You know everyone, don't you, Jackie?' Vermillion embraces her.

'No, I don't.' Jackie glances at Roger.

'I'm sorry.' Vermillion turns to him. 'This is Roger Bewdley from 4th Battalion. Jackie and I shared a flat in Heliopolis.'

'I know.' Roger moves closer to Jackie. 'You used to share with Barbara. As I recall you had a reputation ...'

Jackie raises her eyebrows.

'... as the best-looking threesome in Cairo.'

'We just liked to be sociable, didn't we, Vermillion?' Jackie says. 'All sorts of people dropped in. Those were happy days! Vermillion, do you remember how Simon kept turning up?'

Frank looks at Vermillion. Why are they all talking about Simon?

'That was in '43 when everyone had left Cairo,' Vermillion looks at the floor as she speaks.

'He took Vermillion dancing every night.' Jackie says, turning to Roger. 'Do you like to dance?'

'Roger wants to stay here for a few nights, Jackie,' Vermillion says. 'Margery has agreed. Is that all right?'

'I don't see why not.' Jackie smiles at Roger. 'Since Vermillion moved out, the place feels jolly empty with just Margery and me.'

'I thought Mike had been staying,' Vermillion says.

'That was in the past,' Jackie glances at Roger again. 'Mike swanned off long ago.'

'Come on Vermillion,' Frank touches her arm. 'We must go to the theatre. Roger, we can meet later.'

CHAPTER 33

The crack of a single pistol shot wakes Paolo immediately. Sitting up he stares into the darkness of the barn.

Silence.

Perhaps it was a dream.

Two more shots ring out.

Bloody hell! Paolo flicks on his torch. 0505. Who's shooting at this hour?

He places his hand over Sandro's mouth, provoking a strangled moan. 'Wake up, Sandro! Quietly! Shh! For Christ's sake! I heard shots. Listen.'

There's no more shooting. But there's banging and shouting some way away.

A woman screams.

Paolo jams on his boots and grabs his things. 'Sandro! Get ready to leave in a hurry.'

After the raid on the van, the partisans had split into two groups. One took the booty to hide it in the hills; the other, led by Spartaco, crossed the mountain heading for his home village. Usually he keeps on the move, rarely sleeping twice in one place and staying clear of Soglio. But last night, wanting to celebrate the raid, he came to visit Carla, bringing ten partisans to keep watch at the edge of the village while he enjoyed the comfort of her bed.

Paolo squeezes Sandro's shoulder as he leaves.

Outside, raised German voices and heavy boots resound in the stone streets. Rain beats down from the black sky, but the air smells fresher after the animal stink in the barn. Light spills from the main piazza into nearby streets.

Shit! The Germans have brought their own lights.

Paolo starts. Something heavy slams against a wooden door. Shouts greet each blow, but the crashing persists. Protests give way to wailing as a final stroke splinters the wood and the door gives way. More shouting. Then prolonged screams.

God, this is awful! Paolo shivers, afraid it had been like this for Mamma.

Paolo remembers Spartaco. He must have got away already. If the Germans or Blackshirts caught him, they would torture him until he talked. Four partisans at a time had been on guard; they must have got him out before *la Volpe* arrived. But how did they know that Spartaco was here? Who had betrayed him?

At the end of the street Paolo peers around the corner. Through the sheeting rain he can see one side of the piazza where German trucks are lined up. Soldiers pull a half-dressed old man out of his house. He tries to button his coat but his hands shake too much. A young woman follows with a child clinging to her neck. They shiver together in the cold.

One by one, six more souls are hauled from the house.

The German officer barks an order. Two young soldiers grab the old man and a teenage boy. As they are dragged away they twist around yelling encouragement to the women who scream back. In a moment the men are gone; the women's cries subside into weeping.

More shouted orders as women and children are impelled across the piazza until they're out of sight. Paolo's blood boils. He grips his gun. He wants to kill those fucking soldiers. How many could he get before they got him? Five or six? Not enough. And how many more would they kill in retribution?

He stumbles back towards the barn. Half-blinded by tears, he fails to notice Sandro in the shadows.

'Listen, Paolo.'

Paolo gives an involuntary cry. 'Sandro! I didn't see you.'

'Listen! Spartaco left with the others. They urged me to go too. I said I couldn't leave without you. They'll wait for us near the refuge. If we go now, we'll catch them first.'

'We can't go yet,' Paolo wipes his eyes. 'The Germans are pulling people out of their houses. They're taking the men away and rounding up women and children. Soon they'll start burning the houses. Sandro! It's just … fucking awful!'

'Come on Paolo. We must go, while we have a chance. You know what they'll do if they catch us.'

'I can't go. Not yet. I must see what happens to the men. They were pushing them towards the church. You wait here.'

'For Christ's sake be careful, Paolo. It'll soon be light.'

Paolo skirts round the end of the village. Dogs are barking everywhere, as the first cockerel crows. The rain begins to ease. The church tower is silhouetted against the sky but it's still dark enough for Paolo to move unseen. From behind a wall he slowly raises his head to survey the area.

Fifty metres away stone steps lead up to the west end of the church. Something or someone is being dragged from the house opposite. The officer shouts to hurry the soldiers. Paolo recognises the dark outline of a priest who mutters a prayer in Latin as they fling him to the ground. A soldier points his rifle at his back. There are gasps and groans from across the road where the men must be penned.

'Open the church!' the officer yells in crude Italian.

'This is a house of God,' the priest clambers to his knees. 'It's for sacred purposes only.'

'OPEN IT UP!'

The priest doesn't respond. The officer walks over and jabs his pistol at his head.

'Open it!'

He looks up at the officer but doesn't move. The officer pulls the trigger and the priest topples sideways, blood spurting over his white collar. A soldier rummages for the keys that hang from a belt beneath his cassock. He slashes at the belt but hesitates before wrenching the keys away.

Paolo turns his head to be sick.

The officer studies the iron keys before selecting one. He swears when it doesn't work. He tries another, and another. Finally, he flings open the west doors. He shouts an instruction.

The soldiers take up the shout as they drive the men towards the church, goading them with their rifles as they trample over the dead priest. Soon they're all inside; only then do they cry out in protest. But the officer pushes them back and slams the door. He orders four soldiers to stand guard and marches the others back towards the piazza.

Paolo wonders what other doors might lead into the church. As if in response two of the guards set off along the building's south side. A few minutes later they re-emerge from the north side, apparently satisfied with what they've seen.

It's almost fully light when soldiers appear with another batch of local men, making about fifty in all. When the soldiers re-open the doors, the men inside try to barge their way out. The soldiers hit out with their rifles to drive the new arrivals in. But the greater numbers inside the church seem likely to prevail.

The officer draws his pistol and fires two shots into the church. Glass shatters on the stone floor. The men shrink back. The soldiers force their way in at gunpoint, pushing the men towards the altar. Others herd the new arrivals, who cower near the chancel step as the doors slam shut.

Paolo waits. The rain has stopped and the sky has lightened to pale grey. Colours are starting to return. The soldiers outside the west door take out their cigarettes. They cluster together as they smoke, exchanging clumsy remarks, trying to ignore the crumpled priest at their feet.

At last the sun rises, throwing a long shadow from the church across the town.

Paolo chooses this moment for a tactical retreat, aiming to get to the rear of the church without being seen. He follows the line of a wall, half-running in a crouched position, with his head well down. At the end, he throws himself over a fence and scales the wall with help from an apple tree.

A dog barks. Paolo freezes but no one responds.

He creeps round to the east end, trying several locked doors. One, set half below ground, appears to lead to a crypt. Paolo tries to break the padlock, but the fittings are new and won't budge.

Gunfire echoes inside the church. Merda! He mustn't delay. He raises his pistol and aims at the lock. Hearing more shots from inside the church he pulls the trigger, praying the report is masked by the clamour above.

The padlock clatters to the ground. He rams his shoulder against the door. The hinges screech in protest but the door retreats. He steps into an unlit corridor with firewood stacked along one side. Above he hears hurrying feet and several shots. Something heavy falls to the floor. Men scream. Footsteps race down the steps towards the crypt.

A man cries out as he sees Paolo.

'Shh! I'm here to rescue you. The door is open.'

The young man scrambles past and is gone.

'Don't go yet!' Paolo barks at two elderly men who follow. 'For Christ's sake, see who else can escape.'

One of the men turns back. The other stands, shaking all over; tears stream down his face.

Centimetres above Paolo's head an explosion rocks the ceiling.

'No one else up there can walk!' The elderly man yells as he nears the bottom step.

'Right, we must go!' Paolo catches him as he trips.

From outside the crypt door, comes the voice of a German. Then the sound of a pair of boots descending. Paolo releases the safety catch on his pistol and flattens himself against the wall but there's nowhere to hide.

The old man squeezes behind the door as the German shoves it open and pushes past.

Paolo can see the German's silhouette against the daylight, but he hesitates, afraid to fire in the narrow passage. As he steadies his pistol, he hears a loud thud. The German sinks to the floor. Paolo rushes forward as the old man drops his firewood cudgel and slips out from behind the door.

CHAPTER 34

After Frank's first encounter with Pizzetti, Vermillion has to wait for ten days before she meets him. She is hopeful their roles at the theatre can continue, but as she readies herself she feels distinctly anxious. So much depends on how she gets on.

What if Pizzetti doesn't like *her* or she doesn't like *him*? Her fears have only been partly allayed by Frank's description and his report that Pizzetti wants them both to stay on.

As the minutes pass, the coming encounter looms larger in her mind. Since lunch she has found it hard to settle. Finally, she gives up pretending to work and spends a while tidying herself. At 1615 she is ready, looking her best.

She wanders across to the window and gazes out. She keeps checking her watch. At 1625 she sets off at a brisk pace. Through the summer the theatre has grown hotter each day and by the time she reaches the box she feels flushed, which isn't what she intended.

'Ah, Vermillion, you've made it,' Frank stands up. 'This is Dottor Pizzetti, who used to run the theatre.'

Vermillion is surprised by the sight of Pizzetti, despite Frank's description. He is taller and thinner than she expected. Frank said he was sixty but he has the air of a younger man. His hair is touched with grey, making him look quite distinguished. He must have been good-looking when he was young.

Pizzetti smiles warmly and catches her eye. Yes, he thinks he still is young.

'Piacere,' Vermillion mumbles as they shake hands.

'No,' Pizzetti says in careful English, 'the pleasure is mine.'

Vermillion gives a half smile but immediately regrets it. She daren't look at his face, but she can feel him watching her.

The lights begin to dim before she sits down. Applause greets the leader of the orchestra and swells to fill the theatre as the maestro arrives. The audience settles for the new season's first performance of La Fanciulla del West.

In the darkness, Vermillion is hit by wafts of Pizzetti's eau de cologne. She wishes Frank were between them but at least he's on her other side. She gently touches his hand and he squeezes her little finger.

Once the curtain rises, however, Vermillion is caught by the energy of the music and by the unusual grouping on the stage, with a lone woman surrounded by thirty men who look up to her. Vermillion finds the sight intriguing but oddly unsettling.

Fanciulla is set in a miners' camp during the 1849 Californian gold rush. The men have come from God knows where, leaving everything behind. They're braced to fight for gold yet they long for a better world. The music reflects their yearning. In this lawless place, Minnie, who runs the saloon, is the one person they all trust. At the end, she persuades them to spare the life of her bandit lover so they can escape together.

Despite its Wild West setting a hundred years ago, Vermillion sees the parallels with Naples now, with men brought from all over the world to fight in a strange country against a common foe. They've left their families behind and are desperate for something or someone to believe in. She feels sure that the Tommies will see themselves in the miners and will warm to the show.

* * *

'That was splendid, Captain.' Pizzetti smiles at Vermillion while talking to Frank at the end of the performance. 'You've done a wonderful thing in bringing the San Carlo back to life.'

'Thank you, Dottore.' Frank looks overcome.

Vermillion beams at Pizzetti, hugely proud of Frank and what he has achieved.

'And of course, my dear,' Pizzetti smiles back, 'I include you in my congratulations.'

Vermillion wants to turn away but feels obliged to look at his face and briefly hold his gaze.

'Would you care to join us for a drink, Dottore?' Frank asks. 'We could go to the Club.'

'That would be a pleasure.' Pizzetti looks at Vermillion. She wishes Frank hadn't extended the invitation.

Once they've found a table, Frank orders some wine. It's airless in the Club and Vermillion wants a drink. Frank starts a conversation with Pizzetti about the history of Italian opera and the role of Naples in its development. In other circumstances this might have been interesting but tonight she feels annoyed as the men drone on. She taps her feet to the rhythm of the band.

She wants to interrupt to say Fanciulla was terrific. She can't think of another opera with such a strong heroine. Not only does Minnie save her lover but unlike most of Puccini's heroines she is even alive at the end. She knows Frank would say the composers weren't at fault; the librettos just reflect nineteenth century society. And he would add that musically the roles of great heroines like Mimi, Lucia or Violetta are at least a match for the men. Vermillion accepts that Frank might be right musically but the stories still matter. She finds it depressing that the women always die, which is why she was thrilled when Minnie rescued her man.

When the men finally end their conversation, Pizzetti turns to offer his cigarettes first to Vermillion and then to Frank. She feels tempted but holds back. She glances at Frank, who seems frozen even before Pizzetti produces his lighter. She wonders what Frank will do. She stretches to touch his hand, which feels moist.

Pizzetti inhales deeply and returns to his subject: Rossini's influence on Naples. But Frank looks pale and withdrawn and only says an occasional word.

When Pizzetti stops again, Vermillion leans forward and asks when he first visited the San Carlo theatre. He smiles warmly and starts an elaborate answer, which he illustrates with enthusiastic gestures and facial expressions. There's something theatrical about his movements, even when he stubs out his cigarette. She senses that he tailors his performance for his audience. Yet, despite her reservations, she feels flattered by his attention.

'Would you like to dance, my dear?' Pizzetti takes her hand before she can resist. 'Captain, please excuse us.'

Vermillion doesn't reply but stands up and lets Pizzetti lead her to the dance floor. He holds her very formally and dances well, rather as Edmund had. She readily follows his lead. As she gets used to his style she looks back at Frank and sees him empty his glass, get to his feet and walk away without looking up.

When the music stops, she thanks Pizzetti and returns to their table but Frank isn't there. Pizzetti again offers her a cigarette and this time she takes one. He seems unconcerned about Frank and asks her how she got involved with the theatre. She explains that Frank needed someone who spoke French. For several minutes they talk about France before the war. She's aware her gestures are more expansive than usual. She isn't sure she likes Pizzetti, yet she feels obliged to perform for him. She wants him to like her.

'I think we need another bottle,' Vermillion hears Frank's reassuring voice and feels his hand on her shoulder.

'Ah, you're back, Frank,' she stubs out her cigarette and looks up at his newly washed face. He still looks pale.

Frank sits down. 'Let's order some food.'

'No thank you, Captain. I shall eat at home.' Pizzetti stands up. 'Thank you, Captain. And thank you, Lieutenant. I look forward to working with you both.'

He turns to Vermillion. She proffers her hand. He takes it and raises it to his lips. 'Thank you, my dear.'

Whilst Frank accompanies Pizzetti to the door, Vermillion grabs her glass and takes a large mouthful. She watches Frank return; before he reaches her, she stands up and gestures towards the dance floor. Frank takes her hand and pulls her towards him as they start to dance.

'Dear Frank,' she whispers into his ear. 'Are you all right?'

'I'm better now Pizzetti's gone. Tonight I found him rather smarmy.'

Vermillion wonders how she would describe Pizzetti. She doesn't think he's smarmy. Charming, yes. But something else. Insistent perhaps, used to getting his own way, which makes him hard to resist, like a sixty-year-old version of Edmund.

She thinks about Pizzetti a lot in the following days but still can't decide what to make of him. He'd been polite and attentive, but she knows she'll have to keep him at arm's length. That shouldn't be hard whilst Frank is around but if ever he leaves the theatre, she'll have to go too: she can't be left in Pizzetti's clutches.

CHAPTER 35

To Roger's intense annoyance, urgent orders to rejoin the Battalion had truncated his leave. On his return he found the Allied armies engaged in a major operation to move tens of thousands of men and their equipment from Tuscany across the peninsula to the east coast in preparation for the next big offensive.

Everything has to be done in the hours of darkness to conceal the activity from the Germans. But while his men toil all night, Roger fears the whole manoeuvre is a waste of time.

When he went on leave the Germans were on the run and he expected the Allies to maintain the pressure as long as the weather held. Instead the Allied action has given the enemy two weeks of respite to occupy their new defensive positions. He can't imagine what the Allied generals were thinking. Any prospect of surprise has been lost: the Teds must know an attack in the east is now imminent.

Whilst Roger is critical of the strategy, he is pleased for the Battalion. They are no longer part of the American Fifth Army which, under the self-publicising General Mark Clark, must now fight its way through the mountains north of Florence. Instead the Battalion has returned to the good old British Eighth Army, under General Leese.

Roger has heard rumours that this whole kerfuffle resulted from a bust-up with the Yanks. Apparently Leese can't abide Mark Clark, who in June – determined that the Yanks should enter Rome first – had threatened to open fire if any Eighth Army units approached the capital.

So much for Britain's closest ally!

* * *

Shortly after Roger's return the Colonel summoned his officers.

'Good morning, gentlemen,' Mortimer gestures for them to take their seats as he strides into the tent. 'It's good to see you all so bright and early.'

Roger feels bored already. He returns to the daydream he was having before the Colonel arrived.

Roger hears the bathroom door open and Jackie's bare feet in the corridor. He holds out a glass of gin as she appears wrapped only in a towel. He smiles as she takes the glass in both hands, leaving the towel held in place miraculously by a twist of fabric above her bust. He feels a tremor of excitement as she loosens his tie. Roger admires her tightly crossed legs and starts to stroke her thigh. Slowly his hand slips beneath the towel ...

The Colonel clears his throat. 'We have plenty of good news to celebrate. In France the landings in the south have been successful and in the north Paris should soon fall. And don't forget how far we've come in Italy since we landed in Sicily. This summer we've seen: Cassino in May, Rome in June, Arezzo in July and Florence in August. All fine achievements, thanks to heroic efforts by your men.'

Roger wants to return to his reverie. It's less than two weeks since he stayed with Jackie and his memory of that time is still arousingly fresh.

The Colonel clears his throat again as he points at the map. 'From here, on the east coast, you can see we have a clear run north to the Lombardy plain!'

Colonel Mortimer looks around the group of fifteen officers from 4th Battalion. Most of them are young and keen. At twenty-seven Roger is the oldest, apart from the Colonel and his Adjutant. But they all look older than their years. Even the recent arrivals have aged in *Sunny Italy.*

The prospect of the Lombardy plain doesn't appeal to Roger as it does to Mortimer. It sounds too much like Norfolk. Roger had been happy in Surrey before his father died. Of course he was never taken in by the story of the sudden heart attack. But it still came as a shock, just before he left for Egypt, when he learnt that his father had killed himself following the '29 stock market crash. Why didn't his mother tell him at the time? And why did she bring it up so much later when he'd pretty well forgotten his father? It was like her refusal to re-marry: mother was often irrational.

Roger stares at Stansfield, one of those bright-eyed chaps who has scarcely finished officer training. Judging by his puppy-like face, he has never had to fight for anything.

'In just three months,' Mortimer continues, 'we've driven back the other team by two hundred miles and now we've reached their last defences before the Alps. With one more push, we can turf the buggers out of Italy!'

Roger conjures up Jackie again. He pushes her back as her resistance weakens. He likes to feel her struggle …

'But before we can finish off the other team, we must break the Gothic Line.'

The Colonel waits for the next map to be displayed.

'The Gothic Line is typical of their defences. It extends along the Apennines, snaking across the peninsula from south of La Spezia in the west to a point just north of Pesaro on the Adriatic coast. There are two lines linked together with a depth of about ten miles. That may sound impressive but remember it's only as strong as the troops who man it. And for three months the other team have been on the run. Intelligence clearly shows that they're ready to crack.'

The Colonel looks at the map again.

Roger reverts to thinking about Jackie's lips. God, he'd give anything to kiss her. He uncrosses his legs.

'The Poles are here on the right, near the coast. On their left are the Canadians. V Corps is here, starting a dozen miles from the sea and extending inland.'

The Colonel grins as a new map is unfurled.

'This is a detailed view of the defences. Within the overall Gothic Line, we refer to the two principal lines as "Green I" and "Green II". Green I starts with the Foglia river where the other team have built the usual concrete bunkers with machine-gun posts on both banks. And there are minefields and wire all along here together with an anti-tank ditch. And in the hills behind there are artillery and tank emplacements overlooking the whole area. Yes, it's quite impressive.'

Shit! Roger briefly closes his eyes. He wants to keep them shut and think about Jackie. God, he wants to see her again. Why had he wasted his time on that wild goose chase with the Contessa when Jackie was there for the taking, right under his nose? God, what a bloody waste!

'How will we break this line?' Mortimer pauses to look around the table.

Roger opens his eyes, afraid the question wasn't rhetorical.

'The answer is simple,' Mortimer continues. 'We'll break it the way we broke the lines at Alamein and at Cassino – by a massive aerial bombardment targeting the other team's bunkers and gun emplacements. Then our artillery will soften up the whole area, clearing the mines and wire. And once the other team's resistance is broken, we'll advance on a broad front.'

Roger leans back. He has heard this all before. They always promise a bombardment to obliterate the enemy. But when the shelling stops the Germans reappear unscarred. At Cassino they still held out after every building had been flattened. And Mortimer hasn't even mentioned the rather pertinent fact that the Germans have more divisions in Italy than the Allies. Roger wonders what happened to that old rule of thumb that any attacking army should outnumber the defenders by three to one.

* * *

After the briefing the Battalion's three companies start their advance.

Leaving the transports three miles from the front, Roger leads C Company on foot through gently rolling hills in the golden light of a late summer afternoon. All around, the vines are laden with fruit. But the men are tense as the thunder of heavy guns fills the air. At least now they're on the move, but Roger's efforts to get them singing prove unsuccessful.

They cross the Metauro river – where the carcases of wrecked tanks bear witness to fierce fighting four days ago – and head towards the Foglia. South of the river they find a recently-abandoned farm with chickens still foraging in the yard. The men devote much energy and little skill to chasing them. Eventually the men tire, flopping down in the shade, knowing that they face a long night.

Roger settles near his three Platoon officers to outline the plan.

'Stansfield's Platoon will cross the river first and head for the group of farm buildings ... relieving F Company from 10th Battalion.'

Roger pauses as the guns erupt. 'Then Evengate's Platoon will cross ... passing through Stansfield's Platoon ... and advancing towards our objective at point 217.'

The stink of cordite carried on the light breeze makes Roger look up.

'Finally Temple's Platoon will join Stansfield's ... together they'll fan out behind Evengate ... with Stansfield on the left and Temple on the right.

'Shouldn't we wait at the farm buildings and send out some patrols?' Evengate asks. 'We don't know where the enemy are, or their strength.'

'No, George. The Colonel is clear we must advance at once. Intelligence says the Germans are yet to man their positions. They've left a small window for us to climb through, before they close the door.'

'Whether it's a window or a door, Sir, we could be cut to pieces.'

'There's always a risk, George. But if we can break through now, we'll avoid weeks of costly attrition.'

'Don't worry,' Temple puts his arm on Evengate's shoulder and grins. 'We'll be right behind you.'

Roger smiles. 'Tell your Platoons that once we're through this line, it will all be plain sailing. We just need one more push.'

Stansfield and Evengate smile back enthusiastically.

'Come off it, Roger,' Temple says. 'They said we needed one more push when I arrived last year. I didn't believe it then and I don't believe it now.'

'I told you to tell your men. You don't have to believe it.'

'Shouldn't we tell them the truth?'

'You mean tell them that half of them may die tomorrow and many more will cop it before we clear the Gothic Line. If you told them that, they'd all go on the trot.'

'Roger's right,' Stansfield says brightly. 'It's our job to set an example.'

Temple wanders away, shaking his head. Roger leans back, resting his head against an apple tree, but the endless booming of the guns ensures he doesn't sleep. Occasional shells or mortars explode nearby but Roger stays put. He can't be bothered to find an empty slitter. He shuts his eyes and returns to thoughts of Jackie.

'Excuse me, Sir, it's urgent … from Battalion HQ.'

Roger sits up slowly and takes the field telephone.

'Major Bewdley? A message from the Colonel. F Company has crossed the river and secured its objective. They're digging in. C Company must be ready to advance at 1800. Good luck, Major.'

Roger sends Private Roberts to find Temple while he tells the others to have their men ready at 1755. 'We advance at 1800 sharp.'

Already the sun is dropping behind the hills, but the Allied medium bombers keep pounding away, throwing up columns of dust and dirt. Even at a distance Roger feels the ground shudder; he imagines this is how an earthquake feels.

Roger watches a plane – it looks like a Spitfire – as it loops down in flames. Burning fuel spews across a neighbouring field, setting hay bales alight. Dense smoke climbs into the sky. It's a grim way to go, but he still resents his mother's interference when he wanted to fly before the war.

With the light fading, C Company starts to move forward Section by Section, using the cover of buildings, walls, hedges, ditches, trees, even stationary tanks. They shield their ears as they pass batteries of heavy guns and intermittently they throw themselves to the ground as the Germans target the road. Progress is slow but they make it to the riverbank without loss.

At Roger's signal the first men from Stansfield's Platoon gallop into the water, which quickly covers their knees as they wade with forceful strides. As the river gets shallower on the far side, they quicken their pace again and scamper up the bank. Then, with water spraying off their legs like dogs after a swim, they sprint towards the farm buildings where F Company is still maintaining fire to pin the Germans down.

Before the first men reach their goal, the second group is into the water. Occasional German shells disrupt the operation but within minutes Stansfield's Platoon has made it.

Roger signals for Evengate to lead his Platoon across. He feels pleased with how things are going. Perhaps it's true that the Germans haven't manned their positions.

It's too dark to see F Company moving back but Roger soon hears the splashing of exhausted legs dragging through the water. As they approach the near bank, Roger sees that several men are out on their feet, hardly awake. Several hundred yards to their right he hears the clang of metal where sappers are constructing a bridge, intent on getting tanks across by morning.

Roger waits for the signal that Evengate's men are in position before moving forward with Temple's Platoon. By then the waxing moon has begun to sink.

Beyond the farm buildings a track climbs towards point 217 between terraces of olive trees supported by stone walls. Where the track starts the way is clear but where it narrows and bends to the left several thickets of wire have survived the Allied bombardment.

With his Platoons in place, Roger orders the Sergeant Major to distribute a measure of rum. Evengate crouches beside the right-hand wall as he gathers his Platoon. He signals for the Company's mortars to target the copse, and starts to creep forward. His men follow in single file. As the track narrows, Evengate begins a crouching run until a flare illuminates the track. Evengate freezes. Heavy machine guns – two or possibly three – open up from the copse at the top of the hill.

The men nearest the farm turn and run. Four make it back to cover but others stagger and fall. Evengate himself is trapped. Slowly he scales the wall. At the top he starts to roll his legs onto the level ground. But another burst of fire catches him. His body thuds back onto the track. Roger feels this like a punch in his kidneys.

Other men have been hit. Roger shudders as they scream in shock and pain. The heavy fire continues until the men lie in silent heaps. Most of the Platoon is lost.

Now the enemy artillery joins in, landing shells in the lane. Roger watches with growing disbelief. How has this happened? He has always taken pride in caring for his men. His stomach tightens as he hurries away from the farm buildings before bending to be sick. God, what a horrible taste! He pulls out his flask and takes a swig of brandy.

'The Colonel wants you.'

Temple hands him the field telephone without looking up. Roger takes it and turns away.

'How is your advance progressing?' Mortimer asks. 'Don't let the Canadians beat us to the ridge.'

'Badly, Sir.' Roger wants to be sick again.

'Keep pushing forward, Major. The Company on your right is going well.'

'We've lost most of Evensgate's Platoon. Machine guns on the ridge are firing straight down our line of advance.'

'Try approaching from the left. There's open ground shielded by a wood.'

'We haven't swept it for mines.'

'Major, the whole bloody area has been bombed. Any mines will have detonated.'

'We'll send a patrol to test the ground.'

'No, Major! Your next Platoon must advance! The General insists that we clear the ridge tonight – before the other team can reinforce.'

'Yes, Sir … I'll send Temple's Platoon.'

Roger takes Temple with him to survey the route before the moon drops behind the hills. The meadow is roughly square, some two hundred yards along each side. And the ground is pocked with craters, suggesting the Colonel is right about the bombing.

'Good luck, Antony,' Roger rests his hand on Temple's shoulder.

Temple watches while his men form up. Then he sets off in the lead, gripping his Tommy gun at the ready. The men follow: some stick to his footprints; others take independent lines.

'Watch out for booby traps in the wood!' Roger shouts suddenly.

Then there's silence again, except for the heavy guns.

Temple is ten yards ahead. Behind him the men curse as they advance. Some take long strides hoping to get across in the fewest steps. Others shuffle sideways placing the least weight on the ground and keeping their legs close together: their greatest fear is surviving without their personal equipment. In the long moon shadows, the men's movements look like an other-worldly dance.

Roger clasps his hands together. Temple is nearly halfway across. He used to doubt his pluck but tonight he's coming up trumps. Roger thinks of Evengate and his lost Platoon. Jesus, what a ghastly waste.

A bright flash brings Roger back. Corporal Dutton, the man behind Temple, goes down. Temple turns and starts to come back.

'Keep going, Lieutenant!' Roger bellows. 'For Christ's sake, keep going!'

Temple hesitates. Behind him two men reach Dutton, who has been with the Battalion since North Africa. They squat beside him, administering first aid before signalling for a stretcher.

Temple moves forward again.

Roger turns to two of Stansfield's men who are standing nearby. 'Huggins and Bennett! Quick, take a stretcher! Recover the wounded man!'

Huggins glares at Roger. 'Yes, Sir.' He swears loudly as he sets off.

A shell explodes close to Dutton, followed by a blast on his far side and two more on the left. Did the shell trigger all these mines or was there a tripwire?

Temple turns again. He starts retracing his steps. Another flash. Temple's body is tossed into the air. As it thumps onto the ground, more explosions are triggered. Some of the men keep moving forward; others turn back.

Roger opens his mouth but can't speak. He needs to throw up again. Jesus, what a shambles!

Briefly he considers taking command and leading the last men forward. But that wouldn't be right: C Company needs its commander.

'SERGEANT,' Roger yells, 'SIGNAL A WITHDRAWAL.'

CHAPTER 36

Frank hears a gentle knock on his office door.

'Avanti!' He looks up. A Neapolitan stage whisper emanates from behind the door; Giovanni is warning that the Brigadier has arrived.

Frank jumps to his feet, again regretting Huggins' departure.

'Good morning, Captain,' Carburton shoots a disapproving glance at Giovanni before turning to close the door. 'You and I need a quiet word.'

'Good morning, Sir.'

Frank doubts they can have a quiet word: the boom of Carburton's voice is usually audible right down the corridor.

'Well, Captain, how is the theatre going?'

Frank opens his mouth, but Carburton hasn't finished.

'I'm glad to see Pizz ... etti arrived at the start of September, so the theatre is now in good hands.'

Frank again tries to respond but Carburton gestures for him to wait.

'As you may know, Captain,' Carburton shows his crocodile smile, 'next week I shall be leaving, leaving Naples that is. It will be good to have a change, but I shall miss running this show. Though I say it myself, you and I have made a bloody good team.'

Frank can't speak. He never thought Carburton would leave. Battling against his opposition has been a constant from the moment Frank reopened the theatre. But success had tamed the Brigadier; he had even erected a plaque in the foyer recording his role in the reopening the theatre whilst the war raged.

Frank swallows. 'I'm sorry you're leaving, Sir. I'm grateful for your support in getting the theatre back on its feet. May I ask if there's any more news about your boys?'

Carburton squints at Frank before lowering his eyes. 'The bloody Japs have held them for more than two years. At last we're driving the buggers back, so it can't be long before they're freed. Poor lads, those Japs are a cruel bunch.'

Frank wonders what the Brigadier really wants. Is this a diversionary sally before he launches his main assault? Frank wonders what his target will be today.

'You asked about the theatre, Sir. I think it's going pretty well. Dottor Pizzetti has only just arrived but already we're arranging for some of the stars from Rome to sing here ...'

Frank falters; Carburton clearly isn't listening.

'Intelligence may still need you, Captain!'

'They didn't seem to want me in Rome, Sir.'

'Quite so, Captain! But this isn't for Rome. They may need you in Florence. The Germans have finally withdrawn, leaving the place in a frightful mess. And the natives have some notion that *they* liberated the city. They want to run the place on their own, after they've bumped off all the Fascists, which seems to be most of the populace. Dealing with those partisan johnnies should be right up your street. And you'll probably feel at home with all those paintings of bloody saints. What do you say, Captain? It would be better than returning to the front.'

Frank swallows, trying to digest the implications, especially that final barb about avoiding the front.

'It sounds interesting, Sir. Should I tell Dottor Pizzetti?'

'Not yet, Captain. But I'll let Intelligence know that you're ready to start. They'll approach you directly.'

'I'll wait to hear.' Frank starts to get up but sits down again when Carburton doesn't move.

'Captain, we've worked together pretty well. And I have to say I admire the way you handle yourself. You showed plenty of guts in re-opening the theatre. I didn't always make it easy, but you stuck to your guns when you wanted to stage an opera. I applaud that.'

Frank has never seen Carburton like this; he fears an explosion is coming.

'Captain, you've always listened to my advice even when you haven't followed it. Now there's something I want to tell you, man to man. I believe the time is coming for you to take another bold step.'

For a moment it looks to Frank as though the Brigadier's eyes are welling up, but then he blinks.

'Frank. May I call you Frank? I believe you're quite attached to Lieutenant Henthorpe. You've chosen very well. Like me she admires your boldness, but she expects you to go on being bold. That may mean leaving Naples to do something else worthwhile. You're loath to leave her of course but, believe me, she'll be far more impressed if you're bold than if you just hang around here.'

Carburton gets up abruptly. Frank hurries towards the door but the Brigadier gets there first.

'Goodbye, Sir, and good luck. Thank you for your bold advice.'

The Brigadier raises his eyebrows. 'There's no need to say

goodbye. I'm off to Florence too. Our paths may well cross again. Captain, good day.'

Frank closes the door and leans against it.

Well, well, well. So Carburton is finally leaving. Will their paths ever cross again? Frank had battled for almost a year to contain him. But now with one jerk of the reins he has changed the relationship again: dangling a role in Florence and offering advice about Vermillion.

Frank frowns. He doesn't want to think about Florence. He takes a deep breath.

'Damn and blast!'

Carburton's departure marks the end of an era. Frank's time in Naples is almost over: from now on nothing will be the same.

'Goodbye, Brigadier!' he says out loud. 'Goodbye, Vermillion! Goodbye, theatre! Goodbye, Frank!'

CHAPTER 37

'Must you go so soon, Vermillion?' Margery looks up with wide eyes. 'I'd like to talk about Edmund, if you have a minute.'

Vermillion had dropped in at her old flat to collect her last few things, not expecting Margery to be there.

'I should be at the theatre. Margery. I've got thousands of tickets to sell and with fewer troops around since the landings in France. But a quick cuppa would be nice.'

'I worry a lot about Edmund.' Margery fills the kettle and arranges the crockery on a tray. 'I forwarded the Contessa's letter. But was that the right thing? You know Edmund much better than I do. Will he think I'm interfering?'

Vermillion laughs. 'I had a letter from Edmund out of the blue in which he announced that Frank should return to soldiering. He added that he'd written to tell the Brigadier.

Our relationship ended three months ago, yet he still wants to run my life, and Frank's. No, Margery, *you* weren't interfering!'

'Edmund has a strong sense of right and wrong.' Margery smiles quickly before lifting the tray and heading towards the sitting room. 'He believes every soldier should serve at the front. He doesn't think it's fair that some men are there for months on end while others never hear a shot fired. I think he's right that the job ought to be shared.'

'I don't disagree.' Vermillion flushes. 'But does Edmund say the same about the baby?'

'What do you mean?' Margery doesn't look up from pouring the tea.

'Will Edmund take responsibility for Eduardo?'

'The Contessa became pregnant. You can hardly blame Edmund.'

'Really?'

Margery flashes an angry look.

'I'm sorry Margery. I just feel cross with Edmund. Why did you send him the letter?'

'I thought about it a lot.' Margery clasps the hot teacup. 'I couldn't get rid of the thought that Eduardo might be his. And Edmund has lost so much already, I couldn't take this away. It may sound silly, but I kept thinking that after his … after losing his legs, he might not have another child.'

Tears fill Margery's eyes. 'I'm sorry.' She pulls a small handkerchief from her sleeve and dabs her eyes. 'I couldn't deprive him of Eduardo, if that's what he wants.'

* * *

Vermillion stays with Margery for too long and has to hurry to the theatre. The sunshine is still warm, but the air is fresher and the shade cooler than in August. She feels pleased to be outside.

Perhaps Margery was right to forward the Contessa's letter. Secrets between lovers always spoil things; they make life too complicated. *She* should have told Frank at once about that encounter with Simon. She had meant to, but somehow the time was never right. But would there ever have been a right time? Delaying unwelcome news just makes things worse. She must learn to tell Frank about difficult things even at awkward times.

Vermillion had felt dreadful when Jackie went on about Simon in front of Frank but at least she didn't say he walked her home. No wonder Frank was cross when she finally told him. But he accepted her explanation and hasn't raised the matter again. Dear Frank!

Despite being in a hurry, Vermillion takes a short detour to collect her post and is relieved to find no letters. She feared that Edmund might write again. What he'd said about Frank was bad enough. But he also expressed regret that their relationship ended suddenly. Bloody man! How could he say that, after *he* broke it off! She has had quite enough of his interfering!

A tremor runs through her body. She reduces her stride and takes a deep breath, letting the air out slowly. Why does she feel so cross? It's not like her. And things have been better for the last few days. Frank had struggled in the summer heat but now he's sleeping better although he often wakes in the night. She wishes he wouldn't drink so much, but she knows it's just because he's anxious.

Frank's worries had begun with the fire and then there was Pizzetti to deal with. Now Vermillion fears he will soon leave the theatre. But how will he cope? And what will she do? Should she visit Y Section? Would Captain Ashdown let her return to monitoring German communications. But she wouldn't want Frank to know.

NO! She mustn't think like that. She must tell Frank. There can't be secrets between them. Oh dear, she has so much to learn.

Vermillion enters through the stage door, conscious that there's no one there while still half expecting Huggins to appear, excited about the liberation of Paris. She prays that things are going well for him at the front.

She hurries up the steps hoping to find Frank. Unusually

the door to his office is closed. She stands outside wondering whether to knock. She listens but can't hear voices.

'Are you alone, Frank?' she calls.

'Hello, darling,' Frank opens the door. 'Sorry about the door. I closed it when Carborundum left, in case he returned.'

'Was that the effect he had on you?' she laughs. 'Is he grinding you down?'

'He came to say goodbye. He's leaving Naples next week. It feels like the end of an era.'

'You don't look too sorry. Has the old crocodile lost his teeth? Or wasn't that all he said? Are you off to run the opera in Rome?'

Frank takes her hand and pulls her towards him.

'AMG has already decided about Pizzetti. They no longer need me here, but Intelligence may want me in Florence.'

'Good heavens! That's marvellous! No, I don't mean that, Frank. You know I'll miss you terribly, but Florence is an interesting place. You're bound to like it there.'

'It could be interesting.' Frank sits down at his desk. 'But I hear the city's in a dreadful state after a month of fighting. Every bridge has been destroyed, except for the Ponte Vecchio where the buildings at both ends have been demolished leaving vast heaps of rubble. And the partisans are taking revenge against anyone they think is a Fascist. It sounds pretty depressing.'

'You'll soon have it sorted out. And then I can visit you.' Vermillion stands beside Frank's chair and puts her arm around his shoulder.

'But I don't want to leave the theatre,' he puts his arm round her waist, 'And I want you to be all right. At least you can stay at the theatre.'

'I wouldn't like it here without you.' Vermillion looks away. 'I can't be left alone with Pizzetti.'

'Perhaps you should talk to Ashburn,' he pulls her towards him. 'Y Section will be thrilled to have you back. But don't worry, darling, Intelligence didn't want me in Rome. Why should Florence be different?'

CHAPTER 38

Roger struggles to come to terms with the loss of so many men. He knows he wasn't responsible for what happened, but he felt a heavy burden of sorrow as he wrote letters to seventeen families. Some of the men he hardly knew but others had been around since the desert; he feels their loss acutely.

Despite the exhausting campaign, Roger now finds it hard to sleep and when finally he does drop off he often has lurid dreams.

* * *

A German machine gun post has held up the Battalion's advance for several days. Today Roger's Company is leading an assault on the position. This is especially important because a VIP party is observing the operation.

Roger needs to look at his smartest as he salutes the troops before they march to their starting line. At dusk he signals for the advance to begin and then turns proudly towards the VIPs. General Leese is in the centre with Mr Churchill on his right. Suddenly Roger feels anxious. There's a woman on General Leese's left. Roger focuses his glasses on her. No! What the hell is his mother doing there?

Roger moves away and almost stumbles on the uneven ground. Looking down he sees that instead of his usual black boots he is wearing slippers. He cringes, trying to hide his feet behind a tussock of grass. He doesn't want anyone to see, especially not his mother.

As the advance begins he hears the sound of heavy gunfire but other than intermittent flashes there's little to see. From behind his right shoulder he hears the sound of a single Spitfire which he has called in to support the infantry. That should deal with the machine gun! He just hopes he gave the right grid reference.

He had made a point of also giving the controller the VIPs' grid reference to ensure that they were kept safe.

The plane banks away from the German position, heading towards the VIPs. It must be some sort of fly-past.

No! He can't! He mustn't! The Spitfire is diving towards the VIPs. The plane's engines are screaming. NO! He opens fire.

Roger is about to throw up. He cries out as he wakes.

CHAPTER 39

Frank hears nothing from Intelligence and with the Brigadier gone he has no one to ask. He feels annoyed; he starts to suspect it was just some cock and bull story, intended to provoke him.

But as the summer fades he feels more reconciled to taking the days as they come. He still sleeps badly and has disturbing dreams; and the skull remains an occasional visitor. But he has learnt to keep these things to himself and feels at last he's regaining his grip.

Now that Carburton has gone, Frank can see more clearly his influence on the theatre, where his shadow had hovered for so long ready to swoop if Frank stepped out of line. By comparison Pizzetti is straightforward and Frank finally starts to believe that he wants them both to stay.

The news from France and the Eastern front is encouraging but hopes of the war ending in '44 are receding. Pizzetti won't even guess when the war will finish but he is determined to plan ahead. Yesterday he reviewed next year's performance schedule which Frank had prepared. And this morning together they sketched an outline for '46.

'Let's pop over to the Galleria for some lunch.' Frank smiles as Vermillion hurries into his office. 'I feel the need for a glass of something after that session with Pizzetti.'

'Do you mean now?' She asks with a serious expression.

'Is there any reason to delay?' Frank laughs as he gets up.

Vermillion hesitates; she doesn't look at him.

'I collected the post while you were with Pizzetti.'

She pauses again.

'There was a letter from Pen. Her husband has been wounded in Burma. Poor Bill. She is dreadfully worried, not knowing how he is. They're moving him back to India, apparently, but that's still so far from home. I feel awful for her. I wish there were something I could do.'

'I'm so sorry, Vermillion. I hope they'll bring him home soon.'

She hesitates again, glancing down at the desk before gazing at Frank. Her face is taut with worry.

'There's a letter for you as well.'

She slips it onto the desk, face down.

Frank glances at the sender's name, which is upside down, but there's no mistaking the oversized "B".

'Oh no! Not ruddy Bewdley again! What the hell does he want?'

'If he's booking his next visit,' Vermillion says, 'tell him to write to Jackie.'

Frank snatches up the envelope and stares at Roger's scratchy writing. He feels a sudden chill. He looks at Vermillion; she seems quite calm. Perhaps there's nothing to fear, but already he's starting to sweat. He needs that drink. He considers leaving the letter until they return but an abyss is opening in his mind.

He grips his penknife and slits the envelope. Inside is a solitary sheet. He glances at Vermillion who smiles fleetingly; fear is infecting her too.

He looks down at the letter.

8th September 1944

Dear Frank

I'm writing to tell you about Corporal Huggins. He has proved to be an excellent soldier since he rejoined the Battalion, displaying great courage as we attacked the enemy lines. In yesterday's advance he was hit. Sadly, despite our

best efforts, he died from his wounds. He was popular in the
Company; we shall miss him.

I thought I should let you know. You may want to write
to his family.

Yours ever
Roger

Frank's head sinks forward. He pushes the letter across the table and buries his face in his hands. He rocks slowly back and forth. Tears trickle between his fingers and run down the backs of his hands. Drops spatter onto the desk.

'Not Huggins too!'

Vermillion wraps her arms around his shoulders and presses her face against the side of his head. She clings to him, whimpering in his ear. 'Frank, that's terrible.'

'Damn the bastards, the bloody bastards! DAMN! DAMN! DAMN!'

Frank's shoulders start to convulse. 'Darling … Vermillion … I'm sorry … I can't stay here … I must go to fight.'

PART IV

– October 1944 –

CHAPTER 40

Looking down from eight thousand feet, it's hard to tell there's a war on. In the autumn sunshine, the countryside appears serene, except for the eruption of molehills as shells hit the ground.

But Simon isn't here for reconnaissance. In his new role – the result of big changes in the aerial war – he is circling near the Adriatic coast, close to Rimini, awaiting his next orders.

* * *

After the Normandy landings in June, the Germans had withdrawn their fighter squadrons from Italy, depriving their troops of air cover. With effective control of the skies, Allied bombers have already achieved their key objective of destroying the main bridges in occupied Italy, forcing the Germans to use ferries or temporary night-time pontoons to bring supplies across the many northern rivers.

The Allied air forces have therefore adapted their role to provide tactical support to the infantry and Simon has taken the chance to transfer to a ground attack squadron.

He still flies a Spitfire, but the modified Mark IX fighter is very different to his unarmed reconnaissance plane. In addition to the machine guns and cannons of a normal fighter, this plane carries two 250-pound bombs, clipped under the wings. Being fast and manoeuvrable, the plane can dive onto its targets, releasing its bombs from below three thousand feet. This makes it far more accurate than a normal bomber and therefore more suitable for supporting the infantry.

Simon had leapt at this chance to move to a squadron flying fighters. But at his new base he quickly understood that ground attack lacks the romance of aerial dogfights. In fact the system is more like an airborne taxi rank, with planes circling close to the battlefield awaiting instructions from the infantry about the next target, which might be a tank, a machine-gun post, a truck or a heavy gun.

Time is of the essence with these attacks. Orders often come after troops have mounted an attack and have discovered that the enemy has survived the initial bombardment and remains present in force. Then the squadron can come to the rescue. But these tactics are new and like the rest of the pilots Simon has learnt about low-level flying by trial and error.

With substantial support from the air, the Eighth Army's assault on the Gothic Line started well. Having taken the Germans by surprise, Green I was quickly broken. But the Green II defences at Gemmano and along the Coriano ridge proved more resilient.

Then the weather broke, bringing torrential rain. And for much of September, rain and persistent low cloud made flying impossible. The army's advance slowed and the pilots grew frustrated. Being grounded forced Simon to mix with the other pilots, which he finds hard. For years he has flown alone; now stuck at the base he can't get away from the others, most of whom are young and inexperienced and have only ever flown fighters. To Simon, they're a different breed, flamboyant and egocentric, quite unlike the more reserved reconnaissance pilots.

The younger pilots are also competitive. There is camaraderie between them until one of them starts to falter. Then the group instinct is to stay away, as though whatever bogey afflicts him could be contagious.

To Simon, most of these pilots are living on the edge, swinging from over-exhilaration to self-indulgence. They seem to have little room for other feelings. Increasingly he feels like a fish out of water. As a pilot he is far more experienced, yet he struggles to hold his own. When forced to engage, he takes to saying he has a fiancée. He even shows photos of Vermillion to prove he does like girls. He feels ashamed for doing this, especially when they ask questions about her and why she never writes. He prays she'll never hear about his lies.

The pilots' principal solace is alcohol. Simon has tried this before and has learnt that in the long run it offers little help. This provides another reason for him to steer clear of the crowd. During the prolonged bad weather, he has therefore spent much of the time on his own, dreaming that soon he will be with Vermillion.

* * *

The absence of air support during the assault on Green II had led to losses of more than a thousand men a day. Nonetheless, before the end of September a combined force of Greek, Canadian and New Zealand units had liberated Rimini at the edge of the great northern plain.

And while the Eighth Army was struggling near the coast, the American Fifth Army had begun its advance across the Apennines in early September. By the end of the month it too had broken through the Gothic Line and was only thirty miles from Bologna. It was hard to know where the fighting was tougher: in the mud of the low-lying plains or in the cold of the mountains.

Today the weather is clear and Simon is again airborne. Grass airfields are still unusable but his squadron operates from Fano where the Allies have laid a matted runway of Pierced Steel Planking.

As he circles, waiting for instructions about the next target, Simon's thoughts stray to Vermillion. Today her photograph is safe in the pocket of his flying jacket because he can't take the risk of it floating around in the cockpit when there's serious flying to do.

Simon looks down again, aware that thousands of miniature soldiers are slugging it out on the ground. The war is far worse for them. Soon he will fly through heavy flak but when it's over he will return to the safety of the base. He can't think why anyone would join the infantry when the odds of surviving on the Gothic Line were like the Somme in 1916: in other words, pretty bloody lousy.

Simon understands of course that the plight of German troops – subject to constant dive-bombing – is also dire. British troops had spoken of this terror in '40 during the German blitzkrieg. But how else can the Allies break these defensive lines? Simon has no doubt that the Germans are getting exactly what they deserve.

He starts to hum: "I can't get started with you ..."

But the tune is interrupted by a voice in his ear. He notes down the coordinates of the Nebelwerfer that will be his next quarry. He finds the point on his map and sets his course; he'll be over the prey in two minutes.

He sees the ridge ahead and scans the edge of the copse for the multiple mortar-launcher. From the Allied line a flare arcs up to guide him towards his target. Yes, there it is: twenty yards south from the corner of the copse. He adjusts his course slightly.

He watches as the target disappears beneath his starboard wing. He holds his course until it reappears behind the wing. This is his cue. He rolls the Spitfire onto its back and begins a looping dive down towards 3,000 feet where he'll level out the right way up and release his bombs.

The plane accelerates rapidly. The engine screams and the air rips at the canopy. On the level the plane has a maximum speed of less than 400mph but he's well over that already. The maximum permissible speed is officially 450mph, but in their dives the squadron pilots regularly exceed this.

Simon's plane starts to buck as ack-ack shells burst nearby. Speed is important to get through the flak intact. He scans the dials: 460 ... 470 ... 480. As he pulls out of the dive his body weight multiplies, pinning him into his seat. Blood floods away from his brain making it hard to see. Close to blacking out, he fights to hold the plane. Only just conscious he hardly notices the black puffs of bursting shells that pursue him.

The plane levels out, but the flak still throws it about. Now Simon must focus on jettisoning his bombs. He has to do this blind: there isn't time to search for the target. He follows his standard routine of simply counting to three, confident from past experience he will be in the right position.

He grips the bomb release, aware that on these converted Spitfires the release mechanism can be a problem. Every day, pilots struggle to discharge their bombs. Some have even landed with a bomb wedged beside the undercarriage. Recent orders tell them to bail out if this happens.

"One ... Two ... Three."

Today Simon is lucky and his bombs fall away cleanly. Now he must escape. At only 3,000 feet the plane is at its most vulnerable, flying through a barrage of flak. He pulls back the joystick and accelerates to the maximum climb speed.

At 8,000 feet he is largely free from flak. He banks to confirm the Nebelwerfer has been destroyed. Otherwise he would have made another run to strafe it with his cannons.

Another successful sortie. Simon shakes his head with relief. No longer sweating, he suddenly feels cold. He will fly two more sorties today. And then there will be tomorrow. But he must come through. He has to be there for Vermillion when the war finally ends.

CHAPTER 41

For Vermillion the weeks since Frank's decision have flown by. Having still heard nothing from Intelligence, he finally wrote to Roger asking to return to 4th Battalion. Vermillion briefly protested until she saw it was pointless: Frank had made up his mind.

Vermillion had found waiting for Roger's reply was almost unbearable. But eventually it arrived saying simply: "expect you soonest". After that the time passed even faster with Frank handing over all his work at the theatre. Then finally he received his orders to attend a training camp for officers returning to active service, in the hills north-east of Rome.

Frank leaves tomorrow at dawn. They had decided to spend their last whole day together away from Naples and Frank had chosen to visit the historic site of Paestum on the coast to the south of the city.

Frank points excitedly at the Greek temples as he takes her hand and sets off to walk the last half mile. 'I've wanted to come here ever since I saw these monuments in the distance a year ago.'

Vermillion likes to see him so animated. But why has the prospect of rejoining 4th Battalion had this effect? She fears the realities of the camp will bring him down to earth with a jolt.

'I saw the temples from the Salerno beachhead,' Frank continues. 'After we got ashore, the advance stalled. The German artillery were pounding us from the hills so we were stuck. It seemed just a matter of time before they drove us back into the sea. Then briefly the smoke and dust cleared and I glimpsed these ancient temples twenty miles away. They appeared as a symbol of hope. I promised myself if I survived that one day I'd take a proper look. But I never dreamt I'd come here with you.'

He squeezes her hand and kisses her.

'They do look remarkable,' she looks up at his smiling face. 'It's hard to believe they've been here for two and a half thousand years. It's extraordinary they've survived.'

'Especially with the Yanks landing right here. Mind you, it's quite surprising that any of us survived.'

They walk on in the autumn sunshine. Frank enthuses about the ancient Greek settlements across southern Italy and the importance of Hera, the goddess of women and marriage, and Athena, the goddess of wisdom and just war, to whom the three temples were dedicated.

Vermillion wants to be positive, to leave behind the past weeks which have been so hard. The news about Huggins was a blow for her too, which was amplified by its impact on Frank. And of course Pen's letter about Bill came at the same time. At least when she replied to Pen she could say that Frank was rejoining the infantry.

They stop at the first temple to Hera and walk inside. Frank surveys the rows of columns and looks up at the immense sky. 'It makes me feel very small.'

Vermillion looks around cursorily before turning to Frank. 'Do you really want to go?'

'Most of me doesn't. I've been incredibly lucky to spend a year in Naples with all the excitement of finding the theatre and watching it blossom again. And I've had a marvellous time working with you and slowly – despite my best efforts – falling in love. And then making the wonderful discovery that you were fond of me too.'

He grasps her hand and begins to walk.

'Darling Vermillion … I love you so much. But you and San Carlo weren't what brought me here last year. I came here to fight, to drive the bloody Germans out. Then I heard the call of the theatre and I did all I could to put it back on its feet. And I believe that raised morale. But now I'm hearing a different call. It started before poor Huggins died, but I turned a deaf ear then. Today it's an insistent call which I can't ignore.'

'I know it's important to you, Frank.' Vermillion half turns away, looking towards the sea. 'And I'm trying to listen. But I can't understand a word. What are you trying to say?'

'I'm sorry …'

Frank stops and takes a deep breath. For a while he studies the ground.

'There are times in war …' he edges slowly forward with Vermillion half a pace behind.

'There are times when the only hope for the future is to fight. It's pointless to fight alone so we fight as a group. And strange things happen when you join a group. Your priorities change and your comrades become as important as you …'

'Oh Frank! Listen to what you're saying! You sound like an army recruiting song.'

'God forbid! I know war is terrible and its consequences are ghastly. I know that because I've seen them. Yet there are moments which bring men together, calling forth their humanity. I came to Italy as part of the Battalion. And soon I'll be with them again. How can I stand aside and dodge the rest of the war?'

'This is ruddy Roger's doing!'

'No, Vermillion. The messages are everywhere; you can't ignore them.'

'But Frank, every soldier in Italy is called a D-Day Dodger – even the ones at the front.'

Frank stares at the ground, shaking his head. 'I loathe war and I'm not much of a soldier. Being under fire is terrifying. At Salerno I felt I was going mad …'

He looks at her worried face and takes her hand.

'I'm sorry, Vermillion, but I can't stay on the sidelines anymore, watching the others battle on. I should be there, doing my best for them, and for you and our friends. And for my family, such as it is. I love life and I want to spend my life with you. But I must live for the best in myself. I can't live in fear. I can't hide myself away and emerge when the danger has passed. I have no choice!'

As Frank looks away she sees the tears in his eyes. Once the breeze has dried them, he turns to face her again.

'If I'm killed, I want you to know that I lived as best I could and I have loved you with all my heart and all my strength.'

Vermillion blinks before she looks up.

'I still don't understand. I'm afraid you're going mad. But war is madness of course so perhaps you're just stupidly brave. If you must go, please promise not to be *too* brave. You must come back. The war will soon be over and the world will return to peace. We should be part of that new world together. And please don't tell me what to think if you're killed. But I can promise you this: if you throw your life away, I shall never forgive you!'

She lengthens her stride.

'Vermillion, I'm sorry!' Frank takes her hand to slow her down and tries to kiss her but she pulls away.

'Frank, there's something I have to tell you.' As she turns to face him her eyes are shining. 'I won't sit and wait in Naples after you've gone! As you suggested I have talked to Ashburn.'

Frank swallows. 'Are you returning to Y Section?'

'No, it's being restructured and they can't take me back.'

'I'm sorry, Vermillion.' Frank exhales. 'I'm sure Pizzetti will be happy for you to stay.'

'No, Frank. I do love you but I can't stay at the theatre waiting for your return. I won't be stuck like Pen. Although the Section can't take me back, Ashburn said Intelligence needs translators. There are thousands of partisans and POWs to be interrogated as the front moves north.'

Frank swallows again. 'But that could mean moving closer to the line. You'll be much safer here …'

'Frank! When you say I'll be safe in Naples you sound like Edmund. If it's all right for you to go north then it's good enough for me! Frank, wherever I go, I shall carry you in my heart and I hope you'll carry me too.'

Frank studies her face in silence.

'Dearest and most precious Vermillion …'

He extends a trembling hand.

'… I'm an idiot. Of course you'll follow your own road. You're so precious and I want you to be safe. But you're also spirited and remarkable. I shall worry about you every day but I shall also give thanks for your courage. I shall remember how lucky I am to know you and love you. I love you very much.'

He takes her hand and leans forward to kiss her upturned face. She clings to him, knowing she must soon let him go. At length, he raises his head and gently smooths the tears from her face.

'I had a vivid dream last night,' he says. 'No, not one of those awful ones. This time the war was over and you and I were together in an unfamiliar place. It made me think that we should meet as soon as the fighting stops. We don't know where we'll be, of course, but it should be somewhere in the north. When we saw La Gioconda I was reminded that I've always wanted to see Venice. Let's meet there as soon as peace is declared.'

'It would be wonderful to have that to look forward to. But I'll only agree on one condition.' She looks up and smiles. 'We must stay at the Danieli. My father always told me it's the best hotel in the world.'

'Darling, I can't wait. Now we must pray that the war will be over soon.'

CHAPTER 42

'Why's he so bloody late?' Paolo flicks his cigarette end onto the track below. 'Porca miseria! Sandro, if they've caught him they'll skin him alive.'

'Shut up, Paolo!'

Paolo and Sandro have found recent weeks dispiriting. After the excitement of the bridge and the hold-up, the reprisals in Soglio have kiboshed the partisans' activities which depend on support from the local populace. They have enough ammunition which they have used for some small-scale operations. But Paolo wants to kill more Germans and he feels his skills are being wasted. His only hope is that Falcon will have some better news.

Sandro drops down from the bough of the tree and retrieves the remains of the cigarette.

'Why are you so jumpy, Paolo? You know the English are always late!'

'But even Falcon is never *this* late.' Paolo lights another cigarette. 'If they've got the poor sod, they'll soon be looking for us.'

'SHUT UP!' Sandro scrambles back onto the branch and settles beside Paolo. 'Are you trying to drive us both mad?'

Despite the steady rain, they have a clear view of an ancient shrine carefully placed where two tracks cross. Beneath its broken roof, Paolo can make out a figure, which might be a Madonna. But it could also be a *strega*, a local witch, offering a second line of cover if Mary can't help. Paolo doubts that either would provide much protection from the Blackshirts or the Gestapo.

'Look!' Sandro points along the narrower of the tracks.

Beyond Sandro's arm, Paolo sees the dark figure of an old man pushing a bicycle up the hill.

'If it's not Falcon, who is it?'

Paolo stands up, ensuring his feet aren't visible from the track. He draws his pistol and watches the figure, wrapped in a heavy cloak, shamble up the hill. He stops at the shrine and opens his cloak to take out three fir cones which he places in front of the shrine.

'Good morning, Falcon!' Paolo clicks on the safety catch and drops to the ground. He stretches his right hand towards the man, who throws back his cloak as he turns.

'Good morning Pigeon, Swallow. Let's go this way.' Falcon points along the track that winds up through the dripping woods. 'We can talk as we go.'

'Have you seen *la Volpe*?' Paolo asks.

'There were Germans and Blackshirts down on the road but none up here in the hills. They daren't leave the valleys, unless they come in force.'

'There were hundreds of them in Soglio.'

'That's typical of their *raking* operations,' Falcon says, 'when they take reprisals.'

'It was terrible. They locked the men in the church and the women and children in the walled cemetery and then …'

'You don't have to tell me, Pigeon. It's always the same. How many did they kill?'

'They say it was one hundred and seven, including twenty-three children …'

'And others fled across the hills.' Sandro adds. 'God knows what happened to them.'

'Were any partisans killed?'

'No. They left before the Germans arrived, apart from Swallow and me. We escaped later.'

'Carla was killed as well.' Sandro says.

'That was different,' Paolo says. 'She wasn't a real partisan.'

'Who was Carla?' Falcon asks.

Paolo snorts: he has no wish to remember her.

'She was a *staffetta*, carrying messages.' Sandro ignores Paolo's attempt to silence him. 'This is important! She was the reason Spartaco visited that night. He wanted to celebrate with his girlfriend after the raid.'

'How was she killed?' Falcon asks.

'Spartaco was certain someone had betrayed him,' Paolo interjects before Sandro can continue. 'He swore that if he discovered who it was, he would kill them. He gave Sea Eagle the job of finding out what happened.'

'What did he learn?'

'It took a while before the story emerged. Apparently Carla visited a hairdresser in the valley that afternoon. She was excited and wanted her hair to look special. When the hairdresser asked whether Spartaco was expected, Carla just smiled.'

Paolo checks Falcon's reaction before continuing.

'Spartaco listened calmly to the report. But when it was over, he took out his pistol and pointed it at Carla's head. "Is it true?" he asked. "I didn't say you were coming, I promise," she replied. "Is it true you smiled?" Spartaco's pistol was still pointing at her head. Carla opened her eyes wide, as though she thought he was joking. "I didn't tell him," she grinned. Spartaco stepped forward, pressing the pistol against her temple and pulled the trigger. It was awful ...'

Falcon looks at them in turn and shrugs. 'Have the reprisals affected the group's operations?'

Sandro turns to Paolo.

'There's been a big change,' Paolo says. 'Before the raid, people were excited with the Allies only thirty kilometres away. When the wind was from the south they could even hear the heavy guns. Liberation was close. But now they're angry and afraid, not just in Soglio but throughout the area. They've demanded that the partisans go away. They were already afraid of the Germans but now they're terrified of Mussolini's

Black Brigades and their summary hangings. Without salt they can't keep meat through the winter: they fear they may starve to death. They begged us to leave them alone; then they threatened to denounce us. Without their support, we're buggered. What the fuck can we do?'

'What does Spartaco think?'

Paolo looks down at the clouds nestling in the valley. 'He says it's good for the movement to have some martyrs.'

Paolo wants to inveigh against Spartaco and his crazy political ideas, but aware that Falcon is thinking they walk on in silence.

'I'll talk to Spartaco,' Falcon says eventually. 'He'll have to suspend his operations until the Allies arrive. Then his men can use their knowledge of the terrain to assist the Eighth Army.'

'Will Spartaco agree?' Sandro asks.

'Does that matter?' Falcon says. 'The weather has made flying impossible so he can't get more supplies. He's got the German ammunition, but he needs other things like explosives. Without new supplies, he'll soon be CB.'

'CB?'

'Confined to Barracks. Unable to function.'

'THIS IS CRAZY!' Paolo spins round, glaring at Falcon. 'Don't you understand? It's not a bloody game or a summer sport! Thousands of partisans have been hunted down and murdered or worse. They've risked everything. You can't just hang them out to dry!'

Falcon grins awkwardly. 'I know you're frustrated, Pigeon. But if local people won't support the partisans, Spartaco has no choice. He must suspend operations.'

'And in the meantime,' Paolo says, 'we're expected just to sit here. It's a bloody long time until the spring!'

'If Spartaco doesn't get supplies, you know he'll blame us,' Sandro adds. 'And he still has plenty of bullets.'

'I've thought about that! After I've talked to Spartaco, you'll leave with me. Someone will take you north; there's a new partisan group which needs your help.'

'Where is it?' Sandro asks.

'I can't tell you yet.' Falcon pauses. 'You'll be briefed during the journey. First I must find Spartaco.'

CHAPTER 43

'SQUA...AD! BY THE RIGHT, QUI...ICK MARCH!'

The Sergeant Major's baritone blares out across the make-do parade ground while horizontal hail pecks at the officers' faces as they march briskly ahead.

Despite the constant call for officers to return to active service, the bureaucracy proved absurdly slow and it was already November when Frank arrived at the tented training camp in the Abruzzo region.

'I am a soldier!' he repeats to himself, as icy water seeps down his neck. 'I am a soldier! I am a soldier!'

Frank must ignore these discomforts. He doesn't have time to think: not about the weather; not about anything.

'I am a soldier! I am a soldier! I am a soldier!' He must maintain the rhythm. 'Left … left … left, right, left.'

The square of thirty-six officers is now a hundred yards away. In the murk of the grey dawn they're almost out of the Sergeant Major's sight.

'SQUA...AD! HALT! ABO...OUT TURN! FORWA...ARD MARCH!'

They turn the other cheek to the weather and stride back towards their distant controller. 'Left … left … left …'

Frank finds some comfort in the tempo of the march although his mind longs to be elsewhere.

'Squa...ad, halt!' Frank almost misses the order. He sways forward as the troop stops abruptly. He just holds his balance, avoiding the extra step which would provoke the Sergeant Major's wrath.

'Stand at ease! Stand easy.'

The Major in charge of the camp steps forward. He looks smart despite the sleet.

'Good morning gentlemen. Day seven of your course. Breakfast will be at 0800. At 0830 you'll report to the Assault Course. Then at 1030 we'll meet at the sand table for a test on tactics. At 1130 you'll be at the shooting range and from 0100 you'll practise advancing under a creeping barrage. And don't forget your helmets; we'll be using live shells. Thank you, gentlemen.'

The day wears on. One mortification follows another until Frank's body and mind ache with stiffness and exhaustion. Hour by hour his world shrinks to the army's standard priorities: eating, drinking, sleeping, defecating and staying alive.

Frank's extraordinary year in Naples is now only a dream.

* * *

Idiota! Frank trips on a guy rope. He shines his torch into the darkness outside the tent and wonders what on earth he's doing. *Io son sempre un idiota.*

Why had he been such a fool? What possessed him to abandon Vermillion and the theatre, his two great loves? Was it a noble gesture or does it just confirm he's mad?

He starts to sing quietly:

"Quanto è bella, quanto è cara.
Più la vedo, e più mi piace …
Ma in quel cor non son capace
Lieve affetto ad inspirar."

How beautiful she is, and how precious.
The more I see her the more she attracts me …
Yet I cannot inspire
Affection from her heart.

Moved by the poignant melody, which he had sung to Vermillion on the theatre roof, Frank doesn't hold back.

216

"Essa legge, studia, impara …
Non vi ha cosa ad essa ignota …
Io son sempre un idiota,
Io non so che sospirar.
Chi la mente mi rischiara?
Chi m'insegna a farmi amar?"

She reads, studies and learns.
She knows about everything…
Whilst I am just an idiot,
And can only sigh.
Who will open my mind?
And teach me to be lovable?

'Is that you Frank?' Lodge calls. 'Are you coming to the Mess?'

'I was thinking of turning in.'

'Come on, Frank. A pint will settle you down. You can sing us all a song if you like.'

They grope their way across to the tented Officers' Mess. Frank doesn't feel like socialising. He had felt like this when he arrived in Naples, still reeling from the effects of Salerno. Then, his efforts to avoid his fellow officers – with their endless banter and superficial optimism – led him to explore Naples and discover the theatre. But here, miles from anywhere, there's nowhere to explore.

The mood in the Mess is subdued. The confidence in '43 that the war would soon end has given way to the grim recognition that they still have a long way to go. A year ago, many of them placed bets on making it to Rome or even Florence by Christmas '43. How wrong they were. It took until June '44 to reach Rome and until August to get to Florence. Now no one will bet. Their main speculation is whether they personally will survive to see the New Year.

The officers are a curious assortment who have followed disparate paths through the war. Some have had desk jobs that are now redundant. Several had suffered *holiday wounds* and have finished their convalescence. Others have been ill, often with complications from malaria. Most still have pet complaints, mainly bad backs. The shared privations of the first week's training have brought them together, forging new friendships, but Frank doubts these will endure once they leave the camp.

He picks up the playing cards, which have already been shuffled and cut, and starts to deal.

'I was in Sicily briefly,' Lodge says. 'We crossed the straits of Messina with Monty and fought our way up the Adriatic. On leave in Bari, I met the lovely Raffaella. I enjoyed her company and brought her presents and gave her money to buy food. We began an affair. How was I to know she was a prostitute or an *easy girlfriend*? I really thought she liked me.'

'No bid,' Frank says.

'One heart.' Lodge takes a gulp of beer. 'But once I was back at my unit, I developed symptoms of the clap.'

'No bid,' Wood says.

'When the MO saw me,' Lodge continues, 'it didn't half cause a rumpus. Mind you, if it hadn't been for Raffaella I'd still be at the front.'

'Three hearts,' Black says.

'Four hearts,' Lodge says when Frank doesn't bid. 'They told me VD was self-inflicted and threatened to reduce me to the ranks. But they've lost so many officers that they offered me an alternative: demotion to Lieutenant and an assault course to cure the clap …'

'Double,' Wood says.

'Oh, what the hell! Redouble!' Black grins.

'No bid.'

'No.'

'No.'

'It's four hearts redoubled, Lodge. That could be expensive.'

'We'll see,' Lodge smiles as he sees Wood's lead.

Frank winces as he works out how much it could cost if they lose.

'What's an assault course for the clap?' Black asks as he lays down dummy's cards. 'That assault course today wouldn't cure anything.'

'Thank you partner,' Lodge takes the first trick from dummy with confidence. 'Not a real assault course! It was far worse. They put us in a special camp for a week. Every three hours – day and night – we lined up for injections of bloody penicillin. God, we had sore behinds.'

Lodge quickly draws trumps. 'But the worst thing was getting up twice during the night. They didn't wake us: we had to wake ourselves. And if we missed just one injection we had to start the whole thing again. I tell you it was bloody torture.'

Lodge counts his tricks. 'We made five. I think you'll find that's quite expensive. That camp almost killed me, but it did the bloody job. Now I'm clean as a whistle.'

'You can keep your fucking whistle away from me!' Wood says.

'It suits the Army to make it tough,' Frank says. 'They don't want us catching VD just to avoid the front.'

'Well, if that's their aim,' Lodge says. 'I can tell you they've bloody well failed. I met chaps in there who said the first thing they'd do when they left was to find a girl to reinfect them.'

'They say VD makes you sterile,' Wood says.

'I don't believe that for a minute,' Lodge says. 'They just say that to frighten us.'

Lodge and Black go on to win the rubber. Frank and Wood are silent now as they concentrate on their cards.

'I'm done in,' Wood says as he and Frank win the second rubber. 'And we're up at 0530 tomorrow.'

'Come on!' Black says. 'One more round before we hit the sack.'

'All right,' Lodge says, 'but only one.'

'Did you hear about the chap,' Wood says, 'who had a bad run at poker? Finally, he picked up a royal flush and said a prayer of thanks that his fortune had changed. Then a shell exploded nearby, showering them all with earth. The others

219

ran away. The chap chased after them still holding his cards.'

'That was an unlucky run,' Black laughs while the others groan.

'I wish they wouldn't use live ammo,' Wood says after knocking back more beer. 'Anyone would think they want to kill us.'

'It's their way of reminding us what it's like at the front.' Frank takes another gulp of beer. 'Not that it's easy to forget, even after a year away. Where did you see action?'

'Where didn't I?' Black says. 'In North Africa. Then in Sicily I was hit in the arm. Lodge complains about the VD hospital. The place where they treated me was no better. No one stayed there for a day more than necessary. I wrote to my CO, begging him to get me out.'

Wood turns to Frank. 'What about you?'

They listen in silence as Frank tells his story about North Africa, Sicily and Salerno. And then his time in Naples ending with his decision to leave the theatre to return to the front. He doesn't mention Huggins, of course.

'Bloody hell, Frank!' Lodge says. 'You gave up all that to be here. You need your head examined. I shall tell the MO in the morning you need a psychiatrist!'

'What makes you think we're here to help the bloody army?' Black says. 'When did they ever help us? I'd desert like a bloody shot if I thought I'd get clean away. The trouble is, when they catch deserters they don't half knock them around. POWs are treated far better.'

"Here's an order, Frank,' Lodge says emphatically. 'As soon as you can, you're to find yourself a woman with the clap. That'll sort your head out and delay your return for a good few months.'

Frank looks away, thinking about Vermillion.

'You're not one of those, are you Frank?' Lodge shifts his chair away.

'No.' Frank pauses. 'I was married before the war, but my wife was killed in the blitz.'

'I'm sorry, Frank.' Lodge pauses. 'My advice is still to catch the clap.'

'I'll leave that to you,' Frank downs the last of his beer. 'Perhaps you're right. Perhaps I *was* mad to leave it behind. But if I hadn't, I wouldn't be here with all of you. Come on lads, it's time to catch a few winks.'

CHAPTER 44

Vermillion has felt trapped in a no man's land ever since Frank left. Waiting for her transfer to Intelligence she continues to work at the theatre, but she misses Frank and can't wait to get out of Naples with all its reminders.

It therefore seemed heaven-sent when Margery suggested that Vermillion should join her on a trip south of Naples. She accepted without a second thought but now they've arrived, she's afraid she has made a mistake.

Vermillion glances at Margery, amazed she looks so neat after the slow journey from Naples. Standing in front of the grand house, Margery seems slimmer than ever without her nursing uniform. Her back is turned to Vermillion who is standing slightly behind her.

'Edmund said the house was beautiful.' Margery raises an anxious hand and clasps the bell pull. 'He said it reminded him of home.'

Vermillion responds inaudibly.

'There must be somebody here!' Margery's tugs on the rope, provoking a distant ringing.

'Did you say she's expecting us?'

'Her letter was clear; but we're rather early.'

Vermillion is silent. She knew this visit was important for Margery but she didn't understand why. It was only while they were driving that Margery let it slip: Edmund had made her come, insisting she should see the baby. But if this is just a favour for Edmund, why does Margery seem so tense?

Vermillion sighs. Had Edmund also ordained that she should accompany Margery? Damn Edmund! Their relationship is over; and she doesn't care about his past flings. Yet he is still trying to direct both their lives. She wonders how Margery can stand it. If Edmund had told *her* to visit his putative son, she'd have been livid.

Vermillion stamps her feet. The sunshine is bright but its warmth has gone and there's an autumn chill in the air.

'Shall we wait in the car?' Vermillion clambers back and slams the door. How would she have felt if Chiara had had Frank's baby. Would she have agreed to visit or would she have turned her back?

'Have you heard from Frank?' Margery rubs her hands to warm them. 'You must miss him.'

'It's early days, of course,' Vermillion smiles weakly, 'but it does feel odd. Frank was already at the theatre when I arrived and now the place feels empty without him.'

'You must be proud he chose to go.'

Vermillion feels an inundation of emotion.

'Let's hope the fighting is almost over,' Margery adds.

Vermillion peers through the windscreen, unable to speak.

'Frank and I have agreed,' she says at last, 'that when the fighting stops we'll meet again for a night, even if it means going AWOL.'

'How romantic! Do you know where?'

'Don't tell anyone.'

Margery nods.

'In Venice.'

'Why there?'

'I'm not really sure. But people say the Danieli is marvellous.'

Now Margery is silent.

'Have you seen Simon?' she asks eventually.

'No! Why?'

'Nothing really. I bumped into him last week and he asked about you. He knows Frank has left. He may look you up.'

'Bloody Simon! I wish he'd leave me alone! With any luck I'll join my new unit before he reappears.'

'Are you looking forward to leaving Naples?'

'I'll be sad in a way but it'll also be a relief. For me it has lost its charm. And since Frank left, I've been batting Pizzetti away.'

'You said he's over sixty …'

'But he still gets quite fresh …'

Margery peers through the windscreen, looking for signs of the Contessa. 'Do you think she's had second thoughts about recognising Edmund as the father?'

Vermillion is about to say there's no point in guessing, when she hears the echo of a horse's hooves from along the street.

'That must be her!' Margery flings open the car door. 'Edmund said she liked to ride.'

Watching the Contessa dismount, Vermillion experiences an unexpected surge of indignation that she had slept with Edmund. But why should she blame the Contessa when Edmund openly admitted to having affairs whenever Vermillion wasn't there?

'Welcome!' The Contessa smiles warmly, extending her right hand while holding the reins with her left.

'I'm so glad you could come,' she continues in Italian. 'How was your journey? I hope I didn't keep you waiting. I always ride after lunch while Eduardo sleeps.'

The Contessa studies Margery as she passes the reins to a servant. 'You must be Margery. Welcome.'

She turns to Vermillion. 'And you're Lieutenant Henthorpe. I've never seen a woman in military uniform.'

'Please call me Vermillion. And may I ask your Christian name? I've only ever heard your title.'

'Ah!' The Contessa smiles warmly. 'My name is Maria Immacolata. But that's too much for every day. Please call me Maria.'

The Contessa turns to Margery. 'Please come inside, it's getting cold. Shall we go straight to the nursery? Eduardo should be awake.'

Margery doesn't respond; Vermillion senses her agitation.

'It would be lovely to see him!' Vermillion fills the gap.

'When was Eduardo born?' Margery asks as they arrive at the second landing.

'Almost five months ago.' The Contessa points ahead. 'The nursery is *this* way.'

The Contessa leads them into an airy room filled with old-fashioned toys, presumably passed down through the generations. In the middle a young woman sits on a nursing stool with Eduardo in her arms. She shifts her position as though preparing to stand but the Contessa gestures for her to stay.

Margery walks slowly forward, bending towards Eduardo who gives a big smile and then looks towards his mother for reassurance. Margery bends down until her head is at his level.

'Ciao Eduardo, come stai?' She stretches her hand towards him and he grabs a finger. 'Bravo, Eduardo!'

Margery turns towards Vermillion. 'Doesn't he look like Edmund?'

Vermillion steps closer. He's certainly a fine-looking baby with distinctive blonde hair. She wonders whether Edmund looked the same at this age. Or is the likeness no greater than any other fair-haired child?

'There, that's Edmund's smile,' Margery laughs. 'May I take him?'

She gathers Eduardo and his shawl and holds him against her chest. His smile dissolves into dismay. She envelops him in her arms and cuddles him, but this is too much. Eduardo's bawling quickly fills the room.

'Please don't cry, Eduardo,' she whispers in English. 'You're safe with me.'

He continues to wail until Margery hands him to the Contessa who speaks to him in baby talk. Once he is calm, she passes him to the nurse. Margery watches; she looks bereft.

'Let me show you to your rooms,' the Contessa says. 'I expect you'd like a wash after your long drive.'

* * *

'I hope you'll have a glass of wine,' the Contessa welcomes them into the panelled drawing room. 'What did you make of Eduardo?'

'He's lovely,' Margery smiles. 'Such a jolly fellow.'

'And what will Edmund think?' the Contessa asks.

Margery puts down her glass. She opens her left hand to reveal a small photograph which she passes to Vermillion who studies the picture of a baby harnessed into a pram.

'That's Edmund at six months.' Margery says. 'Can't you see? Eduardo is just like him.'

She turns to the Contessa. 'Edmund will be delighted. He has seen Eduardo's photo, but he wanted me to see him in the flesh.'

The Contessa gives a slight smile. 'Will Edmund agree to be his father?'

'I know he will.' Margery picks up her glass. 'Here's to Eduardo and his father!'

The Contessa embraces Margery. Vermillion joins in the celebration but she can't help wondering why Edmund wants to get involved with a boy he may never see.

'I shall talk to the notary tomorrow,' the Contessa says. 'But I fear it may take some time. The war, and Edmund being in England, will slow things down. But if Edmund agrees we'll sort it out in the end. I'm sure it's for the best …'

The Contessa's voice falters. But she steadies herself and raises her glass again. 'Here's to Eduardo and his father.'

* * *

They spend a pleasant evening with the Contessa, talking about Italy and England before the war and what the world will be like when the fighting ends.

In the morning, they visit the nursery again. Margery carries Eduardo around the room, pointing out some of the treasures. He shows an interest in a red-painted bus, so she tells him about the buses in London. Vermillion can see that Margery doesn't want to put him down as she asks the nurse about his routine. And when the time comes for them to go, Margery blinks away tears as she kisses him goodbye.

The Contessa doesn't reappear until they're ready to leave. She greets them warmly but she looks drawn. It occurs to Vermillion that she has been crying. At the car the Contessa wishes them a safe journey and embraces Margery tightly.

'Shall I drive to start with?' Vermillion asks.

Margery nods as she turns back towards the house. The Contessa is standing at a window holding Eduardo and waving. Margery waves back.

Vermillion takes her arm. 'Come on Marge. We really should be off.'

For a long time they drive in silence. Vermillion wants to talk about what has happened, but she isn't sure how to start.

'I just pray it all goes through.' Margery says at last. 'He's such a lovely boy. I couldn't bear it if something went wrong.'

Vermillion glances at Margery. 'Why should anything go wrong? The Contessa seems clear about what she wants.'

'She's clear now ...' Margery hesitates '... because she wants to remarry. But what happens if that falls through?'

'If she doesn't marry, she'd have even more reason to want Edmund acknowledged as the father.'

'I'm not worried about that!' Margery turns to Vermillion. 'I'm just afraid she might decide to keep him!'

'Goodness. Are you thinking of adoption?'

'Not exactly, but Edmund plans to bring him up in England. That's why I had to come.'

Vermillion is silent as she digests this news. 'Will you take him to England with you?'

'Edmund can hardly collect him!'

'Marge! That's marvellous. Congratulations! When do you hope to go?'

'That may be some time. I have to stay in Naples until Eduardo is handed over and I can't leave the hospital before the fighting quietens down.'

CHAPTER 45

With little progress at the front during November and early December, tempers start to fray. Some in the Eighth Army blame the generals, some the shortages of men and ammunition, and others the weather. A few blame the Americans and rows about Allied strategy. Everyone asks why the hell they're here.

On the grapevine Roger learns the next push towards Bologna has been delayed until after Christmas. Already he's reeling from Joan's letter in which she threatened to leave him. He had written back at once, insisting she should pull herself together. But he feels shaken; he needs to see Jackie again.

Refusing to wait until January, he engineers another seven nights of leave in mid-December, provided he's back by the 18th. This gives him little time to welcome Frank, but Roger feels sure that Frank can look after himself. There's no need for Roger to change his plans.

Having completed the long journey to Naples, Roger is determined to enjoy life up to the hilt. Being with Jackie is as marvellous as his daily hot bath.

'Come here, darling.' He clasps Jackie around the waist, pushing himself against her and almost losing his balance. 'Hold tight, beautiful!'

'Not yet, Roger!' She peels his hand off her bottom. 'Wait till we're back in the flat!'

'Come on Jackie, it's time to celebrate! It's almost Christmas and we're still alive!'

'Happy Christmas, Roger, for ten days' time. It's wonderful you're alive, but I need to get you to bed.'

Faced with the steps up to the flat, Roger steadies himself, but trips at the first attempt. If only Jackie wouldn't hang on so tightly, he could make it quite easily. He braces for another try, wishing the steps would stay still. He stumbles but Jackie has her arm around him and hoicks him up.

After scaling the first flight, Roger feels more confident; he mounts the remaining stairs in a series of charges. But as he gains the fourth floor he nearly falls again.

'BUGGER!'

He rights himself and stands to attention while the landing sways.

'Is this where Ba … Ba … Barbara died?'

'Shh, Roger! Don't wake the neighbours!'

'Aren't they having Christmas too?'

'Quiet! I've got to find my key. There. Shh! The others are probably asleep.'

Jackie tiptoes along the corridor with Roger shambling after her in the dark. A light dances somewhere ahead. Roger sails forward but then capsizes against Margery's bedroom door.

'SHH!'

'It's silent as the grave over here! Except for the ringing in my ears!'

'Is that you?' A woman's voice emerges from the patch of light.

'HELLO!' Roger answers although he's not inclined to stop and chat.

'Hello, Vermillion,' Jackie whispers. 'You remember Roger. We've been out on the town.'

Roger follows Jackie into the sitting room. He gazes at Vermillion who's sitting on the sofa with a book. God, she's bloody pretty!

'Hello, Roger. How's the Battalion? And how's Frank?'

Roger grins.

'Happy Christmas, Vermillion! We're all as fit as fleas. How are you? You look bloody marvellous. We must have a chat, my dear, before I return to the Battalion.'

Roger shimmies towards her and drops onto the sofa.

'Jackie,' he turns, 'what is there to drink?'

'I think you've had enough, Roger.'

'Don't be beastly, Jackie! It's Christmas! Aren't I allowed a bloody drink?'

'All right, I'll get you a beer.' Jackie calls from the corridor. 'But then you must come to bed. We need you at your best for tomorrow. Don't forget, we're going to a show.'

'All right, I've had a few drinks …' Roger beams at Vermillion '… but I have to say you look bloody marvellous.'

'Happy Christmas, Roger.'

Roger detects that Vermillion is no longer smiling and the clouds are gathering. What must he do to make the sun shine again?

'We were shocked to hear about Huggins,' Vermillion says.

Roger's face lengthens as he tries to bring Huggins to mind.

'How was he killed, Roger?'

Roger feels burning in the back of his throat and fears he may throw up. He turns away and swallows.

'That was a dreadful business.' He turns back to face her. 'Corporal Huggins was very brave, my dear. An excellent soldier.'

'But what happened to him, Roger? How did he die?'

Roger grins, trying to get his thoughts straight. 'You don't want to hear about that, not at Christmas.'

'I want to know, Roger. Please tell me.'

'Well, if you must know, it's perfectly simple. The Corporal was shot, my dear! That's what happens in attacks on enemy positions. Men get shot!'

From the corridor come the sounds of more greetings.

'Margery is back, Roger,' Vermillion gets up. '*She'll* be pleased to see you.'

Roger clambers to his feet and sets off to track down his beer but encounters Margery in the corridor.

'Roger! How lovely to see you again! I've been wanting to thank you for bringing that letter from the Contessa. You'll be amazed to hear what's happened since.'

'Glad to have been of service.' Roger pulls himself up to full height as Jackie arrives with his beer. 'Ah, thank you, darling.'

They trundle back to the sitting room. Margery takes Roger's place on the sofa beside Vermillion. Roger is ready to protest until he catches Jackie's eye. Very carefully he pulls up two chairs.

'I was telling Roger how grateful I am,' Margery addresses Vermillion. 'Without his visit to the Contessa none of this could have happened.'

'What's the news about Edmundo?' Roger takes a gulp of beer.

'Eduardo!' Margery giggles. 'You know we went to see him. He's a lovely boy: the spitting image of Edmund ...'

Roger stops listening. He can't be bothered with Margery's prattle. If only she would bugger off to bed. He looks at Jackie and then at Vermillion. Blimey! It's obvious who's the pretty one. But he doesn't want to talk to Vermillion.

'Roger, what have you done today?' Margery asks.

'Jackie and I ... we went out.'

'Where did you go?' Margery smiles.

'The Teatro delle Palme,' Jackie interjects.

'I'm turning in.' Vermillion stands up. 'I've an early start at the theatre.'

'When are you leaving Naples?' Roger smiles.

'I'm off to my new unit any day.'

'Oh! That's a shame!' Roger approaches Vermillion. 'I don't suppose you'll be here when I next get leave.'

Vermillion offers a cheek, which she withdraws at the critical moment, leaving Roger to kiss the air.

'Good luck, Roger. Send my love to Frank. And please look after him.'

Roger's eyes rest on Vermillion as she walks away. God, he'd like to follow her!

'I'm off as well.' Margery kisses Roger's cheek.

'Come on, Roger,' Jackie says when they're alone. 'We'd better get to bed.'

'I haven't finished my beer.'

'Leave it in the kitchen. It's not coming into my bedroom.'

CHAPTER 46

Frank had dreaded the prospect of Christmas from the moment he rejoined the Battalion. And now the day has come, he sees the same unease in each man he meets. Beneath all their seeming jollity is a void. Their thoughts and cares are elsewhere: in the past; or the future; or a thousand miles away at home.

Even the longed-for Christmas mail, which had raised their spirits a week ago, has already been learnt by heart, or forgotten.

Frank has experienced a scramble of emotions since rejoining the Battalion: missing Vermillion; missing the theatre; missing life. And Christmas amplifies these feelings a hundredfold.

He arrived at the camp just as the autumn rains gave way to winter. The snow, which began with occasional flurries, soon settled; and now the flat landscape is a uniform white.

Already in early December, the Battalion was at a low ebb. The men grumbled openly about the broken promise that the Gothic Line would be the final push. And now they face an icy winter of attrition with little prospect of relief. With seven Allied divisions having left Italy for southern France since the summer, the D-Day Dodgers feel abandoned again.

The officers make light of these concerns, joking that Jack Frost deserves a medal for solving the problem of desertions. Men going on the trot had been a big worry in the summer but no one will risk it in the snow.

The Battalion has done what it can to mark the festivities and the men welcome the change of routine. But even their Christmas lunch had been marred by the rumours that other units had butchered local cattle and had eaten fresh meat.

For Frank the Christmas post had brought a card from Vermillion with a welcome pair of thick socks. It was therefore a happy surprise when another letter arrived yesterday with the news that she is moving to Rome in early January to join Intelligence. She also mentioned she had seen Roger, who was evasive about Huggins' death.

231

But most of her letter painted a picture of her happy memories of last Christmas when an audience of more than two thousand had attended the Christmas Day concert at the theatre. And after the performance they had relayed the King's broadcast, linking the troops to their families listening at home. She recalls her immense pride being there with Frank. And then on Boxing Day they had reopened the theatre as an opera house, with a performance of La Bohème.

Frank struggles with this flood of reminiscence and his thoughts keep returning to that remarkable time. He couldn't see it then but now he's clear that already last Christmas he was falling in love. How had he been too blind to notice? But knowing this now makes him long to see Vermillion even more.

Last night he thought about Vermillion as he fell asleep and she was still in his mind as he woke. He felt bereft. And hours later his mood hasn't lifted as he attends the Christmas service, arranged by the chaplain in a snowfield, because using one of the churches that pepper the countryside isn't an option: they are closed to the Church of England.

Frank bows his head against the biting wind, wishing at first he had stayed away. But hearing again the Christmas story – of the birth of an innocent child bringing light into the darkness – he is warmed by feelings of hope. And queuing before the makeshift altar, he feels close to the people who matter most: to Vermillion; to the men all around him; to his mother; and to the generations of his ancestors who also queued with bowed heads to receive the gifts of bread and wine. He gives thanks for them all and for all the good things in his life. And he prays for the end of war.

Despite the cold he doesn't want the service to finish.

* * *

Frank had hoped that a few days at the camp, perhaps a week, would be enough for him to settle in. But now three weeks later he still feels at sea. The training camp was hard physically and mentally but adjusting to life near the front involves a different order of challenge. With no space or time to think, his soul has started to ache.

He still feels like a stranger. And his role in the Battalion doesn't help. When he wrote to Roger asking to return, he saw himself leading a Platoon as he had at Salerno. But instead he is assisting the Colonel while his Adjutant recovers from jaundice. Frank has to do Major Addison's job but without his authority.

It was Frank, as stand-in Adjutant, who had issued the unwelcome order for this briefing on Christmas Day but now the Colonel is late. Frank tries to ignore the scowls from the assembled officers as he stamps his feet to maintain his circulation. Through the fog of cigarette smoke, he glances at the unfamiliar faces. The officers he knew fifteen months ago, apart from Roger, have left – due to wounding, sickness or death.

'For God's sake, Frank, go and fetch the bugger!' Roger declares. 'If we wait any longer, we'll miss the bloody celebrations.'

Frank has seen little of Roger since his return from Naples. He tried to ask about Vermillion but only got half an answer. He's still waiting for a chance to quiz him.

Frank glances at the other officers who clearly expect him to do Roger's bidding.

'Hurry up, Frank.' Roger adds. 'We can't wait all bloody night.'

Frank hastens from the tent. Outside, the camp is dark although a remnant of light endures in the western sky. To judge by the ashen clouds, it could snow again. Ahead, flashes of artillery fire mark the front line but for the most part the guns are quiet. Underfoot the ground is waterlogged; but with the freezing weather the mud has congealed. Frank's leather-soled boots find little grip in the mire.

Laughter emanates from the nearly tents and in the distance Frank hears an unmistakeable song:

"Stille Nacht! Heilige Nacht! Alles schläft; einsam wacht …"

Silent night! Holy night! All asleep; alone awake …

He stops, unnerved by the sound of German singing from across the river.

'Bloody Germans!' He stomps on towards the Colonel's caravan. 'And bloody Roger! Why can't he be more friendly?'

With each step the ubiquitous mud clings to his boots, releasing them reluctantly with an audible slurp.

'Bloody Roger and bloody mud!'

Hoping to make up time, Frank attempts to run. But the slurry covering his ankles has other ideas, causing him to lose his balance and glide gently into a trench beside the path.

'DAMN AND BLAST!'

'Are you all right down there … Sir?' A passing Corporal sniggers. 'Come on lads, help the Captain up.'

'Perhaps he'd rather sleep it off,' the men laugh. 'It is Christmas!'

'Come on, Sir. Up you get.'

'Thank you all. And Merry Christmas.' Frank straightens himself, conscious that one side of his trousers is plastered against his leg. 'I must find the Colonel.'

'He may not see the joke, Sir!'

Frank grins. Gingerly he sets off again. But hearing the men still laughing he turns round as the Corporal lights a cigarette.

'Don't smoke in the open, Corporal! If the Teds see you, you'll get us all killed!'

Frank feels a wave of anger and is still fighting to calm himself as he approaches the Colonel's caravan. He checks no one is looking before taking a swig from his flask.

'The officers are ready, Colonel!' He knocks on the door.

'Thank you, Captain. I'll be there in a jiffy.'

Frank walks stiffly back to the tent. The others are still on their feet, too cold to sit down. Some are smoking but most just stamp their feet and wave their arms. The hurricane lamp overhead spreads a spotty light onto Roger's face as he stares at Frank's mud-caked trousers.

'Haven't you found your feet yet, Frank?'

The others laugh. Frank forces a smile. The others mustn't

know how angry he is with bloody Roger. Perhaps Vermillion was right not to trust him.

'Happy Christmas, gentlemen.' Mortimer marches in. His pink face contrasts with the blotchy grey of the other officers: the heating in his caravan must be a boon.

'May this be the last Christmas of the war!'

'Hear! Hear! Happy Christmas, Sir!'

The officers' united response releases a cloud of vapour into the freezing air.

'I've called you away from the festivities to brief you about our next operation. Our target is Bologna, a vital road and rail junction. We can expect forty-eight hours' notice of our coordinated attack, with Fifth Army attacking from the south and Eighth Army from the south-east.'

Frank knew this operation was coming, but not before the New Year. The Colonel's words come as a body blow. The Colonel nods to Frank; and for a moment he's completely nonplussed.

'The first map, Captain, please!'

Frank picks up the relevant map, one of a set taken from the Italian Army. With a scale of 1:25,000, or two and a half inches to the mile, it shows every house and every bend in the roads and the rivers. The map has been overlaid with the Allied reference grid. And using chinagraph wax pencils on a transparent screen, Intelligence has marked the locations of Allied troops in red, enemy troops in blue and their minefields in black.

'Today the front runs along the Senio River and beside Lake Com …'

'Lake Comacchio, Sir,' Frank emphasises the hard double "c".

'Thank you, Captain. Lake Com … acchio.' Mortimer glowers. 'The Senio River runs north-east from the Apennines towards the sea beyond Ravenna. This is the edge of the northern Italian plain, which extends north-west for a hundred miles across the Po valley as far as the Alps.'

Frank looks across at Roger who raises his hand to his mouth and blows on his fingers. Frank wonders whether he's even listening. Damn Roger! Whatever happens he must tackle him later.

'When the whistle blows for the advance,' Mortimer continues, 'we'll be part of the second wave. Our goal is Imola – here. After crossing the Santerno River – here – there are only minor rivers before Bologna.'

'Tomorrow, you'll move your men forward to their starting lines,' the Colonel goes on. 'I'll brief you then about our plans for crossing the Senio. As you prepare for the advance, I want you to ensure that your men are braced for counter-attacks. We saw at Faenza that the other team can still land a solid punch, even though they couldn't follow through.'

Frank wants to point out that what happened at Faenza was nothing compared to the German counter in the Ardennes which had taken the Allies completely by surprise.

'In preparing for this attack you must remember to conserve ammunition. Our January allocation will sustain only half our normal rate of shelling. Remind the men that shells don't grow on trees. And your plans for the advance must allow for this. Whatever happens, we mustn't run out of shells!'

The Colonel rubs his hands; perhaps the cold is finally getting through. 'Tomorrow night, the men will move to their forward positions. This may not be popular so soon after Christmas and don't be surprised if the other team try a few tricks. Make sure your men are prepared.'

Mortimer looks around enthusiastically. 'Oh yes, I should talk about refugees …'

Frank coughs. Hasn't he noticed they're freezing?

'As you advance, you must expect refugees. If they try to push through our lines, you must move them on quickly to the AMG areas further south. Spies and agents from the other team are sure to be amongst them, along with Fascists. And of course partisans can be a great nuisance. You'll recall those blasted fellows at Forlì who claimed they had liberated the city after we did all the hard work. Just remember, it's not our job to conduct interrogations. Pass them on to Intelligence; let them decide how to handle them.'

236

The Colonel grins. But Frank grits his teeth, reminded of Vermillion's move to Intelligence. At least she is starting in Rome. But what comes after that? He hates not knowing where she is. He does admire her spirit but in his heart he still wishes she would stay in Naples. He wants to know she's safe.

'One final matter, gentlemen. I heard this morning that Lieutenant Smallwood isn't returning to the Battalion but Major Addison will rejoin us tomorrow. Captain Hill will therefore take charge of Smallwood's Platoon as part of Bewdley's Company. Congratulations, Frank.'

Frank can't hide his surprise. Bloody hell. Roger must have known this was coming but didn't mention it. He's glad to have his own Platoon but he must sort things out with Roger.

Outside it's snowing again and by the time they've all filed out, Roger is nowhere to be seen. Frank feels like pushing past the others but he doesn't want to slip again.

Some soldiers are out clearing snow from their drooping tents. Otherwise the camp seems deserted until he hears sounds of merriment emerging from the Sergeants' Mess.

Just then a shadow moves between the tents.

'Get a move on, Frank!'

Frank recognises Roger's voice.

'Hurry up. You've a Platoon to lead.'

Frank turns off the path but Roger backs away. 'Wait, Roger. I need to talk.'

'Not now, Frank. Can't you see it's bloody snowing!'

'Roger, wait!' Frank grabs at his arm. 'Why won't you talk to me?'

Roger jerks his arm free and starts to walk.

'Roger, I hear you saw Vermillion?'

'Frank, forget about Naples. Think about your Platoon. Get them ready to move tomorrow.'

'ROGER, STOP! HOW WAS VERMILLION?'

Roger finally turns to face him. 'She looked terrific,' he grins. 'She was in excellent form.'

Frank clenches his fists and lunges towards Roger.

'Careful, Frank! Don't go rolling in the mud again.'

Frank takes a deep breath.

'There's nothing more to say about Vermillion.' Roger sets off again. 'I spent my time with Jackie.'

CHAPTER 47

Vermillion lugs her leather suitcase a few more yards before sinking onto a wooden bench as a piercing wind tosses leaves and scraps of paper along the platform. She turns away to check her watch. The Rome train is due in twenty minutes but she doubts it will be on time.

She retrieves a tattered copy of the Eighth Army News. After glancing at the headlines, she turns to an article about Lublin, a camp where the Germans had gassed thousands of Jews. She has seen reports of German cruelty but finds this story hard to believe. She drops the paper beside the bench.

She touches her breast pocket. Although her hand is transparent with cold she likes to know Frank's letter is still there. She doesn't need to it dig out: she remembers it word for word. Dear Frank is somewhere in northern Italy, which he says is colder than Naples. She tries to imagine being any colder. Feeling frozen sitting down, she stands up and stamps her feet.

At the far end of the platform she notices several GIs with kitbags on their shoulders. Their uninhibited voices fill the station. She quickly looks away.

She remembers as a child playing on the beach with Pen. Absorbed in the search for rock pools, they lost sight of their mother. Then Pen vanished too. It's Vermillion's first memory of being alone.

She tries to occupy her mind with thoughts about Rome. She runs through what Frank had said. But that was in June, more than six months ago. The city must have changed since then. She wonders what her work will be like. Initially, the prospect of using her languages again was exciting. But now the idea of interrogating Italians seems less appealing. She hopes it won't be long before she moves closer to the line.

Things changed at the theatre after Frank left. Working with Pizzetti was awkward, avoiding his advances. It was so different to those halcyon days when she had worked closely with Frank before Edmund was wounded. That was an innocent time when she hadn't fallen for Frank because she never dreamt he could fall for her. It wasn't until the night of the fire that they discovered they were both in love.

"At last we have plenty of time." How did she ever say that? Since the fire she has had no time. Until now. Today the minutes hang heavy. She looks at her watch. The train is due in less than ten minutes. She glances up. Two of the GIs are ambling towards her. She turns her back again.

Finding herself alone on that beach Vermillion had panicked, until she saw two adults in the distance. With a cry of relief she scampered towards them until she saw they weren't her parents.

Without looking up she can't see the GIs but she senses they're not far away. She won't turn around again. If only someone familiar would appear, even Simon with his offer to fly her to Rome. Secretly she had been quite pleased when he reappeared at the theatre. She had a drink with him at the Galleria where out of the blue he had made this offer.

'I still feel rather guilty,' he grinned. 'You did your bit in Egypt but I never fulfilled my side of the bargain. Now, whilst there's this lull in the fighting, I'm offering again.'

Vermillion almost said yes. She was touched that Simon never took no for an answer and his manner was appealing, like a puppy continually tugging on its lead. But how could she tell Frank? He would never believe it was innocent.

'Don't worry, Vermillion, I won't tell Frank.' Simon said suddenly. 'If you don't tell him, he'll never know. After the sadness of Barbara's death, you deserve a bit of fun.'

'No, Simon. The truth would emerge in the end. I won't betray Frank.'

'Things are pretty dangerous at the front.'

'Don't say that Simon! I've made up my mind, I shall go by train.'

* * *

Vermillion has been in Rome for several days, fully occupied with work. But she is finding it pretty dispiriting to question ordinary people just because their neighbours have denounced them as Fascists, often due to old enmities.

During the day, she can keep thoughts of Frank at the back of her mind. But the evenings are always harder and once the lights go out – often as a result of a power cut – her fears re-emerge. Last night she cried herself to sleep.

Today, with a few hours off, she is pleased to leave work behind. She walks through the centre of Rome impressed by the ancient sites and the splendour of many of the buildings. From the train, she had seen a few bombed buildings on the outskirts but nothing like the devastation further south. And in the centre, there's little sign of damage.

Vermillion stops in front of Chiara's building. It looks solid enough, unlike much of Naples which seems on the verge of collapse. She climbs the steps to the main door, conscious that Frank had been here. He hadn't wanted to see Chiara but at least he learnt what had happened.

From Vermillion's first encounter with Chiara, on the trip to Capri in '43, she has felt concerned about Chiara's predicament since her fiancé's death. The brief affair with Frank was unfortunate: clearly he never loved her.

Chiara had already gone through a lot before the news about her mother and Francesca. Thinking about it here, so close to where it happened, Vermillion feels distinctly sick. She prays that Chiara is coping. If she isn't ... Vermillion can't imagine what she'll do. She just knows she can't ignore her.

Inside, the walls are coated with neglect. Paint, such as it was, is peeling off. As elsewhere in Rome there's no sign of damage from the fighting, yet for years the place has been unloved.

Vermillion hesitates at the bottom of the stairs. Here the building feels damp. Despite the fire, even the steps leading to her old flat in Naples are more inviting. The reek of cats makes her want to turn back, but she cups a hand over her nose and starts to climb.

She stands by the door to the flat wanting to take stock. But, afraid she may get cold feet, she immediately raises her hand and knocks. She tries to fold her arms across her chest but when the cake and other gifts she is carrying interfere, she puts them down on the floor. If there's no reply she will simply leave them there.

Resolving to wait for one more minute, she knocks again. She hears voices and the door opens a little.

'What do you want?' A middle-aged woman pushes a girl away.

Vermillion introduces herself in Italian. 'I'm a friend of Franco, from the theatre … in Naples. I'm looking for Chiara.'

The woman's face breaks into a smile, making her look ten years younger. Vermillion recognises Chiara's sharp features and keen eyes. She takes a rapid breath. Chiara's youth has gone. A year ago, she had called her petite.

'Francesca,' Chiara speaks as though addressing a toddler, 'this is a friend from Naples!'

Francesca looks at Vermillion blankly.

'I've brought you these,' Vermillion stoops to get her shopping. 'How are you, Chiara?'

'Please, come in.'

Vermillion follows Chiara into the dim kitchen where Chiara's mother, wrapped in widow's black, sits at a wooden table. She grips the arms of her chair as she gapes at Vermillion, her eyes darting from Vermillion's face to her uniform and back.

'It's all right, Mamma, she's a friend.'

'Good afternoon,' Vermillion says. 'I'm very pleased to meet you. Chiara has told me a lot about you.'

Mother says something inaudible.

Vermillion smiles and looks away. Behind Chiara, marks on the wall show where a picture once hung.

Chiara follows Vermillion's eyes. 'That was for Il Duce's photograph. Everybody had one.'

Mother watches Vermillion anxiously while Chiara boils the kettle and places the cake on the table. Mother's face moves slightly.

'Make yourself comfortable.' Chiara half smiles. 'Why have you come to Rome?'

'I've left the theatre; I'm working for the army again.'

Mother seems to follow the conversation but doesn't speak.

'Will you be in Rome for long?'

'It depends on the army. Have you heard from Paolo?'

'Paolo, come back!' mother spits out the words. 'Foolish boy! He must come back.'

Francesca doesn't react to Paolo's name. Perhaps she doesn't remember him.

'I'll tell him if I see him,' Vermillion says. 'But I don't know where he is.'

'Paolo come home.' Mother rocks back and forth on her chair. 'He must come home. Stefano will never return. My husband is in Germany.' She crosses herself. 'It's not safe in Rome without a man. Is your man in Naples?'

'No. Franco has left the theatre. He's back in the army.'

Mother nods. She takes a slice of cake and sucks at it hungrily. Francesca watches through large, dull eyes. She doesn't touch the cake in front of her and doesn't respond when Vermillion smiles.

'I had a letter from Sandro,' Chiara says. 'From somewhere in the Fascist north. The Red Cross delivered it but there was no address so I can't reply. He may be brave but he's foolish. If you see him, tell him I forgive him. I just want him home.'

Vermillion wants to ask about the rapes but she can't. She smiles again at Francesca and gets a blank stare in return. She leans back. 'I think I should go.'

'We must open the wine,' Mother nods towards the bottle that Vermillion brought.

'Thank you but I'd rather not in the afternoon.'

'Chiara, the corkscrew?'

'Not now Mamma. Vermillion is leaving. We'll drink some wine tonight.'

Vermillion gets up. She kisses Mother's cheeks through her long lank hair and tries to kiss Francesca without success. She turns to Chiara. 'It was lovely to see you. Is there anything I can do to help?'

'I'll come down with you to the street.'

Chiara gently shuts the door.

'It has been terrible!' She immediately raises her voice as she follows Vermillion down the stairs. 'Poor Francesca! You saw how she is. Her spirit has gone. She's like that all the time, except sometimes at night when she screams in her sleep. I don't know what to do.'

'I'm so sorry, Chiara.'

'And Mamma can't help Francesca. She feels overwhelmed with guilt.'

'What has she done wrong?'

'Don't you know? It was in June. With no money, Mamma and Francesca were starving when the Allied soldiers arrived. Mamma saw two soldiers with piles of tinned food. She begged them to give her some.'

Chiara stops at the bottom of the stairs to wipe her eyes.

'The soldiers were friendly but they taunted Mamma for a kiss. She couldn't stop looking at the food. Eventually she let them come to the flat and she went with each of them in turn. She didn't want to, of course, but she had to get food for Francesca who was already just skin and bones. But when the soldiers were leaving … Francesca, who was hidden away … suddenly appeared … the men came back … they closed the door … one of them grabbed Mamma … while the other one dragged … Francesca into the bedroom … then they swapped around …'

Chiara sobs uncontrollably. Vermillion decides it's enough that Chiara had said they were Allied soldiers. She won't ask her to confirm they weren't German. Clearly ruddy Roger had lied to Paolo. God, he's such a horrible man!

'I'm so sorry,' Vermillion wraps her arms around her. 'That's terrible, Chiara. I'm so sorry.'

Chiara weeps for several minutes, then taking Vermillion's handkerchief she wipes her eyes and blows her nose.

'Chiara, is there anything I can do? Do you need money?'

'There's nothing you can do. We get our rations, which keep us alive. And now the banks have reopened, I have a little money, although the Allies have destroyed the value of the Lira.'

Chiara goes on tidying herself.

'It's different for you, Vermillion. You're clever. You can stand on your own feet. But all we learnt was how to look after a home and a family. We were taught that men would support the family but then they abandoned us to go to war. Now we need them to come home. Until then we live in hope … and despair.'

CHAPTER 48

Frank takes the heavy serving dish and studies the cheeses wistfully.

'I'm sorry,' he says in Italian, 'I can't eat another thing.'

Dottor Enzo Sanudo, in whose house Frank and two other officers are billeted, takes the platter and smiles. He cuts a chunk of pale, hard cheese.

Frank glances at Sanudo, amazed he can eat so much and yet remain thin and wiry. He watches him skewer the cheese and slip it onto Frank's plate.

'You must maintain your strength, Capitano, after a freezing day in the hills.' Sanudo grins as he puts the dish down and lifts a bottle of wine to refill Frank's glass. 'This should go down rather well with the cheese.'

Frank laughs, impressed by Sanudo's dexterity. He studies his face and wonders what engendered such generosity.

'I can't refuse what the doctor orders.'

'I'll drink to that,' Lieutenant Michael Stansfield says in English. 2nd Lieutenant Hugh Purdie and Frank join in a toast to Sanudo.

The Battalion had arrived in the Le Marche region a week ago, for a period of intensive training after the planned attack on Bologna was postponed, supposedly due to bad weather. But widespread rumours blamed the continuing shortage of shells.

They are based in the small town of Sassovivo, which has somehow retained its medieval appearance despite the whirlwind that swept through the area in August '44 when for several days it was on the front line.

The Battalion's other ranks are housed in an old barracks outside the walls. But the officers have been allocated to billets near the centre. Frank, Stansfield and Purdie are quartered in the doctor's house, where every evening the family gathers around the kitchen table to enjoy surprisingly abundant food and wine.

Frank can't quite believe their good luck. He wonders where all the food comes from. During their occupation the Germans had issued dire threats against hoarding of every kind. And as they retreated last summer they engaged in a frenzy of destruction: destroying crops, stealing horses, killing cattle and burning anything that might sustain the Allied armies. Yet in Sassovivo food survived. Perhaps centuries of invasions have taught the inhabitants how to hide their provisions from marauding armies.

Since the officers arrived, Sanudo has talked a lot about the local partisans. Tonight, he is insisting that they liberated Sassovivo before the Allies arrived. Frank listens attentively. He wonders whether the story is entirely true, but there's no doubting Sanudo's pride in what they had achieved. He and his neighbours hold their heads high in the presence of the Eighth Army.

Stansfield waits for Sanudo to finish before asking in hesitant Italian whether all partisans are Communists. Sanudo laughs before explaining there are partisans of every political hue. He is of the left, of course. His outlook is liberal, but he has a strong aversion to the right, and with no Social Democrat partisans in the area, he threw in his lot with the Communists. And everything that has happened since – the killing and torturing of civilians and partisans, the burning of property, and the vicious reprisals – has only increased his hatred of Nazis and Fascists.

Perhaps because the officers now feel settled, the gathering this evening is more lively and Sanudo is especially generous with the wine. He slaps Frank on the back and raises his voice above the background clamour.

'Well, Capitano,' Sanudo strokes his moustache, 'thank God that you British behave better than those hateful Germans! Those butchers who murdered a hundred civilians, mostly innocent bystanders, in reprisal for partisan attacks. They also killed many partisans – twelve were shot right here, in the piazza by the church.'

'Did *you* have to fight?' Stansfield asks.

'I was a partisan because I had to rescue something from this dreadful war. But I didn't fight. I looked after the partisans' medical needs. That was difficult enough. I travelled extensively to care for the wounded. And it was hard getting partisans into hospital, because the medical staff were forced to report anyone with bullet wounds. If the Germans had caught me they would certainly have killed me. Assisting the partisans was considered as bad as being one. Fortunately, the hospital here is run by nuns who took great risks to hide our patients.'

'It was a terrible time,' Signora Sanudo says. 'I worried about Enzo night and day.'

'I give thanks to all the saints that the killing is over,' Sanudo's mother says without looking up.

Frank leans forward to thank Sanudo for his hospitality. But his voice is lost in the hubbub. Seizing his glass, he scrambles to his feet causing the dog to join in the commotion.

'Dottore, ladies and gentlemen,' he says in Italian. 'As the senior British officer present, I want to thank you, Dottore, and your delightful family for welcoming us so warmly to Sassovivo. And especially I want to thank you, Signora Sanudo, and your lovely daughters, Cecilia and Laura, for preparing this marvellous feast. I speak for all of us when I say we are moved by your hospitality. I'd like to propose a toast to the liberation of Italy and the friendship of Italy and Britain.'

The three officers raise their glasses and drink heartily. The family breaks into applause and the dog barks again as Sanudo rises to his feet. He's taller than most Italians and peers down at the seated officers over the rim of his spectacles.

'Thank you, Capitano. Thank you.'

He looks around at the others. 'I find it hard to speak, not because of the tears in my eyes but because of the tears in my heart. Dear friends and representatives of the British armed forces, despite Mussolini's propaganda about the wickedness of the Allied troops, you cannot imagine the gratitude we feel to you and your comrades for ridding our country of the scourges of Nazism and Fascism. We know that what you have done and are doing comes at a great cost. We Italians are ashamed and deeply sorry that for more than three years we fought against you in this dreadful war. But since September '43, we partisans and the CIL have fought alongside you, as we did in 1915. And together we are achieving great things. Let us drink to the liberators!'

Everyone applauds until Sanudo raises his voice calling for calm. The dog takes this opportunity to lift his front legs to the tabletop.

'Silence! Please!' He strokes the dog's head. 'We need some soothing music. Girls, what do you suggest?'

Frank watches the girls as they decide. Cecilia, at nineteen, is two years older than Laura and much more assured. With her long black hair and open face, Cecilia clearly appeals to Stansfield and Purdie.

Cecilia walks to the end of the room and opens the upright piano that stands against the wall. Laura joins her. Cecilia plays a simple introduction to a charming ballad which the girls sing together. Cecilia, the more confident singer, has a clear soprano voice.

This is the first music Frank has heard since leaving Naples; it brings a longing to hear more. He wonders whether he might manage to sing. He clears his throat gently whilst Sanudo discusses with the girls what should come next.

Having won the argument, Sanudo stands beside the piano as Cecilia plays the introduction to "Vivere", a song popularised in the '30s by Carlo Buti. It's the bittersweet tale of a young man who has lost his girl but insists on living life to the full, now that he's free.

"Vivere, senza malinconia! Vivere, senza più gelosia!"

Live, without melancholy! Live, without further jealousy!

Sanudo's voice is a light and subtle tenor which fills the room with warmth. Frank breathes deeply. This is the true sound of Italy, determined to enjoy what the world offers despite life's hardships.

Sanudo finishes to great applause. He looks across at the three officers. 'How about an English song?'

Cecilia glances at Frank from the corner of her eye. Frank looks at the other officers who both shake their heads.

'Capitano,' Sanudo addresses Frank directly, 'would you honour us with a song? Your companions tell me you have an excellent voice.'

Frank laughs. 'I'm grateful for their confidence. But I fear it's misplaced. I haven't sung for a long time.'

He squeezes past the Nonna to get to the piano, wondering what on earth to sing. He empties his glass and places it on top of the piano. Then he sits down and swallows. He flexes his fingers, surprised by the roughness of his hands.

He sits up, pulling back his shoulders, afraid this wine-induced haze will prove disastrous.

'Here goes!' he says to himself, beginning to play a steady march:

'We're foot – slog – slog – slog – sloggin' over Italy!
Foot – foot – foot – foot – sloggin' over Italy –
(Boots – boots – boots – boots – movin' up and down again!)
There's no discharge in the war!

Seven – six – eleven – five – nine-an'-twenty mile to-day –
Four – eleven – seventeen – thirty-two the day before –
(Boots – boots – boots – boots – movin' up and down again!)
There's no discharge in the war!'

Frank is into his stride. His fingers find most of the notes and his voice steadies. Stansfield and Purdie join in the refrains.

Fabio, the only son, watches Frank thoughtfully. Perhaps he's dreaming of becoming a soldier.

'Don't – don't – don't – don't ...'

Frank's fingers falter. 'I'm sorry.' He flexes his fingers and starts again.

'Don't – don't – don't – don't – look at what's in front of you.
(Boots – boots – boots – boots – movin' up and down again!)
Men – men – men – men – men go mad with watchin' 'em,
And there's no discharge in the war!

Try – try – try – try – to think o' something different –
Oh – my – God – keep – me from goin' lunatic!
(Boots – boots – boots – boots – movin' up and down again!)
There's no discharge in the war!'

Frank smiles at Fabio as he starts the final verse of Rudyard Kipling's Boots. Fabio grins admiringly.

'I – 'ave – marched – six – weeks in 'Ell an' certify
It – is – not – fire – devils – dark or anything,

But boots – boots – boots – boots – movin' up and down again!)
An' there's no discharge in the war!'

Sanudo leads the applause. 'Thank you, thank you, Capitano. Your comrades were right. You have an excellent voice. How about another song? Perhaps something less military?'

Frank is relieved to have got though the song. He takes his glass, which someone has refilled, and downs a hefty swig. He looks at Cecilia across the room and wonders whether she would sing a duet. But what songs she might know?

He catches her eye and calls to her. 'Do you know this?'

He starts to play an introduction. Cecilia slips across the room. She flashes a look that says she recognises the music but doubts its suitability. Frank's cheeks burn. Surely she doesn't think he's suggesting anything. But he's committed, so he starts to sing.

"Là ci darem la mano.
Là mi dirai di sì:
Vedi, non è lontano,
Partiam, ben mio, da qui."

There, I give you my hand
There, you agree
Look, it isn't far
Let's depart, my dear, from here.

Frank fixes his eyes on the keyboard as he prepares for the next verse – Zerlina's response to Don Giovanni's attempted seduction. From the corner of his eye he sees Cecilia step towards the piano. She smiles as he looks up. Frank closes his mouth to let her sing.

"Vorrei e non vorrei,
Mi trema un poco il cor,
Felice, è ver, sarei,
Ma può bularmi ancor!"

I'd like to and I don't want to
My heart trembles a little
It would be happy, it's true
But it could deceive me again

Frank grins, trying to hide the panic rising inside.

'Vieni, mio bel diletto,' – Frank can't look up.
'Mi fa pietà Masetto,' – Cecilia sings strongly.
'Io cangierò tua sorte.' – Frank focuses on the keys.
'Presto ... non son più forte.'– Cecilia touches Frank's arm.
'Andiam!' – Frank struggles to stay calm.
'Andiam!' – Cecilia sings sweetly.

Don Giovanni: Come my sweet delight
Zerlina: I feel sorry for Masetto
Don Giovanni: I will change your fate
Zerlina: Soon, I'll lose my strength
Don Giovanni: Let's go!
Zerlina: Let's go!

Now together! Frank wants to look at her but daren't. He concentrates on singing as vigorously as he can.

'Andiam, andiam, mio bene,
A ristorar le pene
D'un innocente amor.'

Let's go, let's go, my dear
To restore the happiness
Of an innocent love.

There's a great burst of applause. Frank stands up. He smiles at Cecilia. Her dark eyes seem larger. They bow together as the others continue to applaud.

'Thank you,' Frank raises her hand and kisses it. 'You sang that beautifully.'

'Thank you, Franco.' She rises on tiptoe and pecks his cheek.

Frank shivers with horror and delight. These feelings are as dangerous as they're unexpected. He turns to Signora Sanudo. 'Thank you all for a wonderful evening. We've had a marvellous time.'

'Thank you for entertaining us, Capitano.' She turns away. 'Now, come along Fabio. Come along girls, you must go to bed. Your grandmother is already upstairs.'

'There's more wine on the sideboard,' Sanudo says gently to Frank. 'But please be quiet when you come up.'

'Yes, Dottore. We'll be as quiet as mice.'

After more expressions of goodwill and more "good nights", the door closes and the officers are left alone.

'Gosh, Sir, you've got a marvellous voice,' Stansfield says. 'No wonder Cecilia is keen on you.'

Purdie laughs as he fills their glasses to the brim.

'It was a pleasure to sing with her,' Frank tries to suppress a smile. 'She has a lovely voice.'

'That's not all she's got,' Stansfield says.

Frank lifts his glass and studies him over the rim; he's hardly older than a boy.

'Sorry, Sir. I didn't mean to be rude but she's jolly pretty. I wish she were keen on me.'

'I prefer Laura,' Purdie says. 'I like her slender figure.'

'Which one do you prefer, Sir?' Stansfield asks.

Frank had hardly noticed Laura but Cecilia has stirred something deep inside. It might be love or romance or simply lust. Whatever it is, it has left his head in a whirl but he's damned if he's going to let on.

'I hope you both enjoyed yourselves,' Frank says.

'Oh yes, it was bloody marvellous, Sir,' Purdie says. 'Better than Christmas at home.'

'Hugh,' Frank smiles at Purdie, 'we've had enough of this formality. Please, no more 'Sir'. I know I must seem very old but I want you to call me 'Frank'. When you say 'Sir' all the time it reminds me of my batman, Huggins. I refused to drink with him until he stopped calling me Sir. He was killed in September. Did you know him?'

Purdie glances at Stansfield who stares down at his glass. 'I didn't join the Battalion until October,' Purdie says.

'I remember Corporal Huggins.' Stansfield avoids Frank's gaze. 'He died soon after I arrived.'

Frank sits forward.

'It was a rotten show.' Stansfield adds.

'It was very sad.' Frank sees an image of Huggins' smiling face. 'He was a very good man.'

'I didn't really know him,' Stansfield continues looking down. 'I just know it was dreadful how he died.'

'What happened?'

Stansfield knocks back some more wine and begins, haltingly, to describe how, as Huggins' unit was advancing towards the Green II defensive line, an Allied fighter strafed them. 'We knew at once they were finished. Something had gone terribly wrong.'

Frank closes his eyes and sees Huggins being shot to pieces. He presses his hands across his mouth to stop himself from shouting.

'That's terrible!' Frank opens his eyes wide. 'What a bloody waste! How the hell could that have happened?'

'It was clearly a dreadful cock-up, Sir.' Stansfield looks shaken. 'But nothing was ever said.'

Frank stands up. 'Now we'd better get to bed. We've an early start tomorrow.'

The others jump to their feet.

'Good night, Sir.' Purdie says.

'Good night, Michael, Hugh.'

'Good night, Frank.'

Frank opens the door and creeps up the cold staircase to the second floor. The house is silent. He wonders whether Cecilia is asleep. As he enters his bedroom, he sees a large shape beneath the blankets on his bed. He carefully removes the bowl of hot cinders and the *prete*, the wooden frame designed to stop the bedclothes catching fire.

The sight of red embers makes Frank shiver. He sinks down on the bed knowing he won't sleep. He needs to think. A wonderful evening had ended with the awful news about Huggins. Bloody Roger! Why hadn't he explained? Does he feel guilty? He damn well should.

Frank tiptoes across to the dressing table that serves as a desk. He angles the candle to avoid facing the flame and starts to write.

CHAPTER 49

'Wait in here, Miss,' the Sergeant grins. 'The Major won't be long ... if you're lucky!'

Vermillion surveys the windowless canvas enclosure. In the distance she can hear the steady thud of heavy guns. The Sergeant told her the camp is out of range for the Germans but she doubts he really knows. She flinches at every blast.

She arrived at the tented camp, ten miles south of the line, during the previous night. This morning she visited the wire cages where prisoners are held until their future is decided. She knows they must be held securely – some of them could be dangerous – but the sight of prisoners caged like animals was shocking. And the sound of their catcalls as she walked past still rings in her head.

After standing for long enough, she sits down on a hard chair facing the large veneered desk and tries to imagine the Major. She smooths her hair and tightens her tie to look smarter. Then she stretches her back, which is stiff from the journey from Rome. But last night she had slept well. Now she can't wait to start work: she has missed the reassurance of a steady job.

She smiles at the thought that she's closer to the line than Frank. She was very glad to learn he's having a good time, although the news about Huggins is awful. She takes out his recent letter and skims through it again.

Darling Vermillion,

How I miss you! I want to feel you near me. I want to kiss you and hold you. I want to hear your voice and know you are well.

A lot has happened since my last letter. In brief, I've been immensely lucky! The Battalion has left the line and is now training intensively. I can't tell you what we're training for but you can probably guess. It's demanding but I'm feeling fitter and have lost a few pounds here and there, mostly there.

Roger is in hospital with malaria. But before we moved, I was asked to lead one of the Platoons in his Company. I'm delighted. There are even some old faces still around and I'm feeling more at home.

But the truly lucky part is being billeted with a delightful family. Dottor Sanudo, a real medical doctor, is a charming fellow who helped the partisans around here. He and I have had some serious late-night chats about the war and what will happen when it ends.

Sanudo's wife, Anna, is a true Italian Mamma. She mothers the whole household, which now includes me and the two other officers from the Company. Stansfield and Purdie are good lads although they are hardly more than boys. They treat me like an uncle.

The elder girl, Cecilia, is nineteen and is pretty, with large eyes and long black hair; Laura is seventeen and good looking in a more diffident way; and finally Fabio is a tall lad of fifteen who is wide-eyed about everything military. He told me that until last summer he had never seen a tractor let alone a tank.

After dinner tonight Dottor Sanudo sang and then I had a go. And the girls sang too. Cecilia had a lovely voice, as befits her name. I thought we might sing a duet and the

first thing that came to mind was 'Là ci darem la mano' from
Don Giovanni.

*After the family went to bed the three of us stayed up
to chat. We got onto the subject of Huggins. Stansfield was
there when he was killed. Apparently, Huggins' unit was
attacking an enemy position when an Allied fighter mistook
them for enemy troops and strafed them. Huggins never had
a chance.*

*Darling, I miss you so much. I love you and long to
see you. I think about you all the time, wondering what
you're doing and how you are. I hope things are going
well. I feel sure you're doing fine. I just pray that I'm
right.*

*Sadly, I see no prospect of getting leave. Instead I'm
focusing on the end of the war and seeing you in Venice. I
must say goodnight now but I shall dream of you beside the
Grand Canal.*

With all my love
Frank

Vermillion folds the letter carefully. She will write back
once the first interrogations are over.

Hearing voices, she stuffs the letter away just as the canvas
door is swept open. She jumps to her feet. As she watches the
Major stride in she is hit by the thought that his head looks just
like an egg which has grown a moustache. The Major stares
back at her, as though something unpleasant has been caught
in his net.

'Who on earth are you?' He looks her up and down. 'Great
Scott! We really are scraping the barrel.'

Vermillion stands to attention and salutes. 'Henthorpe,
Lieutenant Henthorpe, Sir. Intelligence sent me from Rome.
They said you might need help with interpreting.'

'What lingo do you speak?'

'German and Italian, Sir. And some French.'

'And some French! That *will* be useful. Do you know anything about Intelligence, Lieutenant? It's not just about translating.'

'I worked with Y Section in Egypt, Sir, and I've been to several lectures in Rome.'

'Several lectures, eh? That should have cracked it. Tell me, what's the role of Intelligence on the battlefield?'

'The collection, collation, interpretation and dissemination of all information about the enemy, Sir.' Vermillion quotes from the Field Service Pocket Book.

The Major looks up. 'And what about the situation at the front? Do you know anything about that?'

'The Italian front, Sir?'

He raises his eyebrows. 'If I were asking about the Burma front I'd have said. Lieutenant, pull your socks up, or whatever you wear. Of course, I mean the Italian front.'

Vermillion takes a deep breath and lets it out slowly.

'Since the advance on Bologna was postponed, Sir, both sides are spread out along their winter lines awaiting the spring offensive. But there's skirmishing along the near bank of the Senio as we drive the Germans from their bunkers in the floodbanks.'

'And which German units are facing Eighth Army?'

'Units from the German 10th Army, Sir. There's 73rd Corps and 76th Panzer Corps in the east, then 1st Fallschirmjäger Corps and 14th Panzer Corps to the west.'

He strokes his moustache as he studies his notes. 'What reports do you read, Lieutenant?'

'Excuse me, Sir ...' The Sergeant interrupts.

'Quiet, man!' The Major keeps his eyes fixed on Vermillion.

'I've seen all the Eighth Army reports, Sir.'

'Read the Fifth Army ones as well!'

'Yes, Sir.'

The Major turns. 'What is it Sergeant?'

'Sorry to intrude, Major Rummage, but the prisoners are ready.'

'All right, Sergeant, bring the first one in.'

The Sergeant salutes and marches off. The Major sits back. 'You'd better come over this side, Lieutenant. Unless you want to sit with the prisoners.'

Vermillion looks up. The Major is grinning at her. She walks to his side of the table and perches on one of the empty chairs. At least now she won't need to look at Rummage. That *was* the name the Sergeant had used. And wasn't Rummage the fellow that Frank saw in Rome, who spoke such awful Italian?

She lifts her eyes again as a young Italian is marched in. He is well dressed and clearly takes good care of himself. His hair has been recently cut and his fingernails are manicured. He was picked up two days before, crossing the line from the north.

'I was with a group of partisans in Lombardy,' the man says in rapid Italian, which Vermillion translates. 'We had two airmen from the RAF who were desperate to reach their bases in the south. I escorted them across the line. But we were caught in the snow at night and I lost them. Did they make it to their units all right?'

'I don't believe you,' the Major cuts in. 'You never met those men. They died when their plane came down. You don't come from the north. You come from Rome. I think you were sent to spy.'

'No Major! That's completely wrong. I come from the city of Bergamo, north-east of Milan,' he looks the Major in the eye.

'I know where Bergamo is!' The Major studies Vermillion as she translates.

'Tell me about famous people from Bergamo,' she adds.

'Bergamo is very small,' the young man laughs. 'It isn't well known.'

Vermillion is about to respond but the Major raises his hand to stop her.

'Major, this is important!' she says in English before turning to the young man and continuing in Italian. 'Who was the famous opera composer from Bergamo?'

'This is a stupid question!' the prisoner turns back to the Major.

'And what is your *stupid* answer?' the Major asks.

The man glares back at Vermillion. 'I can't quite remember. I'm not very keen on opera. Perhaps it was Maestro Rossini.'

The Major turns to Vermillion who shakes her head.

'If you don't come from Bergamo,' the Major says, 'where do you come from? Tomorrow you'll start your story again. And I expect you to tell me the truth. Do you understand?'

The man jumps to his feet in protest.

'Quiet! Sergeant, take him to the cage!'

As soon as the man has gone, the Major takes out his Players cigarettes and offers one to Vermillion. He lights them both and sits back, stroking his moustache.

'I met a fellow once from Naples who worked at the opera house. He fancied himself as a linguist but when I tested him he couldn't understand a word. He wanted to join Intelligence, but he would never have fitted in.'

CHAPTER 50

The men in Frank's Platoon look done in after a long day of training in the freezing weather. But Frank still sets a brisk pace for the march back to Sassovivo. Dusk is approaching and bloody streaks are slashed across the western sky. Flurries of snow swirl in the biting wind.

The men's grumbling is audible above the sound of their boots. Since dawn they have practised constructing light pontoon bridges, the sort they will use when crossing small rivers. Inevitably many of them got wet and they now feel deeply chilled.

Before they moved off, Frank had shared his hip flask liberally, which lubricated their muttering. Now he maintains the fast pace for fifteen minutes, until he judges they've all warmed up. Then he drops back to the rear of the column and clears his throat.

In their late-night conversations Sanudo has encouraged Frank to sing and to get the men singing too. He described how at the bleakest times the partisans had always remembered to sing to lift their spirits. Frank decides to try the doctor's prescription.

'It's a Long Way to Tipperary ...' he sings at full volume. He signals for the men to sing too. Some don't seem to know the words and it takes several repetitions before the whole Platoon joins in. At that point he switches to Lili Marlene, first in the original English translation and then as the D-Day Dodgers' song.

It still takes a while for all the men to engage fully and produce a lusty growl. But as they approach the main archway into Sassovivo, Frank switches back to Tipperary. Inside the medieval town, the narrow streets and high walls concentrate the men's voices and the drumming rhythm of their feet. Pleased with this effect, they raise the volume.

They pass the communal washhouse where the women shout and wave their fists but Frank doesn't restrain the men. They march on proudly through the central piazza to the far side of the town where they halt beside the old barracks. Frank congratulates them on their singing before announcing: 'choir dismiss!'

Sanudo's medicine seems to work on the men but Frank doubts it will work on him. Sanudo is observant and has noticed his aversion to fire. He has asked Frank about this several times. Finally Frank told him about Barbara. That was quite enough. He just hopes Sanudo will let the matter drop.

Frank turns and walks back towards the central piazza, passing an ox wagon delivering firewood. The empty streets are dark, but the outlines of buildings are still visible against the pastel sky. He finds the place where the partisans were shot in June and runs an eye over the names of the martyrs daubed on a rough wooden board. How shocking they were killed in cold blood. But how many others had died in liberating the town, including British soldiers? Shouldn't their names be listed too?

Frank sets off towards the doctor's house pleased the men have started singing. Provided his own voice holds up he will train them into a choir. He enters the house expecting to see the doctor in the kitchen as usual. Instead he finds him on his knees lighting a log fire in the large hall.

When he notices Frank, Sanudo sits back on his heels. 'Good evening, Capitano. Come and sit over here. You must be frozen after a day outside.'

'Dottore, good evening. I trust the people of Sassovivo are fit and well.'

Frank glances anxiously at the fireplace. He coughs before sitting down with his back to the blaze. Still the tang of burning wood fills his nostrils, and he jumps each time a twig spits.

He gets to his feet again. 'I'm sorry, Dottore. I'm going to my room.'

'Stay here, Capitano, where it's warm. Join me in a glass of brandy. I need something to settle me down.'

'No, Dottore, thank you.' Frank coughs. 'I must go up.'

Sanudo touches Frank's arm as he brushes past. 'Is it the fire again? Have you considered what makes you afraid?'

Frank swings around, clenching his fists.

He glares at Sanudo. 'It's better if I'm alone.'

'Capitano,' he says gently, 'why can't you look at the fire?'

Frank bristles.

'It's all right, Capitano,' Sanudo continues. 'I won't force you. Sit over there while I get you a drink.'

'I'd rather stand, Dottore.'

Sanudo pours a large Italian brandy and hands it to Frank who takes a gulp.

'Capitano, has this gone on for long?'

Frank knocks back some more brandy. The liquid burns in his throat but it isn't the alcohol that makes his heart pound and his skin start to sweat. He moves closer to the stairs.

'It might help if you could talk, Capitano!' The Dottore grasps his sleeve. 'Of course it's hard as a soldier to admit you're not in control. But it can happen to anyone, even the bravest of men.'

Frank half turns. He contemplates the doctor's face, which slowly comes into focus. It isn't handsome but the features are fine and the eyes suggest curiosity about the world and compassion for its inhabitants. But for Frank it's a dangerous face.

He sips the brandy again and walks slowly to the nearest chair where he sits upright on the front of the wooden seat.

'I told you before, Dottore. In the summer ...'

Frank coughs and has to clear his throat.

'... in the summer there was an air raid in Naples. The building where my girlfriend lived was set on fire. No, she wasn't hurt. But a friend of hers went back into the building to find her ...'

Frank stops.

'Go on, Capitano.'

Frank downs some more brandy and glances at Sanudo's attentive eyes.

'The building was full of smoke,' Frank continues. 'However, I found her on the fourth floor. Although she was unconscious, I brought her out alive. But she died a week later.'

'That's very sad, Capitano.' His brow furrows. 'Is that the girl you think of when you see a fire?'

Frank looks at Sanudo's face. He suspects the deep lines are the result of suffering. Frank wonders how *he* has survived.

'Is there something else, Capitano?'

Frank looks at him blankly.

'Is there something else about the fire?'

Frank squeezes his eyes shut and takes a deep breath. 'You've experienced enough unhappiness, Dottore. You don't want to hear about my woes.'

'Go on, Capitano.'

Frank sips some more brandy. He has said enough. He doesn't want Sanudo to know the mess he's in. And he doesn't want Cecilia to hear.

'What else troubles you about the fire?'

Frank thinks about Maggie. If he tells Sanudo about her death perhaps he'll forget about Barbara. So abruptly he launches into the story of Maggie's death in the blitz and how he came home one evening to find the house devastated by a bomb, which had blown the windows out. 'Maggie was in the flat,' Frank concludes. 'She was killed.'

'What a tragedy, Capitano! I'm so sorry.'

There is silence for what seems like several minutes.

'When you look at the fire,' Sanudo asks at last, 'do you remember your wife?'

Frank trembles. He takes a deep breath but before he can respond, the door opens.

'Babbo, dinner is ready.' Cecilia's smiling face appears. 'Oh! good evening, Capitano. I heard your men were in good voice today. Will you sing for us again?'

'Thank you, Cecilia, let's have dinner first,' Sanudo says.

Frank forces a smile. Cecilia is truly lovely. Perhaps it's just as well he has told Sanudo about his troubles. It's better that she knows he's going mad.

'Thank you, Dottore.' Frank mutters. 'I'll join you in a minute but first I must wash my face.'

Alone, Frank feels disconnected from the world outside. He suspects he doesn't really exist. He washes his face in the freezing water; his skin stings after the raw day outside. The burning feels real, but he hesitates before looking in the mirror, in case there's no one there.

When he does look in the mirror, his face appears unchanged, just pinker. And he has lost weight since leaving Naples. Otherwise he seems much the same. So, what has changed? Only what's in his head. He's still the same man, except that now he's mad. But he knows he must keep going, even though it's all a pretence.

Cecilia looks up as he reappears. Her smile illuminates her face so that she seems to shine. But tonight her light doesn't reach him. He's cut off. He smiles as best he can but as she turns away he catches a look of concern. Does she think his loss of interest is due to her?

The others try to make the party go but Frank hardly joins in. The usual silly jokes no longer provoke laughter. Perhaps everyone feels low. Sanudo ensures the wine flows and Stansfield and Purdie try, in faltering Italian, to keep the show on the road. But Frank knows his presence is pulling them down.

As soon as the meal is over, Laura switches on the wireless. Stansfield and Purdie watch as she turns the dial in search of music from an English language station. Clearly she wants to dance.

'Thank you Signora and Dottore for an excellent meal,' Frank says. 'I think I'll go for a walk.'

Cecilia glances at Frank, as though asking what she has done wrong. Frank hesitates before pulling on his greatcoat. 'Buona notte,' he smiles.

Out in the street he stands for a moment, listening to the sounds from indoors. The wireless has been turned up as the music begins. It sounds welcoming. He imagines Cecilia and Laura dancing. Despising himself for his inability to join in, he starts to walk.

The waxing moon spreads a silver light across the town. It has an unearthly beauty, which seems empty and cold compared with the sunshine in Sanudo's house. Frank shivers as the frost penetrates his uniform.

The clock in the central piazza strikes the half hour. Frank wraps his arms across his chest and walks briskly. But after a while he slows. He'll need to keep this up for quite a while, until the others are all in bed. He completes a circuit of the town and approaches the house, but even from down the street he hears music. He presses on, feeling cold, tired and alone.

He accelerates again to jolt his circulation. The clock strikes 2200. Surely they won't stay up for long. He finishes another circuit and again approaches the house, praying they're all in bed. He stops to listen. Silence. No music and no sign of light.

Carefully he opens the front door and listens again. All is quiet. The dying embers shed a dim light across the hall.

'Are you all right, Capitano?' A warm Italian voice addresses him from near the fire. 'It must be cold out there.'

'Dottore!' Frank starts at Sanudo's voice. 'I hope I haven't kept you up.'

'Not really. I was just reflecting on the joys and sorrows of life, with the help of a little grappa. Would you like some? It might help you sleep.'

Frank hears the pleasing ring of the bottle. Sanudo fills a small glass and hands it to Frank. Then he pokes the embers to revive the fire and adds another log.

'Your good health, Capitano!'

Frank tips back the glass and feels a glow of gratitude as the grappa warms his throat.

'Thank you, Dottore, for listening to me earlier.'

'I'm sorry we were interrupted. I could see you found it hard to release those memories.'

Frank studies the embers, where wings of flame are embracing the new log. He enjoys the warmth but he has to look away. He turns to the dim figure of Sanudo. Beside him is that infernal skull. Frank slumps: he hasn't seen it for days.

'When you look at the remains of the fire, Capitano, do you think about your wife?'

Frank looks in Sanudo's direction but all he can see is the skull.

'Not usually … but while I searched the building for Barbara … I thought about her all the time … and as I carried Barbara … I kept thinking … I should have saved Maggie too.'

'Did you remember you weren't there when she died?'

'Dottore …' Frank downs some more grappa and speaks in a flat voice. 'You probably think I'm mad. And you're probably right.'

'Please don't be hard on yourself, Capitano? Terrible things have happened, but you certainly aren't mad.'

'I'm not so sure, Dottore. Often when I see a fire … often what I see is … is … is a skull.'

Frank needs help to find the Italian word *cranio*.

'But it isn't just any skull. Now you will really think I'm mad. The eye sockets … on this skull … are burnt.'

Frank tries to make out Sanudo's expression in the firelight. Will he recognise that Frank is insane after all? And what will he do then?

But Sanudo's face betrays no response. He seems deep in thought. 'Do you always see this skull when you look at a fire?' he asks at last.

'Yes, Dottore, very often. And then my heart races and my hands sweat. I told you I'm going mad.'

Sanudo looks up. In the firelight he appears benign but Frank braces himself for his judgement.

'Why do you suppose you see this skull?'

Frank hesitates. This is too much. He resolves to answer one more question; then it must stop.

'Perhaps it reminds me of the flat – where Maggie died. That bomb blew out the windows. And when I came home there was charring round the window frames. I believe this skull, with its scorch marks, is an image of my dead flat!'

Frank gets up and paces across the room. He halts in front of Sanudo's chair. 'That's all there is. That's why I'm mad. Will you recommend they lock me up?'

'Capitano, please don't say you're mad,' Sanudo smiles. 'You have suffered some awful things and your mind is struggling to deal with them. It isn't about being mad; it's about being human.'

'It seems pretty mad to me. I feel I've lost my grip. Quite simply, I'm no longer myself.'

'You are suffering, of course. But remember that you have been wounded. Not in your body but in your mind, which has withdrawn a little to recuperate. When I ask a probing question you feel hurt, as you would if I pressed a physical wound.'

The Dottore sips his grappa, without taking his eyes off Frank. 'May I continue?'

'No, Dottore!' Frank moves towards the door. 'I'm grateful you have tried to help, but I've had enough.'

'Franco. May I call you that? I know you're feeling great pain. But your wounds might heal better if you exposed them a little to the air. For now I have one more question. May I ask it? Then you can decide whether to answer.'

Frank remains standing. He downs a little more grappa but soon regrets it; it now tastes much too strong.

'Go on,' he says at last.

'I want you to tell me about this skull,' Sanudo says. 'Have you seen such a thing before; a skull with scorch marks around the eyes?'

Frank tries to ignore the new log which is burning strongly. He closes his eyes and studies the image of the skull. He wants to cry or run away. He needs someone to make him whole. And if they can't, he wants to die. He thinks of Vermillion. He must get better for her. He sees her hand stretching out towards him.

'No, Dottore,' Frank looks up. 'I've never seen the blasted skull before. That's enough. No more questions. I must go to bed.'

CHAPTER 51

Paolo and Sandro have worked hard to develop the new partisan group close to Padua, to the west of Venice. But the group, led by the oddly-named Cato, isn't operational because General Alexander has stood down all partisans, pending the Allied spring offensive.

Before Christmas there had been moments of elation with substantial partisan contributions to the fighting in Forlì and Ravenna. But all that is now a distant memory.

Paolo's frustration has grown; he feels hamstrung as he watches the people struggle with the privations of the endless winter. And with no early prospect of the Allies arriving, the Blackshirts with German support are clamping down on every suspect element. The widespread use of torture and the threat of heavy reprisals have made partisan operations impossible.

With little useful to do but constantly on the move, the different partisan factions argue with each other as they seek to build popular support for their political positions after the war. These arguments now threaten to become open fighting.

Paolo and Sandro try not to get involved, but the tensions are never far below the surface.

'No, Paolo! I've had enough!' Sandro paces back and forth across the small room.

'Shut up, Sandro, for God's sake!'

'Don't tell *me* to shut up! I'VE HAD ENOUGH!'

Paolo shifts closer to the disappointing log fire. He hugs himself, trying to stop shivering.

'I'm wasting my bloody time, Paolo! Nothing is happening! You stay here if you want, but I'm going to Rome!'

'Don't be bloody stupid, Sandro! Of course, nothing's happening now. It's the middle of the fucking winter! In the spring the Allies will attack again and we'll finish the Germans off. Then we can go home with something to show for it.'

Sandro peers through the narrow window at the hillside cloaked in snow. 'I don't care, Paolo! Nothing's going to happen for months.'

'You're a soldier in the CIL. You can't desert again. For the third time? Or have I lost count?'

'Of course, I won't desert. But who's going to know if I go to Rome? Unless you fucking tell them? We're soldiers. Why should we hang around with nothing to do until the bloody spring? For Christ's sake, Paolo, let's go to Rome now. Don't you want to see your mother? We'll return long before the Allies attack.'

Paolo is close to conceding that Sandro has a point. It's bloody frustrating being stuck in the countryside, fifty miles north of the front. Falcon sent them here to build links with Cato's fledgling group, which is now trained and established.

But they're still awaiting their first supply drop. Falcon blames the weather but Paolo fears that yet again politics is getting in the way.

'Go on your own if you must,' Paolo touches Sandro's shoulder. 'I'm staying here. Of course, I want to see Mamma. I think about her every day and how she has suffered. And it's all my fault.'

'My family suffered too. They died in the bombing, but that wasn't my fault. And what about Chiara? Her problems aren't my fault.'

'Nor mine!'

'Paolo, the whole thing stinks.'

Paolo is painfully aware that he hasn't seen Mamma and Francesca since his call-up in September '42. God, that's more than two years! And so much has happened since then. Madonna, why did he lie? No one could have blamed him for not going to Rome when it meant crossing the line. But telling Chiara he had gone and that Mamma was well, that was fucking stupid. Mamma may never forgive him. No, he can't visit her until he has taken revenge.

'We should stay, Sandro, to prepare for the spring. When the Allies advance again our task will be to trap Germans as they retreat from the Po river. We need to plan where we can catch them.'

'What's the bloody point of planning, when we don't have the kit?'

'Falcon swears there'll be a drop when the weather's better.'

'And when the hell will that be? It could be months. Let's go to Rome until then. I want to see Chiara to know she's all right. I send her letters but I don't know whether she gets them, because she can't reply.'

'I know you want to go, Sandro. But you can't cross the line in the snow. And even if you make it across you won't be free to move around. You can't say you joined the CIL but have deserted until the spring!'

Sandro glares at Paolo.

'I often have dreams,' Paolo continues, 'about going to Rome and seeing Mamma and my sisters. Sometimes even my father is there. Always I'm welcomed as a hero. I refuse to return as a deserter. And Chiara won't want *you* back, unless you're a hero too.'

'Chiara isn't that sort. What we do in the war won't matter to her.'

'Don't be fucking stupid! Women always talk about peace but really they want security. And that only comes when you earn it. Women close their eyes at the sight of blood but they still expect us to fight.'

'It's all right for you, Paolo. You've got Antonella.'

'That's nothing to do with it. Anyway, I've seen you eyeing Irma.'

'No, I haven't,' Sandro scowls. 'Well even if I have, it doesn't mean a thing.'

'That's your choice. She's a nice enough girl.'

'What if she is? I can hardly pursue her with you looking on, knowing that anything I do will be reported to Chiara. It's bloody off-putting!'

'What about me? Who wants to watch while their sister's boyfriend fucks a local floozy?'

'Is Antonella a floozy too?'

'No, she bloody well isn't. She's from a decent family.'

'Would you rather see me fuck the aristocracy?'

'Shut up, Sandro! That's too political! I don't care who you want to fuck, provided I don't have to know. I hope we'll see Chiara soon; but when we do, I refuse to lie.'

CHAPTER 52

Frank avoids Sanudo for several days. With nothing new to say, he's unwilling to rake over the same old ground. But the skull doesn't leave him: it joins him for their daily training and even while the choir rehearses during the march home.

Damn it! Does it matter whether he has seen the skull before? He stops singing for a moment. There is the skull lying amongst some bones in the desert. He takes up the song again. All right, that was where he saw it first. But there's no point in telling Sanudo.

* * *

'I heard your men singing today, Capitano.'

Sanudo hands Frank a small glass of grappa when the others have gone up to bed. 'They sounded in good heart.'

'Thank you, Dottore. I think they're making some progress.'

'And have you thought about that skull?'

'I've thought about little else.' Frank takes a gulp of grappa. 'Not that thinking does much good. But I've remembered where I first saw it.'

'Are you willing to tell me?'

'It's very mundane, Dottore,'

Frank sits forward.

'We were fleeing from Gazala ... in '42. We had driven all night and were well ahead of the pursuing Germans. Just before sunrise we stopped for a brew-up. The men set up a Benghazi boiler ... made from half an oil drum ... to make some strong army tea ... but I wandered into the desert to stretch my legs ...'

Frank pauses.

'... on the ground ... I saw ... this skull ...'

He feels an urge to cry.

'... lying amidst the flotsam of war ... first there were other bones ... then this skull, with charring ... around the eyes ... I wondered whether the man had burnt to death ... or was it a lifeless skull that was burnt?'

'Why is that important, Franco?'

'That's obvious. It's terrible to be burnt to death.'

'Of course, Capitano.'

Sanudo sips his grappa. 'You said your Battalion was fleeing from Gazala. Running away isn't what an army should do.'

Frank clenches his fists. He wants to hit Sanudo. What does *he* know about the desert war? How dare he suggest they were wrong to withdraw? They were following bloody orders!

He looks at Sanudo again. No, he doesn't want to hit him. He knows he's trying to help. But Frank hates these questions. He slumps back on the chair.

'No, Dottore,' Frank pulls himself up again, 'Gazala wasn't one of our better shows. We did all we could to hold the line. But neither our equipment nor our tactics were a match for Rommel. And we watched each day … it was terrible … '

Frank covers his face with his hands.

'I'm sorry, Dottore. It was ghastly. I had better go to bed.'

'Please stay, Franco. You're very close. Stay for a few more minutes and tell me about the dreadful things you saw.'

Frank's heart thumps loudly.

'It was the same every time, Dottore.'

He knocks back more of the fearsome grappa and drops his head. He must end the interrogation.

'… a handful of British tanks start to advance … towards the powerful German guns … then one of them is hit … and bursts into flames … after several seconds the top hatch opens … a blackened figure appears … he struggles out … then a second one … and another … their uniforms are on fire … they tear off their clothes … rolling on the ground … trying to stop the fire … I'm too far away to hear but I know they're screaming … after several minutes they collapse … and lie still …'

There's a long silence before Sanudo speaks again.

'Where were you, Franco, when you saw this?'

Frank gets up and moves towards the door. 'I'm sorry, Dottore, but that's enough.'

'You're so close, Capitano. I have only a few more questions. Where were you as you watched?'

Frank grips the door handle but half turns around.

'I was behind our defensive line, a couple of miles away. I saw it through my field glasses.'

'And you continued to watch?'

'You're right, Dottore ... I shouldn't have watched ... after the first time I didn't watch again ... through the glasses ... once was enough ... after that I watched with my naked eye ... I couldn't see the details ... but I knew what was happening ... and then I didn't have to watch at all ... I saw the whole thing in my head.'

'And you've thought about this ever since?'

'Of course not!'

Frank faces Sanudo.

'I didn't dwell on what I'd seen. I put it out of my mind. But I wrote a paper about our crazy tank tactics at Gazala and sent it to the Colonel. He was furious. He said I'd been disloyal. He even threatened to demote me. I felt terrible, but there was nothing I could do. I had to forget the whole thing. I've hardly given the matter a second thought.'

'But you *have* thought about the skull.'

'I can't avoid it; it just appears. Is it connected with what I saw at Gazala?'

'What do you think?'

Frank walks slowly back across the room but doesn't sit down. 'Could it be? Could the skull be a shorthand for what I saw at Gazala?'

'Perhaps.'

'But I've always linked the skull with my flat and Maggie's death, because the burnt-out windows looked like the skull.'

Frank paces back and forth; then he suddenly laughs.

'Perhaps Maggie and the flat were never connected with the skull. How extraordinary! I thought I'd forgotten about Gazala. Did the skull come to remind me that those horrors hadn't been laid to rest?'

'Part of you forgot. But another part remembered.'

Frank sits down and stares blankly ahead.

'Franco,' Sanudo asks after a minute, 'how do you feel about Gazala when you think about it now?'

'Pretty awful. Those poor men died in a dreadful way. And I didn't help them.'

'But they were two miles away. What could you have done?'

'Nothing. That was what was so ghastly. There was nothing I could do.'

'And there was nothing you could have done to save your wife. But when there was something you could do, you entered a burning building to save your friend.'

Frank buries his head in his hands. His whole body is trembling. He squeezes his eyes shut, determined not to cry. He breathes deeply and raises his head as he slowly uncoils.

Sanudo puts a hand on his shoulder.

'Franco, you've done very well. It's hard to examine the things that we lock in our hearts. It takes courage to expose those wounds. Now you should try to sleep. Tomorrow you'll discover whether the world seems any different.'

CHAPTER 53

Simon hasn't heard from Vermillion since Christmas, but he can't let her drift away. The war will soon be over and he needs to plan a new campaign.

He trots up the steps to the fourth floor flat knowing Vermillion won't be there but hoping to find Jackie who might have some news.

'Hello, Simon.' Margery's dark eyes study his face. 'How are you?'

'How are *you*?' he forces a smile. 'What's the news about the baby?'

'Do come in. Would you like some tea?'

Simon would prefer something stronger but he advances into the hall. 'Are you sure it isn't too much trouble?'

'Of course not. I'll put the kettle on.'

'How's Jackie?' Simon moves towards the sitting room but then retraces his steps.

'She's firing on all cylinders. She should be back soon; you can ask her yourself.'

Thank God for that! Simon smiles as he saunters along the corridor. The place reminds him strongly of Vermillion.

'How's Edmund?' Simon asks when Margery reappears.

'He's well. Very pleased with his new legs.' She places a cup of tea on the side table near to him. 'He's taking up golf again.'

'Good for him! He has done jolly well. Any chance you can join him at home?'

'The hospital says I can go. But I'm waiting till Eduardo arrives, once Edmund is legally his father. Fingers crossed! I keep thinking it's all agreed but then there's another document to approve or something else to swear with the notary. It's all fearfully annoying. But it'll be worth it in the end. Eduardo is a dear.'

Simon studies Margery as she talks. If anything, she's skinnier than in the summer but she certainly hasn't slowed down. She still has that feverish energy.

'How's your cup, Simon? Let me top it up.'

'Thank you, Margery.'

Simon wonders what he should do. He can't sit here all evening staring at Marge.

'Any news about Vermillion?'

'I haven't heard a thing. But Jackie had a letter. She'll be back soon. Do you want to wait?'

'I may as well … now I'm here … it would be a shame to miss her.'

'You stay there. But please excuse me. I must change. I'm on duty tonight.'

'You poor thing. Nights are hard.'

'Do you fly at night?'

'Sometimes on reconnaissance. Photography requires daylight but we often take off at the night to arrive at the target at dawn. And sometimes I do a special at night.'

'That sounds exciting.'

'Exciting enough. But I'm always glad to be flying. It's better than crawling through the mud and snow like the sodding infantry. Everyone says there'll be one more push to end the war … when the weather improves. I wonder how Frank is getting on.'

Margery sits up, hearing a key in the door.

'Hello! Are you there, Margery?' Jackie calls.

'We're in here, Jackie. We've got a visitor.'

'Oh Lord! Who is it? I look a frightful mess.'

'That doesn't matter. It's only Simon.'

'Hello, Jackie!' Simon adds.

'Please don't look at me.' Jackie appears from behind the door with her ATS cap still firmly on her head. 'I'm not fit to be seen. I must wash my hair.'

'Don't forget, Jackie, I'm on duty tonight,' Margery calls out. 'I'll be off in a minute.'

'Well get the poor chap a drink! I won't be long!'

'Simon, you'd better fix it yourself,' Margery says. 'You'll find everything in the kitchen.'

'I'll have a Martini!' Jackie calls.

'Good luck, Simon. I must run.'

'Goodbye Margery. And good luck with Eduardo.'

The front door clicks shut leaving the flat in silence. Simon takes a deep breath. There's still a trace in the air, as though something has been singed. From the kitchen he hears the water pipes knock under pressure from Jackie's bath. He smiles at the thought of her removing her service dress.

He mixes two dry Martinis and takes a sip. That should encourage her. He smiles again. He tiptoes back along the corridor, pleased at the steadiness of his hands. He places the drinks so that Jackie will be beside him on the sofa where he can lead with his left hand. He sinks down and takes a good swig.

Music! He needs to create the right mood. He hurries across to the gramophone and scans the heap of records in their brown paper covers. But the trouble with records is the need to change them after every song. There's nothing more off-putting than the looping hiss of the needle as it spirals round the final groove.

The wireless is a better bet. He switches it on and waits while the valves warm up. Slowly he turns the dial until he finds an American forces station. Benny Goodman. That's perfect. He turns down the volume and listens. It must be loud enough to affect the mood but quiet enough not to intrude. There! That's just right!

He waltzes back to the sofa and flops down. Far away he hears water draining away. He raises his glass and takes a good swig. Then he hears the bathroom door open and bare feet in the corridor. Perhaps she wants her drink now. He gets up, grabbing Jackie's glass which he clutches to his chest as he turns around.

'Jackie!' He can't hide his surprise. 'Here's your drink!'

'Thank goodness! You won't believe how thirsty I am. I've been up since 0500.

He stumbles towards her with liquid dribbling over his fingers. 'I hope this is all right. Tell me if you need more gin. Cheers!'

Simon tries to ignore the sound of Woody Herman on the wireless. 'How are you, Jackie?'

'Cheers, Simon! I'll be back in a minute. Get yourself another one.'

Simon refills his glass before sitting down and sipping at his Martini. The drink helps him to think. What on earth is he doing? He came to get news about Vermillion. Having a fling with Jackie is the last thing he should do. He is always pleased to see her but he doesn't really find her attractive.

He turns off the wireless just as Jackie reappears in her service dress with a towel around her head.

'I heard from Vermillion last week. She said you offered to fly her to Rome. My word, Simon, you don't give up!'

'Should I give up?'

'I would if I were you.' Jackie takes a sip from her Martini. 'You've chased Vermillion for more than three years but you haven't got very far. There must be other girls closer to home!'

'You may be right, Jackie. But knowing someone for so long means a lot these days. Most of the people I've known have already moved on.'

'You've known *me* for more than three years,' she says. 'Remember, we met on the ship.'

'I haven't forgotten. But you were rather preoccupied, as I recall. And since then a lot of gin has flowed under the bridge!' Simon drinks. 'What are you up to now, Jackie? How's Roger?'

'The last I heard he was down with malaria and they'd moved him to hospital. Poor fellow! I'm hoping he'll get some leave. I could do with a bit of fun.'

Jackie smiles before continuing. 'It's lovely to see you Simon. But I must go and dry my hair. Perhaps you could let yourself out once you've finished your drink.'

CHAPTER 54

As the Battalion prepares to return to the line, their training intensifies. Day after day Frank's men repeat the routines for river crossings under a creeping barrage, with shelling targeted two hundred yards ahead of the advancing infantry. It requires coordination with the gunners and confidence in their accuracy when they practise using live rounds. The training culminates in a crossing at night.

Frank is proud of his men and the way their skills have improved. But they're all increasingly aware of the dangers of crossing the Senio – their first target river – and the many waterways that will follow. Although nothing is said, everyone knows that casualties are bound to be high.

At their final parade even Mortimer acknowledges these dangers and promises help in the form of a new weapon. But he proffers no details and the men gain little reassurance. For months every German they've captured has sworn they will win the war because of their secret Vengeance weapons.

Frank's men could see the Germans were deluded; now they fear the Colonel is deluded too.

Since his last conversation with Sanudo, Frank has approached the Battalion's training with greater vigour, trying to ignore a blizzard of thoughts. When his mind starts to stray to Maggie, Gazala or Barbara, he interrupts, repeating: 'I am a soldier, I am a soldier …' whilst focusing his attention on the task in hand. Then he reminds himself that he was wounded by the things he experienced. Even Sanudo's interrogation hadn't found the basic psychological flaw that he feared might be revealed.

A few days ago he had woken with a clear understanding that Maggie was killed by the blast from the bomb, not by the resultant fire. He had known this all along, but somehow the charred window frames had linked his memory of the flat to his fear of burning.

Now he can see that Maggie's death, the defeat at Gazala and Barbara's death were three separate tragedies not a single combined horror. And the skull no longer stalks him. He thinks of it from time to time and is reminded of the tanks at Gazala. But the image no longer holds sway, causing him palpitations. He has a lot to tell Vermillion when he writes tonight.

For the Battalion's final days in Sassovivo the weather stays bitterly cold. There's still no feeling of spring, which comes late in the hills. Yet even here, as February ends, the days begin to lengthen and the daylight grows more intense. Although the trees are bare, their colour is changing as the buds start to swell.

The spring campaign, which should end the war, is close. Tomorrow the Battalion will return to the line. By and large Frank feels prepared. He knows they must press on with the war if the fighting is ever to stop. Only then will he get some leave and the chance to see Vermillion again.

Marching back from their final training, Frank gets the choir singing. *"We're Going to Hang out the Washing on the Siegfried Line"*.

As he enjoys the steady rhythm and the warmth of the singing, Frank remembers a dream that disturbed him last night.

He's in a gondola drifting along a canal. He leans back, enjoying the surroundings now the war is over. Wondering where Vermillion is, he studies the gondolier. It's Vermillion, controlling the boat with a long pole, more like a punt pole than a gondolier's oar. She stands upright to lift the pole and he sees that she's naked above the waist. Shocked, he tries to reach her, causing the gondola to wobble. With a crash of splintering wood, the craft rams into a warship. Frank is thrown into the water and wakes up.

This morning he was worried that he had had another bad dream. But now, leading the singing, the penny drops that this was a dream about water, not about fire. He feels a surge of gratitude to Sanudo who has helped him face his fears. Frank can see that he never could have saved Maggie or the men at Gazala; it wasn't because he was a coward. Now, facing the prospect of the Senio crossing, he again feels afraid yet somehow he knows this is normal. Perhaps feeling afraid doesn't make a man a coward: it just makes it harder to be brave.

* * *

For the officers' last dinner in Sassovivo, the Sanudos spare no effort. On their return from training the officers find the table laid in the hall where a blazing fire is lit. Frank swallows when he sees it but tonight it only provokes a pang of impending loss. He will miss every member of this lovely family, but especially the Dottore's insight and concern.

At dinner, the hall is lit with candles. There are more courses than ever: spaghetti; meat with garlic and salads; cheese; and puddings. Sanudo produces a series of wines. The usual clamour around the table swells with laughter and intermittent barking.

But alongside all this jollity, Frank hears another note. Is it the acoustics of a different room? Or is it the sound of incipient sadness because in the morning they must leave?

When everyone has been served, Sanudo gets to his feet.

'Comrades and family! I want to say something now

before I've had more to drink. I want my words to come out correctly.'

The firelight flickers in Sanudo's eyes as he looks around the room. 'Dear comrades, for all of us this moment is bittersweet. Bitter because tomorrow you must leave us. But sweet because you who recently arrived as strangers, and foreigners at that, have quickly become our friends.'

Sanudo raises his hands and extends his arms in a gesture of embrace. 'But you brought with you some strange English habits. I will only mention two: you drink your coffee weak when civilised people know that coffee must be strong; and you drink your tea strong when it should have a delicate flavour that is ruined by adding milk. We have tried to teach you better ways, but we haven't had time to resolve these basic deficencies. But let's be positive. At least you know how to drink a glass of good wine.'

Sanudo raises his glass and takes a sip.

'Tomorrow your army will take you away. We don't know where you will go. I hear rumours that you're going to France. But that seems unlikely. I expect you will travel north to attack the Germans and drive them from our country.'

Sanudo looks at Frank who tries not to acknowledge that Sanudo is right to dismiss the official story. Frank knows that tomorrow they will head for the Senio, their start line for the spring campaign.

'Comrades, our thoughts and our prayers go with you all, wherever you are sent. We know that each of you – the Capitano and the two Tenenti – will distinguish yourselves in the battles to come and will make your country proud.'

'We, the whole Sanudo family, will miss you. But as you leave we also feel great pride that three brave soldiers chose to stay with us in Sassovivo. And when this dreadful war is over and peace is restored we hope you will visit us again. Whenever you come, you will be most welcome. This table is big but it's not as large as our hearts, in which you will always find room. And for as long as we live in Sassovivo you will find food and wine … and song.'

'One final thing my dear friends. My lovely daughters have requested that this evening there should be no singing. Instead they have asked that we hear some dance music from the wireless. I can't quite think what they have in mind. But on this special occasion I feel obliged to agree. After dinner Anna and I will retire to bed but you are welcome to dance. As we know you're leaving well before dawn, please forgive us if we say goodbye now.'

Sanudo sits down to prolonged applause. Purdie, sitting next to Laura, clasps her hand. She smiles at him but then glances at her mother who looks concerned. Frank wonders how Laura's parents feel about the relationship. Marrying a good fellow like Purdie would surely be a suitable match. But even if Purdie survives the war and the pair decide to marry, they might choose to live in England. No wonder Signora Sanudo has tears in her eyes.

Cecilia looks at Stansfield and then smiles at Frank; he feels illuminated by her face. Tonight she seems more knowing as though her father has explained. Frank wonders what she thinks? Had it been a revelation that he has feet of clay? Or was she shocked that he had been married before or has a girlfriend in Naples? Perhaps her wide eyes record that she feels sorry for Frank.

He sighs. He knew that telling Sanudo would end any chance of things developing. But he isn't sorry. Cecilia is a lovely girl and he'll miss her, but he's glad that nothing happened between them.

He twirls the stem of his wine glass, lost in thought. Looking up he catches Cecilia's eye. He notices that everyone is silent, awaiting his reply. He prepares to get to his feet but Fabio jumps up first.

'Nonna, Mamma, Pappa, ragazze! I'm very sad that the soldiers are leaving. But please, Capitano, may I come with you. Pappa will tell you I was old enough to carry messages for the partisans. And now I'm strong enough to fight!'

'Fabio, no!' Sanudo bangs the table.

'Pappa, please.'

'No, no, NO, Fabio.' Anna puts her arm around his shoulders.

Frank waits for the clamour to subside and for the dog to be quiet. Then slowly he rises to his feet.

'Fabio, having heard what your parents have just said, we won't take you with us. But I must tell you that I greatly admire your spirit and your desire to serve your country by driving the Germans away. That, however, is our job. It's why we came here, to destroy the Germans.

Frank turns to Sanudo who nods slightly.

'But when the war is over, Fabio – and God willing it will end soon – then we foreigners will return to our homes. And Italy will be free again. That is when *your* work will begin. Fabio, there will be much for you to do to rebuild your beautiful country. There will be buildings to restore, roads to repair and bridges to reconstruct. And there will be millions of people whose lives have been destroyed. Then Italy won't need soldiers. It will need engineers and doctors – like your father – to restore the country and mend people's damaged lives. If you want to serve your country, Fabio, it's better you don't fight; all your strength will be needed to build a new Italy.'

Anna wraps her arms around him. 'You see, Fabio, we need you here.'

'I understand Mamma,' Fabio pulls himself away. 'I shall go wherever I am needed as soon as I am trained.'

Frank takes a mouthful of wine. 'Dear friends, I want to thank you all for making our stay in Sassovivo a special time. Your welcome to three lonely soldiers has been more than we could have dreamt of. I come from a small unhappy family – I was the only child and my father left when I was young – so the family was just my mother and me …'

Frank pauses, distracted by the thought of his father with his *new* family. He clears his throat.

'… of course, I saw other families that were bigger and happier but I never felt part of a large happy family until I arrived here. Thank you for extending your warmth to each of us. One day I hope I may borrow your family again. Or perhaps I'll have a family of my own that I can introduce to you all. Thank you. Thank you, again.'

Frank sits down to cheers. He feels happy but suddenly tired. He helps the others clear away the dishes. Then he says farewell to each of the Sanudos and heads for bed leaving Purdie and Stansfield to dance with the girls.

PART V

– March 1945 –

CHAPTER 55

Rummage looks up from his papers. 'I don't suppose you speak Russian?'

'No, Sir.' Vermillion says. 'Not a word. I'm sorry, Sir.'

'Pity! The next lot are Bolshies. Sergeant, bring them in!'

Vermillion is surprised to find Russians serving in Italy. She is about to raise this with Rummage when the Sergeant reappears with two girls. One, with a wide, strong face and short hair, shouts intermittently in Russian; the other, her long hair matted with dirt, stares vacantly at the ground.

'Bring two chairs, Sergeant.'

Rummage waits until the girls are seated before asking what languages they speak. Apart from Russian they can manage a little German.

Vermillion takes up the questioning and slowly their stories unfold. In '42 they were employed as cooks by the Russian army but when the Germans overran their unit they were taken prisoner. For a while they were treated adequately although the Germans weren't sure what to do with them. But as the war on the eastern front became more desperate, their treatment worsened. Many Russian soldiers were forced to join German units. The girls were raped in their camp and then forced to have sex with the officers, and later with any German soldier.

Finally, the whole unit was moved from the eastern front and the girls were brought to Italy to face abuse of every kind.

Vermillion shakes her head as she listens to their wretched tales. She wants to ask about the German soldiers who abused them but Rummage isn't interested in their treatment. He wants to hear about the German unit that held them, its identity and strength. But the girls know almost nothing.

'Well that was a waste of time,' Rummage mutters as the girls are led away. 'I think I'll have a wash.'

Vermillion can't face another encounter with the quicklime lavatory. She pulls out her cigarettes and notices Frank's recent letter.

She has worried about Frank more since reaching northern Italy. Is it the ever-present sound of the guns or because she spends more time on her own? She's glad that Frank's talks with Sanudo about the desert war have been helpful and that he now feels better about dear Barbara and the fire. She will write to him again tonight.

She drops her cigarette on the ground as Rummage returns.

'Next prisoner, Sergeant!'

A German officer with a patrician air strides in. He smiles at Vermillion who feels an instant wave of anger and disgust towards the handsome young man.

'Good morning, Major Rummage,' he says in fluent English. 'And who is your colleague?'

'This is Lieutenant Henthorpe,' Rummage says in halting German.

'Good morning, Lieutenant,' he smiles. 'I'm delighted to meet you.'

'YOU MUST … SPEAK … IN GERMAN!' Rummage raises his voice. 'What is your name and rank?'

'I'm so sorry, Major,' the prisoner continues in English. 'For me it is a pleasure to speak your charming language again. Does the Lieutenant know I lived in London town for a year? I am an Anglophile.'

Rummage scowls. Standard army procedure insists that interrogations are conducted in the prisoner's language: permitting them to speak in English is thought to give them a sense of superiority, which helps them resist interrogation.

'Yes, of course, Major!' the prisoner says in German. 'Oberleutnant Grupe, at your service!'

Rummage turns to Vermillion.

'Ask him how he became a prisoner.'

Vermillion translates, doubtful that the standard approach will work.

'My unit was camped for the night,' Grupe says, 'after delivering supplies to the fighting units. We were awoken at 0330 by a British patrol scouting for prisoners. We were taken completely by surprise and had no chance to resist. Secretly I was pleased my war was over.'

'You say you were pleased to be captured. Why didn't you desert?'

'That wasn't realistic as we weren't on the front line.'

'Tell us about your military service.' Rummage says.

'I've been in Italy for more than a year. But I've been fortunate. I haven't had to fight against my British friends.'

'But you fought against us before you were captured.'

'I served with a heavy heart. Many of us opposed the war and I never did any fighting; I only organised the army's ordinance.'

'Ordinance used to kill British soldiers!' Vermillion doesn't wait for the Major as her anger flares.

'Yes, Lieutenant, that's terrible.' Grupe shakes his head. 'But these things happen in war.'

'Why didn't you and your friends force Hitler to stop the war?'

'What could we do?' he shrugs. 'We hated the Nazis.'

'But you kept organising ordinance to prosecute the war. You're as guilty as the men who fought.'

'And what about the British who supported Hitler? And their politicians and newspapers who encouraged him in '39 to think he could win? Aren't they guilty too?'

'No!' Vermillion raises her voice. 'They were stupid and misguided. But they didn't permit the slaughter of civilians in reprisals throughout the north of Italy.'

'That's enough!' Rummage intervenes. 'Ask him about his unit and its strength.'

The prisoner smiles. 'There's not much I can tell you.'

'If you're such an Anglophile, why do you refuse to help?'

'I've told you what I know, Lieutenant,' he smiles.

'Tell us about the Russian women in your camp.'

'What women?' The German raises his eyebrows.

'You passed two women as you were brought in. Yes, the ones you held as slaves. Why were they in your camp?'

'I know nothing about them. Perhaps they did the laundry.'

'Why won't you answer?'

'I've told you what I know.'

There's silence while Rummage thinks.

'What will happen to me?' the German asks at last.

'That's simple.' the Major snaps back. 'As you served on the eastern front, when the war in Italy ends we'll pass you to the Russians. You can tell *them* about these women.'

The German rubs his chin vigorously, waiting for Vermillion to translate.

'Take him, Sergeant.'

'No, Major!' he shouts in English as the Sergeant pulls him away. 'Major, I think I can help! I remember about those women …'

CHAPTER 56

The Battalion's return to the line takes place at night to avoid the attentions of the *frontläufer*, the German agents in the border area.

Asleep in the backs of their trucks, the men are unaware as they drive north that each ridge and river they cross marks another battle fought and won. But the men no longer dream of past glories when they were the pride of the British Army: now they just hope that they and the other D-Day Dodgers will somehow survive.

Frank sleeps fitfully for several hours and then stares through the windscreen longing for the light to return. But when dawn finally breaks, the Po valley he sees is different to the one they left in January. The bare trees, the freezing fog and the snow-hardened fields have gone. Now the willows, poplars and mulberry trees are decked in yellow and green. Violets, primroses and purple irises abound. And as the sun rises the sky is blue and the air is clear. Before it was mist which limited visibility across the Senio: today it's the burgeoning foliage.

As the men clamber down from their trucks they also discover a change under foot. The ground, which in January was stiff with mud, is now cloaked in white dust, finer than the desert sands. Soon they will encounter this powder in every crack and cranny.

In the winter they laughed at a Two Types cartoon showing soldiers heading for Bologna through the mud and rain; one says: "give me a sandstorm any day." Now they long for rain to settle the dust.

Leaving their transport well back from the line, 4th Battalion proceeds on foot. But even as the men line up, their minds are gripped by the sound of artillery. They know that the constant drumbeat of the guns will fill their dreams and waking hours until the war ends.

Like other rivers in the flat Po valley, the Senio meanders towards the sea. Faced with centuries of flooding, the inhabitants have raised massive floodbanks to contain the flow. These structures suggest an obvious defensive line, which the Germans have worked slavishly to enhance by tunnelling into the embankments and seeding the surfaces with mines and barbed wire.

The Eighth Army's first objective at the Senio was to seize control of the nearside floodbank. But despite frequent local attacks, progress has been slow and casualties, mainly from mines, have been high. Now in early March, for lengthy stretches, both sides of the river remain in enemy hands.

Beyond this first river are others with similar embankments. And between the rivers lies a latticework of ditches and canals. Most of these waterways are shallow enough for a man to wade through, and generally they present little difficulty for tanks. But for trucks, rebuilt bridges are required. Even in this open countryside, the Eighth Army's progress will depend on how quickly the sappers can work.

Roger, who has come straight from convalescence, is there to meet his Company. Leaving the men to unload, he takes the officers forward to observe their stretch of the river. The Observation Post is hard to get to in daylight as any visible movement is greeted with sniping. To reach it safely the officers have to drop into a crawl trench and cover the last hundred yards on their knees.

Inside the former farmhouse, they clamber up to the attic. There, from small windows, they can see the looming mass of the floodbanks snaking across the plain. But even from the second floor, little is visible on the German side apart from blossom.

Frank is more interested in Roger, who looks better after his malaria. Vermillion in her recent card for Frank's birthday asked him to challenge Roger about what he told Paolo. But Frank wants to know how Huggins died.

Roger stands well away from Frank as he introduces his officers to Captain Seymour, who has served for many weeks on this section of the line.

'Good morning, gentlemen,' Seymour begins, 'welcome to the Senio. The first thing that may have struck you is how small the actual river is – less than thirty feet wide and not very deep. The massive embankments look redundant today, but heavy rain or snow melting in the mountains can fill them bloody fast.'

Seymour turns to a detailed map which he relates to what they can see outside.

'You may have noticed – here and here – there are gaps in the near embankment. The Teds have opened these holes in order to watch us from the other side and to provide a better field of fire. But you can see over here that we've erected screens to spoil their view. So far the buggers haven't intervened.'

Seymour pauses.

'There aren't many places with outlooks over the floodbanks. Three buildings on our side are used as OPs to direct our guns. The Teds have four such buildings, two of which they use as OPs. The other two – there and there – house machine guns. And because of the bends in the river they have lines of fire along both sides. Make sure your men remember this: before they move, they must check whether they can be seen.'

'We've cleared much of the near embankment. And we've marked safe routes through the mines. But things often change. With the Teds on both sides of the river, they sometimes come out at night to lay a new minefield. Make sure your sentries report any sound of digging.'

Seymour points to the near embankment a hundred yards to the left. 'There the Teds are still in residence. They keep half a dozen men in the bunker but usually replace them each morning. From the bunker they have tunnelled right through the floodbank and have mounted a heavy machine gun pointing our way. Finally, there are other smaller positions – there, there and there – which the Teds occupy at night but vacate during the day.'

Seymour invites questions.

'How do the Teds get men and supplies across the river?' Roger asks.

'They use lightweight bridges,' Seymour replies. 'We've also spotted rafts. We try to hit them but it's hard to get a decent shot.'

'What about their positions on the far embankment?'

'We haven't sent patrols across. But we have some idea about their defences. Look at this on the stereoscope. It came from Mae West last week. Tell me what you can see.'

The officers take turns studying the three-dimensional view. They laugh as the image jumps out, revealing the barrel of a gun poking out from the floodbank.

'What's Mae West, Sir?' Stansfield asks.

The Captain smiles.

'The Mediterranean Air Interpretation Unit – Western Section. Everyone calls them Mae West. Reconnaissance planes fly along the river photographing anything new. They pass them to Mae West for assessment. It's well worth buttering them up to establish what they know.'

'If there are no more questions, it just remains to wish you good luck. And to leave you with a final message. Every night we sent out fighting patrols to extend our intelligence about the Teds and their defences. Together with snippets from POWs and the stereographs, this helped us plan our attacks to clear enemy positions or capture prisoners. It wasn't glamorous and sometimes it was messy. But it's a job that must be done.'

* * *

Frank stares into the darkness. The crescent moon has set and the night is silent – apart from the ringing in his ears. Around him the men are restive, waiting to start their patrols.

In five minutes the diversionary shelling will start. Frank finds it hard not to think about Vermillion and her letter which arrived this morning. Thank goodness, she is well, even though she worries about his return to the line.

'Did you hear about the Irish celebrations?' Sergeant Short says in a stage whisper.

'Shh!'

'They had mule races. You know, for St Patrick's Day.'

Frank checks his watch again. Two minutes to go.

A mortar explodes away to the right.

'They had a fancy-dress football match – the officers against the Sergeants! They say the men went mad ...'

Short is silenced by a cacophony of firing all around them. Mortars and shells burst on the far embankment. Brens open up and heavy machine-gun fire cackles over their heads.

Frank blows his whistle.

With diversionary fire continuing, the Germans respond. Mortar bombs explode behind them and a Spandau machine gun fires along its fixed line.

'You're a soldier!' Frank mutters as he steps forward into the darkness. 'You're a soldier. You're a soldier.'

Tonight their orders are clear. They must advance between the white tapes marking the safe areas where mines have been cleared. And once they make it to the near embankment they will clear mines from a new area.

Mortars explode behind them. With fifty yards to go Frank accelerates. He knows they'll be safer in the lee of the floodbank, but his legs will hardly carry him. 'Keep going!' he orders to himself. 'You're a bloody soldier now!'

Flashes and explosions accompany them as they grope their way forward. It's hard to keep going.

'Is this far enough, Sir?' Short asks when they are clearly on the slope of the embankment.

'This will do, Sergeant. Get one group moving to the left, halfway up the bank. And the others along the bottom.'

Shells and bullets are still flying but Frank feels safer here. He can't see the great embankment, but he senses its presence.

The men form a line and start probing for mines in the dark. They poke the ground with thin wooden poles, feeling for anything solid that might be a mine casing. They need to apply some pressure to break the soft ground but not enough to trigger an explosion. When they detect something hard they use a spade at a shallow angle to lift it. And all this must be done quietly, so the Teds don't hear. The work is tedious and hateful.

The diversionary fire soon quietens down and the Germans also relent. There's silence again, apart from the rhythmic poking and scratching of spades.

The sputter of another machine gun causes Frank to jump.

Silence returns. Now the sound of their digging seems to be amplified. Frank feels sure the Germans will hear. But their labours soon reveal several mines.

Mortar bombs swoop overhead in quick succession and explode, away from Frank's men.

Frank feels oddly reassured as silence descends once more.

Voices. At least they sound like voices. Frank strains to listen.

Another volley of shots; this time from the right.

In the quiet that follows, Frank hears German voices from across the floodbank. Are they crossing the river? Frank leads the men in lobbing grenades over the top. He hears muffled explosions. Then something heavy splashes into the water, followed by shouted orders and running feet.

Stillness again. The men keep on prospecting.

A Spandau machine gun opens fire from the farmhouse on the right. It sounds like a whip being cracked. Bullets sing above their heads. Frank's calculation was right that the embankment would protect them. Several stick grenades are flung from the other side. They roll to the bottom of the slope, exploding some way away.

Quiet once more.

Frank hears a rasping sound. It didn't come from his men. There it is again! It's coming from behind him. Frank moves back ten yards. He squats down and tilts his head. The sound of muffled chipping and scraping comes from beneath his feet. Someone is digging underground.

"Well said, old mole! Canst work i' the earth so fast?" Frank mumbles Hamlet's words. He needs to speak to HQ.

As he stands up a brilliant flash floods his eyes. Then a thunderous bang. Stones and earth kick at his head. There's shouting, and several screams. Frank rushes forward. A man, Frank can't see who, is sprawled on the ground. His right foot, which triggered the mine, is all askew. Lance Corporal Thorpe is also on the ground. His hands cover his face. Blood seeps between his fingers.

Frank grabs the field telephone.

'Two stretcher parties. Grid reference S53B42! Urgent! Two wounded! Enemy tunnelling in near floodbank. Request maximum fire at same reference 0330 hours. Target marked with circle of white tape.'

Frank shakes his watch. It hasn't stopped. Eighteen minutes to get clear. He returns to the wounded men. Short is injecting morphine. Frank kneels beside them, speaking to each in turn. Private James is lying still with the shin bone of his right leg sticking out. Thorpe whimpers through his hands, which remain clamped to his face. Frank fears for his eyes.

Mortar shells fly over from the Battalion's lines. Their machine guns open up a new pattern of diversionary fire. The enemy responds with more stick grenades. Two explode only yards away.

Frank loops a length of white tape into a circle and spreads it out on the ground where he heard the digging.

Soon the stretchers arrive. After seeing the wounded on their way, Frank gathers the rest of the Section and leads them back along the embankment a hundred yards.

Above their heads the artillery duel grows more intense. Frank prays the shells won't go astray. As he signals for the men to sit tight at the foot of the bank, a call comes through on the field telephone.

'A message from Major Bewdley. Resume mine clearance on floodbank at once. Stonk delayed until 0545 hours. Remain on floodbank to occupy enemy tunnel.'

Frank swears under his breath. He gets up and distributes a ration of rum. 'Major Bewdley says the stonk has been delayed. We must continue clearing the mines.'

The men grumble as they shuffle back while, against the background of intermittent explosions, Frank tries to quieten them.

"Occupy the enemy tunnel!" he repeats to himself, wondering how the hell they'll do that.

'We'll need more men, Sir ...' Short says, clearly thinking along similar lines. '... if they want us to take and hold the tunnel. We'll need another Section. And tommy guns and more grenades.'

'Sergeant, you're right. I'll inform HQ.'

Frank keeps one eye on his men as they continue to prod and dig. With the other he watches the time and the eastern sky.

After 0500 he discerns the first hint of light. Again he gathers the men and steers them back to their starting line. They don't have to wait long before they hear the men from the new Section entering the crawl trench. Soon they can make out their faces.

'Shh!' Frank tries to dampen their excitement while they wait for the stonk to begin.

As the sky lightens in the east an array of weapons opens up from the Allied side. Soon the enemy responds. But above this cacophony Frank hears the groaning engine of a Stuart light tank heading their way, followed by a second. The first tank lowers its main gun and aligns it with Frank's tape circle. It rolls forward, stopping fifty yards from the embankment. Meanwhile the second tank takes aim at the farmhouse on the left where the Spandau is housed.

Frank holds his breath. The men are silent. They cover their ears, but this doesn't deaden the report as the second tank fires. Frank lowers his hands in time to hear masonry falling. The Germans return fire with several mortars and then a Nebelwerfer launches multiple mortars, making a fearsome noise.

As the second tank withdraws the first tank fires a round, throwing up a cloud of smoke and dust which envelops the Platoon.

'On your feet!' Frank shouts. 'Follow me!'

He gropes his way along the embankment as several mortars fire from Allied lines and the first tank withdraws. Then something far more powerful – probably an anti-tank shell – explodes behind the first tank. The noise is tremendous.

Frank's head rings and he starts to shake. He hears shouting from across the floodbank and many boots on a bridge. He sends the Sergeant to the top of the embankment to observe through a periscope and to throw more grenades to heighten the confusion.

Frank coughs as he stumbles forward through the thinning smoke. Ahead a huge crater has been opened in the side of the floodbank. He clambers over mounds of loose earth. Peering into the rough chamber, he glimpses foggy light from the other side.

Posting guards at the cavern entrance, Frank and Short lead two units forward, one on either side. The air is thick with dust. Frank coughs again. They pass tattered remnants of German uniforms buried in the soft earth. After ten paces the way narrows and they come to a tunnel with a concrete lining, still seemingly intact. Frank leaves his unit in the cavern and presses on alone.

Ahead, he hears shouting in German. A shot rings out. Short flings a grenade well forward which clatters on the concrete floor. Frank presses himself against the wall as it explodes. A man cries out before he falls. Frank presses forward with his pistol ready but when he reaches the man he is clearly dead.

There's a shout of German orders.

'Sergeant! Quick, get back!'

They race for cover as two stick grenades are thrown in at the far end. The explosions are deafening. Frank and Short crouch in the cavern. A machine gun starts to fire. The Germans throw more grenades. A figure appears. Frank's men open fire. The Germans try repeatedly to climb through the opening but each time steady fire drives them back.

Frank confers with Short. They are now effectively stuck. They can't leave the embankment in daylight and they can't advance but they must hold the tunnel until dark.

Short divides the men with a two-hour rota to give them time to rest. Frank picks up the field telephone to report to HQ. He has to hold it with both hands as he starts to shake.

CHAPTER 57

Rummage pushes into the tent. He glares at Morden, sitting at the desk next to Vermillion's.

'What's so bloody urgent, Corporal?'

'It … it … it's this report from the 7th.'

Morden leaps to his feet, saluting at the same time. 'It says …the … the … the Germans are using red crosses to spy …'

'Let me see! Quickly, man!' Rummage grabs the report.

Vermillion has read the report that German stretcher-bearers, displaying red crosses to recover their wounded in the agreed manner, have passed close to Allied positions when returning to their lines.

'Corporal, tell them to broadcast a message, yes in German of course, saying they mustn't abuse the red cross. If they do it again, we'll seize their stretcher-bearers and they won't be returned. That should shut them up.'

'Ye … yes, Sir. At once, Sir.'

'Anything else?' Rummage acknowledges Vermillion at last.

'No, Sir!' They say in concert.

'I'll see you at the conference.'

Vermillion watches as Morden pulls out a handkerchief and wipes his brow. Then he gets out his cigarettes. She takes one and smiles as he lights it. She sits back and inhales. Morden doesn't speak and Vermillion can't think what to say to reassure him.

Sometimes Rummage is perfectly civil, but he can't help probing for any sign of weakness and when he finds one he keeps picking at it. It makes him an effective interrogator but an obnoxious boss. Luckily for Vermillion, he now moves in more elevated circles and of late she has seen him less and less.

Apart from Rummage, she enjoys her job. She still does some interpreting when he sees senior prisoners but increasingly she interrogates alone. She likes to hear the prisoners' accounts of their exploits during the war and to quiz them on their knowledge of the German defences.

Information, which arrives in dribs and drabs, is all recorded and sifted, in case details that are unimportant on their own can be linked with something else to show a pattern. Daily intelligence reports prepared by each unit in the line provide the bread and butter of her work. They often record little of interest but together they add to the web of information around which the intelligence spiders can run. She finds it exciting to be part of this machine as it processes, digests and analyses the enemy's every move.

In accordance with Rummage's instructions, Vermillion's reading isn't limited to the Eighth Army. She also sees reports from the Fifth Army, covering the centre and west of Italy. She knows the Germans now have eighteen divisions along the Italian front, which equates to one man for every five yards spread across the peninsula from Viareggio to Ravenna. And she knows the name and reputation of every German division in the Po valley.

She is also familiar with the Allied units in the area. Here on the plain, in addition to 4th Battalion, there are the 56th London division, the Italian Cremona division, the 78th Division, the 8th Indian division, the 2nd New Zealand division and of course the Poles. And in the mountains further west the Fifth Army includes Brazilians, the American 10th Mountain division and the South Africans on loan from the Eighth Army.

From the prisoners she interrogates come stories of heroism and tragedy, of cruelty and good fortune. And then there are the reports of daily Allied losses. They are presented as dry statistics but she can't forget that Edmund had once been one of these numbers: each one records a life ended or changed forever.

The daily intelligence reports include one from 4th Battalion, which Vermillion finds hard to read. She tried skipping it completely but that made her afraid she might miss something important. Then she tried reading it first, but that increased her anxiety as she searched through the daily bundle. Now she reads the others first to learn what sort of day it had been. Only then does she read 4th Battalion's.

The unread pile of yesterday's reports is diminishing quickly. Vermillion stubs out her cigarette as she turns over the penultimate sheet of coarse Manila paper. She glances at the crude typing and trembles as she picks it up.

Intelligence Summary – 4th Battalion – 30 March 1945 (Good Friday)

Overnight C coy engaged in mine clearance and discovered enemy outpost within near Senio floodbank at R15B63. Cleared enemy from their position.

Floodbank activity continued throughout the night around R15B63 with shelling and Nebels over the whole Battalion sector.

0630	*Enemy counter-attack driven back. Enemy casualties estimated at 8 killed, 4 wounded and 5 POW. Own casualties 4 killed and 1 officer wounded.*
0700	*Enemy broadcast over loudspeakers. Message 'Why are you sitting on the floodbank when your wives are in England?"*
0745	*Enemy bazooka attack on our forward positions at R47B55. Successful response with Piat bombs and 3" mortars.*
1015	*Grenade duel at T61A46 lasted four hours. 2 enemy killed. Own casualties three wounded.*
1430	*Enemy position in floodbank at T19A97 engaged by tanks with several direct hits.*
1500	*B coy attacked enemy outpost at T19A97. Enemy casualties estimated at 7 killed, 3 wounded and 4 POW. Outpost completely cleared. Enemy seen evacuating stretcher cases later in the afternoon.*
1600	*C coy attacked by bazookas but Battalion's Piats ended the action.*
1630	*Tank shot up enemy OP in house at S61A24.*
1835	*Enemy deserter taken at T88A52.*
1930	*We broadcast to the Germans a recording of The*

*Blue Danube and then a report on recent bombing
of German cities. C coy relieved by A coy.*

*All enemy positions on near floodbank are believed to have been
cleared.*

Vermillion takes a deep breath. C Company had been in the thick of it. 'Dear Frank. Are you all right?'

That was Good Friday and tomorrow is Easter Sunday. Is that grounds for hope?

"... 1 officer wounded ..." she reads again. But no indication of how badly wounded. 'Dear God, please protect Frank'.

Vermillion knows, as every soldier on the Senio knows, that a big offensive is imminent. Even the German prisoners she saw today know the attack is coming. But no one knows quite when or where it will happen. Only the most senior Allied officers know the planned date and which of the Fifth and the Eighth Armies will kick things off.

'There's a letter for you, Lieutenant,' Morden smiles as he reappears.

She sits back, wondering what Edmund wants this time. She opens the letter cautiously and skims its contents before folding it and putting it away.

She looks across at Morden hoping for another cigarette. Why had Edmund written to *her*? He's disappointed the Contessa has changed her mind and doesn't want Edmund to bring up Eduardo after all. But why *should* Vermillion write to the Contessa, as Edmund suggests? He should write himself. She feels more concerned for Eduardo and his mother.

How awful for her even to have considered passing him to Edmund.

'Aren't you coming to the lecture, Lieutenant,' Morden looks up and grins, 'to hear the gospel according to Rummage?'

'Of course I'm coming, Corporal.' Vermillion jumps up. 'Rummage says he wants to hear our views.'

'What makes you think, Lieutenant, that this leopard might change his spots?'

Vermillion collects her papers. She follows Morden into the adjacent tent where already a group has gathered, sitting at a long trestle table in front of the Major. She recognises many of the faces from her visits to Rummage's Intelligence truck.

'Good morning, gentlemen … and lady.'

Rummage pauses for long enough to get a reaction.

'You will all have seen from the map that the defences on the Santerno are much stronger than on the Senio. But how will this affect German strategy? HQ has asked me to prepare an *appreciation*, addressing the following vital question. Will the Boche stand and fight at the Senio, or will they pull back to the Santerno?'

Rummage pauses again.

'To help me marshal the arguments, I want to hear the latest evidence about the enemy. Let's start with his morale. What evidence do we have that he's ready to crack?'

'In the last few days, Sir,' a Captain says, 'the prisoners seem more willing to talk. I'm not referring to deserters who always talk. Now even the prisoners we snatch in raids are telling us what they know. They say it's common knowledge that our attack is coming and they fear what will happen to their troops at the front. But they also worry about the news from home: the constant bombing of German cities, the Allies crossing the Rhine, the Russians approaching Berlin. They fear for their families even more than they fear for themselves.'

'Thank you, Captain.' Rummage smooths his moustache. 'It seems our broadcasts are getting through.'

'Yes, Sir. I think they are. Just a few weeks ago they were mostly defiant, still talking about Vengeance weapons. There's been a distinct change.'

'But are they ready to snap?'

'They haven't lost all hope yet. They still talk about a final stand in Austria and the mountains of southern Germany. They dream of escaping to the Alps where they think they'll be safe.'

'May we conclude,' Rummage smirks, 'that their morale is more brittle now?'

Rummage looks around at the nodding heads.

'Good! Now what about the German strategy, Major Fisher? As an infantry man, what would you do in their position?'

Fisher stands up.

'Thank you, Major. Given the Germans' weakness across this whole front, I would fight where the odds were most in my favour. Having looked at the respective defences I have no doubt I'd make my stand at the Santerno. However ...'

'Thank you, Major. Does anyone disagree with Major Fisher's assessment?'

'I agree with the Major, but ...' a Captain from Intelligence says.

'Good, we're all agreed,' Rummage says emphatically. 'The best place for the Boche to fight would be at the Santerno. But is that what he'll do?'

'I wanted to add,' Major Fisher persists, 'that whilst I would plan to fight on the Santerno, I would want the Allies to believe I'd first defend the Senio.'

Rummage frowns. 'And why would you want to do that?'

'To draw the Allies' fire, Major. The enemy knows we precede each assault with a heavy barrage of shells and bombs. If he can make us waste our ordinance on the Senio, then there may be less to throw at him on the Santerno.'

'Do we all agree that this would be their best strategy?'

Rummage looks around the table. Seeing no disagreement, he presses on. 'If this is the Boche strategy, can we attack the Senio without a barrage? Can we save a quarter of a million shells?'

Rummage glares at them.

'But ... Major ... what about Hitler's orders?' Fisher says. 'We saw his orders in the papers we found in Faenza. He has forbidden his armies to withdraw until forced to ... on pain of death.'

'But General Vietinghoff isn't a fool,' Rummage says. 'Would he choose to defend the Senio and see his line broken when he could withdraw to the Santerno and hold the line? And if he plans to defend the Senio why did he fire off that barrage last night. Wasn't he clearing his ammo dumps in preparation for withdrawal?'

Rummage looks around the faces at the table.

'What do you say to that? Come along! British Intelligence is meant to be the best in the world. Let's hear what you have to say.'

Vermillion stares at the table but no one fills the void.

'I wonder, Sir,' she clears her throat, 'whether you'd like to hear about the latest unit reports and this morning's interrogations.'

'Are they relevant?'

'I think so, Sir.'

Vermillion swallows. 'I've read all of yesterday's Intelligence Summaries. None reports any evidence of enemy withdrawal. And normal skirmishing continues all along the line. Could they have withdrawn most of their men without our units noticing?'

'And what has Mae West produced?' Rummage turns to Major Fisher.

'Nothing in the latest stereographs suggests a withdrawal.'

'What should we conclude?' Rummage strokes his moustache.

'There's something else, Sir.' Vermillion looks up. 'Among this morning's prisoners there were three brought forward from reserve who only arrived yesterday at the line. Why were they sent forward if their unit was about to withdraw?'

'Thank you, Lieutenant. That's real intelligence!'

Rummage looks at his papers and runs a finger down the front sheet. At the bottom, he pauses.

'I take it no one disagrees,' he smiles. 'In which case I have my answer for HQ. Thank you, lady and gentlemen.'

CHAPTER 58

Colonel Mortimer is waiting as Frank and the other officers file into the farmhouse which serves as Battalion HQ. 'Find a place quickly and settle down.'

He strides across the dining room to the easel.

'Good morning, gentlemen. I don't need to tell you why you're here. Today, the 9th of April, will live in history as we launch Operation Buckland, the offensive for which you've trained so hard. The Battalion has a vital role in this coordinated Allied attack, which will extend across the whole Italian front. Our purpose is nothing less than to destroy the other team's armies in Italy.'

Mortimer points at the first map, which shows the Italian front dotted with flags – red for the Allies and blue for the Germans – indicating the location of each unit.

'Today is D-Day when Eighth Army will hit the other team with a powerful right hook which will take us across the Senio and the Santerno. All the other team's goods are in their shop window; they have precious few reserves. And when they commit those reserves as they struggle to hold us, then Fifth Army will deliver a strong straight left that will take them past Bologna and into northern Italy. Attacking from the right and the left we shall break the other team's armies south of the Po.'

The Colonel moves across to the familiar large-scale map of the Senio front. The seated officers lean forward. This is the bit that matters.

The Colonel reports on the successful clearing of the near embankment. He describes in more detail the obstacles they can expect on the far bank and the plans for dealing with each of them. He also outlines the scale of the build-up of munitions and the bridge-building capacity that will swing into action once a bridgehead is established on the other side.

'After this briefing you will rejoin your units and quietly withdraw them from the river. The main show will start at 1320 hours with a bombardment from the air. Our planes will hammer the other team in their bunkers. And then the artillery will pound the floodbanks. This bombardment – our heaviest since el Alamein – is designed to destroy the other team's mines and wire because we won't have time to clear the embankments in the usual way. Then the bombardment will move back two hundred yards and the advance will start at 1920 hours led by the Crocodiles and Wasps.'

The Colonel looks at his watch and asks for questions; but there are none. 'Now gentlemen, return to your units and prepare to move your men back from the river. When they're at their starting lines, I'll address them.'

* * *

Colonel Mortimer clambers onto the back of a Jeep.

'Many of you will remember el Alamein.' His voice booms through the megaphone. 'Before that battle ... Monty told us ... we would knock the other team for six ... and that's what we did.' (cheers)

The Colonel's message is clear and confident, yet unlike at the morning briefing he now looks ill at ease. His face seems dragged down by the weight of his responsibilities.

'I have a message for each of you from General McCreery, the commander of Eighth Army.'

> *"The German forces are now very groggy, and only need one mighty punch to knock them out for good. The moment has now come for us to take the field for the last battle which will end the war in Europe."*

'Our job today,' the Colonel continues, 'is to cross the Senio ... and press on towards Bologna ... and beyond.'

'The Senio is a small river ...' (ironic cheers) '... no more than ten yards wide.' (cheers) 'River crossings are never simple ... yet on the western front ... Monty's troops ... have already crossed the Rhine ...' (muted cheers) '... and that river is four hundred yards wide.'

'And don't imagine you'll be alone ... we'll attack the other team ... all along the Senio.' (silence) 'Now let's give them ... a terrific knock.' (cheers) 'Not just a bloody nose ... we want to knock them down (cheers) ... and count them out.' (loud cheers) 'Then we can end this wretched war.' (more loud cheers)

Frank studies the men's faces as they shuffle back to their positions. They look fit and cheerful enough. They believe in the justice of their cause and are sure that Eighth Army will

306

prevail and the war will soon end. But this confidence doesn't extend to their own survival. They know that some of them – one in ten or even one in five – will fall, so that the rest, with their loved ones, can get to the promised land. But if their time has come to be amongst the fallen, they pray they will die quickly, for they fear more than anything being maimed so their families won't want them back.

The Colonel's words have done nothing to reduce their anxieties. It might have helped if he had talked about the enemy's defences and how each element had been addressed. Describing the plan to his Platoon, Frank feels confident about Allied success, but that still can't quell the gnawing awareness that some of them won't survive.

As Frank's men rest in the sunshine, these thoughts flicker through their minds. Some seek distraction by bringing out packs of cards, while others try to read. But most are asleep at the drop of a hat: for Frank this ability is the mark of the seasoned soldier.

With the preparations complete, there is nothing left for Frank to do. He leans back. Looking up, the pale blossom all around stands out against the azure sky. The spring colours have never seemed more vibrant.

He closes his eyes; he needs to talk to Vermillion.

'… my dearest Milione … I wish I could be with you now … to see your lovely face … to hold your perfect hands … and to hear your voice … but I'm afraid I might not listen very well … there's so much to say … I love you my darling … being with you has been the best thing in my life … thank you for that wonderful year in Naples … and thank you for supporting my return to the front … I know it was awful when I left … I'm truly sorry if I hurt you … but whatever happens now, I'm sure I was right to return … if I survive, and I believe I will … I'll return with my head held high … knowing I didn't run away … but if that isn't to be … I want you to remember the happy times … and to know that – DVWP – I will have died doing my duty …'

Frank gets out some paper and starts to write. He must finish before the post is collected.

He lies back and looks up again. Despite the constant ringing in his ears, he hears the growl of the heavy bombers. It's 1320 and the Liberators and Flying Fortresses arrive on cue to pound the German defences. Frank watches in awe as their bomb doors open and their explosive spawn drifts slowly down.

… Frank is at Salerno … looking along the beach … Paestum is lost in the smoke … the Germans intend to drive them into the sea …

He watches the bombs descend until they disappear from sight. Then comes the deep percussion as they explode. 'May the heavies be more accurate today!' He knows that at Cassino too many of their bombs went astray.

A cloud of dust rises from behind the floodbank and begins to spread along the line. Plumes of thick dark smoke record hits on buildings or stores.

… the flat in Ealing … with the windows blown out … Maggie, you never had a chance …

The heavies complete their runs and head south in a new formation. They are soon replaced by the fighter-bombers and then by the Spitfires and Kittyhawks which fire their machine guns and cannons as they dive.

At 1515 this phase of the bombardment ends. The moment they've been dreading is approaching. All the months of studying the enemy, planning the advance, training and building up supplies, are about to be tested. What is needed now is the will – collective and individual – to break the enemy for once and for all.

In a brief moment of silence, the earth catches its breath. Then, with the roar of a myriad guns, the artillery starts its final bombardment. Frank covers his ears. The floodbanks erupt, as though the serpents have awoken and are thrashing their tails. Flames spout from their many heads, spewing out earth and dust.

The shelling goes on and on until Frank finally falls asleep.

But he awakes with a jolt when the barrage stops. His head still resounds to the booming of the guns and his ears ring with their clangour.

When the Battalion's battery pauses, the space is filled by other batteries up and down the river. He can hear distant shells explode and he sees the flashes but the targets are hidden by the floodbanks.

After ten minutes the Battalion's barrage starts again. This deliberate on and off pattern, designed to catch enemy troops as they emerge from their bunkers, continues throughout the afternoon.

Frank watches the sun slowly sink, pausing briefly above the horizon before it disappears. The air suddenly cools. But in the batteries the men in their vests still sweat to sustain their rate of fire.

Frank's watch shows 1807. More than an hour to go. He tries not to look too often but it's only fifteen minutes since he checked before. The guns have been firing for almost three hours, shell after shell after fucking shell. Clearly there's no longer a shortage of bloody ammo.

The smudge of dust and smoke above the river turns to apricot in the setting sun. As the Allied shelling continues, the German guns respond. Several shells burst on the near embankment throwing up fountains of earth. Frank's men abandon their letters and card games and push themselves lower in their trenches. The time for prayer has come.

Frank reminds himself about the Intelligence assessment that the enemy is stretched to man the whole Italian front. But even if they're right it doesn't alter the Germans' advantage in defending a fortified line. Before the Allies can advance, they must break this and the other defensive lines. The empty feeling in the pit of Frank's stomach is growing.

'… Oh God …' he closes his eyes, '… please make me equal to this task … help me not to fail the men … and don't let them see I'm afraid …'

Frank reopens his eyes and peers at the rounded hump of the embankment, now black against the fading western sky.

Towards that blackness he must soon lead his men; tonight there will be no moon.

German shells are landing on the nearside of the embankment in case the Battalion is sheltering in its lee, which in a few minutes is exactly where they'll be. In the twilight, Frank surveys the strained faces all around. He checks his watch again. 1913. Seven minutes to go.

Frank's head rings as the nearest battery pulls out all the stops. He looks towards the south, away from the fog of the battle, where the first stars have appeared.

One more minute to go.

He holds his breath as he signals to his NCOs.

The engines of tanks and trucks rev up.

1920. H-Hour on D-Day. Soon they won't be D-Day Dodgers. On cue, the bombardment of the floodbank ends as the artillery moves its target two hundred yards ahead.

In the fading light dark figures appear from the trenches and dugouts to form up in their units. At Frank's signal they start to advance. Fifty yards to the right is a Crocodile and to the left a pair of Wasps. Frank knows what these weapons are meant to do, but he hasn't seen them in action and he's not sure he wants to.

With two of his Sections, he advances parallel to the Crocodile but just behind. As shells whistle overhead he breaks into a canter on the flat ground. The third Section follows behind, lugging the kit for a pontoon bridge. Beyond the Crocodile, Frank picks out Stansfield's Platoon in the gloom. On his left Purdie is visibly excited, leading his first assault.

The Crocodile, a Churchill tank towing what looks like a tender, heads for a specially built ramp which runs up the side of the embankment. Frank remembers Gazala and the tanks' vulnerability to German guns. Yet he still feels reassured by the beast's proximity. He urges the men to maintain their pace as they approach the lower slopes where the ground has been mangled by bombs and mines.

German shells race over his head; their gunners are firing blind and the shells burst in the trenches the Platoon has just vacated. The ground judders as the Battalion's guns adjust their target to the German batteries two thousand yards away.

Frank heads for the gap between two tattered white tapes, marking the limits of the minefields. Ahead, the Crocodile approaches the top. Frank starts to climb. Soon he will discover the effect of the day's bombardment which should have cleared the enemy from their positions on the far embankment. But experience has shown that troops in concrete bunkers usually emerge unscathed and ready to man their guns.

The Crocodile gains the summit of the embankment and manoeuvres into position. Flurries of bullets clash against its superstructure. Frank presses on but stops when he sees the silhouette of the far floodbank. His Platoon spreads out along the edge of the ridge. To their left the Wasps – based on tracked Bren carriers – are also in position.

Frank stares into the darkness unable to tell where the enemy bunkers are hidden. He just has to trust that each position has been mapped in recent days and the Crocodile crews know their targets.

Frank pulls back as a heavy German machine gun opens fire. There's a yell from one of the Wasp crew. A German shell drops into the river throwing up a plume of water.

At that moment a fireball explodes in front of the Crocodile. With a monstrous roar an inferno of flame streams across the river, cloaking the far embankment with smoke. Frank shudders as the dragon catches its breath and the flames die down. He covers his nose. The air stinks of fuel and seared earth and another smell he can't place.

The Wasps too open fire, hosing the far bank with sheets of flame. The Crocodile attacks another target. Soon the whole embankment is ablaze. Frank lowers his head. He hears screams but God knows from where. Jesus, are there men on fire?

Frank's wireless operator taps him on the shoulder.

'THE COLONEL SAYS GO!'

Frank stands up, blowing his whistle.

Another German shell explodes.

'GO! NOW!' he yells.

Sergeant Short hustles the men over the embankment and watches them slither down towards the black river.

As the Bren teams spray more fire across the floodbank, Frank steps onto the dark slope. Beneath him the ground crumbles and he too slides to the bottom. There's a flash to his left. The earth shudders as a mine explodes. Several men cry out. To the right a shell bursts, spraying icy water across the embankments.

'Come on Sergeant! Get the men across!'

Underhill and Talbot push past with a lightweight boat. They drop it into the water, jump in and paddle across. They scramble onto the bank and hammer frantically to secure the metal posts which will tether the pontoon bridge. Kirkup and Roberts haul the boat back. Then they pull themselves across and clamber up the other side.

A German machine gun on the far embankment, targets Purdie's Platoon. But a belch of smoke and flame from a Wasp brings the firing to an end. Frank knows from the clamour that several men have gone down. Someone shouts for stretchers.

… Frank pictures Purdie with Laura on that last night in Sassovivo …

'Captain!' Short yells from near the water. 'The pontoon's in place!'

'Get the men across, Sergeant!' Frank heads for the pontoon himself.

'STEADY!' Short bellows, as the men run towards the lightweight bridge.

Frank lowers his head. In a few strides he reaches the far side. He clambers up the slope. The earth has been loosened by the shelling. He drops onto his knees and peers over the top of the far embankment. Blackness. Hundreds of yards ahead Allied shells are raining on the enemy. This is where their training should pay off, because to provide an effective umbrella the men must keep close to this barrage.

Frank looks at his watch. 2037. They're pretty much on schedule. At 2120 the barrage will move forward again. By then they must advance two hundred yards. Tonight they lack tank cover: a bridge big enough for tanks should be ready by dawn. Until then the artillery will pound every road to keep German tanks at bay.

'Captain, we've cleared the floodbank!' The Sergeant wipes his mouth.

'Is everything all right, Sergeant?'

'Yes, Sir.' Short turns away and retches again. Frank puts his hand on his shoulder.

'It's a bit a shock, Sir. Seeing what the Crocodile's done. No need for grenades, Sir, to clear the enemy. The buggers have all been fried: their bodies are shrivelled; they look no bigger than kids.'

Oh God! That was the smell! Frank's stomach lurches but he doesn't throw up.

... he sees a soldier with his uniform on fire as he clambers out of his tank ...

Steady! Frank orders to himself. That was at Gazala, not here.

'Well done, Sergeant.' Frank coughs. 'Advance with your Section to point P, near the trees ... take one of the Brens ... and give the others covering fire.'

CHAPTER 59

'Where the hell is Cato?' Falcon glances at his watch. 'We've been waiting for half an hour.'

'I told you he wouldn't come,' Sandro says.

'I talked to him three days ago,' Falcon says. 'He swore he'd be here.'

'That was before the supply drop,' Sandro adds.

'Come on Falcon, sit down.' Paolo signals for Sandro to be quiet. 'We can decide without him.'

Falcon sits down reluctantly. 'Now the advance has started, I want to agree your plan.'

The room where Paolo and Sandro stayed last night feels cold. It's in a traditional stone house, which still retains its winter chill despite the warmer weather outside. Paolo lit the wood fire when Falcon arrived but it hasn't built up much heat.

'Have you checked *all* the bridges?' Falcon shifts closer to the fire. 'Which one is best for disrupting the German retreat as Eighth Army advances.'

'Several bridges are already down, Falcon.' Paolo spreads out an old map. 'But we've checked them all. We've found a key one: near where several roads converge to cross a tributary of the Brenta. If we can close that bridge, it will stop any Germans moving north from this whole sector.'

'And not just Germans!' Falcon says. 'There are rumours of a Fascist plan for a final stand in Valtelina, north of Como. You can tell Cato that if you hold this bridge you'll trap Fascists too.'

Falcon looks up from the map. 'Sandro said the supply drop had changed things for Cato. But he was desperate for supplies. Why the hell has the drop stopped him from being here?'

'You're not going to like this, Falcon,' Paolo says. 'But I think Cato has changed sides.'

'To join the Germans and the Blackshirts?'

'Don't be ridiculous! No, he just thinks he's better off siding with the Communists.'

'That really is ridiculous! He was always dead against them.'

'I'm not saying Cato is a Communist. He is still the same old Liberal who believes in democracy. But he thinks the Communists have changed and now he can trust them.'

'Why the hell would he think that?'

Paolo gets up and starts pacing around the small room. Falcon studies the map and shifts closer to the fire.

'Careful, Falcon!' Sandro says. 'Don't drop it into the flames. It's our only one.'

Falcon shifts the map slightly but keeps reading Sandro's detailed notes about each road bridge north of Padua.

'That looks pretty comprehensive. Well done, both of you. On reflection I'm starting to think that Cato may be irrelevant. It doesn't really matter what he decides to do, just as long as you can take the bridge and hold it till the Allies arrive.'

'I'm glad that's agreed.' Paolo sits down, staring intently at Falcon. 'Look, Falcon, you need to understand that things have changed for the partisans now the Allies are finally coming. Perhaps I should explain.'

Paolo buries his head in his hands giving Sandro time to jump in while Paolo thinks.

'You asked why the supply drop has changed things,' Sandro says. 'It's because of the British refusal to give the Communists any arms. That led the Garibaldi groups – the Communists – to start looting from non-communist partisans. This latest drop has simply raised the tension. Cato says if he doesn't agree to share the arms, then the Communists will simply steal them.'

'Well, that's very clear!' Falcon says. 'We must move the arms immediately and hide them, so they can't be taken.'

'Hold on, Falcon,' Paolo says. 'What Sandro says is right as far as it goes, but it's more complex than that. It's not just about threats. Cato has shifted his position because the Communists have changed theirs. The Communists used to say they needed arms because once the Allies left, they planned to seize power in the name of the people …'

'… all the usual revolutionary stuff.' Sandro interjects.

'The point is,' Paolo continues, 'now the Communists say that after the war they'll support elections. They can say that, of course, because they're certain they'll win. They're happy to gain power without a fight.'

Falcon looks confused. He gets up, walks over to the window and peers out. 'Why the hell does Cato trust the Communists? Hasn't he seen how the Russians have treated the Poles? He had better watch out if any Polish troops come this way.'

'You're right, Falcon,' Paolo says. 'What the fuck difference does it make if the Communists take control either way? But Cato sees this change as fundamental. As long as the Communists support elections, Cato won't oppose them.'

'And then there's his view about Fascists.' Sandro adds.

'I was coming to that,' Paolo says. 'Falcon, you know the Communists had demanded a purge of every Fascist – anyone who held a *tessera* recording their party membership. It was a crazy idea, making half the population into criminals. Everyone disagreed, so now the bolshies are saying that the purge can be limited to just the big cheeses. And Cato has swallowed that too. Remember that before the armistice, Cato worked for the mayor.'

'Stop!' Falcon swallows. 'This is too bloody tortuous!'

Falcon makes no attempt to hide his bewilderment. For the first time Paolo feels sorry for him.

'Forget all this political stuff,' Falcon steadies himself. 'Just tell me this. Are you two joining Cato?'

Falcon's eyes flicker from Paolo to Sandro and back.

'Not bloody likely!' Sandro says.

'We're sticking with the CIL, Paolo says. 'We shall hold the bridge. *Eliminate the Germans first; then deal with the Fascists.* That's our approach.'

'How many others think like you?'

'At least half a dozen,' Paolo says quickly. 'It's the men from the Veneto who side with Cato. They're concerned with who will run Padua after the war.'

'With you two as well, that should be enough to hold the bridge.'

'Don't worry, Falcon. We'll hold it, even if we're only two.'

CHAPTER 60

Rummage grins at Vermillion as he drops a grubby notebook onto her table. 'This is the diary of a German officer. Tell me whether it's of interest.'

Rummage has been making a habit of visiting Vermillion unannounced. Just when she's settled down to work, he appears with a request for some completely new task. Many of these jobs are interesting but they leave her feeling anxious about completing her normal work.

Vermillion lowers her enamel mug and scrambles to her feet. 'Yes, Sir. Shall I leave the Intelligence Summaries?'

'That's up to you, Lieutenant. But I need to know about the diary before we visit the cage.'

She watches him leave the tent before sitting down again. She clasps the mug in both hands. The morning is fine but the sun has scarcely risen and there's still a nip in the air. She gulps some coffee while assessing the pile of papers in front of her: she is probably halfway through. She shivers and takes another gulp. Already the coffee seems cool.

The reports describe the crossing of the Senio. Operation Buckland has started well with both infantry and armour already across the river. But German resistance has increased since they committed their reserves and Allied casualties have been substantial.

She hasn't seen the report from 4th Battalion. She intended to leave it until last, but now she flicks through the remaining reports. Nothing from 4th Battalion. Nothing. She rifles through the papers again. Nothing. It isn't unusual of course: reports are often delayed or lost. But Vermillion catches her breath.

She finishes the tepid coffee and picks up the notebook, trying to refocus her mind.

As she skims through the pages she remembers Edmund's letter which arrived this morning. She needn't write to the Contessa: her engagement is on again and Edmund will soon have custody as Eduardo's father. Thank goodness that's over; if Edmund sends another letter she won't even open it.

She looks back at the German diary which has entries for most days of the last two months. The initial pages are neatly written but that doesn't last and in recent days the writing is disjointed and wild.

The content of the diary follows a similar pattern. Early entries describe the Germans' success in fortifying the line and resisting Allied attempts to occupy the embankment on the Allied side of the Senio. At that stage the author, an artillery officer, seems confident his men will hold firm, still believing in ultimate victory. But recent entries are more telling.

"For days the attacks from the air and artillery shelling have been continuous."

"A wing of Jabos dive-bombed one of our batteries, knocking out three of our guns and causing several casualties. They arrive with such a terrible noise and at such speed that even the strongest men reel in terror. I have to order the men out of the shelters to recover the dead and the dying."

"The men are hungry: last night they tried – unsuccessfully – to shoot a pigeon in the hope of eating meat for the first time in weeks."

"Tonight, we must move the guns back again. It happens almost every night. Discipline is poor. We no longer receive any mail. The men are afraid they won't see their families again."

"More bombing. We lost two self-propelled guns and several men. The infantry is pulling out but we have no orders to retreat. What is the point of going on? We can no longer fight. The army is finished."

Vermillion takes a deep breath as she looks up from the diary. She feels no pity for the author, who has striven to kill Frank and thousands of others in defence of a barbaric regime. But she does feel an awful sense of waste.

'Are you coming, my dear?' Rummage strides back in. 'What did you make of the diary?'

Vermillion jumps to her feet and follows him but then runs back for the diary in case he wants to go through it in detail. She catches up before he springs into the Jeep. She climbs up beside him.

'You won't need that.' He points at the diary. 'I just want to know whether it's of interest.'

'Yes, Sir. It confirms the Germans are demoralised. The constant bombing and shelling have taken their toll. They seem close to throwing in the towel.'

'That's encouraging,' Rummage gazes at her. 'But will we find the same with the prisoners in the cage?'

Vermillion hangs on to the side of the Jeep as they hurry along the broken roads, recently switched to one-way traffic. They overtake heavy lorries, occasional tank transporters and a convoy of empty ambulances, all heading towards the front. But they have to queue to cross the new bridges, some already scarred by enemy fire.

A wing of Allied bombers roars overhead and by the time the planes have passed the rumble of the guns seems louder. Ahead and to the right the morning haze is thickened with smoke. To the left the blue jagged line of the Apennines provides a bookend to the plain. Vermillion wonders when the Fifth Army will emerge from those hills.

The Jeep slows again.

'This is the Senio, Lieutenant!' Rummage shouts.

Vermillion stares at the broken backs of the floodbanks, littered with scorched and splintered spars of metal seemingly planted in the mud. The embankments look like beached leviathans stuck with harpoons.

She hunches her shoulders and hugs one arm across her chest while clinging to the Jeep with the other as they rattle over the bridge. She gapes at the filthy little river. How awful that men died for this.

On the far side the devastation is even greater. The fields are empty and forlorn, pocked with giant craters. Farm buildings are reduced to rubble and the trees are burnt and broken as though autumn has just replaced spring. Vermillion thinks of photographs from the Great War. Is this what her father knew thirty year ago?

She closes her eyes and hangs onto the Jeep for dear life, until they jolt to a halt near a farmhouse which appears intact. Beside it stands the new cage, hedged with coils of barbed wire which spiral like waves. Within, a grey sea of grubby German uniforms ebbs and flows. Some prisoners sprawl on the ground while others stare vacantly, rousing themselves only when a new truckload of comrades arrives.

Vermillion puts her hankie to her nose to temper the smell emerging from the cage. Outside Allied soldiers flaunt their Tommy guns as they saunter past.

'How many prisoners today?' Rummage asks the Sergeant at the makeshift gate.

'Let me see, Sir. We had four hundred and thirty-one but there are twenty-seven new recruits. That makes four hundred and fifty-eight by my reckoning, Sir.'

The Sergeant runs through the breakdown of units and ranks. Rummage marks the list and sets off towards the farmhouse. Vermillion follows.

Several prisoners are brought in. They say they're glad the war is ending but don't speak about the fighting. They don't seem uncooperative but are clearly in a state of shock.

'Are you ready for the next one, Sir?' the Sergeant asks. 'He might be a tad more interesting – he's a deserter.'

'Hauptmann Malzer, did you desert?' Rummage says without looking up.

'Yes, Sir, I deserted because Germany has lost the war.' Malzer waits until Rummage looks up. 'Yesterday was hell, Sir. I have fought in many battles, but that was the worst I have known. The Jabos were terrible.'

'The dive-bombers?'

'Yes.'

'Where were you during the bombardment?'

'Just back from the floodbank …'

'Show me on the map.'

The prisoner takes a few moments to orientate himself but eventually finds the place. 'It was terrible, Sir. The earth shook and the sky vibrated. We couldn't breathe, we couldn't think.'

'And where was your brigade HQ?'

'In a house four or five kilometres behind the line.'

'Show me on the map.'

'I hope I can find it.' The prisoner looks at the map for some time. 'I attended a briefing two days ago. Yes, that must be the building. Looking east we had a view of the church.'

'Thank you.' Rummage writes down the grid reference. 'Sergeant, call in an immediate air attack. Let me know when it's confirmed.'

Vermillion looks at the Captain, trying to imagine how he feels.

'The breaks in the barrage were the worst,' he starts again. 'We never knew when it was safe to come out and move the guns.'

'Was it the bombardment that led you to desert?' Rummage continues writing as he speaks.

'No, Sir, we had been through bombardments before. No, it was the flames. That's what finished the men. How could they fight against an inferno? It was like a volcano … or a scene from hell.'

'The flame-throwers made you desert?'

'Yes, and the chance of getting to America.' For the first time the Captain's face lights up. 'That's where I hope to go.'

CHAPTER 61

Boom! The explosion jolts Frank awake. The target wasn't his slit trench but the bridge being constructed several hundred yards behind. It must have been a powerful shell.

Earlier in the night his Platoon had fought their way across the Santerno. The water was shallow enough to wade but the floodbanks were too steep for tanks. The Platoon was ordered to dig in, until the bridge is ready.

Frank had found some neatly-dug German trenches, where his men quickly settled in. Most fell asleep at once, exhausted by four days of fighting. Frank marvels at their fortitude. He doesn't sleep immediately but at least the fear of nightmares doesn't keep him awake.

Crash! Another shell explodes behind them, close to the floodbank. Shit! The sappers are certainly earning their keep. Near the line they have to work at night, but they can't construct bridges in total darkness and any lights attract more shelling.

Frank climbs out of the trench and walks over to an abandoned farmhouse. He climbs the stairs but even from the top he can't see where the firing is coming from. Spring has provided perfect cover.

He gropes his way back to the slitter and soon falls asleep.

* * *

'WAKE UP, SIR! IT'S URGENT!'

Flaring from another shell lights up the Sergeant's face. There are more flashes and a roll of thunder as Allied guns reply.

'What is it, Short?' Frank sits up.

'A message from Major Bewdley, Sir.'

What the hell does Roger want now? The Battalion's next advance is set for 0800 once the tanks are across.

'They say there's a Tiger at large. Reported at P36W17 last night, threatening our advance. The Major insists we flush it out.'

'Have you looked at the map?'

'Yes, Sir. It's twelve hundred yards, Sir. Towards the north-west. A cluster of buildings. Probably a farm, Sir.'

'Well done, Short. What's the time?'

'0440, Sir.'

'Thank you. You'd better wake the Platoon.'

'One other thing, Sir. We may not have tank support. They're still not across.'

'Tell the men to form up in the farmyard. They'll have cover there.'

Frank gathers his kit and shuffles outside. Above, the sky pulses with flashes of gunfire and exploding shells. Not far away a Verey light illuminates the countryside.

Frank looks at his map. The location Roger gave is at roughly two o'clock from where Frank is standing with his back to the farm. Ahead the flat farmland is punctuated with irrigation canals. They should be easy to cross and will provide useful cover, unless the Germans have occupied them first.

"A Tiger at large." Frank doubts that a handful of rustic sheds could conceal such a powerful tank. Weighing sixty tons, the Tiger is constructed like a battleship with massive armour plating and a formidable 88mm gun which can cripple Allied tanks. The Battalion's Shermans are less than half the Tiger's size. Even at close range their main gun lacks the power to knock out a Tiger. And when hit, the Shermans are prone to brew up. That's why the men call them Ronsons.

Frank rubs his eyes. Little has changed since the desert. Will the Battalion's tanks again be fodder for the German guns? It will be a lucky day for the Shermans' crews if the bridge isn't ready. But can the Battalion advance without armour? Their only weapon against German tanks is the handheld PIAT – Projector, Infantry, Anti-Tank – with its hundred-yard range. And even if fired from that distance, it may not kill a Tiger.

Frank looks up. There's a hint of light in the east. They need to get under cover. At the back of the farmhouse Short catches him. 'It's Major Bewdley, Sir.'

Frank takes a deep breath. Is this the moment to ask Roger about Huggins?

'Frank?' Roger's voice sounds remote. 'Is the Platoon ready? This is important. We'll start a stonk on the Battalion's objectives at 0800. It will lift at 0900. You must be ready by then to attack the farmhouse. What? Yes, I know you're waiting for tanks. They'll be across shortly. But you must advance NOW! The Shermans will catch up. No, we can't talk about Corporal Huggins. Are you clear about your orders? Excellent. I know you can do it.'

Frank sighs as he gathers his Section leaders and tells them to lead the men along the road heading east until it bends to the left. That will be their starting line.

Hearing the drumming of men's boots Frank hums the tune to Lili Marlene. He wishes he could get the choir singing. He stops humming but the tune persists. The words coming from the men's mouths are now clearly audible.

Look around the mountains, through the mist and rain
See the scattered crosses, some that bear no name
Heartbreak and toil, suffering gone
The lads beneath, they slumber on
They are the D-Day Dodgers, who'll stay in Italy

'Sergeant. Quieten the men. We don't want the Teds to hear.'

The Sergeant brings the Platoon to a halt and orders them to stop singing. The sound of their voices is quickly replaced with a thin whistling as they maintain the tune.

'Squa ... ad, sto ... op whist ... ling!

Frank feels a surge of pride as Section by Section the men march away. They have the drawn look of soldiers who have been at the front too long and Frank knows from their set expressions that they now inhabit another world, where all their energies are dedicated to performing their individual duties, and to surviving. Soon they will destroy, for once and for all, this enemy which has harried them for all these years. Bloody Boche! Why the hell are they still fighting? Surely they know they've lost. Haven't the bastards killed enough? Thank God the time has come to knock some sense into their skulls.

As promised, the artillery bombardment begins at 0800. Frank takes this as the signal for his Platoon to advance across the open ground. They move cautiously one Section at a time with the other Sections ready to give covering fire.

The German artillery focuses on the unfinished bridge until a wing of medium bombers appears to target the German guns. Another wing follows, but the enemy shelling doesn't stop completely.

Frank's progress is slow. New vegetation across their route means he can't see their objective and he grows increasingly fearful of an ambush. In flat countryside like this, one well-sited machine gun could kill a whole Section. And the countless irrigation channels slow them down, leaving the men wet, cold and exhausted.

When the Allied bombers withdraw, the Platoon is still some way short of the farmhouse. Frank listens to the steady bass of the guns in the distance, hoping to pick out the sound of the Battalion's tanks. The crackle of sniper fire is all around. On the right a machine gun opens fire just as Frank had feared. But he still can't hear the sound of engines. Either they haven't made it yet or his ears are too deaf.

Ahead to the left a machine gun rattles. Bullets smack against the vines above their heads. Shit! The Germans must know they're coming. Frank orders the Brens and mortars to return fire whilst B Section moves forward again.

Frank crawls to the edge of the field. To the right are more vines but directly ahead is an orchard surrounding the farm. Frank gets to his feet behind the trunk of an old pear tree. The white light from its blossom saturates his head.

Two hundred yards away at roughly eleven o'clock, he can make out some buildings. There's a gaping hole in part of the front wall, probably the result of Allied shelling.

He raises his field glasses for a better view. As he watches, a shadow seems to move. Then the shadow jumps and he hears a loud report. Is that the barrel of a gun, protruding from the wall? Could it belong to a Tiger?

Frank drops onto his knees and crawls back to the Platoon. Behind to the left he hears a commotion as a tank crashes through the vines towards them. He sees the outline of the Sherman. It slows. It must have seen him. He crouches as he runs towards his Platoon.

To his right, near the river, another Sherman crosses the last channel before the farm. It stops and slowly swings its main gun towards the farmhouse. It should have a clear line of fire through the vines. But before it can fire, an explosion throws up a fountain of earth, hiding it completely.

Frank holds his breath. He waits for the tank to burst into flames. Nothing happens at first. Then the tank starts to move, limping slowly away. BANG! Another blast shrouds the tank in dust. Has it been hit? Silence. Then above the dust, black smoke balloons towards the sky.

'Oh God!' Frank panics. What should he do? They must get the men out of the Sherman.

Steady!

'Sergeant! Take two men to evacuate the crew. Bailey, get me the field telephone.'

The other Shermans fire at the farmhouse, provoking another shell from the Tiger, aimed at the Sherman on the left. The shot seems to fall short. But as the dust settles Frank sees the tank's port track is broken. The Ronson is now a sitting duck.

Frank scribbles the grid reference and whirls the handle of the field telephone. 'Sighting of Tiger confirmed. Tell air ops to call in a fighter from the cab rank.'

The German machine gun fires at the burning tank. Frank sees Short again as he nears the tank and disappears from view. The hatch opens and the first man clambers out. Frank wants to keep watching but he turns away.

The tank with the broken tracks fires another round. At the same time the third tank crosses the waterway and turns towards the house. The Tiger ignores it and fires again at the tank with the broken track. This time it finds its target. The Sherman shudders before disappearing in dark smoke.

Frank is sweating all over. He orders the mortar and Bren Sections to keep firing. Anything to cause a distraction. Above, he hears the howl of Allied dive-bombers. The ground shakes as their bombs explode. The German machine gun stops. Silence reigns. Frank sends two men to help with the second Sherman. 'Watch out in case the ammo explodes!'

From the farmhouse comes the rumble of a powerful engine. The Tiger has been driven from its cover. Once it's out in the open, the Allied twenty-five pounders will go in for the kill.

The surviving Sherman accelerates, determined to join in the chase. The crew's only hope is to aim for the side or rear, where the Tiger's armour is less thick.

With the Bren team giving covering fire, Frank orders an advance into the orchard. Through the trees he sees the Tiger scurrying westward, following a narrow track between open fields. Eruptions of earth record the arrival of sighting shells. Above, another fighter-bomber is on the prowl; it risks being hit by the shelling if it doesn't await its turn.

More cascades of earth. Then a deep thud as a shell from a twenty-five pounder finds it range. The Tiger judders to a halt. The Sherman fires another shell. This time the brute explodes. Frank bows his head and closes his eyes. Thank God, the war is nearly over.

CHAPTER 62

Roger isn't surprised to see Colonel Mortimer smile as he starts the morning briefing.

'Gentlemen, I have a message from General McCreery thanking you and your men.'

Mortimer looks round the table nodding at each of the Company commanders. They beam back with the look of men who believe they're winning because they deserve to. Roger lowers his eyes.

'The General is bloody delighted with the success of the campaign. I shall visit each of your units to thank the men myself.'

Roger sits up a little straighter and nods in agreement but joining in with the celebrations is the last thing he wants to do.

'Let's start with an update from Intelligence,' Mortimer continues. 'Can we safely say, Major, that the other team are on the run?'

'The news from Germany is good ...'

'Yes! Yes! But what about Italy?'

Major Addison marches across to one of his charts.

'On 9th April – yes, two weeks ago – Eighth Army launched Operation Buckland with a thrust on the right.' He wields his swagger stick vigorously and almost brings down the map. 'And more than a week ago Fifth Army began its drive in the centre. In that time we've made substantial progress.' He pokes vaguely at the map to identify the key locations. 'The Poles have entered Bologna. And we have crossed the Senio,' (jab), 'the Santerno,' (jab) 'and the Sillaro ...'

Major Addison glances at the Colonel who nods.

'The key to our success has been the speed of our advance. We've denied the other team the time to man their defences; now they're falling back in disarray.'

The Major points to a map of the whole area.

'We've crossed these small rivers successfully. But now we're approaching the Po, a very different river! This crossing presents a new challenge. The river is too wide for the Crocodiles to play a part. It will be more like a landing from the sea. But we're not there yet. Today I want to show you that the Po is a barrier for the Germans as they retreat. No bridges across the Po remain standing. And the other team have no boats of any size. If they flee across the river, they must abandon their tanks and heavy equipment, hoping their men can swim or find small boats.'

Now the Major is rattling along.

'Their only other choice is to make a stand with the river at their backs. But that won't be easy as they lack supplies. They've already abandoned much of their transport for want of fuel. Aerial photographs clearly show they're resorting to carts pulled by horses or even oxen!'

He points at the map 'We now have two further chances to

catch their Tenth Army. Either here before they reach the river or here as they try to cross.'

The Colonel thanks the Major warmly. Roger can't think why. He hasn't told them anything new. And how does he still have time to draw these pretty coloured maps that could come from a nursery?

'Now,' Mortimer says, 'I want to hear from the Company commanders. Let's start with A Company.'

Roger tries not to listen to the description of A Company with almost twenty-five percent losses in the two weeks since the campaign began. And B Company isn't much better.

Then it's Roger's turn.

'I can say with confidence that morale in C Company is high, despite the sad loss of Lieutenant Purdie. Sergeant Short now leads his Platoon. Overall losses have been seventeen percent.'

'Thank you, Major.'

Mortimer quickly runs through the plans for the day's advance. He concludes with a reminder that their aim is to break the other team before they can cross the Po. 'This time we mustn't let them escape, as we did at Messina and Cassino.'

As they file out, the Colonel asks Roger to stay behind.

Roger turns and calls to Frank. 'I need to talk to the Colonel. I'll visit your Platoon this evening. We can talk then.'

Roger turns back. 'I'm sorry, Sir.'

Mortimer smiles indulgently. 'I just wanted to say how sad I was to hear about Purdie.'

'We were very sorry to lose him, Sir, but Short is doing well.'

'How is Hill bearing up?

'I'm keeping him busy, Sir. His Platoon will lead us across the Po as soon as the boats are ready.'

'Excellent, Major. Your Company has done very well.' Mortimer catches Roger's eye. 'There is another thing. I don't want to tell the others yet, but I know you'll be discreet.'

'Of course, Sir.'

Rogers smiles; this might be about his promotion, which is long overdue.

Mortimer smiles but hesitates before he continues.

'As you know, Roger, the war in Europe will soon be over. But it's different with the Japs. They're far from finished. Eighth Army is preparing plans to move some of our units to bolster Fourteenth Army in Burma. It may not happen, of course, but I thought you'd want to know that 4th Battalion might be chosen. Keep it under your hat, Roger. But don't let the men start thinking they'll soon be going home.'

'Thank you, Sir. I won't breath a word.'

* * *

'Damn and blast!' Roger says out loud, not caring who hears. He coughs and clears his throat.

Ahead the sky looks threatening. He can hear thunder in the distance. Or is it just the rumble of the guns? He looks down at the wretched letter. He wants to tear it in half.

'How dare she?'

Heavy rain begins to fall. He folds the letter, stuffs it away and starts walking, following the road north-west towards Ferrara. But the direction is unimportant, he just needs to move his limbs.

After seeing Mortimer, Roger had decided to hang about at HQ, hoping to collect his post. He even visited the tedious Major Addison in the Intelligence truck where he admired the latest stereographs of abandoned German equipment.

He had promised Frank he would visit his Platoon. But bloody Frank wants to talk about Huggins. What on earth is the matter with the fellow? The Corporal died six months ago! Why can't Frank forget him? All right, there was a mix-up, a problem with the grid references. But these things happen in war. Roger wasn't to blame.

Then finally the post arrived. He had waited for months for Joan to write again. And what did he get for his pains? A letter demanding a bloody divorce.

HOW CAN JOAN LEAVE HIM NOW? WHEN THE WAR IS ALL BUT OVER! DAMN HER! DAMN HER! DAMN HER!

She knows he'll soon be home, after three years away! Yet

she still wants a divorce. Well, he'll see about that. If she thinks she can scarper with her fancy man, taking the boys, she's got another think coming.

The rain is heavier now. He passes groups of Italians, at least he assumes they're fucking Italians: they certainly look miserable enough. Old women pushing wheelbarrows and old men wheeling bicycles with two or three children on board, cowering from the rain. They all sidle along with their paltry possessions, giving Roger a wide berth.

Finally he turns back so the rain slants into his face. It's enough to persuade him. He will postpone visiting Frank until tomorrow. Tonight, he'll stay at the farmhouse which will give him time to write to bloody Joan. Frank will understand that Roger needs to be careful after malaria.

* * *

Roger screws up the writing paper, as a shell explodes in the distance. He squeezes it into a ball, lobs it across the room and watches its parabolic descent into the wastepaper basket. When his mother said no to his joining the RAF he should have chosen the artillery.

He gets up and walks across to the window. Careful not to spoil the blackout, he peers around the curtain. Everything is dark except for occasional flashes in the distance. In the morning he'll leave before dawn to rejoin the Company. But tonight he's glad to be indoors, out of the bloody rain. After the shock of Joan's letter, he deserves a decent billet.

He closes the curtains and ambles back to the table. He sips a little brandy and starts his letter again.

'Dear Joan ...'

What the hell should he say? Damn the woman! He'll tell her where to get off. She *must* wait for his return. Then he'll have time to put her straight. *He* will keep the house and the boys. If *she* wants to bugger off, she can go. But she won't get a penny from him.

How unfair on the boys! Waiting for their father to come home and then learning they've got a stepfather instead. Poor little blighters! He must stop her for *their* sake. God, she's a selfish bitch! She always was bloody selfish. The lengths she made him go to, just to make love. And then she complained when he put his hand over her mouth so the boys wouldn't hear.

Roger hears a wailing sound and a heavy thud as a shell explodes. But there are fewer German shells now. He takes a gulp of brandy and looks around the room. How civilised to have a bed, after a good meal and a glass of wine. Better than being under canvas with Frank's Platoon. He smiles at the thought of Frank out there in the bloody rain.

'Dear Joan,
I am reeling from the shock of your letter …'

Roger hears a whistling noise. Then a thundering crash as a shell explodes near the house. He hurries over to the window as the whole building shakes. He flings himself on the floor.

'Bloody hell! That was mucking close!'

He gets up on his knees. He must get outside before the next shell lands. If there's time. A brilliant flash illuminates the room. The floor starts to dance. A roaring noise. And a flooding pain …

CHAPTER 63

4th Battalion continues heading north. Their next goal is Padua, the historic city in the Veneto, where partisans, anticipating the Allies' arrival, have claimed control of part of the city.

Crossing the Po proved easier than Frank had feared. Having abandoned their heavy equipment, the Germans did little to defend the northern bank of the river. And now, with the Allied armies advancing on all fronts and with the partisans in open revolt, the Germans are in headlong retreat, with few units resisting the advance.

Today 4th Battalion is following the New Zealand 2nd Division: a great column of tanks and trucks, long-barrelled anti-tank guns, Bren carriers and twenty-five pounders.

Having led the Battalion across the Po river, today Frank's Platoon is covering the Battalion's rear. The road is flat and only military traffic is allowed, yet their progress along the narrow lanes is slow. They pass a string of villages where the bells are ringing and the residents are out in force, cheering and waving flags. Young girls throw stems of elder blossom as the Tommies pass. Some clamber on board, offering kisses all round. The girls' delight is heart-warming. But the Italian men hold back, resentful of the liberators' effect on their women.

Corporal Johns accelerates as they leave the next village causing flowers heaped on the roof to cascade across the road. Gripping the wheel of the Bedford with one hand and a cigarette with the other, he asks Frank whether the fighting is over.

Frank turns. Johns looks exhausted, as they all do, but a smile lingers on his face.

'It certainly seems that way. But we can't assume anything, Corporal. The Teds have looked beaten before but as the Colonel said they can still throw a hefty punch.'

'They've never surrendered before. Not like they've done in Genoa. And that was to partisans.'

'You're right, Corporal. That was extraordinary. It's only a matter of time before the last pillars of Nazism tumble down.'

'What would Major Bewdley have made of it?'

Frank had felt oddly unmoved by the news of Roger's death, but he pauses, remembering he must write to Jackie. 'I think he'd be pleased that the Battalion is in at the kill.'

'What will you tell your kids about the war, Sir?'

'I don't have any children, yet. But when I do, I won't tell them anything. How could they understand this madness? I will try to convince them never to go to war.'

'Think of all those chaps who should be here. Do you remember Reynolds, Sir? He was at Gazala, when we were the last ones to leave.'

'I haven't forgotten.'

... Frank sees the grey expanses of the desert ... the awful days in Gazala as the Germans ripped their defences apart ... Maggie and their flat in Ealing ... the fire and Barbara's death ... dearest Vermillion ... and Venice not far away...

As they enter another village Johns slows the truck, bringing the last blossoms off the cab roof. Here there are no girls on the street, no welcome and no flowers. Frank sees an old man and signals to Johns to stop. They briefly converse.

'You had better drive on,' Frank says. 'What a dreadful business. A dozen Germans appeared last night demanding bicycles because their transport was out of fuel. When the men refused, they started shooting. Half a dozen were killed, all for a few rusty bikes.'

They drive on, both deep in thought. The silence persists as they pass through a town where the bells ring out in greeting.

'It's about bloody time the Nazis are defeated,' Johns says at last, 'after the awful things they've done. Killing for a bicycle. And those dreadful camps. Did you see the photos of Belsen in the Eighth Army News?'

'I could hardly bear to look.' Frank is silent for a while. 'You're right, Corporal. We must end the war. Perhaps then we can start again and treat each other as human beings. But it isn't over yet. We must keep an eye out for snipers, especially in the trees.'

Despite the reminders of war's horrors, Frank feels more positive than he dares to let on. With German resistance crumbling they've advanced twenty miles in just two days. He smiles. Unless something extraordinary happens, the war is as good as won. And they're less than fifty miles from Venice.

'I heard a whisper this morning, Sir,' Johns says, 'that the Kiwis' next goal is Trieste.'

'Bloody hell, Corporal! That's right around the Gulf of Venice, well over a hundred miles. No wonder they set off at such a lick.'

All morning they follow the rest of 4th Battalion, their route marked every few miles by the Battalion's painted insignia of a red horse on a white background.

The fields look fresh and bright in the April showers, yet the debris of war is everywhere: broken and twisted machines; discarded equipment and clothes; occasional dead animals. The surface of the road is far from flat; it's riddled with bullet holes and pocked with craters where shells have erupted. Even here on a straight road they daren't exceed walking pace.

Frank leans back. Watching the flat landscape unfold, he starts to feel drowsy. 'Pull over here, Corporal. We'll stop for a few minutes while the men stretch their legs.'

Johns steers the truck to the side of the road bringing it gently to a halt. Frank jumps down. 'Everyone out! Ten minutes before we set off!'

As the men set up a Benghazi boiler, Frank wanders on along the road, studying the terrain ahead. To the north-west are the first undulations for miles. From the map he concludes that they're the Euganean Hills, close to Padua.

He raises his field glasses and looks into the distance. Fifty miles to the north are the Dolomites, or at least the foothills. If the air were just a bit clearer, he would see their white peaks. But is he looking at hills or clouds?

He lowers his glasses and observes the road ahead. There's no sign of the rest of C Company. In fact there are no signs of life: no animals and no people. The place is strangely quiet – except for the banter of his men just down the road.

... he sees Purdie and Laura ... they look happy ... poor Purdie ... did Roger write to his parents? ... should Frank write too? ... even if Roger did write, Frank knew Purdie much better ... and then there's Laura ... he should write to her too ... otherwise she may never know that he has died ...

*poor girl … at least she has a loving family … perhaps he
should write to Sanudo …*

Frank marches back to the Bedford. 'Sergeant! Tell the men
to get ready! Get them embussed in three minutes!'

'Yes, Sir. Have you had a cuppa, Sir? Bailey bring the
Captain a mug of the best brew!'

'Thank you, Sergeant.' Frank sees Short's fleeting smile;
even he is playing for time.

Frank gulps down the hot tea. He watches the remaining
twenty-three men as they clamber into the back and settle
down amidst their piles of kit. Many of them are laughing;
they give him a cheery grin as they pass. Frank feels a deep
pang of emotion. He has grown to love these men. Perhaps
when they get to Padua the choir can practise again.

He climbs into the cab and nods to Johns, who swings the
starting handle protruding from the front. The warm engine
catches at once. The Corporal climbs up to the driving seat
and puts the truck into gear.

'Right, Corporal. Padua next stop! That's if we've got
enough petrol.'

'We've plenty, Sir. The gauge says we're half full. And
there's a ten gallon can in the back.'

The Bedford growls with the increasing revs. Johns
crunches into second gear. Briefly they manage fifteen miles
an hour, causing the vehicle to lurch wildly in the potholes.
There are loud groans from behind. Johns laughs as he eases
back to their usual steady pace.

They continue north following the red horse towards
Venice and Vermillion and the end of the war. Frank wonders
where she is. He knows she's with the Eighth Army, somewhere
here in the north, but he doesn't know where. It feels strange
to think she might be close. Roger had seen her at Christmas
but had never really said how she was. Sometimes he gave
the impression he was holding something back. But Frank will
never know. Poor old Roger! How unlucky to die in these dog
days of the war.

Frank glances at Johns. The Italian campaign is all but over, but there's still the war against Japan. There are rumours about the Battalion transferring to Burma. But how could they tell the men? Whoever delivers the message – that they have to go east – may not live to tell the tale.

Johns brings the truck to a stuttering halt. He points up a side road to the left which is bathed in sunshine.

'That's a bit odd, Sir. The red horse clearly points up there although the main road leads straight to Padua. I suppose the Colonel knows what he's doing.'

Johns pulls the truck round and heads off along the single lane road. Tufts of tall grass flick against the axles.

From behind Frank hears a deep moaning, like vast banks of shingle rolling with the tide. Slowly the groans transform into song. Choir practice is starting early.

"A rovin', a rovin',
Since rovin's been my ru-i-in,
I'll go no more a roving
With you fair maid!"

Frank feels a welling of emotion. He could easily cry. Not due to sadness, although there's plenty to be sad about, but because of the nobility of these men who have risked so much to liberate a land they didn't know and will probably never see again.

Frank peers through the windscreen, trying to ignore these feelings by taking in the countryside. They are climbing a gentle hill with woodland on either side. The verges are purpled with wild iris. How surprising that these delicate plants have come through the war. The sight of such abundant life fills him with hope.

The road rises slightly and swings to the right before dipping down to the left. The singing reaches a crescendo as they start the descent, but the crack of a rifle shot brings the choir to a stop.

Ahead, a tree trunk blocks the road. Johns stamps on the brakes. He swings the Bedford across the road. There isn't enough room to complete the turn. He thrusts the gear lever into reverse. They jolt backwards. First gear again. The truck leaps forwards but logs now block the road on the way they came. As Johns brakes again, a second shot rings out. Several German officers come out from the undergrowth, their pistols pointed towards the cab.

'MERDA!' Johns thumps the steering wheel.

'Good afternoon, Captain,' a young German Lieutenant addresses Frank in confident English. 'Drop your pistol from the window. Now open the door. Get out carefully, with your hands up!'

Frank clambers down. He raises his hands and steps towards the German.

'Halt!' The Lieutenant waves his pistol towards Frank's head. 'Now Captain, order your men out – slowly, one at a time.'

One of the Germans checks Frank for weapons. Frank ignores him. 'What's the point of this, Lieutenant? Germany has been defeated. Surrender to us now …'

'Silence, Captain!' He glares at Frank, who is half a head taller than him. 'Order your men to come out!'

Frank signals to Johns. He feels ashamed as he watches Johns scramble down. How the hell had this happened?

'Now the men at the back!'

'Lieutenant,' Frank speaks slowly, 'if you surrender now, you'll all be safe. If you don't …'

'Stop, Captain! When we get to the mountains, you'll never defeat us there!'

A volley of angry German words comes from another officer. The Lieutenant braces himself and yells in Frank's face. 'CAPTAIN! ORDER YOUR MEN TO COME OUT! OR WE'LL SHOOT.'

'Lieutenant …'

'NOW! CAPTAIN! NOW!'

Frank turns towards the back of the truck afraid they may shoot the men and take the truck.

'Sergeant, tell the men to come out … one at a time … with their hands above their heads.'

The rear flap of the Bedford twitches. A first head appears. Bailey squints anxiously at Frank and raises his hands.

'Stand there!' The Lieutenant points at the ground next to Frank.

One by one the men emerge; Short comes last. They line up together, blinking in the soft rain.

'Lieutenant,' Frank says quietly, 'you know what will happen if you get to Austria. The Russians will take you. Is that what you want?'

The Lieutenant looks nervously at Frank.

'Surrender now, Lieutenant, before it's too …'

'SILENCE!' The German Captain shouts from just behind Frank.

The Lieutenant orders two of his men to check the inside of the Bedford. Then he reviews Frank's men, studying their uniforms. He lines up five of them and marches them deeper into the woods.

'Where are you taking them, Captain? Please don't take *them*, take me!'

'You'll come with *us*, Captain. We don't need those men. We just want their uniforms. They won't want to undress in public.'

The rain is heavier and the light is fading when the Germans return, looking awkward in the ill-fitting British uniforms. Frank can hardly bear to watch as they load their kit into the truck. Dressed in their new guises, two of the Germans climb into the cab taking Johns with them at gunpoint. Frank and four of his men are bundled into the back. The remaining Germans get in beside them.

One of the Germans starts the Bedford and they set off back down the road. Frank catches a glimpse of the men they've left behind; then the rear flap is lowered. In the darkness Frank can only guess that the Germans plan to head north, with their cargo of six precious hostages.

He tries to talk to the Germans but stops as a pistol pokes into his ribs. Beside him, Underhill shivers and Frank finally notices it's cold. He shuts his eyes. Venice seems far away.

CHAPTER 64

'We mustn't let the Crucchi get away!' Paolo yells to Cato down in the street.

'Who cares if they escape, as long as they leave.' Cato glares at the first floor window. 'What matters is stopping the fucking Fascists. Mussolini has been strung up, now we must get the rest.'

'You're crazy!' Paolo shakes his fist. 'We can deal with the Blackshirts any time! Let's finish off the Germans first. They're murdering civilians as they retreat. Deal with them now. Then we can tackle the Fascists.'

Cato turns away, shouting something in local dialect which Paolo can't understand. Damn him! He always does this. How can he and Paolo be comrades when Cato has all these secrets?

'If we delay, it may be too late!' Cato shouts in Italian, waving his Tommy Gun for emphasis. 'The Fascists will have taken control. They won't call themselves Fascists, of course. But they'll be the ones in charge. Just mark my words!'

'You've seen the orders from Falcon.' Paolo fingers his pistol just in case. *Hold the bridges until the Allies arrive and don't let the Germans escape.* Come on, Cato, let's catch some Germans.'

'Who wants to help the Allies? This is our country. We should be the liberators. We don't need the Allies anymore. They'll only fuck things up.'

'All right, Cato,' Paolo speaks in a stage whisper, 'we'll deal with the Fascists as soon as we've dealt with the Germans. But we must stop them killing Italians as they retreat. Come on! It's time to take revenge!'

'Go to your bloody bridge, Paolo! I'm going into Padua. If we can stop the fucking Fascists taking over, we'll get our city back.'

Paolo slams the window shut and hurries downstairs. The group has already divided. Cato has nine of the others –

all from Veneto region. The remaining six, including former prisoners of war and two from distant parts of Italy, are staying with Paolo.

Paolo brandishes his pistol, tempted to tackle Cato. Why the hell had he trusted him? He swore he wasn't a member of the party, yet now he sees the Allies as an enemy.

'Come on, Paolo,' Sandro grips Paolo's arm. 'Don't let Cato spoil our plans. We're ready to give the Crucchi what for. They ruined our country. Now they can bloody well suffer.'

'Damn Cato!' Paolo pulls away from Sandro. 'At least he has left us the truck.'

'It was no use to him. He could hardly have crept into Padua in this noisy brute.'

Once their equipment is loaded, Paolo takes the wheel of the ancient Fiat. Driving by the light of the moon, they follow minor roads around the northern outskirts of the city.

About a kilometre before the bridge, Paolo brings the truck to a stop. After concealing the vehicle in a copse, they set off on foot, carrying their weapons, including a light machine gun. Ahead, to the north-east, the first hint of light is visible in the sky but away from the moonlight everything is dark.

They walk silently, following the road but keeping outside the trees planted at intervals along the verges. They avoid the road itself where they'd be easily visible.

A dog barks, some way off. Paolo freezes. If other dogs are nearby, they'll be set off too. He waits for a long minute. There's no further sound; there can't be any houses here. Paolo steals forward as far as the next bend; then he signals for the others to join him.

The dog barks again. Silence returns. From his vantage point in thick bushes, Paolo gets a first glimpse of the bridge, which is still intact. While the others give him cover, he moves forward again to crouch behind a fallen tree.

Here, the black river is only a few metres wide. It is marked by a line of poplar trees. The road runs parallel to the river until it swings right through ninety degrees to cross the bridge and then veers left, continuing along the far bank of the river. On both sides there are solid brick parapets.

Paolo studies the deserted structure. He guesses he's eighty metres away, although he knows that judging distances in low light is difficult. He looks around, going over their plan for holding the bridge. His thoughts are interrupted by the noise of a vehicle approaching from the same way they had come. He signals to the others to keep down.

The vehicle slows as it approaches, until he can just make out an ancient truck with high sides open at the back, the sort used to take produce to market. But that isn't its function today. In the front are two German soldiers. Paolo flexes his trigger finger. The brakes grate as the truck stops twenty metres away. The tailgate rattles and six men drop heavily onto the metalled road. Two of them drag a detonator from the truck.

Fuck! They've come to destroy the bridge. That means the rest of their unit has fled. Paolo signals to Sandro to advance along the far side of the road to observe the other side of the bridge.

The Germans work in pairs: two carry explosives; two roll out lengths of cable; and two command the centre of the bridge with their submachine guns.

Sandro signals he's in position.

Once the truck is unloaded, the driver restarts the engine and drives slowly over the bridge. The other Germans are now in Paolo's sights.

He opens fire. Other partisans join in, taking the Germans completely by surprise. One of the pair on the bridge falls at once. The other turns and fires once. Then he falls too. The rest drop their equipment, scrambling across the bridge, until they too succumb.

Paolo keeps shooting even when the bodies are still. Finally he starts to count. Seven bodies. Where is the eighth? He stands up and walks slowly towards the bridge, stepping over the mangled corpses. He approaches the prow of the bridge. No sign of the missing German. He looks over the wall to the left. Then he crosses to the right-hand wall. Still nothing.

Ahead the wall curves to the left beside the road. He fires a volley of bullets at the top of the wall and walks forward. Two hands rise slowly from the parapet. Then a helmet and a head. Paolo fires another burst into the man's face until he topples backwards out of sight.

'Eight!' Paolo spins round. 'Not a bad haul!'

He smiles at Sandro. 'Dump the bodies over there.' He points at the wall where the last German fell. 'And back the truck onto the bridge so no one can pass!'

A grin spreads across Paolo's face. If the other members of this unit have already retreated perhaps the war really is near the end. Now he has taken his revenge on the bastards he can go to Rome and be a hero.

The other partisans move the detonator, cables and explosives onto their truck. They have hardly finished when the lookout gives a long whistle. Paolo orders everyone to their places.

They wait. And wait. After several minutes Paolo leaves his vantage point to clamber up to the road. What the hell are they waiting for? In the dawn light, he sees two German soldiers dragging a handcart loaded high with bags and boxes. One shouts to the other as they chart a drunken course; they both laugh.

Paolo waits until they've passed. Then he fires at the first soldier who slips under the cart which comes to an abrupt halt. The other soldier spins around; Paolo shoots him in the chest.

'That makes ten!'

Paolo directs two of the partisans to clear the cart and the bodies from the road.

'There's plenty of wine here,' one of the partisans calls. 'No wonder they couldn't walk straight.'

Paolo glares at him. 'Leave the wine alone. We still have work to do.'

'Yes, Sir,' he says in English, breaking into a run.

In a couple of minutes the handcart is unloaded. Paolo walks slowly across the road to inspect the catch but is stopped by another whistle. He signals his men to get out of sight.

In the distance, Paolo sees a khaki-coloured truck approaching fast.

'I think it may be British.' Sandro says.

Paolo peers at the truck until he can make out three figures in the front. Sandro must be right; the uniforms are British but one of the soldiers has striking blond hair.

The truck speeds towards the bridge. Paolo stands up. 'STOP!' he shouts in English. The blond soldier pulls out a pistol and fires at Paolo. The bullet fizzes past him and thuds into the trees.

'FUCKING GERMANS!' Paolo fires a burst at the windscreen. The truck hits the end of the parapet with a crash of splintering glass. Liquid pours from under the engine.

Paolo runs to the front of the truck to get a shot at that fucking blond. But the man leaps from the cab, shooting at two partisans who both slump to the ground. Paolo fires after him but doesn't get a clear shot.

Paolo sprints to the back of the truck. 'Give me cover,' he yells to two of the partisans. He unclips a grenade as he searches for a gap in the canvas to slip it into the truck.

'HELP! HELP! WE'RE BRITISH PRISONERS. THERE ARE ALSO THREE GERMANS …'

'Throw out your weapons.' Paolo clips back the grenade. 'Come out with your hands up!'

Silence.

'TEN, NINE, EIGHT …'

From inside Paolo hears angry German voices.

'SEVEN, SIX, FIVE, FOUR …' he continues.

A German voice bellows a great curse.

'Throw out your weapons!' Paolo shouts again.

From inside the truck a shot rings out, followed by two muffled ones. The truck starts to rock as a fight develops. A piercing scream grows strangled. There are intermittent gasps for air.

Then the truck settles into silence.

Shit!

Holding his gun in one hand, Paolo tries to open the canvas

flap with the other. Sandro comes to his aid. Paolo grips his gun in both hands, braced to fire if required. Sandro pulls back the canvas a little. Paolo glimpses the wretched scene of eight men in British uniforms. Four are covered in blood. He can't tell if they're wounded or dead.

'Sandro, get them out! I must find that fucking blond.'

Paolo heads towards the front of the truck. He hears a single shot. He turns, firing a burst at the blond German before he ducks behind the parapet.

'That's ten ... eleven! I can't remember.'

Paolo feels a burning sensation. He drops his gun, thrusting out his hands to steady himself against the truck.

'Sandro! Tell Mamma, it was eleven!'

His legs weaken. He feels Sandro grasp him as he slips down to the ground ...

CHAPTER 65

Vermillion doesn't look up in response to Morden's quiet cough.

She is still digesting the results of her previous interrogation. Little more than a boy, the prisoner was full of Nazi fervour, despite the news that the Americans and Russians have met up on the Elbe. What had unnerved him was the Allied use of flame-throwers. With tears running down his cheeks he described their effect.

"There's no defence against a weapon like that! In our cramped bunker the four of us were friends. But when the attack came we feared being burnt alive. We fought with each other to escape; the others didn't get out. I used to believe we would win. But without weapons like that I'm not sure."

Corporal Morden coughs again; Vermillion finally looks up. 'What the hell is it this time?'

'I'm sorry to bother you, Lieutenant. There's an urgent message … from the Major.'

Vermillion stares at the papers piled in front of her.

'He needs you for an interrogation. An Italian: he thinks he may be a spy.'

Inwardly she curses Rummage. 'Tell him I've enough bloody work. Look at all this!'

'He won't be very happy …'

'I know, Corporal,' she sighs. 'Don't say anything. I'll come in a minute.'

Morden sets off but turns back to face her. 'There's news that Turin and Milan have fallen to the partisans. I heard it on the wireless, Lieutenant.'

Vermillion watches him saunter away, his boots scraping on the stone floor of the council offices where they are currently based. If Milan has fallen, the war in Italy is all but over, thank God!

Frank had sent her an encouraging letter for her twenty-fifth birthday. But is Frank still all right? She can't bear the not knowing much longer. It's hard enough during the day but at night it becomes unendurable. Is this how Pen had felt all that time waiting for news? Thank goodness Bill has made a full recovery. But he remains in India and may yet return to the front.

Vermillion pulls herself to her feet, tidies her hair and sets off along the empty corridor but takes a moment to remember which way to go. She walks down the grand staircase and along the hallway to the mayor's office. She knocks and opens the door, without waiting for a reply.

'At last, Lieutenant!' Rummage's head jerks in her direction, in what she takes as a greeting.

'Good morning, Sir. The Corporal said you wanted to see me.'

Rummage points at the hard chair beside him. She sits down wearily and looks around the large room. How strange that only days ago a Fascist mayor and his staff had strutted around in here. Many of their papers and photographs remain, although there are notable gaps. She wonders where the Fascists are now. Have the Allies interned them all or have the partisans bumped them off?

Rummage reads from the file.

'Benfatti, Alessandro. Born Turin: 10th March 1924. Claims he's an Italian soldier fighting with the partisans. Says he rescued some British soldiers.'

Rummage looks up. 'Frankly, my dear, it's a fairy story. The fellow's a spy. He claims not to speak English but he understood well enough when I asked if he'd like a cigarette. Interrogate him in Italian but I shall ask the questions. Is that clear, Lieutenant? Good. Sergeant! Bring the prisoner in!'

The door opens and the Sergeant pushes the young man forward. Wearing a torn Italian uniform, he holds himself upright despite the Sergeant's prodding from behind. As the Major is ignoring him, he glances at Vermillion and his face breaks into a boyish grin. Vermillion lowers her eyes, trying not to smile.

'Sit down!' Rummage says in English. 'Sergeant, wait outside.'

Using Vermillion as interpreter, Rummage asks about the prisoner's background, his upbringing and his call-up in '42.

'What did you do when the armistice was announced?'

'We walked out of our barracks … in Bologna …'

'Ah! You deserted! That's a serious offence!'

'We didn't want to be captured by the Germans. We walked from Bologna to …'

'I don't need to know about that.' Rummage interrupts. 'Let's start from where you deserted. What did you do then? Disappeared into the woodwork, I suppose.'

Vermillion studies the young man's face. What he's describing sounds rather like Paolo's story.

'No, Sir, we walked south until we crossed the line.'

'I see. So you've crossed the line *before*!'

'Only on that occasion.'

'And then you say you joined the CIL. When was that?'

'In June '44.'

'Really! Nine months after deserting in Bologna. WHAT THE HELL WERE YOU DOING ALL THAT TIME!'

'We lived in Naples …'

Vermillion studies the prisoner. Was he Paolo's friend who leant out of the window that day in March '44? Then she was desperate to find penicillin for Edmund, because the hospital had run out. She had to find Paolo whose knowledge of the black market was her only hope. She only glimpsed Sandro's face and hadn't really taken it in. But something tells her this is the same fellow.

'That doesn't interest me.' Rummage smooths his moustache. 'You said "we". Who were you with?'

'My comrade, Paolo Baldini.'

It is Sandro! Shortened from Alessandro, of course.

'Did he join up too?' Rummage asks.

'Yes, we joined up again together.'

'Where is he now?'

'He was killed two days ago …'

Vermillion lowers her head and rubs her brow. Poor Chiara and Mamma. How awful that Paolo should die as the war ends.

'Well, that was bloody convenient!' Rummage looks to Vermillion to translate but she won't say this in Italian. 'Could you tell us how it happened?' she asks instead.

'We were serving with a group of partisans. Falcon, the British liaison with the partisans, ordered us to capture a bridge, north of Padua. We planned to hold the bridge until the Allies arrived.'

'Who was in this partisan group?' Rummage asks. 'How many of you were there?'

'We had been eighteen. But there was an argument. Cato, the leader, took nine of the men. They headed for the centre of Padua to drive out the Fascists. It's happening all over Italy where partisans are taking revenge …'

'We know about that! How many of you were left to take the bridge?'

'Only eight.'

'Was the bridge defended when you arrived?'

Sandro describes how they found the bridge empty but then intercepted some Germans who had come to blow it up. Rummage questions him in detail about the detonator and explosives. He listens carefully to the answers, stroking his moustache with growing vigour. Thank Heavens! Rummage is getting bored. Perhaps he's starting to believe him.

Rummage sits forward. 'You say you *rescued* some British soldiers? How the hell did you manage that?'

'We were holding the bridge when a British truck appeared, moving fast. A soldier in a British uniform fired his pistol at us. But we could see he wasn't British. He had such blond hair. He was a German in a British uniform. We shot at the windscreen and the truck crashed into the bridge. Then we heard English voices shouting from the back. There were shots from inside and sounds of fighting. When we opened the back, the mess was terrible with wounded and dead. We separated the real British soldiers from the Germans and drove them to a field hospital. That's where we were arrested.'

'Which unit were the British soldiers from?'

'I don't know, Major. We were racing to get them to hospital. And I was shocked. My comrade had just been shot by that bloody German. Paolo died in the road as I held him ...'

'Thank you, we don't need the details. Now Corporal is there anything *useful* you can tell us?'

'I know one of the British soldiers.'

'How could you possibly know him?'

'I met him in Naples. I'm sure it was him. He recognised me when we opened the back of the truck.'

'I'm not interested.' Rummage says.

Vermillion fails to translate so Sandro continues. 'He was a friend of Paolo, my comrade who was killed.'

'What was the name of this British soldier?' Vermillion holds her breath.

'I don't know his real name,' Sandro says.

'Enough of this nonsense!' Rummage splutters. 'Sergeant!'

'He was very big – almost two metres tall.'

It must be Frank.

'I said that's enough! What's the use if you don't even know his name.' Rummage brings proceedings to a close. 'Sergeant, take the prisoner away.'

Vermillion puts her hand to her mouth as Sandro leaves.

'I'm sorry, Major!' Sandro calls over his shoulder. 'I never knew his real name. We called him Generalissimo.'

It *was* Frank.

'Sandro,' she calls. 'Was Franco wounded?'

'I'm sorry, Lieutenant, I don't know.'

'Mad! Completely mad!' Rummage turns to Vermillion. 'Are you all right, my dear? You look rather pale.'

'Yes, Sir. But I can vouch for the prisoner. He isn't a spy. And the tall soldier he recognised is my boyfriend.'

For a moment Rummage is lost for words.

He fumbles in his pockets. 'Have one of these, my dear,' he proffers a cigarette.

'No thank you, Captain. But I'd like to pop out for a minute to get some air.'

Vermillion hurries into the street. After a few yards she stops to light a cigarette of her own. She breathes in deeply and raises her head. She looks down the road to the piazza where the horse chestnuts are dressed in white flowers.

From what Sandro said, Frank had survived the struggle. Sandro saw him after the fight was over and Frank recognised him. But, of course, he might have been wounded.

'Dear Frank,' she says out loud, looking up at the clear sky. 'Dearest Frank, wherever you are. Please, please, don't die. Not now the war is over. You've been so brave; you deserve to enjoy the peace. If you're wounded, I shall nurse you and make you better. I didn't do well with nursing Edmund but I will look after *you*. Please, Frank, please stay alive, so I can find you.'

She drops the end of her cigarette and treads on it gently. Then she dabs her eyes and takes a deep breath. How extraordinary to encounter Sandro. She hopes he will soon be released. Before he is moved she will send him a note to say Chiara has forgiven him. And she will give him a letter for Chiara who will be distraught at Paolo's loss. Vermillion hopes she can be proud of what he did.

CHAPTER 66

Simon stirs as the thunder reaches a crescendo, crashing in great waves. He comes to with a jolt as the applause washes around him. Below their box, the stage curtains part. A plump, middle-aged man emerges. The audience erupts again.

'Bravo! Bravo!'

Some people are on their feet. The applause intensifies. Simon feels obliged to join in.

'Why are *you* applauding?' Jackie claps vigorously. 'You slept through the final act.'

'I closed my eyes to concentrate.'

'Perhaps that's what you intended. But once they were shut, you couldn't resist. You went straight off. It's hardly surprising after all that wine. At least you didn't snore!'

'All right, I nodded off for a minute. But I heard the important bits.'

'... like the applause!'

Only after several minutes does the audience quieten, so the singers can withdraw.

'Come on, Jackie. Let's not bother with the Club. It's bound to be a scrum. Let's stroll to the Galleria.'

'Does it still rankle that Frank threw you out? Even though you were horribly drunk.'

Jackie's right. He loathes being reminded that he'd made such a fool of himself. And tonight, Vermillion's friends will be at the Club; he'd rather not be seen with Jackie. It's not that he has designs on her: he just needs to keep in touch to hear news about Vermillion.

'I bet Frank wishes he were here,' Jackie says, 'on the night of the German surrender.'

Bloody Frank! Surely he has bought it by now, after the heavy fighting around the Po.

Simon wants to ask about Vermillion but he catches himself in time. 'We're bloody lucky to be here!' he declares. 'It's not often one is present when history is made.'

The audience surges out of the theatre onto the Piazza Trieste e Trento.

'Give us a kiss, darling!' A soldier grabs Jackie and lands a smacker on her cheek. His friend has better aim and kisses her lips before Simon pushes him away.

'Come on Jackie. If you're going to kiss every Tommy, we'll be here all night. Hurry up, I need a drink.'

From the Galleria comes a medley of drunken songs which echo in the narrow streets. Pushing through the crowds they hear voices from all over the world. Raucous baritones compete with the chatter of Italian girls, many of whom are attached to servicemen, but some in groups of five or six cling excitedly together.

The crowd is awash with speculation:

"Hitler is dead."

"George VI is in Naples."

"Japan has surrendered."

"British troops in Italy are embarking for India."

The crowd cheers or boos each rumour as though at a pantomime and then breaks into gales of laughter.

In nearby streets, groups of Italian youths watch with resentful stares. Some make scissor signs at local girls, threatening to shave their hair if they go with foreigners. Others swoop on a lone Tommy walking with his girl. More soldiers join the brawl and twenty young men exchange blows until the MPs appear.

'They'll be glad when the soldiers have gone,' Jackie nods towards another group of Italians. 'But will they take the girls back? And will the girls want them, after what has happened? The peace won't be easy.'

They find a bar in the Galleria that's awash with gaiety. They squeeze in and empty several glasses of wine while joining in the singing.

Simon orders more wine.

'Come on Simon, let's go back to the flat. The fighting may be over but I'm still on duty tomorrow.'

Simon doesn't reply. Instead he grasps her hand and marches her homeward. Perhaps he sets too fast a pace because soon she starts to hiccup and then convulses in giggles. Every few seconds a plosive sound erupts, echoing along the street.

'Shh, Jackie! For heaven's sake, be quiet!'

'I'm trying to … but … hic … I can't control it … hic …'

'Come on, Jackie! Hold your breath until we're at the flat. It isn't far now.'

They hurry on in silence until the next hiccup explodes.

'Shh!'

They reach the palazzo and walk through the gate into the courtyard. Simon takes her keys and unlocks the door at the foot of the circular staircase. Despite a muffled outburst, they reach the fourth floor in silence. Simon puts the key in the lock and turns it but the door stays shut.

'Someone's closed the bloody bolts!'

'Hic …!' The eruption resounds down the staircase.

'Shh!'

Jackie takes another deep breath.

'Who the hell has bolted the mucking door?'

Simon hears footsteps inside. The bolts are pulled back and the door opens.

'Hic!'

'For God's sake, be quiet!' Margery says. 'I knew you'd be drunk when you returned. That's why I bolted the door.'

'Hic …!'

'Jackie, be quiet! It isn't funny!' Margery closes the door behind them. 'Please remember, he's asleep!'

Simon looks at her quizzically but suddenly smiles. 'Well done, Margery, you've found a new man.'

'Don't be silly, Simon. It's Eduardo. I'm taking him to live with Edmund.'

'Well done, Margery,' Simon grins. 'We must celebrate your having Edmund and Eduardo. That doesn't happen every day. And there's the German surrender. Come on, Margery, what have you got to drink?'

'Simon, you've had quite enough. Hic …'

'But Margery hasn't had any. What can we find for her?'

After a lengthy search, they find a tepid bottle of white wine and Simon half-fills three tumblers.'

'To peace!' Simon flops onto the sofa.

'To peace!' the others raise their glasses.

'And to Eduardo and Edmund.'

Simon refills their glasses.

'And to Barbara!' Jackie says. 'Poor Barbara!'

'And Vermillion!' Margery adds.

'Have you heard anything from her?' Simon asks as casually as he can.

'I had a letter a few weeks ago.' Margery smiles at Simon. 'She seemed okay.'

'Jackie, what's the news from Roger?' Simon asks, for completeness.

'Not a bloody word, I'm afraid. I hope he's all right.'

'Margery, is there any news about Frank?'

'Vermillion said he was fine.'

'He's done well to get through to the end,' Simon says. 'He seemed quite low after Barbara died.'

'Perhaps he hasn't come through,' Jackie takes another swig of wine. '4th Battalion took a battering near the Po. Perhaps none of them came through.'

'Poor Vermillion!' Margery says. 'She found it hard when Frank left. But before he went, they agreed to meet in Venice as soon as the fighting stopped. They planned a rendezvous at the Danieli. Poor girl, how will she feel if Frank doesn't appear.'

'Surely he'll let her know if he can't make it,' Simon says brightly. 'Although I suppose the message might not get through. One can never be sure these days.'

'She's not the only one,' Jackie says. 'Hic … there must be millions of women … waiting for someone … some of them will never return … or won't be the person they're expecting … hic … oh sorry, Margery … I wasn't thinking of Edmund.'

'That's a wretched thought about Frank and Vermillion,' Simon says.

'They should know pretty soon.'

CHAPTER 67

'Why Venice, Miss?' the driver asks.

'It's Lieutenant, not Miss,' Vermillion looks away. 'I've wanted to see the city and its canals, ever since I was small.'

'Is it safe to go alone, Lieutenant?' He grins. 'Or are you meeting friends?'

'Yes, Lance Corporal … my friends arrive today.'

'I see you've brought your holdall,' he grins, 'just in case.'

Vermillion doesn't want to talk. She gazes through the windscreen at the flat landscape, now dressed in vibrant green. They pass orchards filled with blossom. Somehow most of the countryside has escaped the war and the crops are bursting through. Wild flowers are everywhere.

They pass many villages which appear unmarked. But the roads are crowded with people carrying heaps of belongings as they head for home now the fighting has ended. Yet there's little sign of rejoicing. Even where the bells ring out, the people seem crushed and exhausted.

They pass elegant Palladian villas approached by avenues of horse chestnuts, their pink or white flowers standing up like candles. But they also see scars of the struggle: burnt-out vehicles and animal carcases; even unburied bodies.

It had been in the middle of the night that Vermillion decided to go to Venice. After recalling each word of Sandro's she couldn't sleep and when she did nod off she had disturbing dreams. Tossing and turning, she was suddenly clear she must go today. Frank had said they should meet "as soon as peace is declared". And with the German surrender the fighting has ended in Italy. To have any chance of seeing him, she must go to Venice.

Of course, she still doesn't know what happened to Frank. Sometimes this lack of news feels encouraging but then the sight of a ruined house or dead animal reminds her how easily lives are destroyed. These fears increase her resolve to go to Venice, in case Frank is there. There are plenty of reasons why she may not find him. He could still be in hospital but at least he might send a message. Then she would know he's alive and where he is. She could even try to visit him.

Still unable to sleep she rose early, catching Rummage before he began his interrogations. He seemed shaken by the sight of her pallid face as though he feared she might faint. Without further debate he agreed a 48-hour pass.

Immediately she ran to Ordinance to find the first supply truck heading for Padua. There she picked up this second truck, which is ferrying a group of Tommies to Venice for the day. As she clambered into the cab she wondered whether this was the sort of truck that Frank was in when he was taken prisoner.

She tries to picture what had happened as they struggled with the Germans. She repeats Sandro's words. "When we opened the back, the mess was terrible with wounded and dead." "He recognised me when we opened the back of the truck." That means Frank was alive. Had they turned the tables on the Germans? But who had been shot? And who had died?

She stares out through the windscreen as they head across the Veneto, the breadbasket of Venice in its glory years. Mile after mile of rich agricultural land, much of it still cultivated despite the war. Vermillion can see that the scenery is beautiful but it doesn't touch her. She feels alone. She hasn't eaten or slept or settled. Her fears about Frank have taken over.

'Have you seen the mountains, Miss … Lieutenant?' the driver points in front of her.

To the left, beyond the green plain she sees the blue foothills of the Dolomites. She thinks she can see some snowy peaks but they may be clouds. So those are the mountains that the Germans were yearning for. Thank goodness so few of them made it.

* * *

Ahead, the light suddenly changes with wide expanses of water on both sides of the road.

'This is the lagoon,' the driver laughs at Vermillion's surprise. 'There, straight ahead, Miss. That's Venice.'

As they rumble across the causeway, Vermillion watches the city rise in front of them until it floats on a shimmering sea.

'My goodness! Thank you, Corporal, for the ride.'

A queue of military vehicles leads into Piazza Roma where a dozen tanks are lined up. Vermillion can't imagine there's a need for such armour: they must be tourists too.

She climbs down from the truck and says goodbye. She looks at her watch. 1420. Frank hadn't suggested a particular time, but she had hoped to reach the Danieli by noon in case Frank arrived for lunch.

The time isn't her only concern: today may not be the right day. Frank had said the day after peace is declared. In the autumn that seemed clear enough: now it seems dreadfully vague. But yesterday was the armistice so she's keeping her fingers crossed.

Despite having no clear time to aim for, she knows she musn't delay. But which way to go? She feels small in the middle of the piazza with military vehicles all around. She straightens her tie and adjusts her beret. Then seeing a stream of soldiers tumble from the truck, she follows at a distance. Soon she sees the prows of boats on the Grand Canal bobbing up and down like restive horses.

Walking on she sees the gondolas are crammed with soldiers lolling on mounds of cushions. They look more like trippers than part of a victorious army.

'Come with us, darling!' Two Tommies grin hopefully. 'We'll give you a ride!'

'No, thank you,' she smiles. 'I shall walk.'

She buys a map at a news stand and plans her route through Dorsoduro and across the Accademia Bridge. She feels safer now she's walking and can leave the crowds behind.

Venice, which was liberated several days before the armistice, appears untouched by the war. The inhabitants go about their business as though nothing has changed. La Serenissima has survived another occupation intact.

Despite her map, Vermillion struggles to navigate through the narrow streets, many of which come to dead-ends beside small canals. Several times she has to go back. Despite her urge to hurry, she slows down and is glad to wander in the sunshine. She stops in the middle of a narrow bridge and watches a boatman work his way along the tight and winding waterway. There are no visitors here. The boats are crammed, not with tourists but with household supplies or building materials: things relating to a world at peace.

In time she finds the Grand Canal again, having cut out a large loop. She contemplates the succession of elegant buildings that jostle for the best position from which to admire and be admired. Each one is different in shape, colour and design, yet they form a harmonious whole. And all this against the background of gleaming water and the brilliant sky.

Amazed by the beauty of the place she climbs the long slope of the Accademia Bridge and looks east along the canal as it broadens into the lagoon. She raises her eyes to the heavens and shakes her head in astonishment. She has never seen such a glorious man-made scene.

The sun beats down on her face and for a moment she feels at ease. In the silence she notices the absence of distant guns. A clock chimes the hour. 1500. Other bells take up the refrain. She hesitates before pressing on, as she feels a pang of fear about what she may find.

'Come and join us, gorgeous!' A soldier sings from a gondola in a mock-Italian song. 'Come here, where I may love you!'

Vermillion shakes her head as she hastens on her way, passing through the cloisters into Piazza San Marco. Here soldiers stand around in groups bargaining with the sellers of trinkets and pigeon food who scurry from group to group.

She maintains a steady pace while taking in the Byzantine façade of the San Marco Basilica ahead. At the end of the piazza she turns right and stops to wonder at the view past the two great columns and across the water to the island of San Giorgio Maggiore. She is dazzled by the fascination of the place.

She walks to the end of the quay, feeling she has come to heaven but is brought down to earth by baying groups of Tommies as they step heavy-footed from gondolas onto the quay.

She studies the map again and looks along the gentle curve of the shoreline knowing that one of the palazzos is her destination.

Feeling a hole in the pit of her stomach, she takes a deep breath and braces herself to keep control as she marches past the Palazzo Ducale. She stops outside the Danieli where a tall Major approaches her.

'May I help you, Lieutenant?' he asks in a distinctive New Zealand accent.

'I'm looking for a British officer.'

'Any British officer?' He grins. 'Or a particular one?'

She grimaces but then smiles. 'Captain Hill of 4th Battalion.'

'I don't know him myself,' the Major says with a serious expression. 'But we've seen a lot of the 4th since we crossed the Po. I suggest you ask at reception. Let me show you where it is.'

Vermillion follows him through the hotel entrance. As he goes he exchanges remarks with other officers. It seems there are New Zealanders everywhere.

'This is reception. Pasquale here will help you.'

Vermillion wishes the Major would stay. His calm presence is reassuring. Now she feels anxious and alone, watching Pasquale busy on the phone.

She turns to look at a group of officers near the piano who wave pints of beer as they sing.

'May I help you?' Pasquale asks in strained English.

'Good afternoon,' she says nervously. 'I'm looking for an English officer. We'd agreed to meet here.'

'What is your name, Signorina?'

'Lieutenant Henthorpe,' she spells out the letters of her surname. Her hands shake as he flicks through the papers on the desk.

'Yes, signorina, a British officer left a message earlier. He will meet you in the bar … at 1700.'

CHAPTER 68

A message from Frank!

Vermillion feels a swirl of relief. Her response to Pasquale is inaudible as she takes to her heels, needing to go somewhere that is big enough to accommodate her feelings. She rushes onto the pavement but turns away from San Marco and the throng of servicemen, hoping to hide her tears.

'Oh Frank, you've made it! Thank you, God! Thank you, Frank! I was so afraid I'd never see you again.'

She passes the church of Santa Maria della Pietà but doesn't look up, only aware there are fewer people here. She pulls out a small white handkerchief and dabs her eyes.

She takes a deep breath, raises her head and notices the warm sunshine. She looks at her watch. 1550. She manages a smile. Just an hour to wait for Frank. It seems a long time. But how absurd! She has waited for six months already. It can't matter how long she waits, now she knows he is near.

She turns around and walks back past the Danieli. She hears more New Zealand voices; they seem to have taken over the hotel.

'Any joy?' the tall Major asks as she passes.

'Yes, thank you. He's due at 1700.'

'I'm so glad!' he beams.

She strolls back to the Basilica di San Marco and walks inside, unprepared for the world of golden mosaics. Her head spins as she tries to take it in. She sits down and closes her eyes, absorbing the peace of the place. It feels like another miracle. She is so fortunate and so blessed. She gives thanks for the wonderful things that have happened since she reached Naples eighteen months ago.

A scrapbook of images flickers through her head. In time the scenes slow down. Starting to feel tired and hungry, she opens her eyes and studies a mosaic of various saints. She contemplates each one for several minutes. Finally, she checks her watch. 1640. She stands up and stretches discreetly before hurrying towards the Danieli. She should have time to powder her nose before joining Frank in the bar – unless he sees her arriving.

The hotel is still busy and she sees no sign of Frank. The men are mostly New Zealanders but there are also some Americans and several Italian men in pristine linen suits. She wonders where such fabric came from.

She takes her time getting ready and finally emerges at 1705. Leaving her holdall at reception, she takes a deep breath and walks apprehensively towards the bar.

She shivers, seeing the face in front of her. Her hands race up to cover her mouth until she has to grasp the back of a chair to steady herself.

'Simon!'

Struggling not to cry, she can hardly speak. 'What are *you* doing here? Where is Frank?'

Simon grins as he gets up and pulls out a chair. Vermillion sinks down.

'I'm sorry to surprise you, Vermillion. I knew you planned to meet Frank. So I thought I should come, just in case he doesn't appear.'

Dreadful thoughts cross her mind as she stares at Simon.

'WHY SHOULDN'T FRANK APPEAR? SIMON, WHAT DO YOU KNOW? TELL ME! TELL ME, SIMON!'

'I don't know anything, Vermillion, I promise. I haven't

seen Frank since last summer. He'll probably turn up soon. But till then, I'm here. Perhaps I can get you a drink while you wait. You look like you need one.'

Vermillion hesitates. She pulls herself to her feet but her legs shake as she inches her way around the table. She doesn't sit down again until she can see the entrance and can monitor the new arrivals.

'Simon, how the hell did you know we were meeting here?'

'Margery told me.'

'Bloody Margery! It's nothing to do with her!'

Simon signals to the waiter.

'Margery just said how awful it would be if for some reason Frank couldn't make it.' Simon looks straight at her. 'I'm sorry Vermillion, I don't want to upset you. I just couldn't bear to think of you waiting in vain. I thought if I were here, then at least you wouldn't be alone.'

Vermillion doesn't respond. She feels sick. She starts to twist her opal ring around her finger.

'Simon, please don't interfere,' she says at last. 'I'd find it easier to wait on my own.'

Simon raises his glass. 'Well, here's to you, Vermillion, and here's to Frank. I hope he's safe. And here's to you and me and to knowing you for more than three years.'

Vermillion is silent. She slowly turns the stem of her glass, still afraid she may cry.

'I'll drink to Frank,' she says at last.

As she sips the wine she looks over Simon's shoulder where the tall Major registers surprise: Simon is clearly not a Captain from 4th Battalion. Vermillion shakes her head and he gives her a thumbs down.

She drinks some more wine as Simon talks about recent events: Mussolini strung up in Milan; the reported death of Hitler; and the end of the war in Italy. He reminds her that fighting continues in Germany and speculates on what might happen next.

Vermillion tries not to listen: her attention is on the new arrivals. More Italian men are joined by some women dressed up to the nines. Vermillion marvels at their jewellery and the lavishness of their clothes.

Simon turns to see what she's looking at.

'It's pretty disgusting, isn't it? Wealthy Italian men kept their wives and mistresses in Venice throughout the war, knowing that neither side would bomb the city. And now the men have arrived to avoid the civil war.'

'Is there really a civil war?' Despite feeling sick she continues to sip her wine.

'Just you wait, Vermillion. The Communists are hell-bent on purging the Fascists, which means anyone they disagree with. They look to Russia of course and claim the Russians won the war, with the help of the partisans.'

Vermillion doesn't respond. She thought she had glimpsed a shoulder in the crowd. But it wasn't Frank. She looks at her watch. 1820.

'Frank, please come soon! I can't go on like this!'

She keeps sipping her wine, not wanting to talk or listen to Simon. Drinking is all she can manage.

The minutes pass slowly.

1830.

'Shall I book a table for dinner, Vermillion? They say the restaurant is marvellous with a wonderful view.'

Vermillion tilts her head and turns away. She had heard something.

'Were you listening, old girl? Shall I book for dinner?'

'Can you hear that?' She glances at Simon.

'It sounds like singing,' he says. 'It's early for the men to be drunk.'

'But can't you hear *what* they're singing.'

Simon rolls his eyes. 'Oh God!'

Vermillion pushes back her chair which topples over with a crash. Her leather shoes clatter on the hard floor as she hurries from the bar. A waiter jumps back as they almost collide.

'Scusate!'

The barman watches impassively, used to such behaviour when a girl has a tiff with her boyfriend.

Vermillion makes it into the hall, pushing her way through the throng. She smooths her hands down her uniform as she goes. The street is crowded but people have started to scatter as a troop of twenty soldiers marches towards them, singing. The column is headed by a tall Captain with his left hand in a large bandage.

'Toreador! Toreador! Toreador!' he sings.

'FRANK! FRANK!'

She knows he can't hear her but she keeps repeating his name. He looks weather-beaten but his head is held high. He sings lustily; she can hear his voice above the sound of his men.

'Frank, please can you stop!'

'Platoon, halt!' Their boots smack down on the quayside. 'Stand at ease!' The boots hit the pavement in unison and for a moment there's silence. Then Frank breaks away from the men and marches towards the hotel.

'Frank! Thank heavens it's over!'

She runs towards him and he lifts her from the ground with one hand and swings her round and round.

From behind him comes a deep growling sound as the men start to sing:

'Daisy, Daisy, give me your answer do ...'

Frank marches back to them with a beaming smile. 'Choir, dismiss,' he shouts as the next verse ends. 'We parade here tomorrow morning at 0800 sharp. Until then, enjoy Venice. And the drinks are on me.'

Vermillion takes his right hand. It feels rough, no longer like a pianist's.

'Are you all right, darling? Were you shot?'

'Only slightly.'

She wraps her arms around him. Behind him the tall Major grins, giving her a thumbs up.

'What happened to your hand? Are you really all right?' She gently extends her arms to get a proper look at him. 'You look amazing, Frank. Where were you hit?'

'I'm the luckiest man alive. A bullet caught my side but it was only flesh.' He smiles. 'Yes, I know, I've plenty to spare.'

She wants to hear the whole story but first she reaches up to kiss him. It seems like an eternity before he lets her go. She takes a deep breath and almost grasps his bandaged hand.

'Milione! How wonderful that you're here. You look so well, my treasure.'

'Frank, thank God you came. I heard you were in hospital. I want to know what happened. But first you should rest. Let's go and book a room.'

'I need a drink. And then you must tell me how you knew I'd been shot.'

They walk hand in hand towards the hotel. A crowd which has gathered breaks into applause. As they approach the entrance Vermillion remembers about Simon. Wanting to avoid a scene she steers Frank along the quay towards Santa Maria della Pietà, following the route she took earlier.

'It was a strange coincidence,' Vermillion says. 'One of your rescuers at the bridge was Sandro, Paolo's friend. He was brought to us for questioning. He didn't recognise me but he described the rescue of some British soldiers from Naples, one of whom he called Generalissimo. So I knew you were alive, but Sandro said there was fighting in the truck and several shots were fired. He didn't know who had been wounded or killed.'

'How extraordinary that Sandro should rescue us! Was Paolo there too?'

'Paolo led the group but a German shot and killed him.'

'Oh no, I'm so sorry.' Frank says. 'They were very brave. They saved my life, our lives.'

'It's awful for Chiara and her mother. They've suffered so much and now this as the war ends.'

'We must visit them. I want to thank them face to face.'

'What happened, Frank, in the back of that truck? How did you survive?'

Frank takes a deep breath. 'It was pretty gruesome. There were four others from the Battalion with three Germans wearing British uniforms. They planned to use us as hostages as they headed for Austria. But when the partisans stopped us and we heard shooting, I grabbed the German Captain next to me. My hands were tied but I still got him by the throat. That's the advantage of large hands.'

'How dreadful. And how brave of you to tackle him.'

'That wasn't the end of it. While I was throttling him he tried to claw at my face but my arms were too long so he dug his nails into my hand. Then one of the guards drew his pistol. Roberts and Bailey grabbed his arms but he still took a pot shot, which caught me in the side. I was losing blood and eventually passed out but not before I'd finished off the Captain. And Kirkup and Underhill overpowered the other guard.'

'How extraordinary you all survived. How did they get you to hospital?'

'I don't really know. I was all patched up in bed before I came round. But this afternoon they said I was well enough to see visitors. And out of the blue the whole Platoon arrived, with news of the German surrender. I told Short I had to come to Venice so he distracted the nurses while I snatched my uniform and scarpered.'

'Thank you so much for coming. But it might have been better if you'd stayed in the hospital. I'd better take you to the hotel to rest.'

They stroll back hand in hand. Vermillion looks across the water at the island of San Giorgio Maggiore as she struggles to comprehend how fortunate they've been.

'Darling Frank, please don't be angry.' She stops as they near the Danieli. 'You remember Simon, the pilot. He turned up this afternoon, uninvited. Margery had spilt the beans about our plan. He said he didn't want me to be alone if you couldn't make it.'

'Don't worry, Milione,' Frank grins. 'Even with a bullet in my side I can deal with Simon.'

'No Frank, please don't hit him!'

'Of course not, but I might drop him into the canal.'

'No, let me go in first and tell him to stay away.'

'All right, I'll wait for five minutes. Then I'm coming to find you.'

Vermillion walks briskly into the hotel and across to the bar. But Simon isn't there. The waiter says he has left. She goes to reception where Pasquale confirms that Simon has gone but he hands her a slip of paper.

Dear Vermillion

Please give my best wishes to Frank. I'm glad for your sake that he came through. I shall return to base.

As I've already paid for my room, please be my guests.

I hope you know I love you. And I won't forget you. How could I? But I know I've lost you, again. And I've pursued you for long enough. Now I must accept defeat with such grace as I can muster. I wish you the very best for the future.

I'm also returning your photo which came with me on every flight.

Yours ever
Simon

Vermillion takes a deep breath as she walks slowly back to Frank. The sun has set; lights are coming on along the waterfront. Frank turns and beams at her.

'The business is done,' she says. 'Simon has gone and has left us his room.'

Frank takes her hand and looks out across the lagoon. 'On the theatre roof a year ago, you said we had plenty of time. You weren't entirely right then. I hope you're right now. But let's not waste a minute, Milione. Let's get ready for dinner.'

ACKNOWLEDGEMENTS

Embers of War follows on from my previous novel Theatres of War but can be read on its own. I had written Theatres of War as a single novel with no thought of returning to the subject or characters. However, whilst working on a different story, I found myself wondering what happened to the characters after May '44. The only way to find out was to write a second novel, starting where Theatres of War had ended.

History

In the acknowledgements to Theatres of War, I referred to some of my main sources of inspiration and they are relevant background to this work too. However, Embers of War follows the Italian campaign up the peninsula into northern Italy and I found *Italy's Sorrow* by James Holland a particularly valuable source for the later stages of the campaign and its impact on the Italian population. With regard to Allied support for the partisans, I read several accounts including *The Secret War in Italy* by William Fowler.

For information about the military campaign in the Po valley, I found no better source than *The Road to Trieste* by Geoffrey Cox (later Sir Geoffrey Cox) who had served as the chief intelligence officer with the 2nd New Zealand Division.

The scenes described in both novels are entirely fictional and the characters are invented and are not based on real people. Nonetheless, as far as possible, I have respected the background events that occurred from '43 to '45.

When it came to the military actions this created a dilemma because I was determined that nothing should take away from the bravery and sacrifice of those who fought in the actual battles. I therefore invented the 4th Battalion and the engagements in which they fought at the Gothic Line and at the Senio. Although these accounts are wholly fictional they are intended to mirror real battles.

The description of Frank's encounter with Beniamino Gigli is fictional. However, his autobiography "The Gigli Memoirs" does refer to an encounter with an unnamed English officer who in June '44 came to investigate accusations that he was a traitor.

Trauma

As characters in Embers of War experience trauma caused by the war, I read two accounts by soldiers who were traumatised during the Italian campaign.

Alex Bowlby's *The Recollections of Rifleman Bowlby* gives a vivid account of his experience in the infantry in '44 which led to his breakdown. Although I had met him in Hampstead in the '60s, it was only much later that I read this account of the harrowing effects of trauma on the soldiers involved. I also read *Mussolini: His Part in My Downfall* by Spike Milligan. Once I got past the stream of puns and jokes, I found this a poignant account of a man overcome by the experience of war.

Looking for a fuller understanding of the subject I turned to *Trauma* by Professor Gordon Turnbull which includes many moving accounts of his work with people overwhelmed by the flashbacks, nightmares and sense of isolation that can follow traumatic events. I summarise in the following paragraphs my understanding of some of the book's key insights.

Traumatic Stress Disorder is caused by exposure to an event/events outside the normal run of human experience over which the person has no control and which makes them feel under threat.

Such experiences can lead to panic attacks, which are adrenaline surges causing heart palpitations, sweating, feeling out of control. The original attack can be obscured by shame, guilt or anger. The person may be especially vulnerable if he or she has already experienced traumatic events, especially where there are similarities between the two occurrences.

Symptoms include flashbacks (re-experiencing the traumatic event as if it were happening now), hypervigilance, nightmares, insomnia, irritability, anxiety, numbness (the shutting down of emotions, the inability to have feelings, and social withdrawal).

In Post-Traumatic Stress Disorder (PTSD) the flashbacks are like panic attacks but are characterised by vivid recollections of what was seen, heard, tasted, touched, or felt at the time of the trauma. With panic attacks the person is aware of here and now; with PTSD they're back there reliving the horrors.

After trauma, sufferers often try to conceal the reality from loved ones. Symptoms are expressed in arguments, brawling or domestic violence. Sufferers often use alcohol, not to get high but to feel normal.

Historically PTSD symptoms were seen as evidence of a character defect, not as a natural response. In WW2, Lack of Moral Fibre often led to demotion. More recent treatment views PTSD as a normal reaction to an abnormal event: the flashbacks and dreams are part of coming to terms with the psychological injury caused by the horror. The key question is therefore not "what is wrong with you?" but rather "what happened to you?"

Music
'Quanto è bella' comes from the libretto of Donizetti's L'Elisir d'Amore, written by Felice Romani.

'Dovunque al mondo' comes from the libretto of Puccini's Madama Butterfly, written by Luigi Illica and Giuseppe Giacosa.

Erstarrung (Numbness), the fourth song from Schubert's Winterreise (Winter Journey) song cycle, is a setting of the poem by Wilhelm Müller.

'Vivere' was written by Cesare Andrea Bixio.

'Là ci darem la mano' comes from the Libretto of Mozart's Don Giovanni, written by Lorenzo Da Ponte.

The English versions of these arias and songs are rough translations by Frank (and the author): they should have sought Vermillion's expert help.

Rudyard Kipling's poem 'Boots' was set to music by PJ McCall (an alias for Peter Dawson).

The song of 'The D-Day Dodgers' was sung by troops to the tune of Lili Marlene. The anonymous words, of which there are many versions, were a response to rumours that Lady Astor had used this expression to describe Allied troops serving in Italy. It seems, however, that there is no record of her saying this and she always denied it.

Map
I am grateful to Paul Futcher for preparing the Outline Map of Italy 1943–1945.

Editing
I was greatly helped by editorial advice from Richenda Todd at a critical point in finishing the book. I am also grateful to friends and relatives who commented on drafts of the novel. The final text was proofread by Timothy Gorman, who patiently pointed out things I had overlooked. Whilst acknowledging my debt to them all, I must take sole responsibility for the novel and any shortcomings.

And finally, heartfelt thanks to Sally who cheerfully accompanied me on the expeditions required to research this story and on the lengthy journey which turned the story into a novel.

RJJ Hall
London – February 2020

For exclusive discounts on Matador titles,
sign up to our occasional newsletter at
troubador.co.uk/bookshop